The Loyal Republic of Mutley Shepwell

David Pickering

For Pip,
who makes the grass
grow greener

CONTENTS

ACKNOWLEDGMENTS

Very many thanks, to Pip most of all, and to Jonny for encouragement, also to David Cook and Seth Turquand-Cook for the cover artwork and design, to Chris Cook and Nick Smith for reviewing earlier drafts, and to Guy Browning, Jenny Weaving and Ellie Bensted for reading early versions.

1
CRIME AND THE
MODERN CHURCH WARDEN

Had you been driving through the farthest reaches of darkest Oxfordshire in the early summer of 2027, you might have stumbled across a particularly beautiful valley in the upper reaches of the little River Amble, a patchwork of hedgerows, fields, and woods, the one road through it flanked by exuberant cow parsley. As you drove up from the south, you would have come to a medieval bridge of crumbling, golden stone, next to a charming, lopsided ancient church.

Ahead of you, at the north end of the bridge you would have seen a dark metal sign, with Gothic lettering proclaiming: "You are now entering Europe." Beside it, there in the heart of Middle England, you would have found a red and white sentry box, unmanned, its gleaming white barrier pole obligingly raised and, above the sign, a painting of a shield: on the shield, the red and white of the cross of St George, on which were quartered a golden crown, a golden cross, and two golden keys.

Had you wondered as to the cause of all this, you would have done well to look to your right, into the churchyard beyond the old, gothic church, where something large was hidden from view by a temporary structure of corrugated iron and huge plastic sheets. Of course, you would also have needed to go back in time, to the previous summer. Suppose you had managed that, and been able to observe what was happening in the small hours of a night in early June the previous year, not long before dawn, this is what you might have seen.

The moon sent down a faintly mysterious gleam on the edge of the church warden's spade as he dug gently into the churchyard soil. The Bonifer monument cast a shadow over his face, in spite of the helpful torch provided by the Justice of the Peace.

"I wonder when was the last time a church warden got sent to prison for grave robbing," mused Bob Corns, who was that Justice of the Peace. "And such a handsome grave it is," he added amiably.

"Do shut up, and think of the reasons why," said the warden, George Sneed.

Bob replied, "We're doing this for the village, and for Europe. At least, I am." The loves of his life were French wine, German politics, and the Italian wife who had left him when she felt England no longer welcomed her; he felt he owed it to them all to heal the breach his foolish countrymen had made. Bob was always ready to share his thoughts with a grateful world, or an ungrateful one, come to that. When not bringing justice and peace from the bench, his day job was as landlord of their local pub; both roles gave him ample opportunity to dispense his wisdom.

While he talked, Bob leaned on his shovel like a true British workman and kept the torch trained on George. He had a dodgy back, did Bob Corns, so, for him, the spade was always more of an ornament than a tool. He left the actual digging to lesser men, who hadn't had a long evening running a pub before they got there.

As George dug stubbornly on, he reflected that he hadn't got involved just for the village, let alone Europe. For him, it was family, and the England he loved, not the politicians' version. He looked across at his friend Des Martin, also digging steadily, and thought to himself, others are doing it for England too, and they have their own reasons as well.

What neither he nor any of the rest of them knew was that in a few short months, their vision of England would be breaking into the dreams of politicians, of media stars, of bloggers, tweeters, writers, broadcasters, gossips, analysts, critics, pollsters, commentators of all stripes and kinds. Their village dream would find resonances not just in their own country, but also far beyond. Their story would run wild across network after network of the wires, the radio waves, the screens, the image roads and information superhighways that connected the news and gossip of half the world.

Looming through the darkness, returning with an empty wheelbarrow, came the tall, craggy figure of Richard Tranctard, usually known as The Old Tank, who was carting soil away to a discreet dump in the garden of his vicarage, for he was vicar of that beautiful Gothic church, St Martin's-in-the-Meadow. For this purpose, The Old Tank had forsaken his usual black clerical shirt and dark suit for more workmanlike cords. He still wore a jacket, though, the most battered old tweed jacket George had ever seen. In this garb Richard trundled back and forth to the vicarage garden, on the other side of the churchyard, by the river. As the moon caught his shock of white hair it looked as if only his head was moving, the rest of him wrapped in shadows, just a disembodied head slowly gliding through the dark.

The sound of a strange-looking car swinging to a stop brought George out of reverie. Mary Wilkinson, now Richard Tranctard's fiancée, was coming over with a hamper of refreshments in hand. Mary, like Richard, had dressed down for the occasion, in her case to stylish jeans and black sweater.

"Your car's a terrible driver," she told her fiancé. He shrugged.

Most of the village had been relieved when he'd been persuaded to join the guinea pigs testing self-driving cars, because his own driving was so bad. When the Woodville brothers had set up their research centre in Traitor's Wood, just across from the church, they'd needed volunteers to test the technology in rural conditions, and his parishioners had queued up to volunteer their vicar. Yet somehow his car seemed to have imbibed something of its owner's crankiness. Perhaps it was because it was an early model, and the software updates never quite seemed to iron out its faults. He called his car James, just so he could say, "Home, James, home, and don't spare the horses!" Maybe that was what got the car so confused.

Mary returned to the car and emerged with a hamper, from which she brought out thermoses of coffee and tea, and flapjack for the troops.

"Getting any joy?" she asked her fiancé, as his tall figure loomed back through the darkness, pushing the wheelbarrow back. He ran a hand through his sweaty hair, which made a flyaway silver crown for his lean face, and made him seem even taller. She used to say it took attention away from his big nose, if anyone else had the temerity to praise it. Her own shoulder-length straight hair was still more blond than silver, without artificial aids of any kind, setting off the delicate bone structure of her face, which had quite a few admirers.

Her fiancé replied in unusually subdued tones, to the surprise of most. George smiled to himself, knowing the cause. A few weeks ago, at the annual service for the village sports teams, Reverend Tranctard had got a little carried away. In the course of a sermon on "the true beauty is inner beauty," he was trying to warn the young men in the congregation not to put too much stock in outer beauty and waxed a little lyrical. With all those young sportsmen there, he felt a need to warn the young, and so he said: "After all, gentlemen, if you meet her at your office or socially, at the pub or at a party, you see her looking her best. But she knows what she looks like first thing in the morning, on a very bad hair day, when she looks in her mirror and surveys the dreadful truth."

It was perhaps a little tactless, especially with his fiancée in the congregation. Coffee time after the service was rather more interesting than usual, and the rest of those present looked on in awe as they saw The Old Tank get a verbal roughing up of the kind they'd never have imagined him receiving, ending with the words, "Perhaps you'd rather not be saddled with the dreadful truth, and perhaps she'd rather not be saddled with you." With which words Mary made a magnificent exit. All agreed it was quite the most entertaining post-church cup of coffee they'd had in a very long time.

In the weeks since, certain church members had taken to intoning quietly, when they saw their vicar approaching, "Behold the dreadful truth." To everyone's amusement, The Old Tank was being unusually deferential to his soon-to-be better half; with their nuptials impending, even he knew he had to behave.

It was an engagement that had shocked the village. No one had ever thought The Old Tank would get married. He was almost the dictionary definition of the crusty bachelor. When a tiny, colourful, and acerbic business-woman called Mary Wilkinson had semi-retired to the village a couple of years ago, the village gossips had been at work at once. The smart money had been on Bill Stone, if he'd finally managed to shake off his long and unavailing devotion to Alicia Cornwell; others wondered if Mary might even detach Johnny Berensford from his current partner, although his long sequence of short-term Eastern European and Far Eastern companions suggested a rather different outlook. Those who liked to think they were in the know wondered about Bob Corns, not long divorced.

Instead, Mary had waded in to take a leading role in that most traditional of High Church survivals, with a determination to shake things up, and she and the vicar were soon knocking spots off each other in stormy meetings. Perhaps that was what did it.

Visually, they made a comically contrasting couple. She was petite and expensively dressed, wearing the kinds of clothes she'd wished she could afford when she was younger. He was a shabby sartorial shambles, craggy and tall, still with much of the muscle that had made him a pretty good second row in his rugby days. They moved totally differently: her quickstep to his lumbering march, little and large, fast and slow, power dressing and rumpled untidiness setting each other off, in every way the attraction of opposites.

She liked to say that he was such a dinosaur she'd had to marry him, to build him his own Jurassic Park, within which she could start him on the path of evolution. Other times she just said she'd taken pity on him, or that she'd sacrificed herself to save any other woman the fearful prospect.

The Old Tank's view, needless to say, was quite different. Having, as he put it, evaded the romance police for rather longer than most, he felt he'd been snared at last and run up the white flag, only to give her a project to keep her busy in retirement. Instead of clients at work she had to be polite to, he was going to give her a live-in client at home, one she didn't have to be nice to, unless she felt so inclined.

A number of the village's sages liked to think that The Old Tank's massive calmness was such that he rather enjoyed the acidic affection his new love specialised in. She had to restrain her remarks with others, but could let loose the full dosage with him, knowing that nothing could unsettle that impenetrable calm, or perhaps hoping that one day she would find something that could. Not much chance of that, though, he was pretty much impervious to criticism, and seemed to derive only amusement from it. It was as if, in her case, love was not blind so much as given X-ray vision, and a scalpel; romance as attempted character surgery, on a patient so robust no surgery could very much affect him.

Des Martin grinned across at George, he'd been present at that most entertaining coffee time too, although no one knew why. He'd had half a lifetime of waving his wife off to church on a Sunday morning, while he got on with the gardening, then when they arrived in Mutley, he announced one day: "That church. Got my name on it. I'm coming," and that was that.

He often seemed to be miles away during the sermon, if not asleep, and quite often hopped out to the vestry to start making the coffee while the service was still in full flow, but there he was every Sunday. Des was like that. Maybe he just liked the people. Maybe he was trying to gain a new respectability in his old age. Indeed, it was a pretty respectable lot they were, reflected George, to be out grave-robbing on a summer night.

At least it was a beautiful spot to start a life of crime. St Martin's had originally been built back in Saxon times, a modest structure. Then a village knight, one Sir Peter de Thurslay, had gone to court and prospered and become treasurer to King John. That ended in tears, with Sir Peter accused of treason and vanishing away to France. King John's son Henry, however, was a gentler soul and allowed the erring knight back.

He returned a changed man, devout, retiring, having changed his name to Sir Thomas, after the apostle who doubted Christ. He also returned with enough money to rebuild the little church in grand late Romanesque style, next to the old stone bridge over the Amble, with a small square tower at the east end. This was in the days when the village of Shepwell was down in the valley by the river.

In the early 14th century an unusually wealthy lord of the manor rebuilt the bridge and the church. For the church, he added a huge north aisle, in Gothic style, bigger than the original church, with a much taller tower at the west end. His timing wasn't good. Just as the builders finished, the Black Death struck, and the entire village migrated up the hill, leapfrogging the little hamlet of Mutley on the way and taking position towards the top of the long limestone ridge that looked north to the Cotswolds and south onto the quiet valley of the little River Amble, a valley that had maintained its agricultural tranquillity all through the centuries, until now.

Meanwhile, St Martin's was left marooned, bracketed

by its two unequal towers. Even the Victorians had left it alone. The church remained untouched, like a medieval relic adrift in the modern world. Only the ancient vicarage was left beside it, at the east end of the churchyard, a charming higgledy-piggledy structure, with one end late medieval and the modern end merely Jacobean, all delightful for the visitor and enormously inconvenient for the resident.

The churchyard itself was sufficiently scenic to draw many a visitor into a ramble, after they'd toured the medieval glories of the church. It was doubly bounded on three sides, first by an ancient yew hedge, then a rather tumbledown stone wall outside it. On the south side there were just the willows beside the river, not that the River Amble was much of a river in these parts.

As the last of the flapjack went down and The Old Tank trundled off with another load of soil, Des looked at his watch, then looked at the sky, which was perceptibly lightening to the East. He gave the usual warning call. "Time's up, time up, time's up," he said, "The early birds will be up and trotting soon. We need to get the fixings back in place, and us back to the village."

So they set the corrugated iron barrier back in place, locked the padlock on the makeshift gate they had entered by, and put the Health and Safety notices back in place. "No entry: Unsafe Monument," went the first sign, and the others too. Then everyone went their separate ways.

This morning, like most mornings, Des and George finished the clear-up and went home last, walking wearily up the path up through the woods to the village. As they left, George mumbled to Des, "How long do you think we can keep this up? We need to find it soon."

"Elf and Safety rules the world," said Des, "We could keep those covers round it for months, no one would blink. They all think we're still waitin' for the restorers. There's time." But he wasn't feeling as sure as he sounded.

As they left the churchyard, through the rather picturesque lych-gate on the north side, neither thought to look back. If they had, they might have noticed a slight stir of movement on the eastern edge of the churchyard, where some rather distinguished old yew trees joined in with the hedge. On the east, for some reason, the yew hedge had gone into decline, and the trees butted into it in places, and all in all, it was gappy and just looked untidy. Perhaps because of the trees, the churchyard's stone wall was at its most crumbly at that point.

Through that uncertain boundary crept two very quiet feet, and once the coast was truly clear, those feet swiftly went up to the 'Keep Out – Danger: Hazard' signs, and two equally quiet hands lifted a piece of corrugated iron aside and slipped in, just for a few short minutes. Then away again before any early dog walkers should disturb the silence.

As George and Des went up through Church Copse, they heard pounding feet ahead. Should they happen to bump into anyone on the way home, their only excuse for being out at that hour was a remarkably early morning walk, and they suspected that it wouldn't look convincing. For a moment Des looked at George and George looked at Des, then they both turned towards the thicket of holly and hawthorn on the left of the track. It seemed to offer the best cover.

The footfalls were coming fast and heavy down the hill. George paused, unsure if he should try to hide or just bluff it out. Des turned back and yanked at his elbow, urging him on. George seemed frozen, then at last he moved. Too late: before they could step three paces, round the corner surged two tall, blond, heavily muscled men in matching red tracksuits. George froze, but Des relaxed.

"Mornin', Borises," he said cheerfully. "Goin' in for the Olympics, are we?" The two red tracksuits half-smiled, half-grimaced, for they were going pretty fast, and, politely rounding the walkers, they shot off down the hill at an impressive pace.

"How d'you know their names?" Said George.

"Call 'em all Boris, they don't seem to mind," said Des. "Anyways, cheer up Eeyore, they're alright, I know 'em, they're two of the Russian's Russians. See 'em when I does jobs up at the Hall. They won't ask any questions, don't care what the village is up to, 'slong as the boss is alright – see." George sighed with relief. The Borises were indeed the least likely people in the neighbourhood to raise an eyebrow at seeing them. They resumed their slow pace up the hill, skirting the muddiest parts of the path. Des looked thoughtful: "Was The Old Tank right? Are we sure it's here?"

"We're not sure at all," replied George. "It was his best guess, and if it isn't here it could be anywhere up at the Hall, and, God knows, there are more places to hide it there than anyone is ever going to find. It needs to be here. Time's running out, the national park deadline's coming up, the bulldozers are ready to roll. And, not that you'll mind, I was hoping we could do something before this corruption of a coronation. At this rate, they'll be through all the negotiations and he'll be on the throne before we find it."

"Quite a jamboree, eh? With the blessin' of every religion, and none, that's the line, right? Cheer up, George, won't be so bad, us all gets a day's bank holiday," said Des, with a pat on the back. "Funny old business, in't it?"

"Funny for you, Des. Not so funny for some of us. She'd never have done that, never have gone near it."

"She's gone now, George, the world has moved on."

"The world, maybe. Mutley Shepwell, never. Nor St Martin's. Never."

"As you like it, mate. For me, I don't mind the world movin' on, and I don't care about all this Europe rubbish. We're better off without all that. For me, it's our village, concrete all over our green space, and bein' sneered at by the Cotswolds, that's what's gettin' my goat. We're not having some government moron with shiny shoes ruinin'

Mutley Shepwell. We'll find it, you'll see. I trust The Old Tank. Anyway, see you later, at *The Old Bells*."

It was a thought that cheered both of them up. For George, *The Old Bells* was his pub, Mutley's pub, named after the bells that rang in St Martin's for centuries, in both towers, till Cromwell's lot took them away and melted them down to make cannons in the Civil War. Sometimes he was lured up to *The Red Ship* in Shepwell, but usually they met here. Richard Tranctard also preferred it. It was his local, and he got on very well with the landlord, even if that landlord, Bob Corns, was totally agin the Church and all its works, which he called "The Rotary Club with hymns." The funny thing was that he still turned up to every major church function, if only to complain, and trotted down the hill to clean the church every January, devout atheist though he was – not only taking a turn on the rota, but the most unpopular month at that.

2
THE OLD BELLS

It was an unusual pub in many ways, *The Old Bells*. For one thing, at this establishment there were three flags along the south fence of the pub garden: the Cross of St George, the twelve stars of the European Union, and the Red Flag. A curious combination; what made it even odder was that the landlord described himself as a "capitalist Leninist." It wasn't what communism was for he believed in, it was what it was against. He was against the class system, against the City of London, against the rich, against religion, against private schools. In fact, he was against aristocracies of every kind, down to (or should one say up to) objecting to Crufts, because it was celebrity culture for dogs, and gave snobs the chance to extend their snobbery to their breed of pet.

This set of attitudes may have been why none of the Thursloe-Cavendish-Bendykes had ever been seen in his pub. It didn't get much trade from outside the village either; *The Red Ship*, up the hill in Shepwell, was the gastropub, and it had the view down the hill, people came from miles away for its food. *The Old Bells* had the older villagers' hearts, however, and most of the younger villagers' too.

Bob's objections to English snobberies had make him a Europhile, as every European country seemed to him more equal than his own, most of all Germany: he had spent part of his youth there, and returned convinced that Germany's post-war politics had created an egalitarian model society beyond Britain's dreams. He even pointed to the success of the German football team as the product of classlessness in action. Brexit had been for him a shock he'd not yet recovered from, the betrayal that had locked us in at the mercy of our own elites. He remained an optimist, though. Bob was congenitally optimistic, it was one of the things that made him get along so well with the Tranctards. Though their views were so opposite, they were united by their cheerfulness.

Bob's positive nature convinced him that the breach with the European Union could only be temporary. His view was that England needed Brussels to save it from Westminster.

The next evening, the conspirators took a night off their excavations and went to *The Old Bells*, as it was Mary and Richard's last night out as single people. When George and Des arrived, Bob was talking cricket to the regulars at the bar, and in the cosy end by the fire you could even see Alicia Cornwell and Bill Stone, who had condescended to come down to *The Old Bells* for once, in honour of the occasion. Mary was about to disappear into the final preparations for the wedding, to which a large chunk of the village were invited. Even Bill was going. In spite of his oft-stated boast that the only way you'd get him into a church was in a box, he wasn't about to miss this party.

They started off discussing the wedding, with great excitement in certain quarters, until Mary had to head home to make some calls and do some wedding business. She didn't leave without a final sally at her fiancé. George, who'd been busy passing round the nibbles, was rash enough to refer to the ever-encroaching bureaucracy of our times as "Just a cross we have to bear."

"Like Richard," added Mary.

"Not too late to cast off that cross, my dear," her fiancé submitted.

"And leave you at large to endanger the neighbourhood? Better to have you under lock and key where I can keep an eye on you. I'm doing this for the public good, you know."

"Another drink, my treasure? Surely you need to drown my sorrows."

"Not a chance. I'll need all my wits about me, married

to the likes of you," she said, but she smiled as she said it.

"Yes, dear," he replied. She kissed him, with a twinkle in her eye, and left.

At that point, The Old Tank announced that he had wedding talk coming out of his ears and it was time for a break. Half of the table looked disconsolate, but soon Bill Stone and Alicia Cornwell were launching into their favourite themes. Alicia was a pillar of the village, but she and Bill were arch-grumblers about most things. Had there been a village Olympics for complaining, they would have been hot favourites for two of the medal positions, almost nailed on for silver and bronze, with only their friend Alexander Livingston ahead in the betting for gold.

Alicia and Bill launched in. Brexit came first. Bill was a repentant Brexiteer, convinced that it had been the ruination of his business career, his big venture importing top of the range German cars. The post-Brexit trade deals made his cars more expensive and the competition cheaper, while all the uncertainty made his customers nervous about splashing out on the expensive toys he sold them. Alicia objected to Brexit for breaking up the UK. The loss of Northern Ireland she could perhaps have lived with, but her family roots were in Scotland. She talked of Brexit almost as the amputation of a part of her soul.

Between the two of them, they could moan for Britain about almost anything. If the pub had been serving them the nectar of ambrosia, and they'd been waited on by angels, with background music from celestial choirs, they'd still have complained that perfection isn't what it used to be. Richard Tranctard had had enough of this and he managed to divert them, only to find that the evening news had given them a whole new bone to chew.

"Leaving the Brexit fallout aside," said Bill, with a slight undercurrent of bitterness, "There is something else, though. As Alicia keeps reminding us, even though the politicians are keen to tell us how high our country's independent star has risen, and to promise the world to all the big and important people, they still aren't bothered with us. Didn't you see the news? Our delightful government's national park commission has just decided that we're not in the Cotswolds, so we don't qualify for all the grants they'll be doling out. Our only chance of some funding for this village, gone."

Usually they found themselves in a minority with their whinges, but when it came to this national park moan, most of the table was with them, outraged that the Cotswolds were going to be a national park and Mutley Shepwell wasn't going to be in it. "It's just a shot to please the new parties, so they can do some deals with them after the election," said Bill. "They've cheesed off everyone so much, they need to give us a few pressies to keep us sweet. They're just planning ahead to save their own skins."

Alicia pointed out that MPs had been moving further from those they were meant to represent for a long time. She said that was why the village branches of the parties died. Bill piped up in support: "Entirely their own fault, of course. When we were members, the local branches got to choose their candidates for Parliament. It was our power and our privilege. Now little cabals in central London parachute in their favoured friends to rule over the peasants in the provinces –"

"We're not peasants, thank you," interrupted Alicia, icily.

"Speak for yourself," he retorted, for Bill was never daunted by Alicia. "The Stones have been good peasant stock for centuries. But that's not the point, our rulers have disconnected. They've brought it on themselves. What's the use of them, anyway?"

Alicia needed no further invitation: "None whatsoever. They're worse news than criminals. We have the police to clamp down on crime; no one holds politicians back. Who needs crime when you've got a government to ruin the country?" She was getting more of an anarchist with age.

Des and Peggy and Richard laughed. The Old Tank

was leaning back in his chair, as usual, he always seemed to nab one of the big, comfortable ones, with arms to it, to be fair to him, he needed the space. Actually, all the chairs were comfortable at *The Old Bells*, although shabby, and a motley collection, but the armchairs were the best. It was the other way round at *The Red Ship*: stripped oak furniture treated and carved to look amazing, but the chairs did your back in after a while.

Richard leaned forward and grinned: "Don't hold back, Alicia, do say it like it is – thanks, Des, Doom Bar seems appropriate, eh, on the eve of my wedding? Bill, you should have some too, I may be going to my funeral, but you always look as if you're coming back from one."

The Old Tank continued: "Give our politicians a bit of credit, Alicia, they are trying, at least. They may take our money four years out of five but they're keen to send it back to us when general elections hove into view. Understandable, really, just a shame none of that money seems to be coming to us. This national park debacle, it seems to remove our last hope of help from government funds. But who is really to blame?"

"Blame it on the Tories, for losin' the last election," said Des, knowingly. That had certainly been a shock, but Labour's beautifully choreographed defenestration of its last, unpopular leader had been perfectly timed for a pre-election surge in support, just when all the tangles of Brexit negotiations had taken their toll on the government.

"Blame it on the Scots," said Alicia sagely. "They could have stayed, they were doing alright, didn't need to strongarm their way to another referendum and scheme their way back into Europe without us. With them going, Labour and the Lib Dems are terrified they'll never get in again, we'll have Tories forever, so they're talking about a grand coalition with the new parties. That's why they keep handing out sweeties, and why they're trying to push this Senate thing through, so at least they'll keep a hand in the Upper House."

"Blame the Greeks, then," volunteered George, "If they hadn't left the Euro, the EU might not have been so keen to let the Scots in."

Alicia, needless to say, remained determined to blame the Scots. She was rather fond of Greece, especially now holidays there were so cheap, paying in drachmas.

3
LONDON VERSUS ENGLAND

The announcement that they'd been left out of the national park got quite a few teeth on edge in the village, but worse was to follow. The government declared that it was finally going to break the planning logjam that had seen house prices rising and rising. Even Brexit had only dented them for a while. Having started by putting the brakes on development in reaction to the last Tory free-for-all, the government was about to take the brakes off again. The prime minister talked, as prime ministers so often do, about returning power to local communities and then he announced that he was taking it away instead, but in a good cause. He pontificated about how, for too long, planning had been a political football, and then declared that the government was going to stop all that.

The new plan was to exclude all politicians, local or national, from a say in planning decisions, by creating a non-political National Agency for Planning. Across Britain, eyebrows were raised at this news. The government claimed that, for any of its decisions, local representatives would have a full right to have their say, alongside other interested parties. The prime minister insisted that it bore no resemblance to the Tory-created national planning agency his own government had abolished. Round the country, eyebrows were hitting the roof by this point.

The cabinet, with a sigh of relief, handed this new National Agency for Planning responsibility for all projects of major significance, including every major residential development, claiming to have taken the politics out of planning and put it into the hands of impartial experts. The decision-making panel was made up of six non-political eminences, plus a civil service moderator from the Cabinet Office. Bob Corns summed up the village's reaction: "Six turkeys and a mandarin; that's a helluva Christmas lunch, but it's no way to concrete over Mutley Shepwell."

It wasn't just their village, groans were heard all over Britain. Not many had much trust in this panel of experts. Anger resounded in a thousand pubs and a million kitchens, but the government was determined and was on schedule to have the NAP up and running in record time. The NAP was soon dubbed the Nappy Band, but its edicts would very soon be law across the country, with no right of appeal. Part of the point was to take some of the pressure off London and the near South-East by diverting development to points further west and north.

The prospect of seeing its beloved fields concreted over, as much as anything, made Mutley Shepwell a cause looking for a rebellion to hitch its wagon to. Europe loomed larger for some, of course, but Europe was a long way away, and not everyone blamed Brexit for everything, although quite a few people still blamed it for something.

The particular reason that the Nappy Band's arrival was greeted with such horror in Mutley and Shepwell alike was that everyone could see the big fields to the west of the village being lined up for a vast new development, practically an entire new village, built right over the view that had been the glory of Mutley and Shepwell for hundreds of years. Endless painters had tried to capture the beauty of the woods and fields stretching west along the valley of the Amble, tourist guides and trip advisors queued up to praise it, and it was about to vanish under housing estates.

Moira Brenchley, the dynamic chair of the parish council, had been mobilizing opposition for months, and soft-soaping the county council planners with great care, only to have the decision snatched far away to London magnates beyond their reach. It sounded as if there was not much hope for protest to the Nappy Band. This started to crystallize a lot of feelings, general unease becoming anger

21

and resentment. Bob spoke for many, again, when he called a protest meeting and announced, "They've concreted over the home counties, they've let the bulldozers loose in every village east of here, now they're coming for us." Never had the parish council heard such a roar of approval.

Half the houses on that side of the village had been built for the view south and west. All the houses along the ridge stretching west from Shepwell were lined up for the best version of that same view. It had stayed pretty much the same for hundreds of years: small copses, large fields, ancient hedges, St Martin's church, and the medieval bridge. On a bright summer day the wheat gleamed golden all the way down the ridge to Traitor's Wood at the bottom.

Now it was about to be taken away from them. Not only that, Traitor's Wood itself was changing. As well as their entire view to the west being turned into housing, the wood below the village had been sliced up for a new Enhanced Reality Research Centre. The planners had promised that the new high-tech centre would be unobtrusive, yet somehow the plans seemed to have developed after being approved, with strange, gleaming glass structures rising up through the treetops, for high tech research and development.

The story behind this new centre made locals' blood boil. It was a murky business. Over the hills beyond the Amble, to the south of the village, in a gracious parkland, was the palatial manor house of Nigel Woodville, one of the famous Woodville brothers, of whose riches many tales have been told. Nigel was somewhat fascinated by new technologies and wanted to research the burgeoning number of different kinds of ways of creating virtual realities for entertainment purposes, and modifying the real world with artificial intelligences, and getting robots to do much of the work of the world. He explained his plans for robots as "creating a new servant class," which didn't endear him to many.

Nigel Woodville's interests ranged from the kind of helmets and bodysuits that immersed their wearers into an entire artificial world, like being inside a video game, to the increasingly sophisticated robots who could form entire staffs for the weary millionaire. He insisted that soon robots wouldn't just be for millionaires, that his researchers would be producing bargain models that could be 3-D printed cheaply enough for everybody to have robots to clean their houses, mow their lawns, wash their cars, make their tea, guard their homes, do their shopping, and organize their lives. His marketing people said that in years to come, the only work would be quality work. Less sympathetic types said that robots would be the slaves of the future, while unwanted humans would be left to rot on the ash heap of their prospects.

Alongside all the practical research, Nigel had a sideline dear to his heart: one of his favourite hobbies was his Formula One team, and he nurtured a dream of one day having a robotic autopilot able to drive his cars to victory, without the need for the prima donnas who drove for him at present. He was sufficiently interested to want his research centre near enough for him to be able to pop in and disturb the scientists who did his bidding for him, but he didn't want his own view spoiled. So he had somehow, in record time, got planning permission to build it in Traitor's Wood.

No one knew exactly what the deal involved or how he persuaded the planners to let him build amid that pristine beauty. It became something of a scandal and evidence that the old planning system just didn't work. Never mind that Traitor's Wood had been pretty much undisturbed for centuries, no one had ever thought to get any kind of legal protection for it till it was too late. As a result, strange structures had appeared between the ancient trees, and more were constantly being built.

Allegedly, almost all the trees were being preserved.

Except the ones that weren't. The paths along the fringes of the wood were still open, including the one by the river to the ruined chapel, but ten metres into the wood, huge fences topped with razor wire rose amid the trees. There had been dreams of a legal challenge, but all potential challengers quailed before the Woodville brothers' vast resources, and so, next to the bridge over the Amble, right across from the church, there was now a gleaming steel gateway, and beside that a gleaming titanium sign announcing the Woodvilles' Enhanced Reality Research Centre.

One unexpected side effect was that the village had become a test bed for advanced technologies. A number of villagers had had taken up the Woodvilles' researchers' offers and made their car their chauffeur. It wasn't just cars either, free prototypes of all sorts of robots were available for testing purposes, for anyone who didn't mind being monitored and having their data built into the next stage of the research. These "domestic assistants," as they were categorised, went under the brand name, Perfect Companions. They may not have been perfect as companions, but they certainly made useful servants. As a result, many villagers had ceased to do their own vacuuming or make their own tea or tidy their own houses or wash their own dishes or mow their own lawns.

This had rather divided opinion in the village. There were four main groups: the refuseniks, who turned their backs on these new machines and the intrusion of the data collection; the early grumblers, who employed the machines but moaned endlessly about their shortcomings; the hesitant futurists, who appreciated having jobs taken off their hands but worried about the data constantly being beamed from their homes and cars to the research centre; and Big Brother's Boys, as they were dubbed by the rest of the villagers, who didn't care about the data, couldn't see any downsides, and rejoiced that their village was finally at the forefront of a changing world. Overall, most of the village admitted that being guinea pigs for the next generation of technology had its advantages.

That may have been a positive, but the list of negatives stretched ever longer: the destruction of the view that made the village, the government's various unpopular plans, exclusion from the new Cotswolds National Park, and a deeper sense of alienation from the powers of London, a sense that went back a long way. On top of all that was the never-ending austerity imposed by successive governments over the years since the financial crash, a permanent hangover that never cleared up: the village was not poor enough to get what funding was available, nor rich enough to manage without.

In addition, there was huge irritation that the promised post-Brexit prosperity appeared to have stopped at London. After a brief dip during the Brexit negotiations, the capital had started booming again, with all the new global connections seeming to begin and end there. The new riches didn't seem to filter out to the rest of the country, in spite of all the promises politicians had made about the flourishing future Brexit would lead to. After all, the only thing easier than to make a promise is to break one.

All this had slowly built up anger in many hearts. A resolutely unpolitical corner of Middle England was coming to feel it was on the wrong end of too many political decisions, and this wasn't fair. Together, all these factors gave Richard Tranctard a ready audience for his plots and plans. Before those plans could progress further, he had a wedding to attend, his own. He left *The Old Bells* for the last time as a single man. As he vanished down the hill, George Sneed and Bill Stone lifted a glass to him. The landlord joined them. As he liked to say, "If I don't show I like what we sell, how will the customers trust it?"

Bob got Bill and George another drink, to make them a captive audience. In spite of his tendency to do this, Bob was a popular man in the village. Few minded his strange opinions because he expressed them in such friendly and genial ways. His appearance was not the most prepossessing. He had been said to look more like a side of beef cut into human shape than a human being really should. He was certainly red-faced, fleshy, stout and always badly dressed. His head was totally bald on top but still thickly forested round the sides with vigorous black hair. He blew around the village in a gale of words and people felt he was a character who livened things up.

Bob was soon ruminating about the state of the country. Others in the village were irate about local concerns, but Bob Corns always preferred to look at the big picture, Europe most of all. Besides, as a pub landlord, he was less disturbed about the prospect of the vast new development than most; it wasn't likely to be bad for business. "Since they took us out of Europe, we've lost our bearings, country's gone off course since they cut us loose, we need to get hitched back to the rest of Europe, get our stability again, save us from the snobs and experts and educated idiots, the Establishment. We need Brussels to save us from Westminster. That's what counts." He thumped his glass down a bit too hard, and it slurped good beer over the table.

"What counts for you, maybe," replied Bill.

"What counts for Mutley Shepwell." Bob Corns laughed and went back behind the bar, with the parting shot, "Want to know my views, just look at the flags." Being the landlord, he liked to have the last word, and he generally did. As they finished their drinks and got up to leave, he leant over the bar, and beckoned to Bill and George. "Think it'll work, The Old Tank's idea?"

"What do you think?" asked Bill, sourly. "We all know it's mad, but what can you do? Might as well go down fighting, since we're surely going down. Politicians! That's the trouble with them, it's when they get ideas."

"You know what it is," replied the landlord, "Ever since that Brexit referendum, it's London against England, that's our problem. Mark my words." With that he went back into the kitchen to wash up some glasses. George and Bill walked back home, but their thoughts were with the wedding on the morrow, and with Richard Tranctard's mad idea.

4
SUMMER WEDDING,
AUTUMN MARRIAGE

The next time they saw The Old Tank, it was his wedding day, down at St Martin's. The church looked wonderful. The service itself, and the reception, organized by Mary, went immaculately. The flowers were magnificent, with white and yellow roses at the heart of most displays, sprays of gypsophila, delphiniums and lilies, a delight of scent as well as vision. The service was the Church of England at its most stately, grand old hymns and grand old words (*Book of Common Prayer*, naturally).

The grandest of those words were the vows themselves. Bride and groom looked humbled when they spoke them. Richard's usually resonant voice faltered as he uttered commitments he had never thought he would make. Mary, on the other hand, was radiant and spoke her vows with a bell-like clarity. There was a resonance to the service that was felt by the hardest and least romantic hearts.

The only negative comment came from a perhaps best nameless person at the back of the church, who looked at the bride and groom standing at the front and whispered that it was a bit Beauty and the Beast. George wondered if he should point out that The Old Tank mightn't have been quite so bad looking if he hadn't played so much rugby in his youth, but he didn't like to whisper in the service, so he kept his peace. Richard Tranctard did always remind him of a not-quite finished statue hacked from low-grade stone by a not very gifted apprentice sculptor, who'd started with enthusiasm, then lost interest half way through.

Nobody else cared about that. The magic of the moment carried all before it. The marquee for the reception was raised in one of Bill Stone's last fields, which he'd kept as it had the best view of all of them, and he could rent it out for occasions such as this. They kept the sides of the marquee open so they could enjoy the remarkable views down the valley of the Amble, those very views that were about to be built all over.

It was a glorious summer's day, and very hot. When not wilting into their drinks, the guests enjoyed themselves immensely. The food was a feast, tables piled high with a mad collection of Richard and Mary's favourite dishes from round the world. It was a buffet so no one had to be trapped with the wrong company. A swing band played remarkably danceable tunes, which were also easy listening for those more concerned with talking or drinking than dancing. The village folk, at least the more curious amongst them, enjoyed meeting representatives of different phases of Mary's life.

The wedding breakfast was mighty fine. When they got to the speeches, there was a certain expectancy. Mary's father and mother being dead, her sister, Vivienne, made the opening speech in their place. Vivienne kept it simple, and enormously polite, full of thanks to all, especially their parents, with a note of regret that they weren't able to be there. Then she sat down and the bridegroom stood up.

His speech began, ""It may have been a mistake, I put an ad up: cantankerous old codger, 60,000 miles on the clock, seeks renovation expert not afraid of major challenge. Does provide tea in bed. – Afterwards, I thought I could have worded it better, but it's amazing what a woman will do for a nice cup of tea in the mornings. In addition to the normal wedding vows I've had to promise that, from tomorrow onwards, a morning tray of tea will be provided each morning. And so marriage enters me on a new career in domestic service. The funny thing is, I'm rather pleased at the prospect. Strange to find someone you're so pleased to see that delivering her tea for the rest of your life becomes an entrancing prospect.""

The bride had, of course, right of reply, it being a twenty-first century wedding. Her speech started off: "60,000 miles, I should be so lucky. His letter should have started, 'Horse-drawn carriage, seeking to be drawn into the modern era, seeks one careful lady owner.' Fortunately, I'm rather fond of this horse-drawn carriage. He may be slow, and about a century out of date, but he's terribly reliable, and honest to a fault." Their speeches warmed up from there, spoken and received with glee and amusement on both sides, as their marriage began the way it would continue, with genial sparring on all occasions.

The dancing was less energetic than at some younger weddings, but enjoyed just as much. George didn't dance, although Moira and Alicia and Mary's sister all tried to inveigle him onto the dance floor. He sat with all the storytellers and reminiscence-mongers who charmed or bored the younger guests as long as they could keep them there, with their stories of weddings past and romances broken, thriving, or just surviving.

Bill Stone and Johnny Berensford, with a little too much champagne inside them, trapped young Jimmy Armsbell and Jem Wansfield-Diggersby in a corner, eager to impart their wisdom to the young. Bill and Johnny waxed lyrical about the tyranny of marriage and overshared somewhat about their divorces. They warned the young men about quite a lot of things. Bill surprised them by blaming his own divorce on Brexit, and the way it ruined his import-export business. The stress drove his marriage apart, he said.

Bill's appearance rather complemented the gloominess of his words. Tall, grey-haired, and lean to the point of being gaunt, his tendency to dress in black just added to the air of depression he carried round with him. Having warned the boys fiercely to avoid the entanglements of all forms of relationship, Bill then rather undercut his own advice by admitting that he was very lonely on the farm these days, and even his mad brother Stephanos was better company than just the chickens. Johnny rather unhelpfully pointed out that Bill wouldn't just have chickens for company if he hadn't sold off almost all his land to fund his various business ventures.

Bill was practically crying into his champagne by this point. Having started by extolling the single life, he ended up by asking Jimmy and Jem if they knew of any romantic social networks for the older gent. Johnny Berensford roared with laughter and warned him, "Don't order a mail order bride. They get so crumpled in the post." He should know, thought Bill, with a grimace which Johnny didn't notice because he was so pleased with his own joke that he laughed till he fell off his chair. Bill went to help him up, giving Jem and Jimmy a chance to escape back to the dance floor. At the other end of the table, George said very little. He just sat back and listened, smiling gently, keeping his own stories to himself.

The bride and groom left, in a horse-drawn carriage, but the band played on, into the evening. As George sipped one glass of wine too many, he once more found himself lost in his thoughts. Weddings always took him back to that great day when he and Tabitha were united. The strange thing was that wedding day had always been a blur in his memory, and yet it was a blur brighter than almost any other past chamber of his mind. After a while those bright images became darkened by the years of cancer and treatment and pain, and slowly fading, and of his son Paul and the sadness of that story, and it was all too much. He turned from wine to whisky and kept his thoughts to the recent past. When the music ended and the last dancers parted, he set off to walk home.

Trudging up the hill, he savoured the calm and quiet of their own village at night, but he couldn't help imagining the loss of peace if the huge new development arrived. George knew the history of Mutley Shepwell as well as anyone and he just couldn't see what was about to be built as anything other than a rupture with what had gone before.

As he walked past *The Old Bells*, it struck him that the two village pubs reflected different aspects of the village story. It would be hard to explain to the outsider quite why the two pubs were such a world apart but, for George, something like their little conspiracy could never have been hatched in *The Red Ship*. That difference between the two pubs seemed to him to say something about the two original villages, Mutley and Shepwell.

It was three original villages, actually, after the Black Death had caused Shepwell by the river to migrate wholesale up the ridge. From that time on, there were Mutley, Upper Shepwell and Nether Shepwell. Upper Shepwell was ranged around the crossroads at the top of the ridge that rose gently from the River Amble, with Nether Shepwell slightly below and to the West, and Mutley a little further down the slope, once neatly gathered around its own crossroads, more recently straggling up the hill towards the Shepwells.

Nether Shepwell had slowly grown down the hill to meet Mutley, till the villages almost joined, bar a line of tiny fields which were not, in reality, much bigger than back gardens; apart from that thin green line, they had effectively joined up, and the three villages were, for practical purposes, if not in the minds of all the villagers, one village. Some residents still wrote their address as "Mutley," "Upper Shepwell," or "Nether Shepwell," and the ancient parish boundaries were still all mixed up, for medieval reasons, but people who like to think of themselves as practical tended to view Mutley Shepwell as one place.

The question still roused lively debate, however, and proud loyalty, as to which of the possible options you belonged to, and if you asked the residents their address, you might hear any one of the four possible village names, with Mutley Shepwell probably gaining slowly. In all three villages, most buildings were in Cotswold stone, but there were little outbreaks of red brick here and there. Some

Shepwellians liked to suggest that the further down the hill you went, the more was built in brick, the less in stone.

Not many visitors even guessed at the history of the tiny stream that ran so picturesquely from west to east along most of Mutley's North Street, before being banished into a culvert beneath the main Burford Road, and reappearing to cheer the cows in the fields beyond, below the manor. Bar a couple of old stone markers, cracked and half hidden by hedges, there was nothing to indicate that for centuries it had actually been a boundary.

The Shepbrook was its name, and it marked the meeting of Mutley and the Shepwells. The two Shepwells were once separated by an even smaller stream, the Little Shepbrook, but this had been banished underground for most of its length, except on the north-western edge of the village, where it began, and was permitted above ground for a short while to provide a charming edging to some rather fine gardens. It blended so well with their dry stone walls.

In spite of the Little Shepbrook being conspicuous by its absence for most of its length, long-term villagers were almost universally aware of its line, the now invisible boundary between Upper and Nether Shepwell. In fact, some of the residents of Upper Shepwell still liked to refer to their neighbour village as "The Nether Regions" and the now-defunct village bakery, safely located on the north side of the Little Shepbrook, had enjoyed referring to itself as The Upper Crust. Nether Shepwellians in their turn had often enjoyed a little looking down of the nose at their neighbours further down the slope, beyond the Shepbrook, while Mutleyans grumbled at snooty folk up the hill, and boasted of a real community spirit in their part of the village.

George would never have joined in those grumbles, or the boasts, but in his heart he was proudest of old Mutley, pub, church, shop, village green and all. He still loved the Shepwells, just not quite as much. Of the two, Nether Shepwell came closer to his heart. He couldn't bear to watch his tripartite village ruined, yet he was afraid he was about to have to do just that, unless their little plot found a way. As he climbed the stairs to his bedroom, he didn't know that they were about to find a whole new source of support for their spirit of rebellion.

5
TAKING LIBERTIES

A couple of weeks later, after the Tranctards returned from their honeymoon, there came an evening shrouded in a quite unseasonal mist. In the early evening, George popped in to the vicarage to talk to the vicar about the church roof, as church wardens do. Richard Tranctard was looking unusually, fiercely, angrily serious. He waved away George's attempt to talk about the roof and its troubles.

"Have you heard the latest?" The Old Tank said grimly. "They're calling it The Recreational Substances Bill. Now they're legalising drugs."

George could hardly believe what he was hearing. As he drove home, so shocked he almost went into a hedge, the thick mist felt to him like a response to the murky business done that day by the government. Before bed, he broke with habit and watched the evening news. The prime minister proudly declared that the government had discovered a way to reduce crime, rake in more taxes, and make Britain a world leader in a global industry. That global industry was the one producing what used to be illegal drugs, and were now recreational substances. Other countries had legalised some of these, Britain was not just going to catch up with that, but streak ahead, with blanket legalisation plus health warnings. The prime minister described it as a blow for personal freedom: "To those, stuck in the past, who say, 'Is this moral?' I say, 'It would be immoral not to.' For too long the taboos of the past have held our freedoms back."

George waited for a roasting from the opposition but just heard the sound of purring on all sides, with the new head of the Conservative party standing up to say he wasn't supporting the legalisation of drugs in spite of being a conservative, but because he was a conservative. The Tories had switched back from safe'n'steady mode to proving they'd 'got with the programme' with their new young leader. Instead of the two sides of parliament opposing each other, they were so busy slapping each other on the back, it was practically a group hug. George staggered. Most of the media were purring too.

Next day, still mentally staggering slightly, he wandered up the hill to Mike and Jane Singer's house to sort out a little parish council business. Mike and Jane were old friends of his, and very well connected in the village. Their twins, Ben and Becky, were back from university, and Becky happily announced that she'd been really organized and already had her first session with her university's online personalized careers auto-adviser, Chelsea. "Chelsea is really quick, she's already got a new section for recreational substances and updated the one for development planning, to allow for the NAP."

Ben turned to his mum: "Lots of jobs in recreational substances, they say, if you've got the right qualifications. I used to be quite good at chemistry. What d'you think?"

Her mother opened her mouth: "As a mother –" That was enough for her son's antennae, and before she could finish the first sentence he was disappearing up the stairs. Ben explained it to Becky later, giving her the benefit of his worldly wisdom: "When she says, 'As a woman,' it's time to run for the hills. If she says, 'As a mother,' put your jet boots on."

Jane watched them as they vanished up the stairs, then turned to her husband. The only part of him that had moved during that little exchange was his eyebrows, which had hit the heights. He shook his head mutely as his wife asked, "Is this the future you want for our children? Well, I don't. Not here. Not in this village."

George watched thoughtfully, if awkwardly, and mumbled his sympathy. They knew he was with them on this one. Then he popped home for a quick bite before the Parish Council meeting. As he turned in at the gate, he saw Molly's little orange head peeping over the lower edge of the bay window of his front room, waiting for him, as ever, her round orange head contrasting oddly with her tubular green body and her blue wheels.

"They might be good at research, haven't a clue about design," he thought for the hundredth time. Molly's loyalty would have been touching, if she hadn't been a robot. He did value her cleaning skills and help with his paperwork, but her algorithms didn't really extend to a real conversation, and no amount of research seemed able to come up with a robot that could make a decent cup of tea: coffee, yes, tea, no.

Molly took his coat for him and brought his slippers, attentive as ever. His meals were quick and spare, with Tabitha gone. He tried to make them healthy but he wasn't sure that ham on toast, with a couple of boiled eggs, really counted. At 7.20pm, as always, he twitched the curtains of his front room and looked out to see if the Old Believers were still carrying on their protest. Sure enough, Bill Stone and Alicia Cornwall stalked stiffly past, and he knew without seeing it that Bob Corns would be striding up the High Street to rendezvous with them at the Village Hall at 7.30pm precisely.

In their younger days they had campaigned to have the starting time moved back from 7.15pm to 7.30pm, and when that start time had been moved to 7.45pm, to accommodate commuters who couldn't get back from work for 7.30, the Old Believers had still carried on arriving at the same time they always had. "Thus far, and no further," was their motto. So do yesterday's pioneers become tomorrow's guardians of tradition

George knew that as he and others arrived, at 7.45 or a little before, each of the Old Believers would cast a look at their watches. Nothing was said, yet they maintained their early arrival, and that look as others arrived, years on. Perhaps it was partly that it had become a handy social rendezvous for the three of them.

The Parish Council meeting was gloomier than ever, although it was a beautiful summer evening. After quick expressions of shock at the government's latest, they got down to the village's business. The mood wasn't helped when you had to edge through the makeshift scaffolding that held the porch of the Thursloe Hall up, just to get in, then negotiate your way round the buckets catching the drips from the roof leaks, if you wanted to get to the Nutkins Room, going past the boarded-up main meeting room on your way.

It was more bad news about the national park. "That's it, then," said Alicia, with gloomy disdain, "They don't care about us, they'll never let us in."

"Tell us about it, dearie," said Peggy Martin. "How many years we been fund-raisin' for a new village hall? Just one of their fat Village Improvement Grants and we'd be made. But no chance for the likes of us. Just more money for the fat cats in the Cotswolds. Do they need the money, I ask you? Even their rabbit hutches are thatched. Their little pooches probably get caviar for breakfast. They'll just use the grants to gold plate their war memorials. It's such a waste."

"It's not over yet," repeated Moira Brenchley, their weary yet dutiful chairman (no chairpersons in Mutley Shepwell, please, and chairs were what one sat on, as Alicia liked to remark). "There is one last review, reporting at the end of the year. If we can find an "overriding historical or other reason" why they should include us in the national park, we can still get in. And that will protect us from the nasties of Nappy."

"You think we have a ghost of an earthly?" demanded Alicia, "The whole thing's a fix. It's just a way of shovelling money at places that don't need it before the election. The government's chucking money everywhere to try to keep the other lot out. They want to make sure it's them next year, even if they're just part of a grand coalition. They shovel money at everyone else, but we're not important enough. They won't bend their boundaries for us, they'll dump their housing on us instead. And who cares, we'll manage, we always have."

"Remind me," said Bill Stone, "Remind me just how we're going to manage to fix this hall, or get a youth club, or fix the Rec, or sort out the drains. Or fit in a village-worth of new houses, with no facilities. We can't get the grants, we can't raise the money. If we can get into the national park, there's so much lard, we're in with a shout for all we need."

"But we can't," said Peggy, "It's these politicians, they're so busy looking after each other, they don't care about ordinary people."

"Or even people like us," added Alicia hastily. She wasn't going to be referred to as "ordinary people." One of her ancestors had been the Mayor of Truro in the seventeenth century.

"We're stuck between the Devil and the deep blue sea; the Tories unleashed the developers last time, now the coalition are doing the same; no one's standing up for the villages," announced Alexander Livingston. Alicia listened with more respect than she accorded any other member of the parish council.

Alexander was, after all, a retired professor, who had taught history at Oxford. His enemies in the village liked to point out that he had taught history at Oxford Brookes, the newer and less prestigious of the two universities resident in that ancient city. Alexander himself held firmly to the view that any fully signed up member of the history professors' guild was as good as another.

The discussion went this way and that for a while, or rather round and round the same old houses they'd been going around for ages, as they tried to work out how to persuade an ungrateful government to let them into its plans, despite its refusal to listen. As usual, they ended without any agreement. Des asked if anyone wanted to go down the hill to the pub, but they couldn't even agree on that. Moira was off home. Alexander, Alicia and Bill wanted to go up the hill to *The Red Ship*, while George, Peggy and Des insisted on going down to *The Old Bells*, which Bob rather had to return to – even his long-suffering staff liked to see him occasionally.

When they arrived Richard Tranctard launched in about the drugs legalisation bill, and that kicked things off. *The Old Bells*, had rarely seen such anger, except from Bob Corns, who loved to prove that he was a communist who believed in freedom, so enjoyed telling them all that everyone should be free to do everything. He also loved to disagree with as many people as possible on any given issue. They ignored him after a while. Des wobbled a bit at the start, till Peggy shut him up.

"Just drink your beer, and be glad that isn't spiked, and no one's banned it and told you to smoke summat instead," she told him, sipping her white wine.

George, Richard, and Peggy were united, for once, but once they'd seen off the landlord, gloom descended. Bob never admitted defeat, of course, he just remembered that he did actually have other customers, and a staff who liked a hand every now and then. For the rest of them, frustration was mounting ever higher. They'd been angry before, and only Richard Tranctard had any hope that they could make their protest heard in any way.

At the end of the evening, Richard gathered Mary, George, Bob, Des and Peggy in a corner. He suggested that this bit of news might bring them a few more conspirators. George and Mary were nervous about the idea.

"What if we tried to find out?" Richard said. "What have we got to lose?"

"Nothing," said Bob.

"Nothing," said Peggy.

"Not a lot," said Des, when Peggy nudged him.

"What does George think?" said Mary.

Everyone looked at George. He shrugged uncomfortably and shuffled his feet. "I suppose we could try." And that was how the next stage of the conspiracy started, with that night in *The Old Bells.*

6
PRESENCE AND MEMORY

At the end of the evening, George walked home down the hill, saying goodbye to Peggy and Des at the corner. Usually, he paused on the way home to enjoy the little side street he lived in, South Street of Mutley, full of 70s mock-Georgian villas. The front gardens were small, but about half were statements of love and skill: no fewer than four of the horticultural club committee lived in South Street, plus a past winner of the overall Champion's Cup, and it did show, some of those front gardens were tiny miracles. Tonight he didn't pause to admire, though, he felt too low. His only observation, as he went in, was that his own garden wasn't what it had been; only one to look after it nowadays.

He turned in the little black iron gate, shutting it neatly behind him, as ever. He reminded himself, as usual, as he stepped past the Georgian green front door, that it was needing a coat of paint again, gave Molly his coat, and thanked her for her efforts during the day – he could never have said why he thanked a robot, it just seemed the polite thing to do. Then he went through the hall to the conservatory at the back, while Morsel roused herself enough from slumber to wag a tail with sleepy enthusiasm.

Morsel was his little dachshund. If people asked about her name, he showed them pictures of her as a puppy, half the size of a teabag, and about the weight of a postage stamp. Normally she greeted him with frenzied excitement, barking furiously, dancing about his feet, then running up the first few stairs and lifting her head to ask to be picked up. At night, however, sleep overcame her. He didn't hold it against her, he knew he was her second greatest friend, after her food bowl. (Unusually for a dachshund, she was a dedicated foodie).

Once Morsel was asleep, and Molly shut down and re-charging for the night, he was alone. On one side of the conservatory was a second extension, halfway between a lean-to and a proper room. He called it his study, although he didn't have so much to study these days, and it was too cold in winter to spend very long there. His desk was there, and his photographs, the favourite ones, of his wife and son and daughter and his little grand-children, of parents and friends and cousins, and the many dachshunds of the past – he and Tabitha had kept quite a menagerie once, now it was just Morsel.

A few special photographs of Tabitha and Paul brought back memories too painful, he didn't feel strong enough to look at them every day, so he kept them in a cupboard, on the wall opposite the door, at waist height between the bookshelves. He opened it now. In it were three tall candles, kept safe within tall glass cylindrical fittings, and beside them, certain very special family photographs, including the one of the great day when Tabitha received her medal at Buckingham Palace. Beside it was a photo of her with their son, smiling, that same summer.

Amazing how like he was to the old man looking down at his photo, thought George, but always better looking, and so much more able. He could have done so much. That photo consoled him some days and twisted his heart on others. It was the last good one, taken one summer day in the village, before Paul moved to London and the drugs took hold.

He bowed, a strange, solemn bow to the photographs and his memories, blew the hint of a kiss to his last picture of Tabitha, blew out the candles, changed one that was getting too low, and locked up the cupboard. That cupboard, for him, was where he kept faith with those he had loved and lost. For him, it was the centre, and the well-spring of decision. It was the place he returned to always.

Hearing the drugs announcement sent him back there, to his little shrine, amid his fears for an England he felt he was losing. When he wondered why he'd signed up to The Old Tank's little army, he returned to those photographs.

He shrugged his shoulders as he walked up the stairs to bed. It might be a mad scheme, he told himself, but you've got to do something, and if it's mad, so what, the people who run the country have gone mad, why not the rest of us? Something had happened to him, he didn't really understand what. The anger had been building for a long time, enough to make him a conspirator even before the drugs announcement, but that, for him, had really gone beyond any boundary. He was so angry, he almost didn't feel like himself any more.

He wondered if he should pin on a badge saying, "I've never done anything like this before." In all their respectable company, he himself was one of the most upstanding of all: retired tax inspector, if that gained entry to polite society; church warden; pillar of the horticultural society, previously school governor for many years. He was the sort of person often described as salt of the earth, if he was remembered enough to be described at all.

He was an easy man to forget: middling height, middling weight, hair of middling grey where it remained, around the large bald patch; eyes of middling brown, a very average sort of face, easily forgettable, pale but not very pale, eyebrows still darker than the hair above, modest and unremarkable features. All his life, he had often been mistaken for someone else, anyone else. He dressed in pretty unremarkable ways, too. His wife used to lament that his favourite colour in clothes was mud-brown, or, if not, grey; if blue, it had to be the dullest kind of navy.

All in all, George was not the sort of person you'd expect to see launching into a criminal career in retirement. Of course, whether or not this was strictly a crime was debatable. No one was planning to profit from it. Officially it was down as repairs to the Bonifer monument, according to the faculty that had got them permission to put up a kind of huge tent over the monument and start digging. Officially, though, it was being done by Des Martin's heritage preservation company, and, officially, they were all his workmen, brought in on contract for this job. He was even meant to be paying them, officially.

On George's way to bed, he woke Morsel up so he could talk to her: "What's up with all of us, then?" He told her all about it, in his most confidential voice. She jumped up onto his bed and snuggled by his side happily, and was asleep in a moment. George took a little longer, though comforted by the warm bundle snoring against his toes.

In the days that followed the drugs announcement, George was startled to find that the reaction wasn't solid round the village. To his distress, he found opinion sharply divided at both *The Red Ship* and *The Old Bells*. On one of his rare visits to the former, for Alexander's birthday lunch, he found Alicia trying her best to argue Bill and Alexander round, without much hope. George joined in, shifting uneasily at intervals on one of those elegant but somehow uncomfortable chairs. He thought they were making progress, until Bill retreated onto safe ground:

"Supposing I did agree with you, what can we do? The Tories aren't exactly trying to set the clock back. They've hardly rebuffed the idea. They're just claiming that the Government will waste the revenues on tax breaks for the middle classes, and boosting the welfare budget. They saw the pound signs and they just went straight for it. Their Mr Shadow Health man was in the papers saying it'll kill fewer people than tobacco and booze, and make more money for the taxpayer. He was practically claiming that people who take drugs are public benefactors. They won't be using up our money claiming their pensions now, will they?" George reeled. What kind of defeatism was this?

Then, on the news, he saw a delegation from the Confederation of Small-Scale Recreational Substance Producers (the newly formed trade association for those respectable businessmen formerly known as drug dealers). They were being ushered into Number Ten, whence the prime minister's spokesman soon emerged, to announce that the government looked with great sympathy on the plight of the small producer, in light of the massive market share already being taken by the major pharmaceutical companies as they pushed into this new market. The government would certainly consider tax subsidies and other aid for the threatened small-scale businesses who had so eloquently made their plea.

This only got two minutes on the news, hardly news at all any more. When the original announcement was made it led to a media feeding frenzy for about a week: a national debate, broadsheets, tabloids, magazines, TV, radio, internet, assorted celebrities blessing the world with their deep thoughts on the matter, all sorts of professional pundits taking their moment in the limelight. A couple of weeks later, the subject hardly merited a mention. The media caravan had moved on and this was yesterday's story in the country at large, but not in Mutley Shepwell.

It proved the catalyst for their most important recruit so far. Soon George was back at *The Old Bells*, in a grubbier but comfier chair, listening to Richard Tranctard expounding his latest refinements to their little plot to the usual crew, along with their newest conspirator, Moira Brenchley herself. Moira was village aristocracy – the kind whose name earns a special respect from their fellow villagers by service and friendship. George would never have thought she would join them. Moira was one of those who usually remained unmoved by governments and their tricks, but her sister's life had been ruined by drugs and she was angry now.

That was her personal reason for joining them. Her public reason, as a devoted servant of the village, was the government's shabby refusal to stretch the boundaries of the Cotswolds to include their humble abodes. She was a woman who cared deeply about the village, indeed she was practically the village's model citizen. Thirty years teaching in the village primary, twenty of those as head, endless attendance on committees, judging of horticultural society entries at the village show, planning of village fetes. Her efficiency was legendary.

It was her service to the village, though, that was most admired. Divorce, it was said, had been her loss but the village's gain. Before it she gave her time to family life; after, she was the slave of the village, and the children who passed through her care at Mutley Shepwell CofE Primary, not to mention the waifs and troubled souls whom she looked after in the village. They all took the place of the daughter who died and the husband who left. Her nephew Jimmy Armsbell had benefited too, she had always been the most devoted of aunts, and supported her troubled sister enormously as well. She had probably done more than anyone else to bring Jimmy up, truth be told, and she and he together did their best to keep his mother on the straight and narrow.

She still dressed every inch the old-style head teacher, on every occasion, smart jackets and skirts in tasteful pastels, hair immaculately bobbed in the same style she seemed to have had for decades, greyer now but otherwise remarkably unchanged, almost a female Dorian Gray, and never anything less than perfectly turned out. Her hair was a curious kind of pepper and salt: silvered on top these days, but still dark elsewhere, except the two silver locks that came forward either side of her forehead, almost to frame it; they showed up strikingly in gloomy light.

In honour of Moira's arrival, Des Martin had given their little band of conspirators a name. Moira liked things to be clearly labelled. They now called themselves The Guy Fawkes Club, after another gentleman who enjoyed plotting and had a bone to pick with Parliament.

Bob Corns abandoned his pretence at working to come and join them for the evening, at their usual table, at the back, looking out at the flags. The usual suspects were present, drinks in hand. Perhaps they should all have a secret handshake, Des suggested helpfully. Richard started in. Moira was soon interrupting. She may have been new to the conspiracy, but she wasn't shy. She wanted to get on to the issues around the national park, and she objected to his long discursions into ancient history.

"Now, now, Richard," she said. "Forget all that. What you say might even be true, but let's get back to brass tacks: we need to be part of this national park, and we ought to be in it. As the Association of Local History Associations told us, there are thirteen different definitions of the Cotswolds, and six of them include this village. Our precious government could include us in the park, only they're not being generous. They're just sitting in London issuing their almighty decrees, as usual, and not listening to the likes of us. We need to get their attention. Your plan might just manage that. Can you explain it a little more clearly?"

There was a general murmur of assent, running through the little group in that snug corner of the pub. The Old Tank was in his element. "Pull up those chairs a little closer then, and let me tell you the next part of how this could go. Not a word goes outside this bar, mind." And the chairs were drawn up and he went through the plan, bit by bit, pint by pint.

A few nights later, George found himself digging beside Moira and no fewer than four even newer conspirators, Bill Stone, Alicia Cornwell, Alexander Livingston and Johnny Berensford, all now officially enlisted as part-time contractors for Des Martin, alongside their day jobs. George wondered how it had come to this, digging under cover of night in his own churchyard. Not exactly illegal, he liked to think, or at least not against the spirit of the law. Old Lord Bonifer wouldn't really mind, if he could come back to give his opinion. Hopefully not, anyway.

7
OLD FRIENDS AND CHERRY TREES

As the evenings slowly became a little shorter, and summer started to think about coming to an end, the conspirators were still digging. During the day, builders' lorries, vans, and massive machines continually invaded Traitor's Wood across the road, but the nights remained a haven of peace. It was the best of late summer weather ("a pleasure to be a criminal on a night like this," as Bob put it), yet they still could find no way to the entrance they were sure there must be, somewhere, an entrance to Lord Bonifer's grandiose monument.

It was designed as a kind of gothic mini-version of the Dome of the Rock. Lord Bonifer had gone on crusade, and he had wanted all who came after him to know it. It was made of the same creamy limestone as the church, with a small dome of solid stone, and gothic arches beneath it, all round the tomb itself, arches that had been submerged beneath the soil for centuries, so that only the pointed top of each arch was visible.

They had now excavated round three sides of the structure, poking and prodding each arch in turn, in the hope that they would find a way in. Still nothing less solid than stone. Hope was fading, and there was a sense of time running out. Beautiful though the arrival of morning was by the River Amble, with a faint early mist dissolving away as the sun came up, and the birds still singing of summer, there was a sense of gloom among the humans there.

George and Des were very silent as they took their usual route: there was a footpath from the north-east corner of the churchyard that zig-zagged up the hill, away from others' eyes, across Church Copse and then up through the woods and glades and copses that formed a patchwork down from the manor to the river on this side of the road, so different from the big fields of wheat on the west side, glowing golden in the morning sunlight. Finally their path turned back towards the village and they said goodbye as they came up to Church Road, the old road that wound its leisurely way from the village down the gentle slope to the River Amble.

On this occasion, Bill Stone waited for them, and accompanied them as far as the short cut up to the road and turned left there, going across to the far side of the village and then along to the old stone farmhouse he inhabited, alone now except for his brother Stephanos (formerly known as Stephen). It had been one of the last four farmhouses around the village that still presided over a farm, until he flogged off most of his fields to raise money for his various business ventures, bar a few chickens and a couple of fields, including the scenic one that he used for wedding receptions.

This left his farmhouse in the same position as eight or nine more old farmhouses, dotted around the fields nearby. They retained their charm but not their land, relics of the days when Mutley Shepwell harboured about a dozen small farms. Now there were just the big three left behind on the north, southwest, and east sides of the village, and most of the southwestern farm was about to be built on, to enrich its landlords, an ancient Oxford college, which said it needed the money for educational purposes.

Manor Farm, on the east side, was still part of the Shepwell Estate, and so its small fields were interspersed between larger woods and copses designed for shooting more than farming, or even just for their scenic value. Indeed, it was believed that the cows who inhabited those fields had been chosen for their looks rather than their profitability: pedigree Jersey and Charolais only.

The tenant farmers of Manor Farm had to work round the enthusiasms of the lords and ladies of the manor, with the actual pieces of land they were allowed to farm forming a patchwork between the wooded slopes that successive Thursloe-Cavendish-Bendykes had lovingly cultivated for centuries, and the Russian still maintained, although he neither hunted nor shot. Various footpaths ran through, which remained open to villagers, as far up the slope as the boundary of the gardens of Shepwell Hall.

George continued as the path ran parallel to the road, behind an untidy hedge. Rather than follow it round the big loop just below Mutley, he decided to take the shortcut up through Tatler's Copse. This little trail got so overgrown in summer that not many used it but, with the aid of a stout stick to bash down the nettles, he managed well enough. As he reached the gardens of the line of houses that faced onto Mutley High Street, he saw something that amused him enough to set him hacking through the stray brambles between him and the fence.

The man hanging from a cherry tree with a telescope to his eye was so intent that he didn't notice the approaching bramble-basher till George called up: "Aren't you a bit old for that?"

To jump convulsively sideways between the branch and the trunk of a cherry tree while simultaneously looking embarrassed, dropping a telescope, turning to see one's interrogator, and squawking, all the while managing not to fall out of one's tree, was a feat surprising in a man of mature years. Des Martin remained a remarkably agile 65. As he clung on to the trunk, he gasped out, "You, is it?"

"You alright up there?"

"I was till you turned up. Never mind. Is me telescope broken? No? Good thing it dropped on the compost, never mind yer hands, you can wash 'em inside. I'm comin' down."

He dropped down with an agility that belied his years, and pulled one of the panels of his smartly painted picket fence back to let George in. "What's up, guv'nor? You're looking mighty miserable this morning."

"What's up with me? What's up with you? Or do you make a habit of hanging from that cherry tree spying through that telescope? I hope you haven't been picking up bad habits in your old age. What would Peggy say?"

"She knows all about it, though she don't approve. – Not so shocked, George, it's just the village show. Look, Joe Bennett's won the garlic section three years runnin'. I'm garlic, George, garlic's me, garlic's always bin me. Seventeen times I've won that cat'gory. Seventeen times, but he's doin' somethin' to his garlic that's rollin' mine over, and I can't work out what. He's out there now on his garden, fiddlin' away, and I'm just tryin' to see what he's up to with it." George looked down at his feet and shuffled uncomfortably.

"No crime in that, is there? I wouldn't touch his garlic, I just want to know what he's doin'. Might be legal, maybe it's not. I'm tryin' to check. Where's the harm in that?" Des shrugged and gestured to the house. "Peggy keeps goin' on about it. Says I'm lettin' my competitive nature run away. I don't see it like that. Never mind, come inside for a cuppa and a spot of breakfas'. Don't say a word about the telescope, mind."

His garden looked wonderful: the whole of the back of the long garden was crammed with veg beds, fruit trees trained along the fences, two sheds and a summerhouse, with just room left between them and the house for a small square of lawn, a few beautifully kept beds of roses, a patio of crazy paving, and a massive, hand-made steel barbeque.

Peggy Martin looked a bit surprised, but she'd always had a soft spot for George. She was feeling less kindly to her husband: "What were you up to, anyway, did I see you getting up a tree? At your age? Fell out of it? Good thing you're made of old boot leather. Don't do it again. I won't be coming to fix you up, silly games!"

Des turned on his patented look of surprised innocence. It was actually pretty good. He had a winning way about him. In his younger days he had often been described as having a matinee idol's looks, several times scouted to be a male model, and rejected it all to stay a builder.

If there had been a competition for Mr and Mrs Mutley Shepwell, Older Generation, he and Peggy would definitely have been leading candidates. Her full-bodied hair was still the object of great admiration at the hairdresser, whichever colour she dyed it, her clothes somehow spoke of style without seeming to try, and, unlike her husband, she had kept her figure; he had certainly kept his strength, but, like Obelix, his chest had slipped a bit.

Three cups of tea and a plate of bacon and eggs later, with Peggy fussing around and saying would he like some more toast, George had been enlightened on a matter he wasn't sure he really wanted to know about. He was very fond of Des, but the growing of garlic had never been a consuming passion for him. George was thinking he really should go.

Peggy prompted him by reminding Des about putting the bins out. When it came to jobs like that she was firmly of the "Why keep a dog and bark yourself" school of thought. George went round the side of the house to help Des. As they wheeled the bins to the pavement, Des re-membered: "What was it had you looking so glum then?"

The happiness induced by a hearty breakfast suddenly faded away. George felt that they'd heard enough about the time ticking away as they scratched round the edges of Lord Bonifer's monument. He launched into his usual complaint about politicians instead, and what they were doing to the country.

Des shrugged. "Oh, that one. Bit above my pay grade, that. I'm just doin' it for the village, rest of the country 'as to look after itself. Not much a builder can do to a prime minister. If I bump into 'im, though, I'll give 'im an earful for you." He thought for a minute. "I know, it's desperate measures time. If you want opinions, we could go and see the pope."

8

THE POPE OF BEER

They weren't the only people thinking of visiting the pope that summer morning. There were two young gentlemen of Mutley and Shepwell who had been trying to pluck up the courage for an audience for weeks. Not that they were at all religious, except where a certain football club was concerned, in which case their devotion was of the most dedicated and worshipful nature. Their need to gain the pope's blessing was because of a different passion.

The full village title of Johnny Berensford was in fact, The Pope of Beer, because his real ale was without error, and his making of stout pretty much infallible, or as near as anyone's tastebuds could discern. At least, that was what his fans said. He didn't disagree.

His actual brewery was down the road in Faringdon. It even looked rather classy, for a brewery. He'd incorporated some old barns on the edge of the town, and built the uglier parts nicely screened away further back, so from the road it actually looked rather grander than your average brewery. Its clientele was richer too, customers who were prepared to pay rather eye-watering prices for what, to the true believers, was a nectar among real ales, and a giant among stouts. The names he'd chosen were Oakenheart ale and St George's stout.

When not supervising the nectar down in Faringdon, his home was a converted wisteria-clad eighteenth-century farmhouse down a lane on the West side of Upper Shepwell, right on top of the ridge, with his garden going down the hill and backing picturesquely onto the Little Shepbrook. His second home was *The Red Ship*, where he could choose between drinking his own beers and other local favourites, while religiously avoiding the standard brands.

He was a generous donor to some local causes, while eschewing and deriding others. He was also an object of great interest to the younger generation because he had been known to give holiday jobs to friends of friends and junior acquaintances, jobs that sometimes even involved helping out with the leftovers at the brewery.

That was what had these two young gentlemen debating whether they should pop in on the pope on their way home that morning. They had spent the previous evening enjoying the drinking holes and dance floors of Oxford and missed the last bus home. After a grimy night on a student friend's floor, they caught the first bus back. Judicious consideration of their appearance might have deterred them from seeking employment at that moment, but the last of the previous night's Dutch courage was still somewhat with them, as their slightly unsteady progress showed, and they were gradually talking themselves into appearing on the doorstep.

They were an unlikely pair of friends in some ways, Jeremy Wansfield-Diggersby and Jimmy Armsbell. The one lived in the big old rectory at the top of Nether Shepwell, the other on the council estate at the bottom of Mutley. Their paths might never have crossed had they not both gone to the little church primary school in Mutley. Jem was sent off to boarding school after that, while Jimmy went to Chipping Camden Community College, but they'd formed a bond.

It was nourished down the years by two shared passions. One was for English history. They'd trailed round many a castle, museum or cathedral together. That enthusiasm had taken them both to degrees in history, followed by launching into a master's each. All the studying created an ever more pressing need for cash, hence their great desire to meet the pope and help him to part with some of his ready cash in return for their services. He was actually

Jem's mother's cousin, but the two branches of the family had never got along, which made Jem nervous. Jimmy was a bit more hopeful, as his Aunty Moira knew Johnny Berensford; Aunty Moira knew everybody. She may not have liked Johnny very much, but she knew him, and that was enough for Jimmy.

Their other shared devotion was something they both saw as a vital part of English history, albeit one rather far from home: Liverpool Football Club. The very night before, when Jeremy saw a Northern gentleman wearing their team's scarf in an Oxford pub, he crushed him in a beery embrace. Then he declared, to his new friend's bemusement, in a cut-glass accent, "I may sound home counties to you, but in my heart, I'm Scouse and I'm proud."

Jimmy and Jem both still wore their "I was born to play for Liverpool" woolly hats all through the winter, and they both had tattoos beneath their hearts of their club's crest, which had caused not a few family ructions. They'd saved their pounds and made a few pilgrimages to Anfield in their time, each one commemorated in photos lovingly mounted on bedroom walls.

As the two friends walked home down the Burford road, they were singing Liverpool's praises, with only the birds to listen to them. The early morning skies of Oxfordshire were serenaded by the cut-glass tones of Jeremy and the Oxfordshire burr of Jimmy, united in a rendition of a well-known song of progress in togetherness, through fair weather and foul.

Fortunately, they had stopped singing by the time they turned down the pope's lane, which might have been a good career move, looking back. It also saved the residents of the former farm cottages along the lane from having their Saturday lie-ins interrupted sooner than they would have wished. Jimmy and Jem were oblivious to the perfection of the lane, with its ancient cottages and converted barns, lichen-covered stone walls, the very last overgrown remains of the cow parsley, a few scattered daisies and ragged robins still peeping through, and, at one end, the beginnings of an invasion of oilseed rape.

They arrived at the front door at round about elevenses, and knocked very nervously. The pope himself answered and heard their petition. He had an imposing presence. Although he wasn't very big, except around the waist, he somehow filled a room. All the bright colours he wore may have helped. From his socks to his ties, via trousers, sweaters, suits, never a dull colour was allowed near him. His pale, pasty face, without being handsome, had a strong bone structure, and a very firm jaw. From his expensive shoes to the top of his bald head, he exuded self-assurance. They felt very small as his deep-set brown eyes looked them up and down. Then the pope spoke: "A holiday job, eh?"

"My Aunty Moira thought you might have something," mumbled Jimmy.

"And Mum says Hello," add Jem, nervously. It was the first greeting his mother and Johnny Berensford had exchanged in a long time.

"Interesting, step in," said Johnny B. They found themselves in a large study, with a housekeeper bringing a tray of coffee. There was a pause while his cat, Chatsworth, decided to install herself on his lap. There is a hierarchy to things: he might be The Pope of Beer, but, as the saying goes, "Dogs have owners, cats have staff," and to Chatsworth he would always be one of the servants. When he tried to reach for the coffee, she nudged his hand to make him stroke her.

He asked the boys to serve themselves, and pass the chocolate biscuits, while he did his duty: a melodious purr arose to prove it, but it was purely performance-related purring, and he didn't dare to pause long enough to drink his coffee, lest he incur the twitching tail and moody silence of Chatsworth's wrath. Thus we find our level in this life.

Once his feline boss was suitably placated, and the boys

had helped themselves to food and drink, he was able to manage enough multi-tasking to deal with human business too. "We don't have anything right now but there might be something in the summer for suitably enterprising young gents. You'd need to prove yourselves to me first, mind." They nodded and mumbled and tried to look enterprising, while wishing their heads didn't hurt and wondering if turning up in the clothes they'd slept in, with hangovers, had been such a very good idea.

"I happen to know," the pope went on, "that they're looking for a few good workers up at the manor for a clear out of the stables and the old yards and a few other things. Mrs Rhodes, the housekeeper, has been asked to recruit a few hard-working lads. You know Mrs Rhodes?"

"Friend of my aunty," said Jimmy, "I know her a bit."

"Good. Tell her I sent you and get yourselves jobs there for these coming holidays. Come back once you've landed the jobs and I'll let you know a couple of things I'd like you to be on the lookout for. Nothing irregular, just a couple of things I'd like looking into, on the quiet. No need to let the Russian know we're looking, is there?"

They looked a bit confused but agreed that there was no need to bother the Russian.

"Mrs Rhodes will help you. She knows what I mean. Do it right and there's a bonus for you, a pretty good bonus it might be, and jobs for the summer, and maybe after that. Got that?"

Jeremy looked a bit stunned. Jimmy coughed a little. "Er, I don't quite know how to say this, er, Sir – "

"You think I'd ask you to do anything dodgy? Or Mrs Rhodes for that matter? Very respectable lady, she's been in the village a long time, and so have I. No, it's a bit of local history. I've an interest, but Russians don't exactly understand these things, do they? What does he know about our village and its past? Best just to quietly check up a couple of things. You lads are both studying history, aren't you?"

"We're all history," said Jem nervously. That was true indeed, especially true of him: history was his great passion, not just his university course.

At that moment they heard the front door open. "'Scuse me a moment," said their host. He went into the hall and they heard the words, "Did you find it?" Followed by a hurried, inaudible muttered conversation, swiftly going out of earshot as it went down the hall and up the stairs. The pope looked bothered when he returned. "Might be a good thing you two turned up. I've heard you're sharp lads, eh? Stay tuned in, and this could be the start of good things."

Next thing they knew they were out the door and walking back down the lane. "How did he know we were studying history?" said Jem.

"Knows your parents a bit, don't he? Dinner parties and that. And my uncle Fred has done a lot of work on that house for him, they might've talked. It was Aunty Moira who told me he had jobs going, maybe he said something to her."

Not knowing that they had just been speaking to one of Richard Tranctard's new conspirators, they walked back down the lane, and down the hill, then Jem turned right and Jimmy carried on down. Jem took a stroll before returning to the Old Rectory. His stroll took him past the wheat, then along the edge of a couple of fields on the north side of the ridge, sometimes containing sheep, now empty, with progressively better views behind him, had he bothered to turn and look back. After a lifetime walking that path, however, he contented himself with enjoying the sunshine and the larks singing their alarm calls to him as he passed, perhaps the most tuneful of all alarms.

Jimmy, on the other hand, cut through to Back Lane, which went down the hill parallel to Shepwell High Street, past gardens to gladden the greenest of hearts; indeed, these were some of the best-kept of all the well-kept gardens of Mutley Shepwell, including two which competed for the most glorious roses on that side of the High Street. It wasn't for nothing that it had been shortlisted five times for Oxfordshire's best-kept village. Those gardens couldn't have been more loved if they were allotments in the Garden of Eden.

9 JERUSALEM IN MUTLEY

George was meant to be getting ready for another night's digging. He couldn't help himself from being distracted, however, when he saw a front garden full of particularly splendid roses. He loved roses, although dahlias and geraniums were his speciality.

Alicia caught him up as he admired said plants. She asked if he could come back for a cup of tea, so they could discuss the intricacies of the situation, but he had a meeting of the history society committee he needed to get to. Fortunately, he was due to drop Morsel in to her first thing in the morning as he was spending a couple of days with his daughter, and Alicia had kindly offered to provide dachshund hostelling services any time he liked. In return, she had retained him to provide personal consultancy services regarding her geraniums, on which he was moderately expert.

They turned down the lane, past George's house, and Moira's mostly picturesque cottage. That is to say, it would have been a picture if its early nineteenth-century frontage hadn't had a 1960s extension added, which was the architectural equivalent of welding the front of an early Skoda onto your vintage Bentley. Curtains twitched as George and Alicia walked by. One of Mrs Mudgery's friends made a mental note. Such sightings often were reported in to Mrs Mudgery, who was the epicentre of village gossip.

Rather later, had their owners still been awake, one or two of those curtains might have twitched in the other direction, and wondered why George, Des, and Bill were sauntering down the lane, as if towards the pub, yet all three turned left, crossed over the High Street, then turned off onto the footpath down towards the river. The curtain-twitchers of Nether Shepwell and upper Mutley might have really worked up a lather had they discerned certain others taking footpaths from other parts of the village, and all wandering casually down the hill, towards the church-yard of St Martin's.

As they arrived, one by one, they worked their way inside the large tent-like set of screens that sheltered and camouflaged the "repairs" to the Bonifer monument. The more they exposed its sides, the better it looked, truly a fine structure. It nestled against the north side of the church, its small stone dome a very, very distant echo of the Dome of the Rock, which Lord Bonifer had seen, but the architect clearly hadn't, not having had the benefit of going to the Holy Land on crusade with his lordship and King Edward II.

That crusade was also echoed in the Jerusalem crosses that adorned the arches round the eight sides of the base, worn over the centuries but still showing a beautiful craftsmanship. It was an almost clear night, with a few high clouds, which became luminously beautiful when one of them passed in front of the full moon. Only the occasional call from the tawny owls in the woods above them disturbed the silence.

They had to be delicate, since the crack in the monument, the crack that gave their nocturnal activities cover, being allegedly the reason for their health and safety work, was steadily expanding to a dangerous point. They had excavated round the first six arches, and were working their way round the last two. Still no sign of any kind of entrance, although Des kept prodding and poking with various implements. Every few minutes there was a little ritual when Bill Stone told him to be careful and Des reminded him that he'd been a builder all his life, and he knew how to be careful.

Those two went steadily but very carefully at it, while George and Alexander Livingston shovelled earth into

Richard's barrow; being the unskilled labour there present, they got to do most of the digging between them, and their backs were telling them all about it.

Bob had been relegated to making the tea and assisting Mary with the delivery of the nightly hamper she brought them to ease their labours. And talking, of course, that went without saying with Bob. Tonight he was wondering if they might find a clue they hadn't been looking for, one entirely more lucrative and perhaps the thing they should have been searching for all along. His musings were interrupted rather brusquely by, of all people, George.

"What's that?" said George Sneed.

They crowded round. At the edge of the side facing the church, following the curve of the gothic arch as it rose up, there was something. It looked like letters. At intervals there were little Jerusalem crosses in some dull metal, studded into the stone. They dug with a will after that, and with great care where they touched that wall. Slowly letters emerged, worn away by centuries of damp.

"What's it all about?" said Des.

"Too much for me," replied Richard, with an air of regret. "Over to you, professor."

"Not that simple, Father. I'll need to trace them out, what's left of them, then take them home and try to fill in as many of the gaps as I can." His words were cautious but there was an air of excitement about Alexander; one of his specialities had been inscriptions, and this was close to his heart. He went off to get his tracing materials and a better camera, while the others removed the last of the earth as delicately as they could.

When the full inscription was revealed, they gathered round, and George heard a sudden intake of breath from Richard Tranctard. His own heart was beating faster. Des did a little dance. Mary hugged Richard, then took care to tell him off loudly, so no one should think she was going soft. Bill's eyes seemed unusually moist. He and Des and Peggy started grabbing everyone for group selfies, standing next to their discovery. A bit undignified, thought George, but rather fun.

At the end of a long night, with the sky lightening above them, promising a clear blue sky, and the birds in chorus along the willows by the river and in the woods above, Alexander took his leave first, with some detailed photographs and tracing. Des and George stayed on longest, as usual, taking rather less professional photographs on their phones, and George even joined in when Des started singing a few merry songs from the days of their youth.

It was a long day of waiting for the rest of them before night came down again, with clouds rolling in from the west this time, and only the occasional glimpse of moonlight when it found its way through a brief hole in that vast celestial flying carpet of cloud. Alexander was waiting in the church porch as the others arrived. He refused to say anything until they were all there, then he took them inside and lined them up along the porch, in front of his 3D projector. When they were all sitting comfortably, he pushed the button and a reconstruction of an arc of medieval Latin words appeared. He pushed another button and the arc morphed into a straight line of damaged text.

"Begins something like this: Some Jerusalem crosses, then, 'Jerusalem stands guard something gap before Rome, and the riders watch over the four winds something something,' then a gap that's just too damaged, then 'Let only those with the hearts of crusaders, No, maybe, who are crusaders in their hearts, Let only those enter within, lest the beasts arise in wrath.' Then more damage, then the Bonifer insignia and more Jerusalem crosses to end it."

"That's it? That's all? Nothing about the other thing? Nothing about the treasure?" Bill Stone was a practical man and he wasn't impressed. Bill rarely was.

Des was also a practical man, and he'd noticed something. "Go back to that first picture, Prof, there's a duck. And cheer up, Bill, might be simpler than you're thinking."

They went back to the first image. "See where the crosses are, the way they're spaced? I had to move a stone screen once, in an old manor house, and they had little holes just about the same places, so you could put poles through and lift it out. How's about we try?"

It was a lot more complicated than that. The metal Jerusalem crosses could indeed be levered out, and a thin wire poked in soon revealed a deep, thin gap in the rock behind each, but it took Bill and Des days and days of trial and error to find metal poles thin enough and strong enough to insert into each thin crevice. Finally, they were ready.

Mary and Alicia joined them for the moment of truth. All of them grabbed something metal, two to a pole. They tried leaning right: nothing. They tried leaning left: nothing. They tried lifting up: nothing. They tried leaning forward: and slowly the entire stone panel inside the outline of the arch disengaged, slowly, stiffly, slowly, and it started to pivot out. Then, suddenly it tipped and Des got a faceful of damp stone as it lurched over on top of him. He just managed to get an arm up to break the impact, and the Old Tank's barrowful of damp earth half-broke his fall, though it left a red weal across his back.

They managed to get it off him, and ended up gently laying it on the floor at their feet, to the sound of Des's grunts and groans, with a soprano layer of Peggy, Mary and Alicia's calls of sympathy overlaid on top. A strange, damp, musty, smell emerged. It smelt like drains that had been left bunged up for a hundred years. It was dark within. Richard and Bill and Alicia shone torches in.

They saw a coffin-shaped tomb, made of some kind of dark stone. It was raised up on a much broader, waist-high slab of cream-coloured local stone, with brasses on the floor on each side of the slab showing four horsemen launching themselves out across the floor. On the dark tomb itself, around a brass of a lordly crusader in his armour, another Jerusalem cross on his surcoat, were four beasts: man, ox, eagle, lion, etched onto the stone at each corner. The workmanship was exquisite. It was marvellously preserved. The gothic traceries round the walls of the chamber were shaped to match the arches on the outside, as if they were about to swing open onto the starlight.

For once, they were all silent. Bill spoke first, with more enthusiasm than anyone could ever remember on his frowning face:

"You little beauty, you!" Des wrapped Richard Tranctard in a bear hug. "You mad old coot, you're actually right!"

Alexander Livingston coughed, looking not entirely happy to see the glory going to another. The rest of them, however, were too happy to care. The celebrations at *The Old Bells* went on late, and George had all he could do to keep Mary and Bill from saying something more loudly than they should. It was a good thing the landlord was in on it anyway, he steered his customers to other corners of the pub, leaving their little corner table, tucked away on the far side of the great fireplace, all to itself.

The most surprising moment, for George, was when Alicia materialised at his elbow as he sat down, a glass of wine in one hand and an unopened bottle in the other. ""And which of us, deep down, actually believed there'd really be anything there? — Special night, George, so I've ordered this bottle of Chateauneuf du Pape. It is your favourite, isn't it?"

"How did you know?" He said.

Alicia just smiled, "Morsel told me." The laughter and stories rippled on around them. Everyone was on top form that night.

10
MRS RHODES AND
THE RUSSIAN'S RUSSIANS

They weren't so happy three nights later. Three nights of searching, three days of trying to keep the day job going, or the day retirement activities for most of them, on far too little sleep. Everyone was getting more and more crotchety. They had found a tomb, but, so far, nothing more. Fuses were getting shorter all the time.

"Where is it, then?" demanded Bill Stone. "The treasure, or the other?"

"I think you can forget the first of those," replied Richard. "We're not treasure hunters, we are here to strike a blow for freedom." (Not all of his fellow conspirators seemed convinced.) Richard went on: "What we've found half-matches the first part of Hobson's recollections, but only the first part. We've found the riders, but where are the beasts? The man, the ox, the eagle and the lion are symbols of the four evangelists who wrote the gospels. They are not the beasts we seek. Where are the beasts?"

That was a question that obsessed them for a little while. Had they but known it, they should have been looking up the hill not down at the tomb. The answer might just have been not far from the eager but clumsy hands of Jem and Jimmy, as they toiled, rather more than they had hoped to, in their summer of work up at the manor.

Ben and Becky were keen to help, or at least get on the payroll at the manor. The twins were old friends of Jem and Jimmy and wished they could be doing their summer jobs with them.

"We've just got these poxy paid internships, doing really boring stuff in the office park in Faringdon for some business friend of Mum's," explained Becky, looking at Jimmy, "We could really do with some proper money, and the manor would be such a cool place to work. I really like Mrs Rhodes."

Jimmy was busy teaching Ben how to play poker better and just grimaced, "We could do with some proper money too, but we ain't getting it in this job."

Jem was most sympathetic, and explained how they really would like to help, but Mrs Rhodes had already said that it was hard enough getting two outsiders through the manor security, which had been quite a business, and they didn't dare to ask her for any more, not till they'd at least got to know her better, and anyway, Jimmy was right, the money wasn't up to much.

To tell the truth, they didn't like their holiday job, to start with. Mrs Rhodes was fine, and usually friendly in her own very formal fashion, once you got past her stiff, old-fashioned manners. She was tall and thin, eyes once blue, now more grey, classical profile, nose perhaps a little larger than it might have been, quiet and precise and very, very thorough, as unbending as the collars on her perfectly ironed white blouses. She was as perfectly punctual as she was perfectly groomed, in jackets and skirts that might have been more at home in a smart office in the City than their little village. She kept her hair long, always brushed into the same long flow it had been since she was a girl, immaculately dyed in one of a range of modest browns, perfectly shaped and never a single hair out of place.

Of all the manor's previous staff she was the only one the Russian had kept on, and you could see why. Her organization was the stuff of legend. Every part of the manor was kept immaculate, and she expected the same standards from her staff, even the temporary ones, as they found to their cost.

They had harboured the illusion that a summer job might mean a bit of relaxed gardening in the sunshine, but she kept them indoors, under her beady eye, and had an endless succession of jobs for them. Jem sometimes wished the Russian hadn't kept her on. Their work ranged from humping furniture in and out of store, to sorting out years-worth of paperwork left behind by the previous owner. Not for any actual use, as Jimmy bitterly remarked, just for the manor archive. She even made them take down every metal curtain ring in the place, clean and polish them, then put them all back up again. If we'd known they were wanting real work, we should have asked for real money, he added bitterly.

It wasn't just that: the Russian's Russians spooked them, the staff at the house, that is, especially the four security men, in their identical grey suits. Those suits were cut nice and loose under the armpits, for carrying guns, or so the boys thought. Jem and Jimmy never really got their names, so they built on Des Martin's naming system and dubbed them Big Boris, Fat Boris, Red Boris (for his hair) and Boris the Scar (for obvious reasons). In fairness, they did admit, down at the pub, that Fat Boris should probably be called Muscle Boris: he might be short and square, but it looked more like muscle than fat, a lot of muscle; nevertheless, they preferred Fat Boris as a name.

Most of the rest of the staff were Russian too, except the gardeners and the cleaners, and some of the office staff were pretty spooky too. The office manager and the various personal assistants lived at the top of the main house, with the security staff based down in the basement, a bit like in the old days, mused Jimmy, although Downton never saw servants like the four Borises. Mrs Rhodes said their basement had its own underground gym and firing range. There were also some rooms at one end she was never allowed to enter.

Very soon, Jem and Jimmy were almost ready to quit and try another summer job, but when they hinted this to Johnny Berensford, he looked so angry that they had second thoughts. Then, the very next day he turned up at Jimmy's house in his Range Rover, took them both off into the garden shed, and quietly offered them a bonus that would double their money, if they stuck it out till the end of the summer. For a down-payment, he took out £500 each in shiny new notes to see them right for the present, and offered to top it up any time they liked, so long as they were discreet about it, and he did mean discreet.

"You boys are young, and you don't know what rests on this," declared Johnny, looking each of them in turn very intently in the eye, while stroking Chatsworth with unusual firmness.

Jimmy tried: "Can't you tell us a bit more, boss? We'd just be happier if we knew what we were getting into."

Johnny shook his head. "I can't tell you now, but hang on in there and you'll find out in time." They looked so nervous that he put Chatsworth down, reached for his wallet and handed over another £500 each.

"Just to make you feel better, boys. You're doing a good thing, you don't need to worry."

They felt it would be churlish to refuse, so they shook hands on it. Once they'd done so he gave them a very serious lecture on the vital necessity of discretion, pointing out that the Russian might not be very happy if he knew they were working for someone else, and you didn't want to upset the Russian, did you? They came away with a nasty taste in the mouth about the whole deal, and, to tell the truth, rather frightened, but they couldn't see any way of turning back.

"You'll just have to button it, for once in your life," said Jem, with unusual vehemence, to Jimmy. Even more unusually, Jimmy just nodded, in silence.

11
THE SINGERS AND THE SONG

The Guy Fawkes Club was in need of new blood, younger blood to be more precise, and more tech-friendly heads. Bill Stone, of all people, was the one to find the answer. Not that Bill was himself a repository of technological wizardry. He'd had a rather chequered career, trying out one business idea after another, usually with disappointing results. In the end, when he had run out of fields from the ancestral farm to sell to fund his business plans, he had been forced to take a job with the Woodvilles, of all people. He had become their Buildings & Facilities Manager, which he found hard after so many years of being his own boss.

He often looked across the road from the research centre where he worked to the vintage Porsche that Mary Tranctard parked outside the Vicarage and mused, loudly and sadly, on the unfairness of life, which dragged a gifted entrepreneur down through no fault of his own, and raised another up, through no virtue of hers. He liked to think that, when it came to business, Mary was as untalented as he was talented, and yet, by what he saw as pure good fortune, she had been as successful as he was not. He had been known to lament that if he'd had Mary's luck, he'd never have hit the financial rocks.

Mary's own business career had seen plenty of reverses. Unlike Bill's, though, there had been ups to go with the downs. She had to admit that the venture which finally led her to her crock of gold had surprised her as much as anyone. A couple of years ago, she had suddenly started making her fortune in used sports cars. It was all because of two court decisions: first, the High Court decided, for the sake of road safety, that all new cars must be fitted with GPS speed limiters, which tracked the speed limit on every road and enforced it from within the engine; then, in another big test case, the judges ruled that all insurance would be void if the speed limiter was turned off or tampered with.

That suddenly made new sports cars a lot less interesting than old ones to the boy racers, girl racers and other speed freaks of the world. The judges had not yet ruled that old cars had to be retrofitted with limiters. Until they did, many customers felt it was time for out with the new and in with the old. Mary's old sports cars were suddenly highly in demand. She regularly raised a glass to the very judges her customers cursed, and praised GPS to the skies; others wished it could be banished, but nothing can be uninvented.

Mary was immensely cheered to finally find herself an overnight success, after all these years. The only person who insisted on being unimpressed was her new husband, who did his best to keep her newfound riches from entering their lives. She found that amusing, and enjoyed finding ways of getting round him. Having in the past often needed help to protect her from her bank manager, nowadays Mary needed all sorts of help with marketing and communications to enable her to make the most of her good fortune. The couple who had sorted it all out for her were Mike and Jane Singer, who travelled the world from Mutley Shepwell with their own design and marketing consultancy.

Brexit had nearly floored them a few years ago, scaring off some of their best international customers, but they had made their way back, and they wanted to speak up for an England that was totally international as far as business was concerned, yet in touch with all its local roots. Mary's cars appealed to them, and they helped her to sell faster than she'd ever dreamed she could. She knew that they would be the people to spread the word about The Guy Fawkes Club's discovery, once a discovery had actually been made, but she couldn't persuade them to take an interest. Mike and Jane were amused to be sworn to secrecy, touched to be asked, and completely incredulous.

At this point, Bill stepped in. He'd managed to put in a good word for the Singers at the reality centre and get them an introduction to the marketing people there, which led to a rush of business for them. They owed him, and they knew it. Nevertheless, to begin with, his stuttering attempts as a recruiter of plotters went no further than Mary's had. They explained that they were just too busy to join some mad crusade.

Their minds changed very rapidly when the coalition unveiled the third part of what was starting to seem a four-card trick from the government, that is, a surprise four-part series of Westminster edicts unleashed on an unwilling country. At the precise moment this third card of the four-card trick was revealed, their family were all in the kitchen, washing up after supper, surfing the net or putting off going upstairs and doing homework. It was what Jane liked to think of as a happy family moment, until it was spoilt when her husband switched on the news on the radio.

It was another announcement from the PM and his deputy: they'd stood up in parliament to announce that it was time to cut the last of the cords linking church and state. "Religion is a private matter," said the prime minister. "I will defend to the death anyone's right to practise their religion, but it has no place in politics or public life in the twenty-first century, or in education. From September next year, this law will end the link between faith and schools."

The PM handed over to the deputy prime minister, who went on for a while about how she was personally a great admirer of faith schools, yet the need to develop unity in the new Britain was such that all schools needed to be focused on core, government-approved British values. Schools should not to be dividing children from each other by teaching other values or faiths not shared by all. Religion and religious education were not matters for the classroom, but for places of worship, where they would always be freely allowed. Much of the media cheered the advent of a properly secular Britain.

Jane was more than upset. She instantly became a one-woman crusade. Her children had been at the village's Church of England school, very happily. She loved that school, and was grateful to it. Even after her children had long outgrown it she remained a governor. She knew what a harmonious ship it was, and how neatly balanced. It had happy links to both the village churches, and had taught basic Christian values for over a century without any great objections; suddenly change was being forced upon it, without consent. Much that had been held dear was being torn away by Westminster dictat.

All round the country, hundreds of other schools seemed to be in the same position. There was much protest from church schools and churches but a great deal of approval from influential sections of the London media, and from politicians of all parties, who seemed to feel this a great advance. The government wanted very much to move on swiftly, but Jane and thousands like her were incensed. Even Mike was up in arms. He and Jane considered together for about five minutes, and decided they'd make their own protest.

They marched out the door and down the road to *The Old Bells*, where they asked Bill to sign them up for The Guy Fawkes Club on the spot. Bill was thrilled, and felt himself practically a spymaster, as he ushered in his secret new recruits. With Mike and Jane's arrival, The Guy Fawkes Club was almost complete. The Old Tank wished for only one more plotter to join their number.

The next morning, Mike was sitting in the kitchen after breakfast, reflecting on the strangeness of things while making the coffee. As he poured the milk into the jug, he poured a cupful for their cat, Miss Moppet. He gave her a cup rather than a saucer because he liked to see her dainty little highness dip her graceful paws into the cup. Then his peace was shattered as Jane swept into the kitchen.

"That girl! That phone!" She announced "And what are you doing about it?"

Mike sighed. They'd often felt that Becky's relationship with her mobile phone verged on the abusive.

"Me? I thought she was your daughter too."

"That ended when we got her that holophone. It was bad enough before, but now it's all-in-one immersion in her magic gadget. Wouldn't be surprised if she's formally applying to be adopted by her social network. Certainly got more time for them than her old mum."

"What's she done now then, Janey? How's she wound you up this time?"

"Too busy videomessaging her thousand best friends urgently to talk to her mother. Says she'll get back to me when she's ready, if we haven't died of old age by then, and tell me if she can fit our plans for the weekend into her busy little electronic life. The fact that she still lives here in the holidays seems to have passed her by, she acts as if she isn't here even when she is. Why come home at all if she doesn't want to talk to us?"

"We still provide food, cashpoint, laundry and taxi services. Anyway, isn't she s'posed to be good at multi-tasking? Couldn't she talk to you as well."

"She was multi-tasking, Mike. She was texting, doing her nails, real-messaging her friends – we should never have got her that augmented-reality messaging thing. Not to mention catching up with all her YouTube favourites. Just didn't have time to talk to her mother. Needs her digital fix before she can stoop to mere actual talking face to face."

"She's young. She's at university and loving it, she and Ben are high as kites, looking forward to life. When they get home, they're still full of all their student joys, still love their student friends, their student life. Would we expect them to come back down to earth just yet?"

"No, no – it's not that, anyway."

"What is it really, darling?"

"She won't help. It's her own primary school that's broke *and* about to have the heart ripped out of it, I took her there when she was so small and so cute, and she won't lift a finger, even for the school, let alone the village hall. How can I stand up at the parish council and call on the whole village to come to the rescue when my own daughter won't do a thing?"

"Well, at least we're trying something, in our own way."

"The Old Tank's madcap scheme? How did I talk myself into it? After one good night's sleep, it seems madder than ever. Pigs will fly on magic carpets before that one works. My head knows better, my heart couldn't say no. But you, I used to think you had more sense. Should have known better, after twenty-five years."

"Thanks for the confidence," he replied.

"It's not your fault dear, your chromosomes let you down. I'm off to talk to sensible people." She swirled off in a buzz of energy and passion. Her masses of once red curls might be artificially coloured now (usually in some shade of auburn or another), but her hair still signalled her moods wonderfully. When she was fired up and tossing her head to emphasise her points, it added emphasis at every turn. It topped off the magnificent chaos of her life.

Her hair also had an incidental effect in marriage: it brought her and her husband almost level in height, diminishing the space that separated them in flat shoes (she usually wore heels, if only to close the gap). He was tall and lanky, even if getting a bit hunched these days. His children liked to compare his hair to ginger candy floss with a hole in the middle, but it was greying now. Appearance-wise, he was rather Jekyll and Hyde. For work, he dressed up surprisingly neatly; at home, he managed to look elegantly dishevelled most of the time, just plain dishevelled the rest.

They were opposites in almost every imaginable way.

As Jane's sister had once pointed out, it even showed in the way they hugged. She was a practitioner of the she-bear hug, after which her friends and relatives tottered off a pace or two to count their ribs. He, on the other hand, was a purveyor of the awkward anti-condensation embrace, always leaving plenty of room for air circulation between his hug and its alleged recipient. His wife never thought much of it as a method of welcoming loved ones, but he didn't like to get too close and personal. She wrote it off to being British and male.

The difference showed in their parenting too: he was the one who organised things, ran the household, remembered everything that needed remembering, from washing to birthdays; she did the cooking, the garden and the creativity. Her creative talents around the house extended to doing almost all the DIY that had transformed an old wreck into a rather stylish and eclectic abode. In it, her family's Georgian dining room furniture somehow harmonised with the most modern cupboards and tables, and their chairs ranged from traditional high-backed leather armchairs to personalised hi-foam sofas in a patchwork of fabrics, computer-made to her own precise design, with frames 3-D printed. They had a kitchen table older than the house and side tables younger than the cat, yet somehow Jane had magicked it all together.

In their marketing business, she was the design side, and did the PR, that is to say she was good at charming the customers; he and his team managed every kind of number, including all the money, and the actual delivery of what she and her team designed. They seemed to complement each other pretty well, and their opposites produced many fewer conflicts than they once had done.

Jane was still fuming, but her focus had switched back to the school. "We can't just rely on your mad schemes. We've got to do something that makes sense. — Maybe we should go and see Lady Venetia. She's always been good to the school. Now there's someone who knows how to be a benefit to her community. Doesn't waste her time on mad old parchments and digging silly little holes. Come with me, Mike, we could pop up before the parish council meeting."

"Go with you? What do you need me for? It's not exactly riveting, taking tea with Her Nibs."

"She's taken a shine to you, dear, and you're so good at buttering her up. The parish council meeting gives you a wonderful excuse to get away."

"We could steal the butter from a farmload of cows and butter her up till Christmas, she still can't help with the school any more than anyone else. And for all her buzzing round trying to look useful, a fat lot of actual use she's been for getting the village hall sorted."

"James lost most of their money back in the last crash. She doesn't have any spare these days, and he isn't bringing his back from France. They used to help the village in the old days."

"Doesn't have any to spare? If she wasn't quite so busy keeping up appearances, she could manage a copper or two to help out. And why can't you talk to the Russian about it?" Mike was buttering himself a second slice of toast, with some ferocity. He never had a second slice of toast at teatime.

"Darling, he's never there. He's always off buying oil wells or small countries or something. And who am I to go and talk to the Russian? It's the parish council who should be approaching him on behalf of the village."

"Such dainty reticence, dear. Never stopped you sticking that beautiful nose of yours in before. Sure you're not afraid of dodgy Russians with rather a lot of burly bodyguards?"

"You're spilling jam on your sweater, darling. It's not that. He wouldn't set the dogs on us. Remember when he bought the place and had us all up for drinks, even Ben and Becky too? He made that elegant little speech about how in Russia they still believe in community. And he still supports the village fete. He still lets everyone traipse all over the manor's woods, all the way up to his gardens. He might do something to help about stumping up to save the school, we just need to do what we can ourselves, first, not put it all on a sugar daddy."

"Didn't know you were contemplating a sugar daddy. Anyway, do our children want money from a man whose enemies find themselves dead on Moscow back streets?"

"Darling, not like you to recycle internet scare stories. Nothing ever proved, you told me so yourself. And certainly no children dead on Mutley Shepwell back streets, or the High Street either."

"What would the kids say if they could hear you now? What would the nuns who taught you say? Whatever happened to those high ideals you used to preach at me? When I married a little Catholic girl, I thought I was at least getting a bit of morals, not that the RC Church is exactly famous for it these days."

"Don't treat me like a criminal! I'm in this for our kids, and for all the other children in this village." With that, she departed at speed, and their usual tea-time amity was comprehensively punctured.

On her way down the hill, she collected Moira, who was at George's discussing the training of puppies. This rather surprised Jane, as Moira had never been known to be interested in a pet before. As Jane arrived to collect her, George was protesting that he was vastly out of date, in this as in other matters. "Oh come on, George, you've judged dachshunds at Crufts!" was Moira's response. Such was George's modesty, Jane hadn't even known his distinguished past on the judgement seat.

"My judging days are long over," said George ruefully, "along with a lot of other things." He looked so Eeyoreish they insisted on taking him along with them. Mary whisked past them in her Porsche, with Richard looking bemused in the passenger seat. The Old Tank had no time for cars, of any kind, except that he was almost getting fond of his strange driverless automobile, which saved him the tiresome bother of trying to drive, an art he'd never mastered.

"Why does she get it to impress the one person who's never going to be impressed by it?" muttered Jane, "Wish Mike would get me one to impress me. I'd give him a proper reaction."

"A bit harsh, Jane," protested George mildly, "Mary's never had any money before, it's only natural to splash out a bit now she's got lucky on limiters."

12
TEA AND CAKE
AND REVOLUTION

For all of Mutley Shepwell, they needed to find what they were seeking, and the whole project was taking so long. George was glad to help the Tranctards with the next step in their plans. With Mike and Jane Singer's arrival, The Guy Fawkes Club was almost complete. The Old Tank wished for only one more plotter to join their number: Lady Venetia Thursloe-Cavendish-Bendyke. Richard and Mary Tranctard were to have been the recruiters, but in the end Richard couldn't be there at the vital moment, as the only time they could find clashed with his monthly meeting with the vicar of Mutley. George was recruited instead, as Tabitha had always been a great friend of Lady TCB.

This regular date with his fellow vicar wasn't Richard Tranctard's happiest day in the month, in fact he referred to it as "the curse"; it always gave him a headache. They were poles apart on every front, personality, churchmanship, theology, politics, you name it, and the vicar of Mutley, Mike Jollyon, known to the village as "Reverend Jolly," had never got over the fact that the Church of England still saw fit to maintain St Martin's-in-the-meadow as the parish church of the separate parish of Shepwell, which actually contained most of modern Mutley within its ancient boundaries. Shepwell might have moved en masse up the hill nearly 700 years ago but the CofE still hadn't got round to moving its parish boundaries.

Due to this omission, the parish of Mutley still covered the top half of the ridge, which meant that, just to confuse those not in the know, it now contained all of Shepwell, ever since Shepwell's move up to the ridge in the 1350s, but only the oldest part of Mutley, the bit higher up the hill than the rest, round the crossroads. As Mutley had grown down the hill, over the years, it had crossed the ancient boundaries and entered what the Church of England still called the parish of Shepwell.

Rev Jolly had been campaigning for years to have the two parishes merged and he hit the roof in a big way when Richard Tranctard was allowed to remain priest in charge of St Martin's even after he retired. Rev Jolly had thought this would have been the perfect moment to do the deed and create a united parish, while sending Father Tranctard on his way, with some rejoicing.

They were at opposite ends of the Church of England, the High Church and the Low, the traditionalist and the radical advocate of change. Rev Jolly was famous for calling for everything to be updated, from technology to doctrines, music to service times. He used to accuse Father Tranctard of trying to take St Martin's back to the 1830s, and the Oxford movement, until he realised the Old Tank took that as a compliment.

Mutley's parish church now embraced every innovation in the Church of England. It tried to run on modern management principles, with modern theology and a smorgasbord of modern styles of worship, supporting an up to date array of good causes and picking up on every initiative promoted by the powers that be in the Church. The vicar even wore jeans on occasion, a crime of which Father Tranctard had never been found guilty.

Old-fashioned sermons had made way for interactive discussion, or for more spiritually creative uses of time. One Sunday recently, instead of a sermon, they wrote their own creeds. The choir had long ago made way for modern computerised music systems, and all forms of video abounded, 2D and 3D. They'd ditched hymnbooks and put the words for hymns up on their shiny new holoscreens. They'd even set up their own social community network on the web.

In spite of all that, to Rev Jolly's great frustration, Mutley parish church still saw fewer people on a Sunday than the retrograde St Martin's. More people from their villages, to be fair; St Martin's had become a refuge for the disaffected for miles around, it was a surprisingly cosmopolitan place. Some of the incomers had even set up St Martin's own net presence, over Father Tranctard's protests, with messaging circles, flexible social networks, and all.

Amid the technological innovations, the flowers remained of Olympic standard, and the music was famously good. Perhaps that was what frustrated Reverend Jolly most, or perhaps it was that he was a great lover of ecclesiastical architecture, and St Martin's was a much-loved building, for all its lopsided oddity.

Half of Mutley parish church was much loved and the other half seriously divided opinion. The original thirteenth-century chapel had been demolished in the seventeenth century by the lord of the manor, who'd decided to celebrate the restoration of King Charles II by rebuilding and rededicating the parish church, henceforth to be known as The Church of Charles, King and Martyr. His rebuilding was delicate and beautiful, but rather small. So, in the middle of the nineteenth century, a well-meaning local magnate had paid for the demolition of the houses behind the church, and the construction of a neo-Gothic extension behind it that was much larger than the original Restoration masterpiece. For architectural purists, it was as if someone had welded the Ugly Sisters to Cinderella.

A hundred and sixty-one years after the Victorian part of Mutley's church was completed, the campaign to have it knocked down had just celebrated its one hundred and sixtieth anniversary. The committee members marked the anniversary by taking a bottle of a particular brand of beer that had just been voted the world's worst and ceremonially smashing it against the west door of "that Victorian monstrosity." They streamed a video of their action, then turned the camera off and very carefully cleared up the mess.

Rev Jolly was less of a critic of the church building than most. He was glad to have acres of space, but not so glad when the heating bills came in. It seemed unfair to spend so much money and still have enough draughts for a small town, and the small congregations of today did seem somewhat stranded in their big old Victorian barn. It was a good location for concerts and bazaars, however, on the crossroads in the middle of the village, with enough space for all comers at special events, funerals, and Christmas.

The name didn't help, though, Reverend Jolly always felt. As a lifelong campaigner for the disestablishment of the Church of England, he felt it a cruel irony that he'd ended up vicar of a church named after a king. Another of his long-running campaigns was to have it renamed, and he'd even tried running sample opinion polls in the village to see which saint the villagers might like to see it named after. He'd thought they'd go for something neutral, like "All Saints," or something popular like "St Nicholas." As it turned out, the number one vote on the ballot was for "St George's Church," with numerous requests for the Cross of St George to fly above it. The second most popular option was to call it "St George and the Dragon Church." He nearly gave up. After that, he made sure not to ask anyone in the village about names.

George Sneed was remembering the naming fiasco as he walked up to Charles, King and Martyr, on their way up the hill. Even in bright sunshine, he felt there was something sinister about that mad Victorian extension and its huge spire looming over the charming Carolingian church in front of it. He and Mary dropped Richard off there, promising to have her ladyship save some cake for him, if his meeting finished in time for him to join them. Somehow the Old Tank seemed to suit the architecture, however much he might dislike passing through the tall, high north doors of the church.

Then George and Mary made small talk as they went up the high street. George was hobbling on a stick today, having turned an ankle doing the gardening. Mary looked at him sagely:

"At our age, we have to look after things that used to look after themselves." George nodded wistfully, and winced his way up the hill.

Mary was picking his brains on geraniums and dahlias, and this kept them constructively engaged as they passed the last of the houses on the east side of the high street, with the Shepbrook discreetly flowing through a culvert beneath. On the last part of the way up to the ridge, the high wall of the manor ran right up to the road on the east side while, on the other side, various lanes and old farm tracks ran off to the west, populated by a mix of old stone farm buildings and cottages, together with an eclectic mix of more modern houses.

Just after the manor wall began they came to a rather elegant black metal gate. Until recently, it had been the side gate of the manor. When the manor had been sold, Lady Thursloe-Cavendish-Bendyke had prevailed upon her son to slice off the bottom corner of its gardens for her, so that she could make this gate the entrance to her new home.

For the manor itself, the main gates were over the ridge, outside the village, with Shepwell Hall elegantly engraved on a huge, dark stone beside them, a stone which the Russian had brought from the Ural Mountains, it was said. Through those gates a very grand drive led up to a massive Victorian frontage, right on top of the ridge, looking north into the Cotswolds. Behind it rather grandiose mock-Gothic cloisters reached back to the original manor, a Jacobean, rather smaller structure looking back down the slope to the valley of the Amble. The cloisters enclosed a formal garden, between the two parts of the manor.

Behind the Jacobean Old Manor, there was a crumbling wing, jutting out at an angle in a rather untidy way from the south-eastern corner. Parts of it dated back to the thirteenth century, notably the old tower and the great hall, once used for dances and parties but empty for a long time now, with the rest of that wing largely store rooms and the old library. It was rumoured that the Russian was going to restore it, but so far his designers had restricted themselves to transforming the Victorian structure. This now combined the original exteriors, restored in tip-top fashion, with dazzlingly postmodern interiors.

Mrs Venetia Thursloe-Cavendish-Bendyke, formerly of Shepwell Hall, now resided in the old Home Farm House of the estate. It was down the slope near Main Road, but with a view back up to the manor house where she had spent so many years. When she first moved there it had been her son she had vacated the manor for, in the time-honoured way, but he had then decided to put the last of the family's fortunes into highly leveraged investments at the start of the last boom. Being, he liked to think, a venture capitalist, or at least that was what his firm claimed to be, he served a brief apprenticeship, then started tucking into high risk investments like a vampire let loose in a blood bank.

He'd timed his arrival well: he started his spree just when the markets finally started to boom again after the years of austerity following the great recession. He jumped onto the gravy train with the family's cash in a snakeskin briefcase and enjoyed the hors d'oeuvres and the main course mightily. Unfortunately, he was still in the restaurant car enjoying a few puddings when the train hit the buffers. He'd ridden high for just long enough to buy himself a chateau in France and a beach-house in Barbados when, a couple of years ago, the crash arrived to spoil his party.

To his mother's everlasting fury, he chose to sell the family home and the family treasures, rather than his new foreign abodes, and live off the proceeds in Provence and the Caribbean. Since then he'd hardly been back to old England. He blamed it on Brexit, said the financial barriers that had risen between the EU and the City had forced him to choose between the country of his birth and the country of his favourite wines. Not to mention that France had been the home of two of his three wives.

He still dabbled in strange and complicated financial deals, which usually seemed to revolve around tax loopholes, but he had at least managed not to crash again, to date. In spite of his exile, she still believed that Brexit was best, while wistfully campaigning for some form of co-existence with Europe that might bring her grandchildren closer, or at least bring them to visit more often.

She was left only with the old Home Farm House, once the farmhouse of the farm nearest the manor itself, but long since used as a kind of dower house. She had a rather large garden, from which she could gaze up the hill to her old abode, cursing quietly, until the Russian magnate who'd bought it, not content with the low, friendly, mellow stone wall along his southern boundary, planted a very high and ferocious hedge all along it. This giant of a hedge combined English yew bushes with something altogether nastier and spikier that came from southern Siberia. He had it shipped in almost full-grown, so in one week she saw her view disappear, in spite of all the most outraged protests a lady whose family went back to the Conqueror could muster.

She seethed quietly in her charming seventeenth-century farmhouse and brooded on former happinesses. Complaining to the Reverend and Mrs Tranctard was one of her pleasures in life. Indeed, complaining to most of her old friends was something of a hobby. The arrival of Mary Tranctard had added to her audience. Richard had always been a favourite, and Mary had swiftly become one. In fact, Mary had rapidly become a fixture in village life, once she'd married a village institution. George was not so much a friend as an object of sympathy; Lady TCB had been enormously fond of Tabitha, and tried to be good to him for her sake. She found him rather dull, but entirely worthy.

When they arrived Lady Venetia was surrounded by some of the last boxes that had remained packed up in the loft since the Hall was sold. When she saw them she waved something that looked like an old glossy magazine at them. It turned out to be one of the prospectuses from the bank her son James had joined after university. "Do you see this? 'Exciting prospects,' they promised, 'Becoming global players,' 'Optimizing resource allocation and synergising technological innovation and financial insight.' Gobbledygook and horse manure. Certainly took James in. Mind you, after four years at St Andrew's, he was just dazzled by the bright City lights, and the money. We never gave him any when he was young. Perhaps that's what made him so greedy."

"But this?" She waved it at them again. "Call that a bank? My Uncle Freddie was a banker for forty years and you know what he told me when he retired? I asked him if he'd had an interesting career and he said, 'If I'd wanted excitement, I'd have joined the circus.' I can still hear him saying it. Banking should be boring, like dear old Uncle Freddie. But these idiots keep wanting to be acrobats and they end up being clowns. When are they going to learn?"

It took her a little while to calm down. Once her ruffled feathers were back in place, she offered them tea with more warmth than some of her guests would have imagined her capable of, before congratulating Mary on her wedding, which, she assured her, ranked high among the many she'd been to, very high indeed.

After the tea had duly been poured, slices of Cook's favourite Victoria Sponge were proffered, a signal honour, as the command to Cook to roll out the Victoria was reserved these days for special occasions, since Cook had so many other things to do, being also maid of all work, assistant gardener, blocked drain clearer and chief bottle washer to boot.

"That said, my dear, I don't know if I should be offering you congratulations or deepest sympathy," added Lady

TCB. "Still, if he's being particularly intolerable, there's always poison."

"I keep a store handy at all times," Mary reassured her. "Don't forget, my last husband died very handily, just when I needed him to."

"How exciting, Mary, should I be calling for the Special Branch and the Black Maria? What did you need him dead for, anyway? I thought you'd wrapped up the divorce years ago."

"Of course, of course. But one of my latest husband's curious superstitions is about divorce; he wouldn't have married me if Jack had still been here to annoy. Fortunately for me, Jack chose to take up extreme sports rather late in life and gave himself a heart attack. I like a man who knows when to enter and when to leave. Shame about the years between, of course. He was always trying to prove how macho he was, one way or another."

"How very convenient, my dear, and not even a need for tedious effort. So helpful when they find ways to shuffle off this mortal coil all by themselves. With Richard in the house, though, you may need to keep the poison cupboard well stocked. Of course, if he behaves, then make sure you wrap him up warmly on winter nights. A beagle on the bed is my solution, or preferably three. He's not as young as he was."

Their conversation continued in that vein. They both seemed to enjoy it. Most people were far too in awe of Lady Venetia to give her that kind of treatment. She looked forward to the Tranctards' visits. Mary was even permitted to advise on the garden, and George to help with a little deadheading. They were still out there when Richard arrived, not having quite found the opening to broach the reason for their visit.

"Good afternoon, Venetia," he began. (He was one of the few permitted this familiarity.)

"Good of you to turn up, Richard," came the reply, "I'll see if the beagles will return the last of the cake." Not that the beagles would have been allowed cake, of course, but she always liked to threaten her late guests by intimating that their food had found its way to worthier mouths. Richard's arrival turned her attention to politics.

"Will the government end its abominations?" She thrust home this sally by poking the Reverend Tranctard with a cake fork, as if he personally were to blame for all the regime's crimes.

Her guests were unable to oblige her with a precise answer, and indeed, after a meaningful glance from his wife had updated him as to the situation, Richard was keen to change the subject. Where others, even Mary, waited on the right moment to introduce a sensitive topic, Richard Tranctard just waded in. He didn't just look as if he'd been hacked out of granite, he sometimes proceeded through life as he were an animated lump of rock, bulldozing slowly onwards, regardless of conventions and obstacles.

He came swiftly to the point and introduced Lady TCB to The Guy Fawkes Club, its membership, activities, and ambitions. She was initially horrified, beginning by asking how he dared disturb her family's graves, and then lacerating the plans with mordant wit. She was particularly irked that the whole thing had begun under her nose, with a revelation discovered by her supposedly faithful butler, Hobson, which he had yet kept from her, and revealed instead to Richard Tranctard. This truly enraged her.

Gradually, George and Mary turned her focus from Hobson's treachery to the problems of the village, and so began to avert her wrath. They reminded her of her family's long care for the villages in the manor of which they had so long been lords. They recited the histories of Thursloes and Cavendish-Bendykes of the past who had sacrificed so much for this valley and its inhabitants. They put it to her that the path of duty lay in following her ancestors in protecting the villages from the depredations of outsiders, such as the Russian and the Woodville brothers.

That was the key. Her hearty hatred of the Russian was

almost equalled by her disdain for the Woodvilles, as jumped up parvenus whose vast wealth could only have been ill-gotten. She began to see that joining Richard's plot would be a way of picking up the ancestral baton.

Finally, her rage subsided and she asked: "Have you found any evidence in your noisome excavations? I do hope my ancestor's repose has not been disturbed in vain."

"Ah, there I am afraid you have me at a disadvantage," replied The Old Tank. "We have duly been digging away for weeks, weather permitting, as you know, with all due care, of course, and have, after digging almost all the way round, finally found access to the original crypt, where Lord Bonifer's monument lies, and there we have, for a while, been stuck. Investigations and more investigations. We may be on the verge of a breakthrough. At the same time, it might be terribly helpful if your ladyship were able to get some more precise directions from dear old Hobson."

He received a look that indicated, with the greatest clarity, that while her ladyship might not be exactly disgruntled, her gruntlement was far from complete. "I have been to that wretched home more times than I care to remember, and each time Hobson's dementia is worse. His confusion reaches deeper by the month, and now he falls asleep more often than he wakes. He won't be able to add anything to his original story. If only the stupid man had spoken to me when he found that book."

"To be fair to Hobson, milady, was he not trying to do the right thing?" asked Mrs Tranctard.

"If you must be so legalistic, Mary, Yes. It wasn't one of the books I'd reserved from the sale, so it was technically the property of the Russian. But I would never have let it go, if only I'd been there, if that wretched son of mine hadn't needed me at just the wrong moment."

"Hardly his fault that time," said Richard. "Double pneumonia invites itself, it does not wait on invitation." She snorted, but in a ladylike fashion, and then her face softened slightly and her attention wandered back to her son's hospital bed in those worrying days.

Mary coughed delicately to return to the matters at hand. "So, we are left with what Hobson told Richard: that something in the book he found indicated that some kind of charter relating to King John's grant of the manor of Shepwell to Sir Thomas de Thurslay remains beneath or between the horsemen and the beasts. Alexander also harbours hopes of finding some clue to King John's treasure that was lost in the Wash, with Sir Peter in charge of it, but Richard thinks that rather fanciful – not that he's in a good position to call anyone's ideas fanciful just at present."

Her husband coughed, and had the grace to look very slightly embarrassed. "A long shot, to be sure. Nothing ventured, nothing gained. At the worst, we'll all have had a lot of exercise. Besides, I think there is more to Hobson's story than the sceptic might think. He was very detailed, back when his memory still served him. It was a good memory, then, and he remembered all sorts of details, including these riders and the beasts. To be a little more precise, he said the note in the book told him it was being fought over by the horsemen and the beasts."

Hobson's former employer frowned. "Do you know? I think he might have tried to tell me of this once. Naturally I told him to get back to his work. It makes no sense."

"There, your ladyship," announced Richard, "We do have some news. We have found four beasts on the four corners of Lord Bonifer's grave: the eagle, the ox, the man and the lion, facing outwards from the corners. Around the grave are four riders, flat metal brasses set into the floor around the tombstone, also facing outwards, as if riding away from him. We wouldn't have known they were the four horsemen unless Hobson had told us his story. Not exactly the average grave decoration, the four horsemen of the apocalypse."

"You still don't know it's them, though, do you?" Mary chipped in. "They could just be decorative horsemen. He was a tournament champion, after all, he might have liked to have four knights on horseback round him. And Hobson said the horsemen were fighting the beasts, only they aren't. These beasts look like the four associated with the four evangelists who wrote the gospels."

"My dear," said Richard, "Bill and Alexander have a theory: they think there may be another chamber beneath. The tomb of Sir Thomas de Thurslay has never been found. There was an inscription on an arch of the Bonifer monument that was something to do with Jerusalem guarding Rome: Lord Bonifer went to Jerusalem on crusade with King Edward II; Sir Thomas went to Rome on a mission for King John. And why would Lord Bonifer have had that vast tomb built in our little churchyard, and a hidden chamber below it, if he had nothing to hide?"

Mary sniffed disdainfully. "The vanity of men knows no limit. Lord Bonifer's little folly is nothing on the tombs the Marlboroughs built for themselves at Blenheim, or the Medici in Florence, or a bishop's tomb or two I can think of."

"My ancestors never had that kind of vanity, you may rest assured," declared Lady Venetia with great assurance. Having resolved that matter, she enquired, "And when will you know for sure about this hypothetical lower chamber?"

"We have sent for some special equipment and we shall be testing the floor of Lord Bonifer's tomb with the latest scientific devices, without damaging it, of course. It all looks very solid, but we will find what lies beneath, and let you know everything. If Hobson was correct, it may be Mutley Shepwell's finest hour."

His hostess sighed deeply. "Richard, I may find it in my heart to forgive your depredations, and the mess you have made of my ancestor's tomb, but I cannot join your mad crusade. Nevertheless, I shall be amused to watch your attempts to shake the halls of Mammon and the towers of the demagogues who rule this country. You may not succeed in upturning their tables, but you can at least blow your trumpets outside their castle gates. Do continue, with my best wishes. Meanwhile, Mary, rest assured that many prayers are said for your survival, being married to this dreadful man." Said without a smile, but with a twinkle, for those who knew her.

It was the most unusual refusal they had yet had, in their efforts at recruitment. Mary rallied. "Isn't 'dreadful man' a tautology? At least this one provides some entertainment, with his mad views and worse clothes."

"I'm glad to see he isn't managing to influence you with those mad views. I had thought that Anglo-Catholicism had mercifully died out in these parts until Richard arrived and began to dress up our services with silly smells and bells. It's good to see that you're resisting his eccentric notions."

"Oh, I don't know. The longer I'm married to him, the easier I find it to believe in purgatory."

On that note, they returned, with her ladyship's blessing, ready for the adventure of the tomb. Meanwhile, with the air of woman who knew that her noble self-sacrifice would probably shipwreck her happiness, if not her sanity, she prepared for a visit to that faithful old retainer, James Hobson, wondering if he might have one of his now sadly rare episodes of lucidity and if, should that happen, he might even remember something valuable. But she knew in her heart that it wouldn't happen and, truth be told, although she'd never have told it, perhaps she went simply to see the old man and give him a little good cheer.

There the matter seemed to end, yet, just four days later, it was her ladyship who came to the Tranctards' door, and, through gritted teeth, asked for admittance to The Guy Fawkes Club. Richard and Mary welcomed her with open arms, tea and sympathy. They almost had the kettle on in anticipation, having been watching the lunchtime news. When Lady Venetia arrived, Richard tried to look surprised, and failed. They signed her up with the utmost amity. With her on board, their conspiracy was complete.

The announcement that made Lady Venetia sign for Guy Fawkes was the fourth card of the government's four-card trick. At the same time as it brought her blood to the boil, it made Bob Corns hit the roof, and had Mary Tranctard pruning roses as if cutting the heads off politicians. To the best of Richard's knowledge, it was the first time those three had ever agreed on any one single issue.

After four years of interminable discussion since the last election, this fourth card was suddenly being brought into law with remarkable haste. It was billed as "Bringing the British Constitution into the 21st Century:" no more House of Lords, on the one hand, no peers in parliament, an elected Senate instead; in addition, goodbye to 'first past the post' for electing MPs, in with proportional representation. There was at once an outcry that the current government was only doing this because they were afraid they would never win an election again, with the Scots gone. The outcry didn't stop the coalition from pushing their plans through parliament at high speed. Rarely have so many venerable trees been uprooted so swiftly.

There was uproar in the weeks that followed, but the government stood firm, except for one thing that it didn't care enough about to fight over. An alliance between King Charles and the Church of England killed off the attempt to put into law that coronations should be secular. The king's coronation had already been delayed for years by interminable negotiations between government, church and monarch, complicated by the Scots' secession, followed by slow-motion changes to various ancient laws, which had delayed the ceremony for so long that no one had the heart to start negotiating again. The government couldn't be bothered to argue, when it was having such a fight over the major changes it was determined to push through.

The nation was left with a multi-faith-and-no-faith coronation. The Archbishop of Canterbury's traditional role was split between her, the Chief Rabbi, the Head of the Muslim Council, the Chair of the National Secular Congress, and the Arch-druid, representing Wales, with other religions represented by New Age and Quaker delegates (a silent role for the Quaker, naturally).

This latest raft of government meddling annoyed Bob Corns, Lady Venetia, and Mary Tranctard for quite different reasons. Mary Tranctard was spitting fury because no bishops in the lords; her late, lamented father had been a bishop, and a good one too. Lady TCB was wroth because no aristocrats in the lords, which she saw as: "The end of tradition, elegance, the wisdom of the ages, the end of good taste and breeding in parliament. The end of England." The landlord was cheering the exit of the clergy and the aristocrats but he was furious because the Senate, the replacement for the House of Lords, wasn't democratic enough for his taste. There, and in the new-style House of Commons, instead of letting local parties choose their candidates and local people vote for the individual of their choice, the seats went to lists of candidates hand-picked by the party leaderships in London. "London versus England again," was his verdict.

All three of them, strangely, agreed that a lot of it went back to the Brexit referendum. Without the hand of Brussels to restrain them, the inhabitants of the Westminster village had become more meddlesome than ever. All three agreed that Westminster needed some shackles put back on it, for England's sake.

13
THE RIDERS AND THE BEASTS

George had cut a deal with Alicia. He didn't like leaving Morsel alone so often, and Alicia didn't like spending her nights poking around ancient monuments, so she had delegated her digging duties to him, and taken on the role of dog-sitter, with some relief. Alicia was very fond of Morsel, Morsel was very fond of Alicia. The one disturber of the peace, when Morsel went to stay at Alicia's, was her cat, Sailor. Sailor was a huge old, fat tomcat, a dark grey tabby of uncertain lineage who regarded the village as his own. George wondered if his unfortunate name had contributed to his somewhat dubious temperament.

Alicia's previous partner had chosen it, just because he liked the idea of hearing her say "Hello, Sailor," when she came in the door. Her partner was like that: when she joined Slimming World, he used to eat cake in front of her, offering her a fork and suggesting "just a sin or two." If she succumbed, he'd call her "the little sinner" for the rest of the evening. Sailor was his cat, really, and he got annoyed when she refused to use the greeting he'd designed the cat's name for. Perhaps Sailor was annoyed too. Either way, Sailor was quite remarkably cranky.

Indeed, Alicia had had to switch vets recently because of an unfortunate incident: Sailor had escaped from the treatment room when the vet's assistant opened the door to go and get different eyedrops. That wouldn't have mattered had a customer sitting in the waiting room not chosen to let their little bunny rabbit out of its cage, at that very moment, so their six-year old could play with it while they waited.

Before anyone could react, the little boy saw his beloved rabbit snatched from his lap, and Sailor had dispatched it in a corner more quickly than Alicia could stop him. It was sternly pointed out to her that this is something of a breach of etiquette: when you take your pet to the vet it is not expected to eat someone else's pet. For once, Alicia's dignity deserted her, and she could only beg the pardon of the distraught child. She changed vets swiftly.

It is not surprising that Morsel was nervous about enjoying the hospitality of Sailor's home. Whenever she darkened the doorstep, Sailor jumped up on top of the furniture and stared down at her from a great height. Morsel used to retreat to Alicia's protection or, if Alicia wasn't around, into her travel cage, looking fearfully up at the baleful eyes of her feline host.

Except that one evening, with Sailor absent, Morsel had been tempted out by a plate of cheese and biscuits, left unwarily on a coffee table too close to the sofa. Morsel could get up onto sofas, and she was so busily joyfully tucking in she didn't notice Sailor's return until it was too late. By the time she got back into her cage, she had a well-scratched nose, and a thoroughly mauled ear.

The pitiful noises that greeted Alicia's return alerted her, and she felt herself an unworthy guardian as Morsel greeted her with pitiful relief. The moment Alicia sat on the sofa, Morsel was on her lap, cocking a wounded ear at her with the air of a war-wounded veteran desperate for morphine, if not surgery. Alicia felt awful, but George was very forgiving. By the time the two of them and the vet had everything sorted out, he was very late for his night-time excursion, and could not stay for the restorative sherry she tried to force on him.

After all that, it was an unusually agitated George who arrived and reported for duty. The Old Tank was looking uncharacteristically uptight himself and dispensed with the usual pleasantries.

"It has to be that stone," he was saying, "We've tried everything else."

"They're not fighting, though," said Des, for the umpteenth time. The four brass horsemen they had found in the tomb, and the four engraved beasts, were not depicted in any sort of conflict, more in perfect amity than perfect enmity. Yet Hobson's memory, when it still worked, had been of words about the horsemen fighting the beasts.

"That's what I mean," said Richard, wearily. "They aren't fighting, so they can't be the ones. We have to go deeper, and that stone is the only thing that might lead us down."

George, Bill and Alexander all looked down at the space at the foot of the tomb. Everywhere else the stone flags of the floor were small and square, but to the right of Lord Bonifer's feet, as he would have looked at it (to the left, from their point of view), between the second and third horsemen of the Apocalypse, or just horsemen, it might be, there was a single long smooth flagstone. "Do you think you could lever it, Des?" asked Bill.

"What's the damage, though?" asked Des. "Could lever it but with that crack on the tomb, it might start to come apart. We're meant to be fixing it not wrecking it."

"We have to try," said the Old Tank, "We've tapped every stone and nudged every crack to try to find a way down. That star is the only possibility." On the floor, at the centre of that long, smooth flagstone, was carved a five-pointed star, with the Roman numerals VIII.X. "If the 8.10 matches the four horsemen, then we're talking the Apocalypse, the Book of Revelation, and it says 'The third angel blew his trumpet, and a great star fell from heaven, blazing like a torch, and it fell on a third of the rivers and on the fountains of water.'"

"So all we need is an angel and a trumpet," mused Des.

For once, Richard was not in the mood for contemplation. "Just get those crowbars in," he gestured to George and Bill. They very carefully obliged, but the big flagstone with the star on it extended under the base of the tomb and as they tried to lift there was a terrible snapping noise, and the crack on the top of the tomb was suddenly much bigger and almost matched by a new one on the vertical stone above the star. The flagstone itself did not move a centimetre.

George looked guilty, Bill looked cross. The Old Tank ignored them. His eye was caught by a glint of something revealed by the expansion of the crack across the top of the tomb, which ran alongside Lord Bonifer's effigy, now separating his right arm from the rest of him. Bob Corns and Des Martin leant across so their lamps could shed light. There was a glint from within the tomb. "Gently now," said George, as Des reached in.

It was a small hunting horn, made of some dark metal, three-quarters of a millennium old but perfectly preserved. Around it wound a Latin motto. Richard Tranctard stared at it, dredging up his Latin. "Let no something stranger ring me, no, sound me, or maybe just blow me," he added.

"Should we get her ladyship down to do it?" Asked George.

"I'm the priest in charge of this church," replied Richard, firmly, "I'm no stranger in this churchyard. I was given the cure of souls here, maybe that even includes old Lord Bonifer's. I'll sound the horn."

He tried, and a strange, strangled sound emerged, half a hunting call and half an impression of centuries of must and rust. It was a strange sound, and hurt their ears, but it was enough: the peculiar tone and pitch seemed to trigger a mechanism inside the stone. Something clicked, and there was a sound as of glass breaking under the stone slabs of the floor.

Before their feet, the star stone slowly, slowly, slowly, with a great grinding noise, began to move. It tilted, degree by degree, and began to angle downwards, opening a gap in the floor at the corner of the tomb as it did so. Their torches revealed a kind of stone ladder going down perhaps eight feet into darkness.

"Here we go," said Des.

100

They lowered a camping lamp and a big torch down onto the floor and then Bill led the way down the stone ladder, into a surprisingly large, triangular room. The steps reached down to the shorter wall at the base of the triangle, a mossy stone floor, the whole triangular chamber was very damp, the stone walls covered in moss and lichen, the floor and ceiling too. Before them was a humbler stone coffin, raised off the floor. On it was an effigy, a knight in chainmail, his face partly worn away, a stone hunting dog lying at his feet.

On the longer wall on their left was a dragon, between two strange creatures, each carved as if ready to leap forward out of the wall: one had seven heads and ten horns, with ten crowns on its horns, and names written on the heads in letters that moss had filled in and the dust of centuries had blurred away. Its body was like that of a big cat, but with an oversize mouth full of vicious teeth, and strange, sturdy un-catlike feet. On the other side of the dragon was a beast with two horns only, a rather mild-looking beast compared to the first, almost like an oversize lamb.

Bill stared at the beasts with his mouth open, but George and Des were looking at the other long wall. On it was a horseman with a head made of crowns and fire, and runes on his chest, and a sword not in his hand but stretching sideways from his mouth. His horse seemed to be standing on some kind of winepress. His right hand held a kind of sceptre, and on either side of him were mailed knights, much smaller, from wall to wall.

"Must of tooken 'em a time to do all that lot," said Des, admiringly.

"Shame they went and buried it for all these years," agreed George. "I wonder if there's a way we could get these open to the public. Would be a bit of a tourist attraction for the village. I suppose Lady Venetia would have a fit."

"Doesn't seem very Christian, though," said Alexander.

"Goodness me, don't you ever read the Book of Revelation?" Richard asked, with an arched eyebrow.

"Funnily enough, hasn't been a major feature of my bedtime reading," Alexander replied.

"Should have been, and then you'd know. On your left, the dragon, the beast from the earth and the beast from the sea. On your right, the rider whose name is Faithful and True, who bears a name that none shall know, whose words are a sword that strikes down nations, who treads the winepress of the wrath of God. And with him the armies of heaven on white horses. Some of them do have crosses on their chests, you know, just a bit hard to see in this light, with all the moss and the dirt."

"So this is it, then," said George, "Where the riders fight the beasts, across Sir Thomas's grave."

"He changed his name, you know," said Richard Tranctard. "He was christened Peter, but he changed it to Thomas because he thought he was unworthy to share a name with the prince of the apostles."

"So where is it, then?" Des asked, always one to get to the point.

"According to Hobson, where the riders fight the beasts, which is over the good knight's very body. You don't think he could have had it buried with him?"

"He went to enough effort to hide it, or at least Lord Bonifer did."

They set to work to try to find the secret compartment that must be there. They tapped walls, floors, ceilings, they inserted knives into cracks, they used Alexander's metal detector, and he even smuggled one of the test robots across the road from the security department at the research centre, which had some sort of new-fangled scanners and detectors that could probe a building's secrets.

Nothing was seen or heard until Alexander's robot stretched out a long metal arm across the effigy of Sir Thomas, and above the shield: the detector beeped – raw excitement ran round the room. They looked at the shield,

Sir Thomas's design, a white background quartered by a red cross, with a crown, and three golden keys, in token of his loyal service as King John's treasurer. The Old Tank looked at it thoughtfully, and with a sudden start his mouth jerked into life: "That's not right. That's not the crest. It's a crown, a cross, and two keys, one in each of the quarters. There's no cross here, and there's a third key – the one that's a little bigger, and more embossed?"

The metal detector confirmed, a slight, small, polite beep. They all turned to Des, who had the craftsmanship. He looked thoughtful and went down on his knees to inspect. The shield stood out slightly from Sir Thomas's body. Des reached under its edges and felt about. Suddenly the whole thing lifted off. He held it reverently in his arms and turned it over. There on the back, mortared in to the stone, could just be seen the outline of a very old, very elaborate, very elegant key.

14

THE MUTLEY SHEPWELL
NEWS & CHRONICLE

A few days after that discovery, the Guy Fawkes Club sat in a crisis meeting in Moira Brenchley's summer house.

"We now have the most useless of all things," mused The Old Tank sadly. "We have a key without a lock. We've searched every inch of that tomb and there's nothing there for this key to open."

"But Richard, it has to be at the manor somewhere," said George. "There must be a lock waiting for that key."

"I took it straight to Lady Venetia and she couldn't place it," said Richard. "She did admit that in the rooms behind the Old Library there was all sorts of old junk that hadn't been looked at in a very long time, and when she sold the place Hobson ran out of time to check everything as thoroughly as he would have liked, so the back store-room and the tower and the cellar beneath may have something hiding somewhere. Seems rather remarkable, looking back, but she was completely distracted by that son of hers."

Jem and Jimmy were still complaining that they had absolutely no spare time, nor any freedom, to go hunting for locks, even though Johnny Berensford turned up one day with a perfect copy of the key: "I took it straight away to a man I know who was able to find some very discreet connections who have got one of the newest 3D copy anything super-machines, and he's made some beautiful replicas. There you are, boys, try it out on any mouldy old locks you find. Must be one of them."

The conspirators met several times over the next couple of days to try to find ways in. Moira Brenchley even attempted to charm Mrs Rhodes. They were old acquaintances, and she was actually allowed to call Mrs Rhodes Sally, a rare privilege. But even for old times' sake, Mrs Rhodes wouldn't contemplate trying to get any more temps past the manor's security. "It's just not possible," she explained, "the checking processes are ridiculous. We only did it for those two because they'll probably come back each summer for the next couple of years, but we don't need any more unskilled labour about the place and I won't be able to persuade Mr Pronotkov's manager any different." With that, she declined.

Those days of fevered discussion left them no nearer their goal, and the conspirators felt they were having a sad time of it as they gathered again in Moira's sky-blue summer house. The golden wheat she had been looking out on had been slashed down to stubble by the harvest and the early summer sunshine had given way to clouds and showers, dampening the mood still further. Even Moira's comfortable scarlet cushions, home-made Eccles cakes and spelt bread couldn't cheer them up.

It was the power of the press that did it in the end. Alexander Livingston put his editorial hat on. He was on the editorial committee of the *Mutley Shepwell News & Chronicle*. It had been formed twenty years earlier by an alliance between the old *Mutley News* and the *Shepwell Chronicle*. Alliance was perhaps not the right word; it had been riven with conflict ever since. That was why it couldn't have an editor. Every major decision had to be made by a committee representing the three old villages.

The Mutleyans complained the Shepwellians ganged up on them; the Upper Shepwellians moaned that the Nether Shepwellians undermined them; all sorts of individual antagonisms produced endlessly changing cross-currents, as committee members joined, got fed up with the bickering, and left. Bill, Alexander, George and Moira were the only long-standing members, and George usually kept his head down, while Bill, as treasurer, restricted his attention to the accounts, which were his private realm. They lamented the lack of interest from the village, they lamented the declining standards of modern life, they could agree on what they didn't like. As for what they liked enough to put into the *News & Chronicle*, however, that was another story entirely: never in the history of human conflict was so little debated for so long by so few.

In the end, in spite of all, from chaos comes invention, and Alexander Livingston, sitting there with his editorial hat on, had an idea. "We could ask the Russian if we could do a little series on the history of the manor. It's certainly got enough of it. I've been wanting to get in there for years. At the fete he went and asked if there was anything else he could do for the village, so we'd just be taking him up on his own offer. We could ask if he could free up Jem and Jimmy to give us a bit of help. Gives an excuse to get into the medieval end, the tower and the cellar, and the Old Library. We don't have to tell the rest of the editorial committee, doesn't matter if they ever agree to run the story or not."

It was worth a try, they all agreed. They sent Jane Singer to ask the Russian's number two about it, entreating her to use all of her renowned customer-soothing charm. Jane had done a certain amount of printing and designing for the manor, and was a second cousin of Mrs Rhodes to boot, so had more of an entrée than anyone else. Sure enough, she managed to swing it.

In the course of business, Jane had managed to spark up a cordial relationship with Nikolai Marisovitch, the aforementioned number two. Most of Mr Pronotkov's business happened on a far grander scale, but there are always humbler matters that need to be attended to, and when Mrs Rhodes couldn't deal with them, Nikolai turned to Jane, who'd taken the trouble to make herself very helpful, in view of the lucrative possibilities involved. As a result, Nikolai trusted her for local knowledge and recommendations, and was willing to do the odd favour in return.

Jane thought this history project might be pushing her luck, so she took along a couple of bottles of a whisky she'd introduced the manor to, knowing it was now a firm favourite, and a rare set of photographs she'd found of the Russian football team's finest moments, as Nikolai's kids were football mad. These gestures were appreciated. On such things do small decisions sometimes hang.

There were celebrations at *The Old Bells*. "Here's your opportunity then," decreed the pope. Johnny Berensford was looking pretty pleased with himself. He grinned beerily at Jane, looking rather as if he'd had a liquid lunch, which is easy to do when you own a brewery, but he did remember to keep his voice low. "I love it when a plan works out. Why do you think I arranged with Mrs Rhodes to get Jem and Jimmy taken on?"

Johnny Berensford was in an uproariously good mood all evening, and doing his best to get everyone else under the table. He also had a lovely time playing with one of the replica keys; they all did, but Johnny enjoyed it the most, and even took it home for safe-keeping in his very own safe, at the end of the evening. For the rest, they were all worrying and going over all the possibilities incessantly, and resisting his best efforts to get them into a party mood. Jem and Jimmy looked pretty worried too, the next morning, when he nabbed them as they exited Jimmy's house, and explained what they had to do. They weren't exactly thrilled. They'd had a heavy night, which didn't help: celebrating a win for their team by separating their friend Tom from his Otherton scarf, scaling his garden wall and using it to decorate his family's old outside toilet, all that had taken quite a while.

They weren't looking very happy as they came in through the side gate of the manor and turned up through the new dark steel gate in the Russian's evil-looking hedge, past the cameras and razor-sharp wires and other things he had threaded through it. They nodded to Big Boris and patted the hounds nervously. "Didn't know Dobermans got that big," had been Jem's comment when he first met them, and both boys still treated all four hounds with the greatest respect. Then they trudged up the slope to the old library. Mrs Rhodes met them with something less than her usual calm: "This is all very inconvenient. I'll need to spend a lot of time over at the main house helping Professor Livingston. You boys will just have to start cataloguing the library and inventory the contents of the tower and the cellar by yourselves." She went over the whole process with them once again: it had been begun years ago but none of the staff had ever had the time for the job. There was a pair of dedicated library tablets waiting for them, state of the art equipment, of course. The moment they clicked the holoscreens into place, Jimmy wanted to play with this neat kit, but a long look from Jem calmed him down.

They both sighed. Jem looked at Jimmy again and Jimmy looked at Jem again; they squared their shoulders and went to work with a feeling of foreboding. They soon checked the old chests and strongboxes in the library itself, as expected they had nothing to do with the new key. So they went into the tower, the cellar, the back storerooms. Time passed. Alexander, after the first few days, only dropped in occasionally.

Having retired from academia, he now worked as a consultant at the research centre, using his linguistic expertise to train robots to speak better. He did, however, manage to get permission to leave his robot assistant, Alfred, with them. Alfred looked quite like Molly, same orange head, similar tubular body, painted grey this time. But he had a bulge on his back and rather longer, extendable arms.

Alexander took care not to mention that the bulge and the arms contained several sensors and detectors, for Alfred was, in fact, a security robot, designed to help customs officers and others with a need to search. As far as Mrs Rhodes and the Borises knew, Alfred was just a personal assistant, trundling after the boys to record their inventory and catalogue. Alexander, had, however, given Jimmy and Jem detailed instructions in how to use the sensors and detectors, when they were alone.

After several weeks of frustration, finding all manner of old junk, and a few genuinely ancient minor treasures, they had worked their way to the storeroom at the top of the old tower. It was actually one main room with three small backrooms squashed in around it, all of them rather dark, with only high windows which were kept curtained for the sake of the old books and pictures. There were no ceiling lights and the desk lights, rather old-fashioned things with sooty grey lampshades, gave good light only in places.

"I know we're supposed to be sorting this out," muttered Jem thoughtfully, "but why did they have to leave so much junk?" There were old bookcases and cupboards against every wall, in different kinds and shades of dark wood, with strongboxes, cardboard boxes, and wooden boxes stacked up in every gap. The boys had to manoeuvre carefully round the boxes to get to the back cupboards and the dark wooden doors into the little rear storerooms. The doors looked so old they might have been the medieval originals. The walls were panelled in blackened oak, and the overall effect was gloomy in the extreme.

Jem and Jimmy worked their way through the cupboards and strongboxes in the main storeroom, then the first backroom. Alfred was behind them – stairs always took him a long time, because he had to lever himself up by his arms, unless the stairs were shallow enough for his tracks to get a grip. Once he arrived, he extended his arms and started surveying the room.

They had him instructed to photograph everything, catalogue it as per their directions, and silently use his sensors to investigate any unusual cavities, temperature differences, surprising materials, or other oddities. Alfred's slow progress gave them a chance to relax for a bit, while pretending to take notes on their ePads. They were pretty sure that the CCTV and other security devices hadn't been installed beyond the entry floor of the tower, but the manor was so full of surveillance and security systems that they were never quite sure they mightn't be being observed, so they always tried to make it look as though they were working.

Finally, as they talked football in low tones while trying to appear as if they were earnestly discussing old books and parcels, Alfred beeped at them. Jem and Jimmy froze. Their criticisms of Otherton were forgotten in an instant. Even football vanished from their minds. Usually Alfred spoke, but they'd programmed in an old-fashioned electronic sound in case he actually found something. With what they hoped was an artful slowness, they recommenced talking about cataloguing, and went to see what Alfred had found.

As they entered the last of the three little backrooms, they noticed Alfred tapping the wall behind a stack of crates and boxes. It seemed solid enough. Yet Alfred's screen was displaying some remarkable readings: metal behind the stone surface and some form of hinges on the left side. On the right, what looked like a lock. Alfred's metal fingers whirled, something clicked in the wall, and a section of stone swung open.

Behind it, there was a deep recess in the wall, with an empty plinth, where once a statue might have stood. At the back of the recess was a wooden panel. When they pulled the panel back, they found a very old and faded fragmentary wall painting. It showed a knight in armour with drawn sword, between two coats of arms. Above the painting was an ornate metal curtain pole, fixed to the wall with big, dark metal brackets, equally ornate, from which an ancient curtain hung. Jem reached to pull it back and it came away from the curtain rings, descending gently to the floor, leaving just a few wisps of ancient material hanging loose.

"Now you've done it," muttered Jimmy. "Better hope

no one remembers that. Anyway, what's it all about?"

"Could be Lord Bonifer, the first one," said Jem, in the same low tones. "Looks like the same coat of arms they have above the door to the old hall. The other one's the pope – the keys, I've done that in our medieval course. Stands for St Peter or something. Don't know what he had to do with it."

"What d'ya paint a picture like that in a store room for? And what about – "

"What about that curtain ring? The one top left."

"Look at the style of it. Get that key out – look, it's the same … "

And it more or less was. Just that one curtain ring had the same carved curves around it, tapering to gothic spear points. Truly a strange curtain ring, in fact hardly a curtain ring at all: it was fastened to the metal pole the curtain hung from. When they reached up to try to pull it off, the pole came loose at one end.

"You're having a smashing time now," said Jem. "Think there's anything else we could break between us, while we're at it?" He smiled, but nervously.

"Me?" Said Jimmy. "Get a chair, you clumsy oaf. Let's see if we can put it back. And we'll need a torch, it's dark in here."

Fortunately Jem's phone had a torch function. Jimmy got up and shone the light on the wall where the pole had come loose: there was an ancient-looking metal fitting. Then he jumped and dropped the phone.

"Oy, that's my phone! And it's broken," said Jem. Jimmy wasn't listening.

"Give me that key."

"What d'you mean? What about my phone?"

"Stuff your phone, the village'll buy you ten, if this is what I think it is. Gimme that key."

"What are you on about?"

"Gimme the key," he whispered.

Jem did, and Jimmy slotted it into the inside of the

metal bracket the curtain pole had hung from. Part of the wall behind it started to open inwards to reveal an opening, a foot or so square, carved from the massive thickness of the tower's ancient walls.

"Give us the torch," said Jimmy.

"The one you just broke, you mean?" said Jem. But the torch function still seemed to be working, even though the screen was cracked all over.

"A box. It's wooden, dark wood. And it looks really old. Quick, take it and let's get out of here." They crept through the main storeroom: no one there. Slowly, they edged down the stairs, Alfred levering himself downwards behind them, tooting to them to wait, till they switched his sound off. At the foot of the circular staircase, the room at the base of the tower opened into the back end of the Old Library. They peeped round the door: still no one there. "Maybe they don't bother to watch this bit," muttered Jimmy hopefully.

Jem whispered to him, "I'll go ahead and talk really loudly if I meet someone. You duck back and hide it if that happens. Once I'm out, I'll bring the car round to the side door of the Old Hall, be ready when I get there." As he handed the box to Jimmy he heard a noise and turned.

Big Boris was coming through the door. "Vat are you doink?"

Jem looked at Jimmy, Jimmy looked at Jem. "Bit of sorting out … "ventured Jimmy.

"Vait here," said Big Boris, and disappeared.

"Not likely," whispered Jem. "I'll just go ahead through the Old Hall. No point in the car, we can sneak out through the walled garden and the orchard." They walked quickly through the Old Hall, trying to look innocent. They made it to the side door on the south side. It opened onto sunshine and green gardens.

"Now," said Jem, "If we can get across the lawn and into the walled garden, we're away." They looked at each other, took a deep breath. Peeped out the Old Hall's side door, stepped onto the lawn, just as Big Boris came back through the main doors.

"Run!" Said Jimmy. He was halfway to gate of the walled garden, Jem streaking ahead, then Jem was through and he was almost there, the grass of the lawn soft and level beneath his trainers. He thought he'd never run this fast. There was shouting behind, and the noise of feet. He was almost at the gate. Suddenly he found he wasn't running anywhere. Something hit him from behind and he found himself on the floor, the box beneath him. A moment later Fat Boris landed on top of him. As his arms were wrenched behind his back, before he passed out, his brain somehow found space to note that Fat Boris really was Muscle Boris after all.

15
BETWEEN THE NEW RUSSIA
AND THE OLD KING

The pope was waiting for Jem and Jimmy's return, with Richard Tranctard. ("Should've brought a fourth for bridge," as he told them.) Instead, they saw a large Mercedes pull up, from which emerged an unusually flustered Mrs Rhodes, accompanied by Boris the Scar.

"Mr Pronotkov would like to see you up at the manor, please," she said. "It's about Jem and Jimmy, they seem to be in some kind of trouble." Her usual air of calm authority was severely shaken.

"Give us a minute," said Johnny. They conferred. Mrs Rhodes was feeling terribly responsible for those two boys, who had been, at least in theory, in her charge. She was incredibly worried for them. Even The Old Tank seemed troubled, beneath his granite exterior. Johnny was uttering words of great sympathy while still looking very calm.

In the end, he and Johnny went, with Bill remaining behind to comfort Mrs Rhodes, update the others and stand ready for, well, anything. Richard Tranctard and Johnny Berensford were unusually silent on the drive up to the manor, not knowing what this foretold, and not knowing if anything they said in that grand limousine would be private.

The car pulled up at the manor and Mr Pronotkov's number two, Nikolai, was at the door to welcome them, tall, blond, handsome, calm, efficient, deferential, neat and elegant in all his movements, wearing a classic dark grey suit as if he'd been born in it. He took them through the usual state rooms – the grand winter drawing room and summer drawing room, where Mr Pronotkov did his entertaining in due season, with their eighteenth century highly ornate furniture and their twenty-first century highly minimalist lights, screens and fittings.

They went on, down a corridor neither knew, to a room none of the village had ever been invited to: Mr Pronotkov's own office. More of a suite of offices, actually, one like a library with a desk in it, another full of sofas and antique sculptures, the third full of assistants and all their equipment. The furniture was a mix of classically elegant and ultra-modern, surrounded by a combination of massive old-fashioned, wall-mounted screens and smaller holoscreens that seemed to be showing endless charts and graphs and reports, of pictures and words and numbers; money and people and information moving round half the world.

Mr Pronotkov was there to greet them, coming forward to shake hands as Ivan ushered them in. Like the four Borises, he wore a suit, but there the resemblance ended. His suits were immaculately tailored, his hair and face immaculately groomed, his English almost perfect, with just enough of an accent to charm the unwary, his movements always measured and calm.

He was of medium height, with dark brown hair, dark grey eyes, which seemed almost black in some lights, and regular features which might have seemed innocuous had it not been for the air of authority that somehow surrounded him. He may have been rather overweight, but the cut of his suits made up for that skilfully, and the memory everyone carried away of him was not of his unremarkable looks but his eyes, which were dark and unfathomable; he fixed them on the person speaking to him, with seemingly full attention.

Those dark eyes gripped whomever he was talking to with what seemed like total attention – but who could know? Who ever knew any of the secrets of those eyes? People melted under Mr Pronotkov's gaze, which combined sympathy and command, somehow hinting at secret understanding and arcane knowledge. Those eyes kept all their master's secrets safe, but seemed to unlock the secrets of others. Once they had gazed into your own you could never be sure that their owner had not glimpsed your deepest treasures, if indeed you did not find yourself blurting them out as the persuasion of his conversation followed in the wake of the magnetism of his gaze, his voice pushing open doors his eyes had unlocked.

His voice was deep and reassuring, in English or in Russian, and seemed to promise that one's secrets would be safe with its owner. That promise was backed up by the almost unnatural calm of his presence. It was rumoured that he had never been seen to lose his temper or show surprise, but then he was rarely seen in public at all.

His retinue usually dealt with human contact for him, except where the rich and powerful were concerned: he rationed his presence for maximum effect; those granted an audience knew themselves favoured and fortunate, found themselves entering as curious suppliants, whatever their business might be.

So far, his routine had never varied: visits to the village were limited to his annual visit to the church fete, which took place in the riverside meadow on the east side of St Martin's, always accompanied by a generous donation or two. His staff did their jogging on the village paths, and a few of them were known to frequent the pubs at times, but even then they kept themselves to themselves. Parades of grand visitors arrived at the manor at weekends, but the villagers might as well have been on Mars for all they saw of those meetings.

So Johnny Berensford and Richard Tranctard were feeling unusually nervous. Mr Pronotkov welcomed them most affably – "Call me Vladimir" – and various minions offered drinks and nibbles of the finest quality, as they found themselves sitting down in the sofa-filled office.

"First, can I reassure you that Jem and Jimmy are very well and will be restored to you shortly. They had a slight misunderstanding with a couple of my bodyguards, but my doctor is checking them over now and they will be absolutely fine."

"They'd better be, if anything's wrong with those boys, we'll calling on the full force of the law," blustered Johnny Berensford.

There was a slight, well-bred wince. "Let us not talk of law, Mr Berensford – Johnny – after all, I am quite ready to waive any charges for the removal from my property of a certain dark, wooden casket. Others might call that theft, but I prefer to regard it as a regrettable misunderstanding. I do, of course, wish to know the history of that box, and why all of you seem so very keen to have it in your possession."

They looked at each other grimly, and then at their host, who met their gazes in turn. As their eyes met his, their resistance weakened.

"You haven't opened it, have you?" said Richard Tranctard.

"Oh no, your boys were most insistent that I should not. I am happy to delay the moment of opening if I am given a good enough reason. Please enlighten me."

Richard Tranctard looked at the pope, who seemed ready to resist, but then his eyes met Mr Pronotkov's, and a moment later, he shrugged and looked away. With an air of immense weariness, Richard Tranctard began: "If that casket is what we think it is, you'll need to open it with extreme care in very carefully controlled conditions. We were going to take it down to Oxford to one of the experts there, whom we happen to know. If it's what we think, it's 800 years old. I suppose I had better explain."

And so, with sadness in his voice, he did. His tale began in the early 1200s, in the reign of Bad King John, who had in his entourage an able young knight called Sir Peter de Thurslay. Sir Peter rose rapidly in the royal service to be one of the king's most trusted advisers. Indeed, being also a man famous for his personal piety (very unlike the king his master), he was the man chosen to negotiate with Pope

Innocent III after that powerful prelate had decided to punish King John over a dispute about who should be Archbishop of Canterbury. King John was most grateful when Sir Peter's embassy to Rome saw the problem resolved, and made him the royal treasurer.

It was a story remembered in Thurslay family legend – later to become Thursloe family legend, and still later, as the family intermarried with the nobility, Thursloe-Cavendish-Bendyke family legend. According, as Father Tranctard put it, to generations of family tales, King John was so grateful to his pious friend that he gave him the manor of Shepwell.

A few years later, when Prince Louis of France invaded and John's throne seemed lost, Sir Peter was one of those barons who remained utterly loyal: this time he is meant to have vowed to the king that if Prince Louis or any other usurper were to take the throne, he would go to Rome to beg the Pope to launch a crusade to win England back for John's family, the Plantagenets.

At this point, according to an ancient TCB myth, King John laughed, amused at such loyalty, and decreed that if he or his successors ever ceased to rule in England, Sir Peter and his manor of Shepwell should be freed from their allegiance to the King of England and owe allegiance only to the pope: "Thou wilt need not go to Rome, for Rome shall come to Shepwell and of Rome you shall be part." Or so the family legend went: it was even rumoured that there had been a royal charter once with all this written down, but it had long been lost.

After that, the story became murky, with rumours of a falling out between the loyal knight and the king. Perhaps said charter had been revoked. Whatever the cause, Sir Peter had become even more religious at the end of his life, and changed his name to Thomas, feeling unworthy to share a name with the prince of the apostles. His end was shrouded in mystery and the place of his burial had long been lost.

About seventy years later, Lord Bonifer had built himself a magnificent tomb by the parish church on his return from the crusades. On the basis of a strange reference Lady Venetia's man Hobson had once come across in the old library, they had decided to investigate Lord Bonifer's monument, in the hope that it might cover and conceal the humbler tomb of Sir Peter (or Sir Thomas, as he was at his death). This had proved to be the case, and Sir Thomas's tomb had revealed a key, which had led them to this casket.

"And you think your charter is in this casket?" said their host with an amused smile.

They nodded. "Perhaps," said the pope, Shepwell's pope, that is.

"I shall have it looked into." There was consternation among his guests, but their host was unmoved. In vain did they point out the Thursloe-Cavendish-Bendykes' rights in the matter. They hadn't taken it with them when they sold, and so, said Mr Pronotkov, with a kind and regretful smile, it would seem to be his. "But you must be keen to see your boys. Bring them up."

His assistants duly did. Jem and Jimmy appeared, somewhat bruised, but on their feet. Their genial host went to greet them personally with a warm handshake, received somewhat warily. They remembered his earlier words, overheard by Jem in a rather less comfortable, windowless room in the basement of the manor, where he had been taken, with an unconscious Jimmy, when he realised that the Daleks were right, and resistance is useless. The Borises were certainly strong, and when Red Boris brought two of the hounds round the corner, fortunately still leashed, Jem's appetite for defiance completely crumbled.

As Jem sat in that prison, with Jimmy slowly coming round, Mr Pronotkov came to visit, all solicitous concern and promises of medical attention. Then he ordered two of the Borises out, and talked to them in the corridor. The only bit Jem could overhear was a small snatch as Nikolai opened the door to let the Russian's private doctor in. The phrase that stuck in his memory was "English rules, not Russian rules." The words made him wonder.

After that, things swiftly looked up. The doctor seemed very competent, and Jimmy wasn't too woozy for long, and claimed he didn't ache too much. Nothing broken, anyway. Nikolai questioned them, but gently, and seemed to believe their repeated assurances that they didn't know what the casket was, or the key (which seemed to have been skilfully extracted from Jimmy at some point). He told them he believed that they were just doing what they'd been told, and said he would contact Johnny Berensford.

Nikolai Marisovitch was the model of soft-spoken politeness throughout, on the model of his master. Nevertheless, his two captives did not look not very impressed until he handed them cheques, the size of which made their eyes open very wide indeed. After that, they were very glad to accept the apology, made on the Borises' behalf by Mr Marisovitch: none of the Borises looked very apologetic, but they all nodded when told to, and shook hands with the boys.

Jem and Jimmy were also suddenly very happy indeed to sign the legal documents Mr Pronotkov's lawyer gave them, waiving any claims in consideration of the compensation offered. They wouldn't be needing summer jobs for a long time, and the possibilities for their next travels suddenly spanned the world. As they gaped at their cheques, Nikolai looked deep into their wide-open eyes and expressed his and his employer's regret in resonant words.

After that, it was champagne all the way. They were led up to Mr Pronotkov's imperial office, where they were mightily relieved to see Johnny B and The Old Tank again. They relaxed enough to try some of the world's best champagne, followed by some of Russia's best vodka (or so their host claimed, and he ought to know). They were then sent off in their own Mercedes, while the older men agreed to meet their host again in a few days. He promised to bring in the very best people to open the casket and prudently examine its contents, and he promised to do so extremely swiftly. He could see how very, very keen they were to find out. As they left, Nikolai Marisovitch was already making phone calls, summoning farflung experts to drop what they were doing and fly post haste to Mutley Shepwell.

16
OF LAWYERS AND OTHER EVILS

The Guy Fawkes Club were an unlikely crew to be con-
spiring. The news from the manor had left most of them
like rabbits frozen in the headlights. Fortunately, Mary
Tranctard had been through plenty of crises in her business career, and was at her best when dealing with them.
She had a cousin who was a very high-powered lawyer, and
owed her several favours, and she had prevailed upon him
to travel down from London to advise them on how best
to proceed when they heard the news they were all waiting
for from Mr Pronotkov.

While Mary wined and dined her cousin to get him in
the mood for a meeting, with help from Moira, the rest of
the conspirators were meant to be preparing. Johnny Berensford was unable to be at the meeting with the lawyer so
had offered his home as the venue for the preparatory session as his way of contributing to the evening.

Unfortunately, without Moira and Mary, no one had
any idea how to prepare. Instead, the assembled company
was scattered round Johnny Berensford's vast and over-
powering sitting room. It was all deep red armchairs and
dark oak furniture, with huge bookcases and an even huger
fire, that you could probably have roasted a small ox in.
The only preparation going on was alcoholic. Dutch courage was being liberally dispensed.

Meanwhile, their host was pontificating. It was another reason why he was called the pope: he loved to hear his
own voice, and he felt the world should love it too. Sometimes he was talking business, sometimes it was music,
sometimes it was beer, and sometimes it was bridge. He
had his favourite tunes, he loved to play them, and it never
seemed to occur to him that there might be anyone who

didn't just love to hear them again and again. He could be a bit like an organ grinder cranking out the same old songs in the corner, oblivious of the fact that the others had moved on to new tunes.

When Richard Tranctard accused Johnny of riding his hobbyhorses to death, Johnny replied that the hobbyhorses needed the exercise, and his hearers were obviously in dire need of mental stimulation, lest their doctors pronounce brain death just a little prematurely.

As their genial host, Johnny felt he had a right to steer the conversation and, naturally enough, was waxing lyrical about the new beer he was creating, and how the focus groups were loving it. His customers may have been fond of the beers he created, but Johnny always loved them more.

One of his proudest moments had come when he'd been burgled and the burglars had left his fine wines and whiskies behind, but taken every single bottle of the ale and stout he'd brewed himself. "You get a better class of burglar in this village," was his happy verdict. The police had never heard a victim praising the discerning judgement of the thief before.

This evening, Johnny was insisting that everyone try some of his new brew, pointing out that they'd be in a meeting with a lawyer for the rest of the night, so needed something to dull the pain. The new beer was a lighter version of his famous Oakenheart. Des Martin suggested calling it Pineheart, or maybe Stripped-pineheart. This didn't go down well. Peggy shut Des up, but the others started in on the game: Piningheart, Shandyheart, Lowcal-heart, Veneerheart, and plenty more, were the names they were coming up with. Johnny sulked and went quiet.

Richard Tranctard asked, "Is the pope tired of his latest bull?'

Johnny glared at him. "You have anything better to say? Haven't noticed any constructive ideas coming from your corner. Got a plan for this evening or are you just relying on Moira and Mary?"

Richard had to admit that he was. He and George and the others said their goodbyes to the pope and his beverages. They went the back way, down Back Lane, and happened to meet Alicia on the corner of Bendyke Row. She had been unable to get to Johnny Berensford's but was joining them for the main meeting.

Bendyke Row was where the Thursloe Hall was situated, along with some of the grandest and oldest houses in the village. There was Cotswold stone all around them, with a climbing rose of great maturity growing up one side of the hall. Sadly its roses were almost gone for the year. The hall itself was in a terrible state, for all the beauty of the stone from which it was made. George and Alicia filed past the buckets in the entranceway, round the blocked up entrance to the main hall with its now sad and sorry and very, very damp stage, and turned into the Nutkins room. The rest of their crew met them, together with a visitor.

"My cousin Giles Prenderby," Mary announced. Giles surveyed them with autocratic confidence. He might have been a little less serene had he known that Mary had explained his impending arrival at the previous meeting in these words: "He hates the PM. They were all up at Oxford together and the first Mrs Lightwing was on her way to being the first Mrs Prenderby. They were engaged, actually, when Lightwing stepped in and stole her. Then he ditched her for the Duke of Dunford's daughter, champagne socialist that he is, so she hates him too. That's why they're willing to help."

Giles Prenderby began with lawyerly caution, leavened with a hint of malicious glee. They say revenge is a dish best served cold, and he had waited thirty years for his, so it was very nicely chilled indeed. "If you can produce what you say you can, then there will be certain possibilities. The PM will announce it's all nonsense to start with, and then we can bring in two medieval statutes one of my assistants has been working on, which suggest your

124

claim could be valid. Constitutionally, it will need to go to the Privy Council, and we can string them along for a while. In the meantime you'll be what is known as a territory of undetermined sovereignty. It might be possible, even if we can't stretch to the precise claim you're making, there might be opportunity, for example, to claim a temporary status analogous to that of Andorra or San Marino, or perhaps something more like the Isle of Man, or one of the Channel Islands, in their earlier more medieval incarnations."

"While we're wrangling with Westminster, we can start bickering with Brussels about your status. They'll look down their noses, of course, but we can claim to be affiliated to the European Union, so we can appeal to their courts too. Our rights would certainly predate most other claims, by quite a way. They'll find it so preposterous they'll tie themselves in knots to kick us out. We can have fun with it all through the European courts while they do."

He certainly looked like a man who was having fun. Lawyer though he was, he couldn't restrain a sunny smile. They looked a bit blank, but he continued smoothly on.

"In theory, you'll have an overlord in Europe, but it seems reasonably safe to say that he'll leave you on your own. Meanwhile, we might just take the chance for a little embarrassment for the prime minister." At this point the lawyerly reticence deserted him, and with something approaching a snarl, he added: "But we need you to get started now, so we have time to make him look a fool before the general election."

"And before the National Park is finalised," added Moira. "We need to kick up such a fuss they can't leave us out. It's where we belong."

Giles Prenderby nodded briefly. Soon he was droning on again, and bringing out various documents that he seemed to expect to be signed without delay. Alicia and Bill were objecting loudly, till Moira silenced them with a few tactful words and asked them to leave her and Mary to review said documents with George, who, being a retired tax inspector, was the council's nearest thing to an expert at inspecting things. Bill obediently nodded. Alicia was somewhat dischuffed. As she left, she doubled back and asked Moira quietly if she could join the review team, at least as an observer. Moira was grumpy, but finally agreed. They said farewell to Prenderby, promising to update him when they had news from the manor.

17
THE TORY ANARCHISTS OF
MUTLEY AND SHEPWELL

It was more than a week till The Old Tank and Johnny B were back at the manor. Mr Pronotkov's minions had phoned to delay slightly, as certain unspecified operations seemed to be taking longer than planned. The summer weather had taken a turn for the worse by then; even so, with a lot of low grey cloud, with the golden corn gone and the fields all stubble and brown, the view from the ridge was still stunning.

Bill Stone and Des Martin had managed to arrange to join them this time. "After all," as Des said, "You don't get invited to a place like that very often." George would have liked to be there, but gracefully stepped aside for Des. Moira Brenchley took the chance to ask him to help her with some gardening matters instead. In fact, his gardening assistance had to be delayed, at the last minute, even though Moira had a perfect afternoon tea already prepared for him, with added Buck's Fizz as a reward for the labourer. All of it went to waste as Bill Stone's brother Stephanos (formerly known as Stephen) created a surprise vacancy and George had to stand in for Bill at the manor.

Bill had been looking forward to the visit but, as so often, his plans were foiled by his brother. Bill was sometimes heard to grumble that he didn't know what was the worst thing about divorce, losing his wife and kids, having to take a job he hated, or having his brother take pity on him. For Stephanos, in later life, was a brother awash with pity.

After an earlier working life as a journalist, he had become utterly disillusioned. He'd gone into journalism when Fleet Street was still the street of shame, and ended up, decades later, tailoring "media product" for unseen masters across the Atlantic, as an outlying part of a "content creation" team for one of the big social media networks. News, gossip, opinion, reviews, speculations, his team wrote it all by the yard.

What they wrote each day was dictated by ever so clever algorithms, which measured the world's appetite for stories, hour by hour, minute by minute, millisecond by millisecond, and issued directions to their human serfs accordingly. The machine measured the beat of the newsworld's heart, but, although it called the tune, it still needed human operatives to do the dance on the machine's behalf.

The system prescribed the shape and size of the content, the human writers coloured it in, and the system then distributed it in myriad different forms to its millions of users. Stephen had started by thinking he'd gone into journalism because he was a free spirit, wanting to uncover truth and to guide his fellow men and women. He ended up believing he was just a co-ordinate in a global matrix.

After all of that, he had decided to retire early, and that the final antidote to a life in journalism would be a retirement trip round India. While there he experienced some sort of spiritual epiphany, cast off the name of Stephen, and henceforth regarded himself as a spiritual guru, Stephanos Stone, seeing himself as having become a rock of wisdom and far above other men, especially his unspiritual brother.

For one thing, while in his life as Stephen he had always gone off to work soberly clad in conventional garb, his dark shoes appropriately shiny, now he was Stephanos he never wore anything on his feet more substantial than a sandal. His explanation? "I follow in the footsteps of the Enlightened. Buddha, Zoroaster, Christ: not a sock between them. Their feet were open to the air of this world, just as their minds were open to the world of the spirit."

In vain did Bill point out that socklessness and enlightenment were not synonymous. His attempts to bring his brother down to earth had simply persuaded Stephanos that fraternal charity required him to come and live with his errant younger brother, to show him the true path. (The fact that he'd run through all his money might also have had something to do with it.) Since Bill was now rattling round a large farmhouse by himself, he agreed to this as a temporary arrangement, and was now wondering how far the enlightened could stretch the definition of "temporary."

He'd just about got used to the chanting from his back bedroom at all hours, but Stephanos's attempts to make him vegan had led to separate mealtimes, and rows when he cooked meat, as Stephanos viewed the smell of frying bacon as an unfair assault on his vegetarian vows. Almost worse than the rows was the making up. Stephanos was perfecting his holier than thou reconciliation routines.

When the new guru condescended to honour the pub with an appearance, Bob Corns had taken to offering him a little Buddha with his beermug, unperturbed by the filthy looks Bill gave him. The net result of his brother's enlightenment was that Bill, having previously withdrawn into his home after the divorce, was now to be found working far longer hours than he used to, and had become quite the life and soul of social life at the research centre. When not working he was out around the village at all hours. He had become *The Old Bells'* most regular customer.

Bill found himself tied up that day in taking Stephanos to a commune near Swindon, to which he was devoutly hoping his brother might become attached. For that reason, he could not join the trip up to the manor, creating space for George to join the party.

When they got there, Mr Pronotkov was smiling. He had a lawyer or two with him. His opening words were: "Congratulations, you were right. Here it is. You may have to have a little trip to Rome to talk to the pope about this." And he showed them an ancient parchment in a glass case.

"Your bad King John was good King John to Mutley

Shepwell, it seems. As you thought, in return for his man Sir Peter's loyalty, he promised your village its freedom if his family ever lost the throne, subject only to the pope in Rome. I believe you may be a little over 500 years late in claiming your independence, did not the last Plantagenet die in 1485? Your Bosworth Field? Your famous Tudors? Should you not have been your own country all these years?"

Johnny, George and Des were fascinated, and gathered round the parchment, but The Old Tank looked a little irked. He wagged a finger with unusual asperity, and burst out: "The famous Tudors, as you call them, might not have been terribly welcoming to a lord of the manor who claimed independence. Henry VIII had a certain way with traitors. If you think what he did to his wives, you can imagine what he did to people he really didn't like. His father and his children also knew how to use an executioner."

"As for the Vatican, though, do allow me to correct you. Coming from Russia, Mr Pronotkov, you may not have noticed a little thing called the Reformation. When King Henry VIII split from Rome, one of the most famous laws of the day began, 'This realm of England is an empire,' and it was made very clear that popes have no jurisdiction in England. If we are set free from kings, we are also now set free from the popes of Rome, I hope."

Mr Pronotkov's lawyer frowned: "If this document made your manor independent of England before Henry VIII's changes, the Reformation would not apply, and you have, in fact, the papacy as your overlords. Of course, your English lawyers might argue that since Henry VIII's laws, the popes in Rome can be your spiritual overlords only. According to that argument, for judicial and governmental purposes, the realm of Shepwell is an empire, independent of all other jurisdictions. It is true that, for spiritual and certain technical legal purposes you are, as it might be, a colony of the Vatican – we, in Russia, can sympathise with your distaste for that. For all practical purposes, however, you are independent."

His lawyerly face creased into what might have been a smile. "According to this grant, you owe taxes to no one, and military service only to the pope. Maybe you should send him some of your young men to be Swiss Guards? If you commit a crime, only the Vatican's courts can try you. They might make you go to confession afterwards."

"We'll skip that bit, but we might have a use for the Vatican when it comes to business," interrupted Johnny B swiftly, "Rome's practically part of the European Union, for business purposes at least, and there could be possibilities there. So we'll put up with the Vatican, for the EU's sake, so long as they don't try to make us religious."

"The Vatican never was very Christian," added the Old Tank, sourly, "or we wouldn't have needed a reformation. We'll have to have words with them about keeping our spiritual independence, even if we want to be legally linked."

Mr Pronotkov's lawyer leaned back and steepled his fingers. "This document seems to raise a great many questions. You are in an extremely unusual position. There are many questions. You will need much legal advice. Your own government will have views. Your current royal family might have an opinion, although the document clearly mentions descent in the male line from King John, and the last such descendant was King Richard III, who died at Bosworth Field."

"As the current lord of the manor, Mr Pronotkov could try to assert a right of jurisdiction, although, you may be relieved to hear, he does not intend to. Besides, the document seems to bypass mere lords and put overlordship directly in the hands of the pope. Then, as you say, the Reformation may have ended that overlordship, or made it merely spiritual. The Vatican may try to offer you guidance."

"Let them try it on," snorted The Old Tank.

"Father Tranctard," said his host reassuringly, "Surely

you do not expect the government to allow you to secede? You are hardly Scotland."

"Of course not," said Johnny Berensford, interrupting, "but we can give those berks in Westminster a good poke in the eye. We have a lawyer who reckons we could take this to the Supreme Court, and make it last a good long time, and that's before we go to the European Court of Human Rights and the European Court of Justice and argue to be part of Europe again. There's a lot of fun and games in this. In the meantime, we'll be, for legal purposes, independent of the government, our interfering new king, and Uncle Tom Cobbly and all."

George coughed, hesitantly. They all inclined their heads at him, and Mr Pronotkov made an expansive, welcoming gesture with his hands. George cleared his throat and, reluctantly, spoke.

"We believe in England. Some of us believe in God as well." (Johnny looked rather startled at this turn of phrase; Richard just smiled.)

"We don't believe in everything being decided in London, by Londoners. We want to take a stand for the rest of us in England. Here in Mutley Shepwell we haven't turned our backs on Europe, and we don't think Westminster is always better than Brussels. In Lord Bonifer's day, everything flowed from England to the rest of Europe and back again, without barriers. It wasn't the EU who invented that. Our village is English, and it's European. We don't need Parliament getting in the way. This charter from King John means we can send a message. If we can get to independence for just one day, we can raise a flag for villages everywhere."

"Yes, indeed," said Mr Pronotkov, with a twinkle in his eye, "A very English secession. So much more peaceful than Chechnya, or even Crimea. But lawyers cost money, and so does publicity. Suppose you create your little republic, just for a season or two: you will need a way of governing yourselves, and of course, borders and passports and internet independence and all these things. Money, money, money. Such a problem, it can be. Yet that is where I might be able to help you."

They looked at him with dawning comprehension.

"I have, as it happens, a number of discussions about tax to make with your Inland Revenue. The arrangements I had made are in danger of being invalidated by new legislation – governments are so keen to collect their pound of blood these days! With the election looming, your politicians seem keen to find scapegoats and – how do you say it? – hang a few of us out to dry? Honest businessmen though we are."

"While you are conducting all your negotiations with London and Brussels, good lawyers might just be able to argue that you are semi-independent for a little while, until your status is settled. To find myself located offshore, while remaining onshore, even for a limited duration, could be very valuable to one such as myself. And perhaps to others. Should the village wish to, say, participate in these special arrangements, there could be a great deal of profit, of value to the community, to be realised."

Now it was Richard and George who looked shocked. Johnny, on the other hand, was most enthusiastic, and Des looked like a man who could see Father Christmas landing the sleigh with presents for all. When Richard tried to object, Des reminded him that it was for the village. After all these years of austerity and services being cut back, who could object? The Old Tank did object, but even George could see the benefit to the village. Mr Pronotkov was most persuasive. The Old Tank might not like the commercial aspect, but he had to agree that a venture like theirs needed funding from somewhere.

Finally Des waded in. "I think we'll have to call a special meeting of the parish council," he said. On that, all could agree, first a meeting of the regular parish council, then an extraordinary meeting, to which the whole village must be invited, to give their views on this rather unusual situation. On this note, business was adjourned and drinks were served, very fine drinks, with very fine nibbles to go with.

As they walked out the gates afterwards, having declined the proferred Mercedes, they all looked happy, except for George, who mused, "What will Lady Venetia say? We've just done a deal with her Private Enemy Number One."

Richard winced, Johnny laughed. Des ignored them, lost in his own thoughts. As they turned down the hill, he said, with a certain awe, "Could be the biggest parish council meeting in history."

And so it was. As soon as they got back, they assembled the conspirators, and worked out a plan, meeting at Alicia's elegant house in Nether Shepwell, with her three sheep gently bleating in the field below them. To get things started before news could leak out, they decided to call an emergency council meeting, at which they explained the novelty of the opportunity. This led to agreement to call an extraordinary parish meeting, open to the entire village, for the very next day. Then they all had to get messaging round their various networks to try to get the news to as much of the village as possible, and Bill and Alicia even took paper flyers round those few villagers known to have rejected all modern methods of communication.

The need for speed even brought Des to the door of Joe Bennett, for the first time ever. To Joe's credit, the frost had always been on the other side of the glass: Des was in almost all circumstances an unusually mellow man, laid back to a point that his wife often found frustrating, but when Joe's arrival ended Des's seventeen-year reign as the garlic king of the Mutley Shepwell Village Show, something stirred deep within. He hinted at conspiracy in the judging, he railed against unfair growing techniques, he resorted to spying, he could not bring himself to even consider that Joe might be better at growing garlic than he was.

It would have been bad enough for Des had one of his established village gardening rivals stolen a march on him, but Joe was an outsider, and a townie to boot. Joe had worked for many years in the Cowley car plant in East Oxford, living in a 19th-century terraced house with a garden far too tiny for his gardening ambitions, while he spent 25 years paying off the mortgage.

When he retired, he found he could trade that in for a large 1950s bungalow with extensive garden (south-facing) in Mutley Shepwell. Joe did so, and was finally able to begin to realise his gardening dreams. He had filled so much of that largish garden with sheds and greenhouses that he was negotiating with the old lady next door to buy the back end of her garden.

Des, however, was appalled, and had maintained a cool distance from Joe which even Peggy found embarrassing, until the need to rope people in to take flyers round the village saw her recruiting Joe, and seizing the chance to make Des go and deliver said flyers to him. Des gritted his teeth, said "I'm doing it for the village," and was about to dump the flyers on the doorstep, with exaggerated disgust, when Joe opened the door, beer in hand, and invited him in for a drink.

Caught by surprise, Des had instinctively accepted the proffered beer before his conscious mind could formulate the word "No," and found himself dragged in to a surprisingly pleasant conversation about soils and rainfall, with Joe most politely deferring to Des's superior knowledge of the village's weather patterns, drainage and precise variations in soil. By the time they'd finished their second beers, Des was wondering if he mightn't have misjudged the man, and when they got to the end of the third, he was starting to sight the beginning of a gardening friendship, garlic or no garlic.

Flyers delivered, messaging messaged, web alerts and notifications circulated, friends and neighbours chased up by phone or in person, the village was soon humming. For most it was a shock, for many a curiosity, for some an annoyance, for almost all who were able to make it, an unmissable event. At the appointed hour, the village's doorways disbursed their humans, the streets filled up, and a small sea of humanity converged on the appointed place.

Without a village hall fit to have it in, they had to hold it in the open, on the scrubby patch of grass behind the village hall that passed for a village green. The weather was unseasonably cool, with a bit of a nip in the air, so Bill and George and the Tranctards gathered together the materials for a bonfire. It seemed appropriate for the members of The Guy Fawkes Club to be providing one.

Des and Joe Bennett managed to nab enough of the drama club's portable stage to create something for speakers to stand on, and rig up a series of lanterns to light up the stage itself and the area around it. Moira, as chairman of the parish council, would chair the meeting, and a lineup of council members and eminent villagers was preparing speech notes frantically. Unknown to most, the lineup consisted almost entirely of the conspirators. There was no attempt at a balanced ticket, or any kind of debate. This was one direction time, for those organizing it, they wanted everyone to see that there was no alternative.

All might have been moot had it rained. Fortunately, it was a fine evening, with a clear sky darkening gently to the east and a beautiful sunset to the west, followed by the last clouds clearing and the first stars gently peeping down from the heavens, as if curious to see what was going on to cause such commotion in Mutley Shepwell.

More of the village turned out than had ever been seen together before. To start with, there was a certain confusion, not to mention scepticism, about declaring independence. It was Moira herself, as chairman, who started the speeches, or should one say, the carefully calibrated propaganda campaign to persuade her fellow villagers to step out into the unknown.

With the clarity she was famous for, she concisely explained the story of their newly discovered document, went in detail through the unusual legal position it created, and waxed lyrical about the Russian's offer of the resources needed to exploit the unique position they found themselves in. She reminded the villagers before her of the parlous situation that the years of austerity had left them in, with no buses any more, no children's centre, no resources for the elderly and infirm, everything needing repairs, from the school and the village hall to the roads and both churches. She put it to them that they'd had years of every service being cut back, and only the potholes growing.

"This is our chance to rebuild the village. Just think of the marketing opportunities. For one short moment we will be unique in the world. If we can get the story out wide enough, we can sell enough unique memorabilia – "

"You mean Tat and Rubbish," muttered Alicia Cornwell, standing sullenly beside her.

"I mean sell enough unique merchandise to get the village hall re-opened, and maybe fix up the working men's club as well. If we really did well, we could even knock the wretched carbuncle down and put up something that didn't make me wince every time I go down to the river. And then there's a new play area for the kids, and building a meeting place for the old people, and something for the teenagers, that'll cost a bit, has to be indestructible – "

"Oy, if we get that Village Hall reopened, we're not having a bunch of tearaway teenagers trashing the place again," burst out Bill Stone, to nods of approval from many.

"That's why we need their own separate place, isn't it? Round the back of the village where it won't annoy anyone. But not so secluded they can get up to total naughties."

"And who do you think is going to want the problem kids over the back of their fence, then?" demanded one heckler.

"That's detail," said Moira very firmly, "If we ever get that much we can worry about it afterwards. But we'll never get near that sort of money if we aren't very, very organized and get this public quick. The government'll shut us down soon enough, and then the taps go off."

Mike Singer backed her up. "We might not like it, but this is the biggest opportunity our village will ever have to get itself set up for life. We've never been famous, no one ever heard of us. If this makes us famous for a few months, we need to harvest those months for all the money celebrity can make us."

Next, Alexander Livingston weighed in. He did so with a certain fastidious distaste, yet he spoke up. This surprised several people who had in the past been on the receiving end of his judicious scorn for all things commercial. Those who knew him better were not surprised. Medieval historian though he was by trade, he had embraced the latest technologies, he fancied himself as a student of contemporary culture, and his disdain for the world of commerce didn't prevent him from dabbling in it when opportunity arose.

His retirement role as a consultant down the road with the Woodvilles hadn't been an entirely popular career choice in the village; he had shrugged off objections with lofty declarations about advancing science in retirement, having advanced history in his previous life. He was helping their engineers to tune in the robots to the ways of speech actual humans use, and helping them with security (another of his hidden talents). Be that all as it may, Alexander Livingston felt that he knew how to step out of academic mode and into the language of the people. He had spent a lot of time preparing his words.

He began: "Mike Singer's right, alas. It's the new alchemy: fame into money, the base metal of celebrity into gold. We've all watched the alchemists at work, the celebs who are famous for being famous and get filthy rich off the back of their celebrity. We've seen them on screen, we've watched them sprawl all over the web, making a fortune out of doing nothing, getting rich for free. Now it's our turn, just for a few months. Are you going to turn your backs on that?"

And so it began, as speaker after speaker conjured up new commercial possibilities in this intriguing window of opportunity. Some of the local farmers were very interested in providing locations for large companies that might want a tax haven address. Mike and Jane Singer led the way in thinking of the merchandising possibilities: their marketing agency was used to producing such stuff for other companies, they rather fancied selling it on the village's account. Various enterprising individuals began to see pound signs.

At this point, and only at this point, the more idealistic speakers were allowed a turn. Moira had carefully calculated that commerce must come first, with the chance to rebuild all that had been run down, before the motivations that actually inspired most of The Guy Fawkes Club were allowed an airing.

Alicia mixed justice with advantage in pointing out the unfairness of a bunch of London bureaucrats denying their beloved village its rightful place in the new national park, when any fool could see it deserved a place in the Cotswolds. She pointed out that the fame they were about to receive might provide the "compelling reasons" needed for the boundaries of the Cotswold National Park to be redrawn in Mutley Shepwell's favour.

Then the landlord of *The Old Bells* stepped up and rather startled the meeting by announcing, "This isn't about money. I like money as much as the rest of you. But this is about one in the eye for London and Westminster. We're just standing up for all the other villages that would like to opt out of the London sneerers' version of England, where we're all just leftovers while London rules and the Two Cities rich boys and girls walk all over us. Do you want to lie down and let them? They blamed us for Brexit, but that was all their fault. They pushed the vote over the edge by making everyone so mad with them, it was all about protest. They told us that after Brexit England would get the benefits but London still managed to hog them all. London is richer than before, with all its new global trading, and England is still as broke as ever."

"We were had. They told us they'd make Brexit work for us, but it's only worked for them in the end. Time to show them. They set off the anger, they blundered into setting off the explosion that broke us out of Europe, we're going to break back in. For a few little months, Mutley Shepwell will be part of Europe again. We're doing it for everyone, not just for us, to show there's still a little freedom left in this country. And I hope, up in Westminster, they choke on it."

Quite a few eyebrows were raised at that speech. Not as many, though, as were lifted to heaven when the Old Tank pointed out that if the village wasn't part of England then its churches weren't part of the Church of England. "King Charles can go and defend someone else's faith, and leave us to have the old Church of England back."

"You're getting a bit of an anarchist in your old age, aren't you?" whispered Johnny B, from the side of the stage.

"Yes," said The Old Tank, as he stepped up to the microphone and warmed to his speech. "But I'm a conservative anarchist. I'm not an anarchist in spite of being a conservative, I'm an anarchist because I'm a conservative. Not just that, I'm an anarchist because I'm a Christian, and our leaders are trying to freeze out God. We won't kowtow to London's godless elites. We're going to be a republic, because we're loyal to the real England, England as it should be. It's not just us. We've got a lot of friends in the new parties. Westminster is overdue a good kicking."

His listeners looked slightly scandalised to hear such a sentiment from a man of the cloth. Richard Tranctard was just working up a head of steam. He got really visionary when he got on to the European bit:

"We want a better Europe, we want to be back in a Europe that's for the people, not the bureaucrats. So we're going to send them a message now, that the people are going to take Europe back: we're not turning our backs on Europe, we're signalling that people want to be part of a better Europe. Westminster failed us, Brussels failed us: they have Mammon, we have God on our side. We're doing this for all the people who never got listened to. We are the prophets of the return, and one day they'll remember that we told other villages to get on their feet and start building a people's Europe."

He stepped back and Mary Tranctard stepped up to quote the last lines of that Chesterton poem, "The Secret People": "But we are the people of England; and we have not spoken yet. Smile at us, pay us, pass us, but do not quite forget." She asked them if they wanted to be forgotten, adding, with a twinkle in her eye, that in her husband's case that would certainly be merited, but the rest of the village deserved better.

That was just the speeches. The receptions the speakers received got steadily more raucous throughout the evening. This may have been due to Bob Corns' delivery of large parts of his stocks, for free, to the punters who were listening. He was not the only donor: amazing amounts of beer and cider turned up, not to mention white wine, and a bit of red, purchased from the local discount supermarket, with the proceeds of a whip round held by the parish councillors themselves and a few friends. Alicia called it a shameless attempt at vote rigging, George looked depressed, and Moira almost protested, but no one else seemed to mind.

There was only one dissident who demanded the right to speak: Rev Jolly himself. At that very point, by some kind of inexorable logic known only to the denizens of Middle England, helped by a little encouragement from Des and Johnny, the whole meeting found itself singing

"Jerusalem," led by the choir from St Martin's. This was followed by a toast: "To the republic." Star Wars fans weren't sure which republic they were toasting, but most of the rest decided that having a toast was a good way to conclude a meeting, and the supermarket-purchased liquid victuals seemed to have run out, so they all finished off with three rousing cheers, led by Bob Corns and Mary Tranctard, the most unlikely of allies, and a toast to "the loyal republic."

After that, the meeting split between the two village pubs, with Bob Corns and The Old Tank, arm in arm, leading the procession down the hill to *The Old Bells*.

For a week that had begun in a pretty ordinary fashion, it was a strange conclusion. The sages in *The Old Bells*, as they considered it afterwards, agreed that the frustration had been building for years, and the four-card trick coming out of Whitehall over the summer, on top of all their other frustrations, had made the village a tinderbox waiting for a flame.

While much of the village drank to their forthcoming independence, Moira, Johnny, the Singers, Bill Stone, and a few others accepted the Russian's invitation to go straight on to a planning meeting over drinks and canapés at the manor. They talked deep into the night, while lawyers and Mr Pronotkov's small army of staff (including numerous extras especially drafted in from Russia and New York) made phone calls. Before morning, all over the country, and beyond, unsuspecting journalistic acquaintances found themselves being lined up with an unusual scoop.

18
THE SORDID EMPIRE
OF COMMERCE

Seated round a table with some of the most highly-paid experts in the world, trying to put a plan together, the parish council felt themselves way out of their league. They were relying on Mike and Jane Singer, who were the village's local experts on marketing and branding, and George the retired taxman, for the tax bit. Across the Russian's giant boardroom table, the Singers found themselves facing the vice-chairman of one of the world's biggest advertising agencies. He had been summoned to the meeting by Nikolai Marisovitch in person.

Alongside him were sitting some of the most expensive lawyers the City of London can provide, and a full set of PR, branding and multi-media marketing experts, with names like Fenella, Tristan, and Cordelia. These experts concocted the basics of a high-speed campaign at that very first meeting, working through the night, and started to roll it out the very next morning.

In the following days they rapidly fleshed out their communications plan, releasing it in stages, not just in the UK but globally. As each piece of publicity was created, it was projected out around the world, in multiple media. Parish Council members found themselves being wheeled in to the manor for media coaching sessions.

Mick's Metal Bashers, the remarkable workshop attached to the village garage, was called in to drop whatever it had on hand and start producing signs for the village, using the republic's new flag as its coat of arms. Unfortunately, the flag hadn't been invented yet, so to start with they used Lord Bonifer's coat of arms as the new republic's sign, in memory of King John's gift, not that King

John's gift had been made to Lord Bonifer, but his arms were more elegant than Sir Thomas's: a silver knight on a white horse on a sable background, riding over a golden crown.

The final design for the new national flag naturally caused a massive argument. Half the village seemed to want to help design it. The arguments could have dragged on for months, but Jane Singer, practical as ever, pointed out that they couldn't use the flag of their new republic for branding purposes until they actually had a flag.

This concentrated people's minds, and in the end they decided just to use the arms of Sir Peter (later Thomas) de Thurslay, since he was, after a certain delay, the author of their good fortune. His coat of arms was a St George's Cross with, in the quarters, two golden keys, a gold crown and a golden cross. The reference to St George reminded people that they were a republic loyal to England, even if not to its current rulers.

Elsewhere, things kept moving on. They needed to move fast to get as much exposure as possible during the rest of the summer lull in the news schedules. Until the major party conferences got going, there would be nothing terribly much to catch the headlines and friendly newspaper and web editors could be persuaded, over a sufficiently good dinner, to give some decent coverage to a novelty story.

"Novelty," bristled Alicia and Moira, but they had to pipe down in face of the combined elegant incomprehension of all the experts. For London folk, "novelty" was the least offensive label that could possibly be applied.

Thus began one of the more unlikely dashes for global news coverage in our days. Bored journalists told their editors they had a scoop and took the chance for a day out in the country, with a rather good meal at *The Red Ship* thrown in, so long as they were willing to listen to Moira, Alicia and Bill tell them at great length about the unique situation of the village and how it really now deserved to be in the national park. The Mutley folk were calling their situation Mexit, the Shepwellians Sexit.

The village drama society had managed to dig out the barriers and sentry boxes they had made for their last summer's outdoor production of *The Great Escape*. They painted over the Nazi insignias with Sir Thomas's coat of arms and set up sentry boxes and barriers (politely raised, of course) on the roads in and out of the village. Mick's Metal Bashers had spent a lot of time putting together very elegant "You are entering Europe" signs.

Mick still felt sore about the Brexit referendum. He'd taken it personally that Middle England got blamed for Brexit, when villages like Mutley Shepwell were solidly pro-European. His own mother had been Polish, her parents staying on after the war; few knew it, but Mick was short for Michal, not Michael. Mick had many reasons for being sure that truly English meant truly European.

Beyond those elegant signs, ten yards further into the village, was another sign: "Welcome to the Loyal Republic of Mutley Shepwell." All signs were decorated with the new country's flag, when it arrived.

Rapid calls were made to lawyers about trademarking the village "brand." The man from the *Financial Tribune* managed to get his Italian colleague to startle the Vatican spokesman into declaring that the Vatican had no designs on the territorial integrity of the United Kingdom, which naturally got members of the British Independence Congress parading up and down Lincolnshire high streets with Union Jacks, chanting "No Popery!" and carting off an effigy of the Pope to the nearest cliffs, where it was tipped over the edge to the tune of "Land of Hope and Glory." Diehard Protestants in Northern Ireland marched in orange to announce that if Rome invaded Mutley Shepwell, they would invade Rome.

The Pope's spokesman, looking mildly bemused, asked if anyone really thought that the Vatican was about to send the Swiss Guards into Middle England to try to take over this village no one in Rome had ever heard of. Numerous journalists practically begged him to try, pointing out what a dull week it was otherwise, yet he politely refused. A London theatrical costumier did manage to get some actors dressed up as Swiss Guards to march up to the checkpoints at the entrance to the village and parade around a bit for the cameras.

The prime minister initially took it all in good part and declared that he could take a joke as well as the next man, but got rather more miffed when the Russian's lawyers and his old enemy Prenderby took a writ to the Privy Council, pointing out that by the decision of King John, Mutley Shepwell was no longer part of the United Kingdom, but by the verdict of Henry VIII's parliament, it couldn't come under the sovereignty of the Pope either, so it had a claim to become its own country, under the jurisdiction of the European Union rather than the British government, "on the model of San Marino or Andorra or Lichtenstein."

The Privy Council would have to meet to consider the matter, but when it tried to set a date, Prenderby and his colleagues proved wonderfully imaginative in finding reasons for delay. At the same time, he and his team were initiating similar proceedings in Brussels, Strasbourg, and Luxembourg, meeting a wall of polite incomprehension, but happily continuing with their applications and filings, regardless.

Down at *The Old Bells*, they weren't impressed with the prime minister. The landlord took it a step farther and lambasted all politicians. "Instead of new faces, we have revolving chairs," he said. As if to prove it, there was a little five-day wonder of a Westminster fiasco just before the party conference season kicked off. The coalition seemed to be in crisis, there was a day of wonderful political excitement when the Prime Minister announced the coalition was unworkable and sacked half the cabinet.

The media went mad and there was talk of a surprise

general election. Emergency discussions behind closed doors were held instead, negotiations found a path to compromise, and a few days later most of the same faces were back at the same cabinet table, some of them at different chairs. In the end, it was dubbed by the press "the night of the short knives." A number of villagers felt that longer knives would have been in order, if not toasting forks, and for both sides of Parliament.

All over Mutley Shepwell, there was a sudden surge of capitalist zeal as villagers began to sniff opportunity on the wind. Neighbour astonished neighbour with one unexpected money-making venture after another. They took every shape and form, finding endless ways to exploit their village's new-found fame. In Back Street you might find Mrs Mudgery and two friends knitting "I was born to live in Mutley Shepwell" woolly hats for babies, in every shade and colour, which her granddaughter then sold for her over the internet.

Down the hill, one of the local farmers was sure that becoming a tax haven would make them all rich, the new Monaco. Others pointed out that Monaco had had a little longer to become the old Monaco, and they'd be doing well to make their fortunes before their window of opportunity closed.

Mike and Jane Singer were at the heart of much of it. Their long careers in marketing had left them with a lot of contacts. Their own family were happy to help. Ben came up with the "Mutley Shepwell: the World's My Village" line of T-shirts; Becky sketched out a line of fitness gear themed with the Mutley Shepwell flag and Ben came up with a slogan for it: "Mutley Shepwell: Fittest Place on Earth." Becky found that embarrassing, but it seemed to sell. Jimmy Armsbell got together with some mates to create the "Another Planet" travel website, where people from anywhere could blog and message together, with a series of rotating straplines, such as "Leave the Evil Empire, join the Republic," and "Villagers: Champions of

Freedom."

A few stood aloof. Des Martin said he'd had so many nights digging that he couldn't sleep properly any more. Perhaps that was why people started waking up to find potholes had been fixed in the night. George Sneed didn't join in the outbreak of commercial mania, nor did Alicia Cornwell.

George quietly left his fellow villagers to their schemes, Alicia was more vocal. She somehow managed to blame this excessive commercialisation on the Scots. She blamed most things on the Scots. She felt their departure had destabilised the country, and all sorts of things were running on strange courses since. She was also bitter about Northern Ireland's departure from the United Kingdom to form a united Ireland, but it was the defection (as she saw it) of Scotland that had really hurt her.

After the last election, Labour and its Liberal Democrat allies had needed the Scottish MPs to form a government and the price had been a referendum in a year, and effective independence in three. The last rites of final independence had been delayed till 2027, mainly so the government could keep the Scottish votes on its side for the rest of the parliament.

It was using them to change the constitution to make it harder for the Tories to get majorities, while it tried to work out how to win a majority next time, without Scotland. For all practical purposes, however, Scotland had become independent in June 2025, after 300-odd years of union. For half of England the Scots' secession, when it came, was a relief, for the other half it was an unforgivable act. Alicia was definitely of the "unforgivable" party.

She ended up having a row about it with Bob Corns. A row was a rare event for Alicia, a very common one for Bob. Alicia might become icily dismissive when offended, but rarely lost her calm. She had remarkable poise, always had her appearance perfectly composed, and didn't like to reveal any disturbance, or other sign of inner weakness.

She always needed to feel in control. Her powerful feelings were kept on a very strong leash. In addition, appearances mattered greatly to her. She was proud of her looks, still very striking, eyes still Baltic blue, the silver hair mixing perfectly into the dark brown. She hated to lose composure and look less than perfectly together. To be lured into a row was very unlike her.

She'd been lured down to *The Old Bells* and left vowing never to darken the doors again. It started with her blaming the Scots, and that set Bob off. He thought the Scottish departure was the best thing to happen to England in centuries, and couldn't believe that she'd blame them, or the last government, for the outbreak of Wild West casino capitalism in their little village. "Thatcher, blame her," he said. He always said these things went back to Thatcher; that was when the public-spirited English soul was corrupted by the machinations of her evil sorcery. For him, she was pretty much the Wicked Witch of the West.

For Alicia, on the other hand, she would always be the first woman prime minister, and a brave and honest woman too, for all her faults. She credited Margaret Thatcher with reviving a country whose greatness had ebbed away. Alicia even had a picture of her tucked away in a corner of her dining room, with Theresa May's beside it.

That was just a brief episode, though, and Moira managed to get them back on speaking terms soon. Bob might lose his temper on occasion, but never for long, and a pub landlord couldn't afford to alienate his customers. Alicia graciously accepted his apology, and even said she might return for George's birthday lunch.

Meanwhile, Moira was endlessly energetic in directing the business of the parish council. She still called it that, although more romantic souls were calling it "the national assembly," "the council of the republic," or "the parish parliament." In fact, one of the profusion of sub-committees their secession had spawned was devoted to just such constitutional issues as choosing new names for all their groups. They all had plenty of other sub-committee work to do, from negotiations with all the companies wishing to try their luck with a Mutley Shepwell branded product, to advising tour companies who'd suddenly found a place for the village in their itineraries, and journalists who'd like to play foreign correspondent while staying close to home.

One of Moira's deals involved the Singers and a couple of consultants who happened to live in the village getting together to form the commercial arm of the new government. They were soon churning out T-shirts, phone cases, teatowels, hats, caps, plates, mugs, and all manner of other memorabilia, including the flags themselves. Soon they were making their own stamps, not that you could use them to post anything, but collectors were buying them.

In a few weeks they had the world's first Mutley Shepwell branded cuddly toys, tins of biscuits (with charming village scenes on the tins), bars of chocolate. In a world of ecommerce, it was fast to get these things made, not just locally, but in other countries, even other continents. Policing their brand was another story. They had to turn to the Russian's lawyers for help with that.

Meanwhile, there was another secession in the village, and it fell to the Singers to sort it out. This led Mike and Jane to withdraw from all the usual business temporarily for one of their most stressful kitchen table conferences. They had to summon Becky back from university. Her father explained to her:

"Someone's got to soften Her Nibs up a bit, and her ladyship isn't talking to anyone on the parish council since she found out about the Russian. She always had a soft spot for you."

Jane had taken a career break when the twins were younger, during which she'd earned a little pin money by helping Lady Venetia with her accounts, finances and general admin. This led to an unexpected friendship between them, which was greatly strengthened in the aftermath of James TCB's decision to sell the Hall. As well as breaking his mother's heart, her son also broke her finances and left them in pieces, upturned and dumped in a heap, together with her, in the Dower House. Those finances might have remained in chaos had not Jane and Mike come to the rescue, with the teenage Becky and Ben.

Ben was soon relegated to help with the gardening, but Becky proved to be rather good with numbers and organization, and much harder working than she looked. She helped her parents to get her ladyship's affairs neatly tied up, with sensible arrangements made for managing the small amounts of land she'd been left with, and the odds and ends of other Thursloe-Cavendish-Bendyke investments from times past.

At the same time, there had sprung up an unlikely friendship between Lady Venetia and the young Becky, whose career she thereafter watched over with touching care. Becky was welcome for tea up at the Dower House any time, and used to help Lady Venetia with patchwork, gardening, flower arranging, and other matters of import in the vicinity.

This friendship had assumed greater importance since the day when her ladyship had discovered the new alliance with the Russian. Her wrath was without end. She called down the curses of every one of her ancestors on the parish council and all its works.

She even summoned workmen to put up a flagpole next to her front gate, so she could fly a Union Jack to show that she had not joined the loyal republic. "I'd rather live in Britain than in a Russian colony," she opined to those who dared to question, and when they pointed out that the Union Jack wasn't really Britain's flag any more, she assured them that the Scots would soon see the error of their ways and return with their tails between their legs, and Britain would be Great once more.

Such was Lady Venetia's disgust at the Russian's involvement, she had gone on television to make a Unilateral Declaration of Independence from the new republic, declaring it decidedly disloyal, not loyal at all. She even managed to get a TV crew to film her petitioning the prime minister to send her a contingent of Coldstream Guards to protect her loyal British enclave, yet the PM seemed reluctant to heed her call. The lads from Mick's Metal Bashers offered to build her some proper fortifications, and some signs to match the ones they'd made for the republic, but their thoughtfulness was not appreciated.

It took Becky's return to calm Lady Venetia down. Becky knew how to charm her ladyship, and while the flag remained aloft and the farmhouse was definitely staying part of the United Kingdom, reasonable working relations with the republic were restored. Jane and Mike could get back to their ever-expanding marketing operations with lighter hearts.

19
THE REPUBLIC AND ITS REBELS

Perhaps the most unlikely outbreak of commercial exploitation came from Alexander Livingston, of all people. At first he lined up with Alicia to look down his nose at such things, sniffing audibly as each new deal was announced, looking pained to hear of yet more commercial delights on the way. Then, one day in *The Old Bells*, over a lunch that became considerably longer than he had planned for it to be, he encountered a television producer sniffing for stories. This charming gentleman, Zac 'Jackboot' Boot by name, was happy to buy drinks for a long-time resident, and in a surprisingly short time had discovered the secret grief of Alexander Livingston's heart.

It went back to his days as an ardent young student, gifted, good-looking and full of hope for the future, dashing about Britain and France trying to make a name in academia with ground-breaking research on King John. He was sure he had accumulated information of vital historical importance, from hitherto neglected sources. In those old-fashioned days, he had photocopied this, hand copied that, photographed items with his own Kodak camera, put together a large briefcase of informational gems culled from monasteries, medieval libraries, the family treasures of reluctant aristocrats, the secret joys of the curators of provincial museums.

After a week of frenzied writing it all up in a little *gîte* near Perigueux, a week in which he felt as if all stars aligned and the muses descended to bestow their gifts, he was ready to drive back to English Academe and make his mark. As he lunched in a small town just south of Poitiers, someone smashed in the window of his Mini and took the vital briefcase. "As if it could have done them any good," he said to countless friends and relatives. Frantic searches, desperate pleas to French police, even an offered reward, all were in vain.

In time, with more research funds painfully begged for, he tried again, but that first flush of inspiration never quite returned, and what he came back with was never quite the triumphant rewriting of accepted history that had once, so briefly, seemed within his grasp. He always looked back on it as the false dawn of his career, the moment when eminence and distinction seemed just around the corner. It was even the reason he had come to the village: he was sure that one of the keys to the mysteries of the last days of King John was that strange ruined chapel between the River Amble and Traitor's Wood.

One of the things Alexander had almost pieced together was the strange story of the king's late falling out with his most devoted servant, Sir Peter de Thurslay. He had been trusted with the most delicate missions, trusted also to guard the king's son and the king's treasure, trusted always.

And yet, in the last year of the king's life, that same Sir Peter became a hunted man, escaping to the invading French with, so it was said, only the shirt on his back, a fast horse, and one small casket. According to local legend, that horse took him galloping out of the back gates of the old manor at the top of the hill just as the king's soldiers smashed in the front gates. The knight went spurring down the hill and over the bridge that crossed the Amble, on his way to exile.

Then, after John's death, Sir Peter, by then a sick old man, who had renamed himself Sir Thomas de Thurslay, was somehow permitted back by that gentler soul, King Henry III, whose childhood he had guarded in happier days. Sir Thomas was permitted his manor once again. He may have been, although sources differ, allowed burial by the river in that tiny chapel, never used for worship or for burial thereafter, frequented only by the almsmen Sir Thomas had employed to pray for his soul. It was a kind of chantry chapel before its time, with a few cottages for the almsmen beside it. Now those cottages were ancient ruins, and the chapel itself a ruin.

Alexander was in his own mind convinced that the chamber they had found under Sir Bonifer's massive monument had originally been intended as the tomb for Sir Peter. Why he had chosen instead to adorn it with the strangest of engravings, and to be buried elsewhere, Alexander was still trying to fathom, after too many years.

His travels to France had largely been in search of Sir Peter/Thomas's children, who had not returned with him when he came back to be buried in his own native soil. Certain indications had suggested that he had hoped they would return one day, yet they had remained French forever, and the manor was inherited by a junior branch of the Thurslays. Two generations later, a member of that junior branch became Lord Bonifer. A few generations after that, when the Thurslays joined their name to the Bendykes, it had become Thursloe, not Thurslay. Sir Peter's story was lost in the footnotes of history.

All this Alexander Livingston had found, in the course of half a lifetime researching King John, with only a couple of badly-received books to show for it, and no appreciation, he felt, for the new light he had shed on a crucial period of English history. Then he met Zac Boot over lunch at *The Old Bells*.

Alexander's good looks remained, though worn and frown-lined now, and before he knew it, he was about to be paid more money than he'd ever seen in his career to front a TV series for American television on the story of this village that had become its own country. He was only going to get to tell a tiny bit of the story he really wanted to tell, about King John and how he has always been misunderstood, but Zac Boot almost promised that another series would follow (Zac was too canny to make binding commitments, yet he made it sound very nearly a sure thing).

With Alexander's capitulation to the sordid spirit of Mammon, Richard, Mary, George and Alicia were the last conscientious objectors. They usually suffered their friends' commercialisation in silence, except when arguing with Bob Corns, who always said that taking money off capitalists on behalf of the people was his communist duty. They could never get him to explain how keeping the money himself qualified him to be a righteous class warrior on behalf of the proletarian poor.

Finally, seeing their ideals for the new republic getting more and more submerged in this happy outbreak of enthusiastic capitalism in the raw, Alicia went on the warpath.

"This profiteering must stop. We're meant to be doing this for the village, for all villages, for England. It's not just a chance to make a quick few quid."

She kept making this argument at meetings of what used to be the parish council, and was now the meeting of the council of the republic. They weren't keen to listen.

Her listeners pointed out that if there hadn't been the chance for a bit of alchemy, of fame into money, most of the village would never have been interested in becoming independent in the first place. Alicia seemed to be alone with the Tranctards and George over this, until Alexander turned up on her doorstep in fury, crying betrayal and theft.

He'd just been on his way to London to sign the contract for his new TV series when he got a message to say that he'd been dropped from the cast, in favour of a well-known TV presenter who knew no history and had never even set foot in the village. "Every time I get a break, the rug gets yanked from under me," he moaned. Alicia managed to combine sympathy with chastisement for his surrender to the spirit of commerce, and even tried to point out that this betrayal might be for the benefit of his mortal soul, an argument he was not very interested in hearing at the time.

He recovered his equilibrium in the end, allowing for the odd outburst of bitterness. Soon he and Alicia were a debating team again of an evening at *The Old Bells*, taking on all comers with their critique of capitalism. Bob Corns even bought them a drink once (a very rare event), saying that they were reviving the pub tradition of free and frank debate.

The Old Bells had always been the home of a good argument but that had been in danger of temporarily dying out as everyone was so busy talking about the wave of business enterprise, until the two of them came back to provide some opposition and stick the knife into the empire of commerce.

Alicia's bitterness was alleviated somewhat when she found a way of utilising the village's new-found fame for non-profit purposes. The roots of her new scheme went back to the secret success of her publishing days. One of the most curious things about her was that, although she longed to lived up to the distinction of the revered ancestors whose images looked down on her dining table, the thing she might have counted as her greatest achievement was something she was deeply ashamed of and never referred to.

Her secret came out in an evening sharing white-wine-shaped regrets with Moira and Mary. The very next morning she forbade them from ever passing on what she'd told them. That didn't stop them from showing her how she could use her knowledge for the good of the republic.

Her dark secret, as she saw it, went all the way back to her twenties, when she'd gone into publishing, into an old and prestigious publishing house, enjoying the ambience, the creativity, the company. Her timing wasn't good. She spent the best part of twenty years in meetings bemoaning the decline of traditional publishing. They lamented it all: the power of the bookselling chains, the rise of internet sales, the mushrooming growth of self-publishing, the ubiquity of social media, the reluctance of millennials to pay for content – she and her colleagues sat through endless discussions, all the while watching their comfortable world slowly decline.

It was Alicia who turned the company round, and her colleagues never forgave her for it. She told them to stop complaining about self-publishing and get on the bandwagon, to use their publishing resources and their name to pull in punters willing to pay them to publish their books. Instead of paying out advances to authors, advances that got bigger as the author's sales grew, they took in advances from authors, which got smaller as that author became more successful.

If the authors were willing to put in additional money upfront, the company provided PR and marketing, on a sliding scale of fees. The authors got to say they had a real publisher, and to have experienced professionals manage the whole process for them. The publisher found would-be writers queueing up to pay hard cash for the right to be published above a respected publisher's name.

Alicia even thought of the name for this new "open entry, assisted publishing" imprint: Guardian Angel books. She hoped it gave the right kind of welcoming feel to the prospective clients. Authors who then made it reasonably big could move on from this new kind of situation to the more traditional, to the usual industry terms, while those who didn't could at least feel they'd had their chance in the sun. The company went from genteel decline to uncontrollable growth.

The price it paid was that its staff moved from an elegant, rather elitist world into a mass-volume factory: instead of relatively few carefully nurtured authors on an editor's list, they churned hundreds through a largely automated process, with marketing, production, PR, all going through similar changes. Some felt it was like moving from a Jermyn Street tailor, producing bespoke suits of the finest, to working in a cash and carry warehouse, piling them high, selling them cheap. The shareholders applauded; the staff sulked, adapted, or left. Few of them forgave Alicia, and she never forgave herself.

As a result, Alicia never mentioned her greatest career achievement, feeling that her notable ancestors would disapprove. Perhaps that was why she had buried herself in the depths of the countryside, far from her old London world and her old contacts. She'd turned her back on it all, except for a little freelancing, and gone back to where (some of) those revered ancestors came from, far from where she'd had her own adventures. Perhaps there were other reasons. Perhaps the disappointment had helped to make her a trifle waspish about others' stories of their achievements.

She had never seen a way of making use of her experience, until now. Mary and Moira pointed out to her that the council of the republic was being deluged with requests for help with PR from independence movements great and small. They were also constantly being offered sponsorship funding from companies desperate to get their name associated with the torrent of publicity this little village was generating. If Alicia could put that funding and those needs for publicity together, she could channel the republic's fame into a better cause than making money.

She took them up on the idea and the republic's publishing arm was born. Online and offline, she dedicated it to every village seeking greater independence, every movement fighting the establishment, every lost cause fighting the powers that be. The village's online existence took on a life of its own and became a forum for manifestoes, academic research, popular protest, religious revolt, every kind of rebel who might want to link hands with fellow revolutionaries. Books, pamphlets, a semi-scholarly journal, all appeared with remarkable speed, with help from Alexander and others.

Emboldened by their unprofitable but righteous efforts, Alicia and Alexander continued the lonely fight against the empire of Mammon, wearily supported by Richard, Mary, and George. In spite of their best efforts, they soon found the story of the money-raising hitting a new low. This episode, which Alicia saw as the Marianas Trench of good taste, began at the Mutley vicarage with the arrival of certain emissaries from the empire of commerce whom no one had expected.

20
THE BRIGHT LIGHTS OF FAME

The usual humble Skoda in the vicarage drive had been joined by a rather snazzy BMW, alloy wheels taking the chance to gleam weakly as the last of the autumn sun peeped through the clouds. Inside the house, the vicar was being propositioned in an unusual way.

"It's like this, Reverend. Reverend Jolly, isn't it?"

"Jolyon to you, Ms – er?"

"Bateman's the name, Linda Bateman from the *News of the Times*, this is my assistant Sam. I'm in the Marketing Department, and we think we have something to offer you."

"I'm not accustomed to reading your rag, or indeed any of your proprietor's right-wing mouthpieces, he's as bad as his father was. The only thing I ever read was your "Raving Reverend" column and the man's dotty, gives the Church of England a terrible image. I don't see what you and the Church have to do with each other."

"It's like this, Reverend Jolyon. You have a bit of a problem with the electrics, don'tcha? And the church roof. Bats in the belfry, is it?"

"Dry rot, actually, not to mention woodworm. What is that to *The News of the Times*?"

"Well, Reverend Jolyon, we're considering making a donation. We're doing a little feature on your independent village here in Mutley Shepwell and we thought we could do a feature on you. Showing our support for your church, and the village. Very respectful, very tasteful."

"Respectful? Tasteful? And how would I explain it to the Archdeacon? There's such a thing as bringing the church into disrepute, you know. Could ruin my career, I'd be a laughing-stock forever. No, we'll raise our own money our own way, strictly ethical means."

"We're very ethical, Reverend Jolyon, no one's as ethical as journalists. And your roof? You really sure?"

"Very sure, thank you. Good day to you, Ms Bateman."

"Wait a minute, Mike," said his wife, Rosemary, often seen in the village as very much his better half. "This kind gentleman is offering money the church needs. We should at least offer him a cup of tea."

Ten minutes later, the offered cup of tea was proffered to the emissaries of the world of journalism, with chocolate biscuits and home-made fruitcake, no less. She ostentatiously avoided offering them to her husband, who was pretending to need to check a few urgent texts. His wife sighed apologetically and explained:

"He's grumpy because it's one of his dieting days. He's doing a religious version of the '2-5' diet. Sends him mad. I call it the Pharisee diet. His motto ought to be 'If it was good enough for the Pharisees, it's good enough for me.'"

In spite of all her best efforts, however, the discussion didn't progress much. Linda's charm and chequebook made no impression. His wife's cajoling about the church roof also fell on stony ground. As she ushered a somewhat annoyed Linda and Sam to the door at the end of a fruitless half hour, she was apologetic.

"I'm so sorry, he's usually pretty flexible. We even have a treasurer who's an Anglican Buddhist, and a church warden who's a druid in his spare time. Good idea, really. Amazing how differently we all believe, yet still get along." Two blank faces looked back at her, and she decided to write this one off to experience.

As she got back into the BMW, Linda Bateman furrowed her brow in characteristic annoyance. The oil slipped out of her voice as she announced to her assistant, "She was alright, shame about him. Let's get back."

There it would have ended, had they not needed to

stop for petrol at Mick's garage on the way out of the village. The garage was the other half of Mick's Metal Bashers, the half that paid for the bit he really loved, the Metal Bashers workshop. This was right next to the garage, making it easy for the curious motorist to pop in. It stood behind a low fence made entirely out of forks of all sizes, from dining forks to garden forks, and its front wall was made of repurposed panels from old aeroplanes, with windows shaped like portholes (they had, in fact, been salvaged from a ship).

Linda left Sam to fill up the car, walked across to the workshop, and stopped dead. Not much astonished Linda Bateman, but she'd never expected such remarkable workmanship in a country village: helmets, shields, weapons, suits of mail for film and TV; bespoke installations for the very rich, everything from hand-made fences like the one in front of the workshop, to vast barbeques made to fit unusual spaces and cook to perfection, and all sorts of strange individual items of furniture or decoration besides.

If you could make it from metal, Mick and his assistants, Charlie and Dave, could make it for you. He left his long-suffering wife, Sally, to run the garage next door, which made the regular income they relied on to fund his love of metal.

Linda stepped inside: the workshop was a treasure cavern of twisted, half-carved metals, with all sorts of commissions in every stage of construction. Mick himself was working on a barbeque shaped like Father Christmas's sleigh (it was for a hotel in Finland), while Charlie and Dave were making a spiral staircase designed to look as if it had grown out of a steel fir tree, for an eccentric collector in Canada.

Mick had often been told that if he'd moved to London he could have been famous, but he preferred to be known only to the cognoscenti, and stay home. He was village born and village bred, and when he died he'd be village dead.

Linda Bateman now proposed to remove that anonymity; here was the location for the photo-shoot from heaven, as far as she was concerned, with Mick and his crew in armour, alongside her Page Four girls. Yet Mick said No. Sam did the sensible thing and went to talk to Sally. Two minutes later Sally was in the workshop and doing the talking. "Come on then, Linda. Just how much are you offering?"

A number was named. Sally Smith took a deep breath. "That's halfway to getting the school a new playground." Mick looked at her, his vast chest heaving and a pleading look in his brown eyes. "Not here. We never let 'em in here. It's our place."

She stared him down: "Our kids were at that school, and our grandchildren soon will be. You don't want little Jenny to have a decent playground?" She turned back to Linda Bateman. "Double it and you can do the shoot here." Mick walked out, breathing heavily. "He'll be there," said his wife. "If he don't listen to me I'll get little Jenny and Shane onto him, he can't say No to them."

Linda's day had suddenly got a whole lot better. "Done, Mrs Smith. And a pleasure doing business with you. Sam will be in touch about making the arrangements."

Indeed he was, and, what's more, additional help turned up. The day before the photo shoot, Jem and Jimmy knocked on the Smiths' door, with their most helpful faces on.

"Good evening, boys. Can I help you?"

"Oh no, Mrs Smith. It's, can we help you?" said Jimmy.

"The thing is," added Jem, in his most concerned voice, "it'll be a busy day for you tomorrow. Contracts, money, talking to the boss, all that –"

"You're not going to have the time to look after your guests, are you, really?" added Jimmy. "We know you'd like to, still remember those nice buns from the school fete, but you won't have the time tomorrow. Now, me and Jem, we could set up a little hospitality station, tea and cake and coffee and things, you know, for those poor, busy girls when they need a break from the photography."

"You feel they might need a little TLC, do you?"

"Emotional support, it's always got to be good, and a nice old English cup of tea. We know you'd do it if you had the time, but since you don't, we're here for you."

"And them," added Jem. And so it was that the next day Jem and Jimmy made the tea, while Sally Smith negotiated with photographer and journalist in the big workshop, then got together with Charlie and Dave to talk her husband round to co-operating.

The apprentices had rapidly come round to the idea of a little fame, but the sorcerer himself was still bitter that his carefully guarded anonymity was about to be sacrificed for a bit of fund-raising. Sally and the apprentices had to drag him into position each time for the photographs. When not dispensing tea, cake and sympathy, Jimmy and Jem were awed witnesses to the photo shoot.

A rather less awed witness was Charlie's partner Jade. She watched him and Dave standing on the metal fir tree spiral steps they had made, waving the village's new flag, surrounded by "Page 4 stunnas." Thanks to the workshop's collective efforts, the girls were wearing very convincing ancient Greek-style armour, holding tridents like Britannia's, and shields emblazoned with the village crest, with huge flags bearing St George's Cross draped behind the whole scene.

The flags had almost kiboshed the whole thing, since Sam had unthinkingly brought Union Jacks, which were now of course an alien country's insignia. Fortunately, the Cross of St George was still acceptable in the loyal republic, since it was not just the flag of England but the flag for all sorts of other entities too, from the long-lost armies of Byzantium to a football team to which the new country still gave its support. The girls and the St George's Crosses surrounded Charlie and Dave, in their blue boilersuits, "to add a bit of colour," as the photographer put it, while the little crease between Jade's eyes became just a little deeper.

"All in the call of duty, is it, dearie?"

"Oh yes," said Charlie happily, "Definitely. Duty, tha's me."

She turned to the models' boss.

"Ms Bateman – "

"Linda, it's Linda."

"Tell me, Linda, you got any contacts with the Chuppendales? Another photo shoot?"

Linda looked quizzical. "You do metalwork like this too?"

"No, but I'm the chair of the WI. We have a history with calendars." Linda was reaching for her mobile before Jade had finished the sentence.

In between times, Jimmy and Jem spared no effort to make their guests at home, with help from homemade cakes they'd wheedled out of Jimmy's Aunty Thelma. They had help: Ben Singer suddenly discovered a devotion to the village school never seen before and took the day off his holiday job to help. Becky Singer insisted on coming along too.

Becky stationed herself next to Jimmy, dutifully making tea and cutting cakes, and here and there sighing rather noticeably as his eyes went past her to the visiting ladies. Where she could she took the chance to keep him busy with trotting off to get more of this and that and keep his contact with the girls down as much as she could.

Not that her efforts made much difference. Jim and Jemmy had even brought along their brand-new business cards: *J and J, Production, Support, Research & Resourcing*. "We do anything, really," explained Jem. "By the way, the numbers are mainly our business mobiles, but we can take personal calls on them as well." Strangely enough, none of the girls seemed to want to take them up on this generous offer.

Jem may not have helped himself by wearing a T-shirt emblazoned with the news that "One plus one does not equal two." He tried to explain, to anyone who would listen, that he was campaigning against the binary understanding of marriage. "Two is just an arbitrary number," he added, trying to look like a man at the cutting edge of the twenty-first century, before trying to open his hearers' eyes to the need to expand marriage to include any number of partners, which he felt was an option that combined the best of tradition with modern insights into the essentials of human autonomy.

Strange to say, no one seemed very keen to listen to his carefully thought-through speeches, except one girl who asked if anyone had been interested in marrying him on that basis. Linda Bateman listened briefly, then looked him up and down, laughed, and announced that marriage wasn't something Jem was likely to have to worry about, unless the research centre down the road found a way to manufacture female nerds.

Jimmy was getting a much better response talking music and sport. Jem felt, once again, that philosophers are always unappreciated in England. In fact, the only person who seemed interested in his ideas was the Reverend Richard Tranctard, who took him aside to give him a dressing down: ""You talk about free love as if it were like free food, or free transport, but those are commodities you can price any way you want, while love is not a commodity and it has no price."

Jimmy leapt in to defend his friend: "It's not as if he ever gets any, Rev, he just likes to talk." Jem wished he were a thousand miles away, till the Old Tank gave him a pat on the shoulder and told him to have a cup of tea and think about it.

Just before the visitors left, one of the Page 4 girls, Petra by name (or perhaps it was stage-name), handed Jimmy back his business card. "Get a lot of blokes wanting my number, keen to give me theirs. Have a look on the back, though."

He turned it over and a simple row of eleven digits made him reel. "No! Really?"

"Really. It's my own mobile, not my work one. You're a bit different from my average kind of fella. If you're up in London some time, give us a call." With that, and a peck on the cheek, she was gone, while he held on to the table.

He didn't even hear Petra's friend Jade whisper "*That?* You gave *That* your number?" Petra went slightly red, "Makes a change, don't it? Anyway, I don't have to pick up the call."

Jem looked after them with incredulity. "Why you? Why not me?"

"Good taste, mate, only possible explanation," grinned Jimmy, but absent-mindedly. He was busy checking coach times and prices to London on his phone.

"What was that about," said Becky Singer, from the doorway.

"Nothing," said Jimmy, absent-mindedly. He was so absorbed in his travel plans that he didn't even notice her creep up behind him and peep over his shoulder. As she did so, Jem was looking back from the doorway at her, with an almost unreadable expression on his face. Then he shrugged and marched back to their hosts, leaving Becky peeping over Jimmy's shoulder at his mobile, with more than a hint of a tear in her eyes.

Perhaps fortunately, her mother arrived to take her and Ben away at that moment. Jane and her son made contrasting entrances, he lagging behind, lost in excitement, lost for words, she edging past the photographer and models in the front hall, with a certain distaste that increased markedly when she saw her daughter's crumpled face.

"Never mind them, darling," she said, with a hug, "It's just a silly game, all that fashion and glamour – it's a business they sell you, it's a game they play, it's just the beauty game, it's not real, darling."

Becky looked down as she replied, "But she's in the beauty game and I never will be."

Her mother hugged her again: "Of course you are, darling, you're a beautiful woman, you're my beautiful girl. And they're just silly, shallow money-grabbers in why-bother skirts. You're worth ten of them."

"I'm glad they didn't bother," mumbled Ben behind her, shambling dazedly into the sitting room with his mouth open. His mother turned her nuclear stare on him and he shut up.

Jane Singer's disdain was as nothing to that of Mrs Mudgery, who had invited herself along to help clear up, and to find out everything that was going on. None of it pleased her. As far as the girls went, her verdict was: "Shop window outfits – everything on display."

She was a woman of strong opinions and she had a few other things to say, all of them unflattering. Mick's father had been her second cousin, so she felt entitled to express her views. She couldn't object to fixing up the school playground, though, and Sally managed to talk her round in time. Sally could talk almost anyone round to almost anything. Thirty years of being married to Mick had given her persuasive powers that could coax blood from rock and make water flow uphill.

That was how it came to pass that Mick, Dave, and Charlie found themselves on the front page of *The News of the Times* that Saturday, it being a slow news day, under the headline "We Salute the New Republic," surrounded by flags, tridents, shields armour, models, and a very large cheque. Mick then stomped off back to his workshop, still fed up that he'd been talked into the photo shoot.

His apprentices basked in their mates' appreciation, and endured their partners' wrath. Jade continued in correspondence with Linda Bateman and Sam, whom she continued to call Sammy. She was determined to upstage anything Charlie could do.

The two village churches, meanwhile, took diametrically opposed views on their village's new independence. Up the hill, Rev Jolly announced that it was business as usual, although some members of the PCC asked if they were now a foreign mission, and the Sunday School took pleasure in "Collecting for the Missionaries" and using the proceeds for their own equipment.

Down the hill, however, The Old Tank and the church wardens took great pleasure in announcing that St Martin's was now part of the Church of England's Diocese of Europe. The Diocese of Europe was rather surprised to discover this, and politely declined to play ball, so The Old Tank started looking elsewhere for a new church home.

George wasn't totally sure about this but Richard and Mary and Alicia were set on it. The church choir rather liked the idea of being independent. The Old Tank sent out a press release about belonging to the true Church of England, which, for him, seemed to have a lot to do with the old Book of Common Prayer.

He'd managed to concoct a version of history that had the true Church of England beginning with the first Elizabeth and ending with the second. This might not have convinced many historians but no one at St Martin's was arguing. The parochial church council started selling souvenirs, and Richard Tranctard started flying the EU flag and the flag of the loyal republic in the churchyard, and wearing a dramatic black cloak at services, in token of his church's new independence. Mary asked him if he'd like her to buy him a red carpet on which to ride his bicycle from the vicarage to the church.

That was just the start for The Old Tank. His sermons started to get truly esoteric. Not that they were exactly sermons, Richard Tranctard was enjoying himself too much: he had a quirky sense of humour at the best of times, and he was soon having a lovely time sending off letters to the Archbishop of Canterbury explaining that, for the duration, St Martin's was no longer part of the

Church of England, until the Diocese of Europe should relent and accept it as a member. He kept refusing all requests to meet the relevant authorities until the final decision had been reached about the status of the village.

Then he really got carried away and one evensong, as part of what was meant to be a sermon, he read out a letter he was sending to the pope in Rome, announcing that although Mutley Shepwell might technically be a fief of the Vatican at present, St Martin's would pledge its allegiance to no pope since the Reformation, and before that possibly only to the memory of the one English Pope, Hadrian, after whom his cat was named. He had actually got as far as suggesting sending Hadrian the cat to Rome to offer homage at Pope Hadrian's grave when the church wardens managed to wave hard enough at him to get him back onto a track somewhere nearer planet Earth.

It was hard to see how their vicar's mind worked, sometimes, but it all added to the interest of a Sunday morning. Soon he was promising that he would announce St Martin's response to this new-style "multi-faith coronation" the new king seemed determined to push through, particularly as there was a push from some of those involved to use a new experimental version of the Lord's Prayer, which began, "Our father and mother, who art in heaven." This proposal had sent Richard Tranctard's blood pressure to new heights, and united St Martin's in disapproval, while up the road Rev Jolly cheered it on.

Mary Tranctard was quite with Richard about the coronation, but her father had been a bishop and she didn't like to see a humble vicar getting above his station in life, even if it was her husband. The last straw for her was when Richard managed to quote Augustine of Hippo, Thomas Aquinas, Martin Luther, and Archbishop Laud in a letter to the Archbishop of Canterbury, a letter which gave a kind of potted history of royal coronations through the ages as a prelude to pouring scorn on the current proposals. Sighing deeply, she gathered the senior members of the church together, and, with them at her back, told him to get back in his box for a while. If granite had feelings, then his might have been hurt, but granite is a hard rock: he listened, smiled, and laid off the grand announcements.

Instead, he started to focus on his secret dream. His true passion, which he'd always thought would be forever beyond his reach, was to found a hospice in memory of his parents. Mary softened as she explained the scheme to George. It was one of the few things she never teased her husband about:

"He was away at university when his father was taken by a heart attack. Then he was a missionary in Africa when his mother got cancer. She didn't like to tell him because she thought the work he did was so vital. He found out too late, from his aunt, and got back to find that she had died alone. Ever since then he's wanted to found a hospice. He's never been able to raise the money, but now he thinks he might be able to."

When it came to fundraising, the fame of the new republic soon showed Richard Tranctard the way to a rather different approach. Early one Monday morning, Mary discovered a convoy of fashionable vehicles outside the church, with her husband inside it, dressed up in his grandfather's clerical frock coat, waving his great-uncle Gerald's fob watch, surrounded by a team from an American fashion magazine, who'd suddenly discovered medieval chic.

As the cameras clicked, her face darkened. Her husband was swift to reassure her: it was all to raise funds for the hospice, and for the church roof. He smiled at her shock: "Think of the good of the church, my dear, and the care of the dying. Impeccable motives. Still, wives have been known to object to even smaller things. After all, women are very articulate about their woes."

"We have a lot of woes to be articulate about. Starting with you, dear one. And don't be so sexist."

"My dear, it was a tribute: women are such good communicators, about all things in life."

She communicated quite a bit about that little fashion shoot, and was not amused to find her husband on the front of one of America's most celebrity-oriented magazines, his rough-cut ugliness surrounded by glamour and elegance, which, she enjoyed telling him, just accentuated his status as the man whom looks forgot. He was more bothered that the ignorant fashionistas had not mentioned the hospice plan, nor managed to incorporate the ecclesiastical history of the revolution.

Up the hill, quite a few of the congregation at Charles, King and Martyr, feeling that they were being rather left out of a once-in-a-lifetime opportunity, petitioned Rev Jolly to leave the Church of England too. He indignantly refused, with the backing of his bishop, who was privately highly amused but felt obliged to be publicly censorious of parishes making unilateral declarations of independence.

At least Rev Jolly avoided the wrath of Mrs Mudgery. After Sally Smith had talked her down from her high perch about the photo shoot at Mick's Metal Bashers, she got to hear about the fashion shoot at the church, and she was not impressed. Her friends and neighbours got quite a speech, ending with words to the effect that if that The Old Tank dared to show his face at the parochial church council on Wednesday, he'd regret it.

Mrs Mudgery felt that things were getting out of hand. She saw herself as the supreme guardian of tradition down at St Martin's, and indeed for the village as a whole. The village, sadly, had never taken kindly to her attempts at custodianship, so she regarded St Martin's as her special fiefdom. Within its walls, she tried to maintain all things exactly as they had been in her childhood. In the case of the church linen, she had succeeded, mainly because she looked after it all, or, as she put it, she did "the holy boiling," meaning that she washed and ironed and starched it all to a state of sinless perfection.

As she pondered the follies of her fellow villagers the

starching of the linen became almost an act of aggression. She was positively a picture of righteous wrath, and the holy boiling that week was done with even more forceful concentration than usual, the altar linen starched to within an inch of its life.

She really boiled over when she saw that Saturday's paper, which featured not just Jade but also the Secretary and Treasurer of the WI, dressed in royal regalia, posing outside the Village Hall on a large litter borne aloft by twelve members of the Chuppendales. These gentlemen were dressed as Swiss Guards, with additional flags and chains. The photos showed the aforesaid gents rolling out a red carpet, on which the rest of the WI committee rode up to the village hall on white horses, wearing crowns, looking a little less than comfortable in some cases, and were then presented with a very large cheque.

The accompanying text explained that the fee for the photo shoot would cover the emergency repairs needed to keep the Village Hall from falling down, and that the WI and Village Hall committee were still seeking sponsors and donors for the complete rebuild needed to make it truly fit for purpose.

Mrs Mudgery resigned from the WI, and it was only the thought of the hospice project that saved Richard Tranctard. Her mother had died in a hospice, where she was greatly and expertly cared for. In memory of her mother, Mrs Mudgery very reluctantly agreed to spare The Old Tank the full measure of her wrath.

Her patience was greatly tested, however, when the *National Eyewitness* got in touch with him, all the way from America. It wasn't just Mrs Mudgery who frowned. The more colour co-ordinated blanched at the combination of American footballers in black and white, stars-and-stripes-wearing cheerleaders, the huge village flag right across the front of the church, and Father Tranctard in a purple robe to which a mere vicar was not really entitled. Mrs Mudgery turned up to frown at that photo shoot too, like the proverbial spectre at the feast, on the pretext of helping with the tea for the participants. Her frown narrowly failed to curdle the milk in the drinks she handed out, though not for want of trying.

But she kept silence at the church and relieved her feelings only when she got home and asked her neighbours Elsie and Joan if they'd ever seen men who looked more like a lump of wood on legs and had fewer brains per pound than the hulking loafers they'd photographed, whom she felt were probably criminals in the making, if not already on loan from America's finest prisons. Then she got on to the cheerleaders, and demanded to know if these girls ever wore anything more than a shop window outfit. Elsie and Joan averred that this was unlikely, although when said girls visited their grannies, perhaps decorum might return.

Mrs Mudgery might have been relieved had she seen Mary Tranctard marching her husband back to the vicarage. Once Mary had managed to stop laughing, some firm words were had. She promised to help him to find other ways to fund the hospice, and Richard's photographic career abruptly stopped. As Mary said to Lady Venetia, he had enough follies against his name already without becoming the unlikeliest fashion model in history.

21
ROBOTS AND RELIGION

Richard Tranctard was hoping to use the money from his photo shoots as a down payment on a building for the hospice he dreamed of. He had long mused about putting in a bid for some of the buildings at the western end of the Mutley Shepwell business park. The eastern half had been leased years ago to the Woodvilles who had made it a "Rural History Experience" for coachloads of tourists coming back from Shakespeare's Stratford and the Cotswolds. It majored on picturesque historical poverty.

A business park might sound like a strange location for a hospice, but it would actually have been a rather scenic spot, were it not for the buildings currently present. The whole business park had been put up on the cheap in the sixties and the end the Woodvilles hadn't taken over had been empty for so long that it was falling down.

It was reputed to be so decrepit and unfit for habitation that even the rats had complained to the council. All the coachtrippers who thought they were experiencing the picturesque history of rural poverty at the other end of the business park could have got a lot closer to the real thing by getting out of their coaches and walking a few feet.

The Old Tank knew he had to wait till these decrepit business premises had finished their brief career as a tax haven. He wanted then to landscape the surroundings, and create a hospice at the heart of the village. Great was his disappointment when he discovered that Stephanos had beaten him to it and put in an offer for that end of the business park, where he proposed starting a new community of all religions.

Stephanos had had the idea a while ago, but not announced his plans till now. Bill was happy. He just wanted his enlightened brother out of the house and didn't mind how big a commune he joined. Richard Tranctard was adamantly opposed, declaring that Mutley Shepwell didn't need a world of new religions when a perfectly good world religion had been happily established on the premises for centuries.

Nevertheless, long before independence was declared, Stephanos had been networking round the world with a view to fund-raising. Never one to think small, he had come up with a plan to hold a world congress of religions, the revenue from which would fund his new dream.

He'd tried to persuade the Enhanced Reality Research Centre's marketing department to sponsor this jamboree, suggesting they could let out all their robots to play through the village that day and make it a "Meet the Future" experience – the future of technology, the (claimed) future of spirituality, and any other futures anyone else wanted to bring along. The Woodvilles' marketing people were initially amused, then annoyed, and finally explained to him in words of a single syllable that they didn't want religious nutters mixing with their robots, thank you very much.

Stephanos had started something, however. The Woodvilles had been trying to work out how to cash in on all the publicity the location of their research centre was suddenly generating. They decided they rather liked the idea of letting their robots take over the village for a day, with the world's press watching. For that, they needed the permission of the council of the republic.

Richard Tranctard opposed the idea mightily and the council seemed set to back him until the tables were turned by, of all people, his wife. The Woodvilles were offering to make very generous donations to nominated charities as part of the deal, and she saw the chance to further the future of Richard's long-dreamed of hospice. Here was a chance for substantial funding.

Richard didn't actually mind the Woodvilles' robots at

all. It was their artificial reality research department he really objected to. Under the slogan, "Better than the real thing," it promised to recreate any experience, any high, any vision, any pleasure, any imagined world. This included all sorts of experiences he thought should not be artificially recreated.

Mary, to his surprise, took the opposite view. Her view was that artificial reality could be used for good or evil. If some chose to use it to indulge their vices, at least they were taking those vices out of the real world and into their own private hells, where their only victims were themselves.

The Old Tank could only feebly demur, and suggest that these new technologies would provide additional avenues for vice rather than removing the existing channels. The rest of the council was persuaded that artificial reality was worth encouraging, even if it only partially reduced the real-world impact of the vice industries. They took the money on offer, to distribute to good causes, and gave the go-ahead for a "Meet the Future" day.

At once the Woodvilles' and the Russian's marketing and PR teams got to work to drum up participation and coverage. For different reasons it suited them to have a spotlight on this ephemeral republic. All sorts of high tech companies bought in. Academic visionaries were recruited at speed to pontificate about the futures of societies. Inventors, planners, futurists, technologists of all stripes were brought in for a one-day extravaganza.

The Russian set up an instant conference centre in the manor grounds, with outposts in the public rooms of the manor and in the village pubs and the village hall. With a speed that only great resources make possible, "Meet the Future" took shape, promising the chance to "live in tomorrow today, for a day".

Stephanos's "Global Conference and Worldwide Manifestation of the New Enlightenment" had become an unwanted sideshow to the main event. It was a strange creature, this Mutley Shepwell festival of religions. The world's better known religious bodies had been united in their lack of interest, leaving the field to all sorts of alternative religious and spiritual groups. Even these had shown little enthusiasm, until Stephanos had brought the dates of his conference forward to catch the moment in the media spotlight.

This brought in a flood of applications. Participants ranged from a Jedi Mindfulness Grand Master, to the Venerable Order of Scientocracy (established in 2017), and the New Age of Eternal Illuminated Wisdom, in the person of Stephanos himself, their rather chuffed host, happy to be with other sandal wearers at last, all brimming with enlightened and mindful thought.

He and Bob took particular pleasure in informing Richard Tranctard that some of the leading members of this festival of religions would be leaders of "the Anglican Continuum." They thought this sounded like a religious version of Doctor Who. On investigation, however, it seemed to be the representatives of various rather exotic churches from all sorts of interesting corners of the world that had once been merely part of the Anglican world, but had since spread their wings to fly off into their own religious universe, where they could unfold in splendour.

That splendour began with their titles, which were far more exciting than the fuddy duddy Church of England had ever managed. There was the Supreme Archimandrite of the Western Antiochian Orthodox Anglican Communion, a marvellously attired gentleman from Benediction, Kansas. His arch-rival and nemesis liked to describe herself as the Patriarchal Archbishop and Primate of the Continuing Anglican Protestant Alexandrian Catholic Eparchy, which was based down the road in Rome, Missouri. There were Archbishops galore, Primates, Eparchs, Archimandrites and Metropolitans. To be a mere bishop was practically equivalent to being a janitor in this title-sensitive world.

Stephanos had even managed to get an endorsement from a Hollywood producer. Curiously, the producer in question was less famous for his mild religiosity than he was for his appearance at the Oscars the previous year. Instead of the usual thankyou speech, he started off: "I'm here as an Official Diversity Inspector on behalf of the fat, the bald and the ugly, who are massively under-represented in this room." Things went sideways from there. He even proposed starting a burger bar in the lobby at the Oscars ceremony to try to get everyone off their diets for the evening, and he set off a hashtag, "#OscarsSoThin". All this won him many hearts, and when he sent an endorsement for the festival of religions, he practically acquired saintly status in Stephanos' eyes.

Thanks to the combined efforts of Mr Pronotkov's and the Woodvilles' PR, Mutley Shepwell had briefly become a hot topic for much of the tech and business media. With so much of the sunshine of publicity shining down, Stephanos and his confederates were determined to creep out of the shade and have at least their fifteen minutes in the sun, however unwelcome their presence might be.

The Woodvilles' technological marvels were due to be manifested, with impeccable, very carefully planned, timing, on the first afternoon of the conference. The "human futures" exhibitors were to be allowed to start first, and show off their visions of tomorrow. Then, very suddenly, there would appear a horde of machines: gardening robots, street cleaning robots, sports training robots, housekeeping robots, automated driving robots, security robots, every kind of robotic creation the Woodvilles' research centre had in stock turning up to welcome the human versions of the future.

That was the plan, and they were given blue skies and sunshine to enjoy it in. Stephanos and his crew had caught wind of this plan and timed their entrance accordingly. As the robots appeared from hiding throughout the village, a gloriously-robed grand procession of abbots, gurus, monks, sadhus, seekers, nuns, priests, archbishops, eparchs, archimandrites and hierarchs started its march down the high street, in the full glare of all the filming and photography summoned by the Woodvilles.

It was a wonderful chaos: the many-coloured religious humans trying to make their way down the high street while an army of robots tried to parade their wares in carefully choreographed manoeuvres that often ran right into the procession. The whole scene was shrouded in vast clouds of incense, and soundtracked by the rising din of clashing chanting from extraordinarily obscure sects. The marketing people waded into the chaos and managed to cut a deal: soon, the spiritual humans and the machines headed off to a marquee outside the village for a vast futuristic feast, where everything from the cooking devices to the cutlery was experimental and future-shaped, while the robots waited on the religious. For bored reporters, it made a grand day out.

The journalists had been duly primed to ask how ordinary, credit-card wielding humans could benefit from a world of robots, what a robot-enabled society might be like, how leisure might overtake work in a world where the tedious jobs were done by machines, and all sorts of other friendly questions of that sort. Reference to any potential downsides of artificial intelligence and robotic workforces were strongly discouraged. All in all, the marketing department felt they'd had a marvellous day, stopping the traffic, managing the religious maniacs, getting their robots to chat up the news crews for them, announcing the shape of the future in a place so redolent of the past.

22

TROUBLE IN EDEN

"You know," said Alexander Livingston happily, "I like to think of us as a kind of border micro-kingdom between Wessex and Mercia, a semi-independent prince-bishopric, without the prince or the bishop. The rest of the country may be splitting into its Saxon regional roots but we're more a late medieval revival: a classier kind of retro, in my view." He sat back and sipped his tea in George's garden.

"The Old Tank wouldn't mind being a prince bishop," commented Des sagely.

"We're not letting him, though," added Peggy. The Old Tank had been known to claim that Alexander wanted to see something like a secular version of medieval Europe, without God, without national boundaries, without intrusive nation states and their endless bureaucracy.

Richard Tranctard rather liked half of that vision, but he wanted to keep God while junking the bureaucrats, the endless rules, the nation states and the Catholic Church. He didn't have much appetite for argument at present, though: he'd imagined they were striking a symbolic blow for freedom and the whole enterprise had been taken over by capitalist zeal so quickly he was altogether dazed.

Peggy and Des had no time for all this retro stuff. They preferred Bob Corns' line that Mutley Shepwell was showing the rest of the country how the 21st Century was going to pan out: get rid of central control and let the locals decide things for a change, under the EU's broad umbrella. Bob put it down to technology, saying that the accounts book and the railway line were tools of central control, the smartphone and the tablet, the tools of liberation. He'd had aspirations to be a politician once himself, and he still liked to make little speeches to captive customers. Alexander preferred to regard big data and the internet as on the side of the big battalions, and took a rather less optimistic view of the future, but they were all enjoying the present.

They were all enjoying the last rays of a little autumnal outbreak of sunshine. It's amazing how the English cheer up when the sun shines for a few days running, especially late in the year when they might have thought they'd had their annual ration.

Stephanos was inspired by a particularly cloudless day to think of starting a beachfront café behind Bill's farmhouse. There wasn't any sea to go with the beach, of course, but a few tons of sand onto the disused farmyard behind the shop, a few colourful marquees, some toys for the children's sandcastle building, and he thought he might have a tourist attraction on his hands. Being a bit busy with global enlightenment at present, he pencilled it in as an idea for the future. The future looked very bright at that moment. Yet, as the saying goes, into every life a little rain must fall, and so it was for Mutley Shepwell.

While all the commercial side of things was expanding with remarkable speed, a very different and more tangled story was unfolding on the political side. As far as international affairs went, perhaps it was the football club that first signalled an end to the republic's days in Eden.

The citizens of Mutley Shepwell may have become a little overexcited in those happy early days when internet blogs from Moscow to Hawaii were full of the world's newest republic, and their little village suddenly became for journalists a new playground. The Prime Minister and the Cabinet were at first on holiday, then busy with party conferences and other bigger things, and had yet to formulate a response to the UDI in their own backyard. Everything seemed so simple.

That air of initial euphoria may explain how the football club came up with what seemed to its committee, at the time, a modest proposal: for as long as they were part of an independent country, they wanted to be an international team. Seemed straightforward enough: they asked the Football Association to intercede with FIFA for them, pointing out that they couldn't be worse than Andorra, really, and if they were they'd be willing to grant citizenship to a few decent footballers from Oxford or Swindon.

To their disappointment, if not their surprise, the bigwigs at Lancaster Gate turned them down flat. They tried the European football authorities, pointing out that they had returned to Europe, and proposing that they could form a kind of enlightened bridge to coax their fellow countrymen and women back to a more European way of thinking. No dice with Strasbourg, Brussels or Geneva, just a blank wall of bureaucracy.

It was the same for the rugby team. When the cricket team tried their luck the letter back began by saying that if Her Majesty's government agreed to Mutley Shepwell's secession, then the cricket authorities would of course consider the request. This sounded at least a little more polite, until the letter ended, "and should the United Kingdom government also decide that the moon is made of green cheese, and the oceans of lemonade, we would be slightly less surprised."

Unnecessary, the cricket club agreed, really quite uncalled for. The international rugby and cricket authorities were similarly unsympathetic to these new Europeans; inflexible in the extreme, it seemed to the village sports teams.

The cricket and football clubs gave up then and there, but the rugby club was made of sterner stuff. In particular, its committee had backbone, and that backbone was provided by the Brigadier. He may have been retired for many years but even the cockiest young flanker at the club would have hesitated to tackle him.

In the days when Britain had an empire, and people talked about the men and women who made it, the Brigadier was just the sort of person they talked about. In the absence of an empire, he had made the Mutley Shepwell rugby club his own kingdom. Hardened prop forwards still trembled as they remembered the day when the previous regime hit its low point with the 78-3 loss to Short Hanborough, a village that thought it was doing well if it managed to muster 15 fit male humans for its team, and was rumoured to resort to escapees from the Wildlife Park to fill the replacements' bench.

The Brigadier watched the debacle in silence, only the hue of his face betraying his emotion, as it went from lightly tanned to part-boiled, to mature beetroot, to volcanic, to goodbye Pompeii. He marched off at the end without a word.

A week later he had engineered an Extraordinary General Meeting of the club at which a raft of ex-military gents (old friends and acquaintances of his), new to the club, ousted the committee, with himself at the head. In fact, they didn't need to oust most of the committee: by the time his speech was halfway through a number were ready to resign, and as he went on and on, rehearsing in painful detail each defeat, each sorry surrender, the committee were ground down to the point where two-thirds of them did resign before the vote, and slunk off home without waiting to see whom their replacements would be.

At the next training session, the changing room had changed. In place of pin-ups were pictures of the memorials to the men of the village who died in the world wars, and in pride of place, Her Majesty Herself, the old Queen, still alive then. Before the next match, the Brigadier pointed to that picture and challenged his team:

"Do you want to be worthy of her? Can you look her in the eye? What about the men of this village who fought and died for freedom? Do you want to honour them or make them turn in their graves? They shed their blood, will you shed yours?" After that, the team would have run through the changing room wall to get onto the pitch, and get out from under the Brigadier's gaze.

They were a team transformed: the new regime began

with a victory, and it had continued with remarkable success. This was not a regime that tolerated failure, and it certainly wasn't going to let the stuck-in-the-mud rulers of world rugby get in its way.

The colour in the Brigadier's cheeks started moving up the gears, the committee donned their combat helmets, weaker spirits dived for cover, and the martial step of the Brigadier was seen, for the first time, marching on the manor, a one-man British army. But, wondered his fellow committee members, would it be D-Day again, or Napoleon's march on Moscow?

When the heir of Waterloo strode up to the manor's big front doors Nikolai, for once, was caught by surprise, and was rattled enough to agree an interview with Mr Pronotkov. Mr Pronotkov, in contrast, was quite unrattled, full of interest, and seemed rather amused by the idea.

He pointed out that, whatever the international authorities might say, his contacts in Moscow could pretty much guarantee the participation of a Russian team, or teams. He also had substantial interests in Hong Kong, Japan and in Western Samoa, which did indeed produce a Pacific Islands' set of teams, a Japanese group of players, and an East Asian 7. The Russian team, it turned out, had to be unofficial, merely a "Russian 7," but to cheer that up they named themselves The Cossacks, in honour of the rather more famous Barbarians, whereupon the Japanese team became The Samurai, the Pacific Islanders The Chiefs, and the Hong Kong-based team The Ninjas.

The Mutley Shepwell International Sevens Tournament was born, together with the Under-21 International Sevens, and two more junior youth tournaments, all populated by teams with generous helpings of imported high-class talent. Journalists who had been about to turn up their noses at this little tournament were taken out to lunch by the most charming PRs, in some of London's finest restaurants, where the details of the hospitality arrangements for the press were explained to them. Being chauffeur-driven to the match from a country house hotel was a new experience to most of those involved, nor were they used to the bubbly on offer being vintage champagne. Having one of the world's best chefs flown in to cater for their every need was really quite refreshing; a journalist could start to feel appreciated.

The dates of the tournament were blocked out on calendar after calendar. In anticipation, space opened for this little rugby tournament in newspapers, magazines, websites, blogs, real-time feeds. It found itself being described as a welcome addition to the international calendar, light-hearted relief from the sometimes overly grim and serious nature of the international game in the modern age, the return of the cavaliers in an age of over-regimented roundheads, and so on.

The council of the republic was jubilant over this. Their next meeting was one long celebration, except for one member who watched it all with furrowed brow: Alexander Livingston. When it ended, Des suggested they all go to *The Old Bells*:

"Let's drink the health of these rugby boys, because they don't drink enough for themselves!"

Alexander politely declined, and beckoned Alicia, Moira, Bill and George to stay behind, and asked if they'd mind foregoing the celebrations at the pub. "I need to borrow you for a little discussion, please, it won't take long, but there's something I have to tell you." He led them back to his dark but beautifully converted barn, tucked away behind the row of houses straggling back from the High Street along Shepherd's Row, on the west side of Nether Shepwell, backing onto the famous view down the ridge and away to the west. Before explaining his reasons for dragging them over, he poured everyone a stiff drink. Then he began:

"I happen to have known the Keeper of the Medieval Collections at the University Library in Cambridge for a long time. We were undergraduates together. He's just surprised us all by taking early retirement."

"Lucky beggar," said Bill, with feeling.

"Not only that, he's bought a big house down in Fowey, the one that TV comic used to live in, the one right at the harbour entrance. Amazing place. Not something librarians can usually afford. He claims his cousin Albert died and left him a pile. Sounds dodgy to me: I've known him over forty years and I'd never heard of any Albert. Not only that, they're cursing him at the UL – The University Library, I mean, over in Cambridge. I dropped in last week when I was at a conference, and his old assistant is mad as can be. David seems to have left one of his collections in a total mess. Any idea which collection?"

They stared at him. "Yes, the thirteenth-century collection. Strange, that, when he was the most orderly man I've ever known. Everything else in beautiful order, but for that one set of manuscripts. They're such a mess, that the assistant couldn't even be sure if everything was there. He thinks that one or two of the unfinished manuscripts are missing parchment, but he doesn't even know. They were David's baby, no one else was allowed near them, and now he's gone and he's refusing to help. They can't quite be sure, but they think they have a bit of thirteenth-century manuscript missing."

Alicia stared, George stared, Moira stared. Misgivings were forming behind their glassy eyes.

"What's that to do with us?" snapped Moira. "Why should we care?"

"Something Mrs Rhodes told Alicia, the other evening. You know they've had specialists in to sort out the dry rot in the thirteenth-century attic above the Old Library at the Manor? Well, they have. Only Mrs Rhodes was very puzzled, because the regular specialists got told to take a day off in the middle, just when The Old Tank and Johnny B were having their meeting with Pronotkov. Right after that, some other men turned up, very scientific types, she said, and totally closed-mouthed, wouldn't talk to anyone.

They went up into the loft and shut her out. But she'd checked it at the end of the day before, and she checked it again after the odd scientists had gone, and she is sure they stripped out timber that was perfectly good, she's sure of it."

"Then she had to sign for a package for one of the Borises. It went to the basement office, where no one's allowed. Only that Boris was being a bit casual, and let her have a peek in the doorway while it was opened, and she's sure she saw a wooden casket, very like the one Jem and Jimmy found. Only the Russian and his team ever saw what was in it when it was opened. Jimmy and Jem aren't sure if the casket at the manor now is the original one or not."

The council of the republic was not amused, or at least those members present. Consternation was the least of it. Moira tried to calm things down. "We don't know anything, we don't have any proof, we can't go spreading rumours," she said. All but one of them saw her point.

"Shouldn't we tell the police?" asked George.

"And say goodbye to all the things our republic is getting us?" Bill asked angrily. "We've never had a break in this village. We've been ignored, bypassed, patronised, dumped on, treated like dirt. We finally get a break, and you want to take it all away?"

As George opened his mouth again, Alicia intervened. "Why find out more, when we know just enough not to really know anything? What's the point of finding out when you know you don't want whatever you might find? Let it lie, let it lie."

"Let it lie," agreed Moira thoughtfully. She stared round the table and, one by one, everyone nodded. George hesitated. If the Tranctards had been there that evening, perhaps their moral support might have stiffened his backbone for the fight, but they had not been invited to this little conclave, and in the end he just looked at his feet and muttered something about needing time to think it over. The other three stared at him. Alicia was the one to break the silence:

"No talking to anybody, now, promise, George, not even The Old Tank. We're very fond of him too, but he is just a bit inflexible." Moira winced fractionally at those last words.

Alexander chipped in: "We need you, George, you're the only one who understands all this tax stuff the Russian wants to do. The village needs you, George. Take some time tonight, then back here tomorrow, same time, to talk it through when you've had time to think, okay?"

They all looked at George with great care and worry. He sighed. "Don't you think we should come clean?"

"We're not unclean, George," Alicia pointed out. "We don't know anything, we just have unfounded suspicions. Not very founded suspicions, anyway. No point in prodding a sleeping dog, it might wake up and bite us." She put a hand on George's arm. "Think how much Tabitha loved this village, she wouldn't want all we've done to go to waste, would she? Think of the village, George."

George looked at his feet and shuffled them. "I need to think about this," he said. "If we don't speak up for our principles, if we silence ourselves, are we still us?"

They gathered round him, and Alicia spoke in her most soothing voice, the one she had used on her most recalcitrant authors in her publishing days.

"Take a long walk, George, and think about the village, think about what it means for the village. Our principles have to include looking after the village, don't they? Take a long walk, and no talking to anyone till we've met again in the morning, okay?" George paused, and they all stiffened and held their breath, then relaxed when he finally nodded and promised.

"Let's come back at six tomorrow evening, here," said Alexander. "There is one thing, though," he added, in his most businesslike manner. "I've had a look into Sir Thomas's tomb, with a team from one of the London hospitals –

oh, don't worry, we did all the paperwork, what do you take me for? They brought up all this gear to investigate the bones, but there were no bones. It's empty. It's an empty tomb. Where once we thought we had Sir Thomas's remains, we have an empty tomb. Where was he buried, then?"

Moira looked thoughtful: "And where we had a key without a lock, now we might just have a key with a lock that was built around it. What lock was Sir Thomas's key made for originally?" None of them had an answer.

23
A LONG VIEW ON A DARK NIGHT

The others may have slept that night, but not George. He had never been totally comfortable with what they were doing, in the first place. George Sneed was, after all, one of life's most unlikely rebels. He sat a long time over an untouched glass of whisky, while Morsel snuffled and tried to fight off sleep beside him. She was trying so hard to stay awake, he even gave her an extra helping of supper, a treat that had always been religiously reserved for the late Queen's official birthday, and his late wife's actual birthday, for those two days alone.

Then, in the small hours, long after he always went to bed, the stars looking down on the village high street saw one lonely form making its way up the hill, then turning left for the shortcut to the walk along the ridge. It was where he'd so often walked the dog with Tabitha, and it was where he went to think.

He'd never been there at this hour. He even saw an owl floating silently above the corn, which he'd always wanted to see, yet tonight he hardly noticed it. The thing he came back to, time and again, was the drugs legalisation. He could remember it clear as yesterday. He had joined the conspiracy before that, but that was the moment that had seared his soul, when he had gone to work on The Old Tank's plan with more energy than he'd had in years. He wished he could talk to the Tranctards, but he had promised not to. He was alone with the darkness and his God.

As he walked through the night, with only the odd call of a tawny owl to keep him company, and the cold stars looking dispassionately down from above, he kept going back to the beginning, to those two evenings. His thoughts circled round: the high and mighty in London and the effect their plans already seemed to be having, a younger generation who just seemed brainwashed and liable to completely go along with the new reality.

They needed help, and the bigwigs of Westminster needed to be shown a thing or two, along with all their friends in the media who cheered as they ruined the country. Little old Mutley Shepwell had this one chance to get one over on them all. A big thing to give up. Did he, did any one person, have the right to spike it for everyone?

He had walked that path for most of his life, in good times and in bad. He had walked it in a romantic haze with Tabitha, on spring days with blossom ahead in the trees, on early summer days with cow parsley and ragged robins rising by the path. He and Tabitha had taken Paul and Elizabeth for their first long walks there, he'd carried his children home on his shoulders at the end of some of them.

He'd walked there with friends and relatives, with village acquaintances, with every dog they'd ever had. He'd walked there in his sadness, too. He'd walked that path with his eyes too full of tears to see the view, or later on, when his tears had dried yet he could hardly see that view for the grief rising up around him like a wall of pain, arching over him to hide the sun and blot out the sky, turning the green fields into a dry land of the heart. He walked it again this night in an agony of conscience, his memories battling his sense of right and duty. He finally trailed home through the darkness with his questions still unanswered.

The next morning, after picking at his breakfast with rather less than the usual enthusiasm, he took another walk. As he turned down Back Lane, Moira appeared. "Going for a walk? Mind if I come?" He did, rather, but couldn't bring himself to say, so they continue to the path at the end of the lane, that angled up to the larger track he'd walked the night before, the one that meandered along the top of the ridge. They talked about everything except the one topic dominating both their thoughts.

It was a dull day, autumn really coming in, with low cloud and a wind that made them glad of their coats, but the view was its usual magnificent self. Even with the fields below them all stubble and brown after harvest, they still made a wonderful patchwork with the hedges, set off by Traitor's Wood at the foot of the slope and the manor's woods and fields over to the left. There there were the fields of grass over the river, dotted with sheep and cows, and Lord Hunter's lands beyond.

Most of those hedges had been there for hundreds of years, the woods for longer, as Moira reminded him. When they got to the top she took care to point out the high-lights, such as St Martin's and the bridge – "Hardly see the bridge if they build all those houses. And on a sunny day the glare from all the solar panels – have to put your dark glasses on to look down the hill." And then her trump card: "Wasn't this Tabitha's favourite walk?" He looked at her with trouble in his eyes, then mustered the courage to admit that he'd rather be on his own.

Moira nodded, understanding. She turned back to the village, while he continued west along the ridge and down across the river to Stokely Overton, and then took the long loop back along the river and eventually back to the bridge by St Martin's and up the hill. It was lunchtime before he got back to Mutley. He'd just started warming up some soup when there was a knock at the door.

It was Alicia, in her dark navy coat of winter wool, hair beginning to be flattened by a very soft rain, which had just begun to fall. "Thought you looked a bit down, George. Brought you these." It was a little tray of winter primroses. "Might look nice in the front garden?"

Without really thinking, he took the plants, saying, "Funny, just got some of these, maybe Alexander could use them." She looked so crestfallen that he added quickly, "Would you like to come for a bowl of soup?" And, wet though it was, Alicia suddenly brightened like a flower after rain, when the sunlight first touches it again.

That evening, they were all back at Alexander's again, and all eyes were on George. He looked more uncomfortable than they'd ever seen him, shifting in his chair like a man in pain. Eventually he got some words out.

"Alright. I couldn't do it to the village. I'll do the tax stuff. The Old Tank, Mary, they'd feel they had to do something, you're right, we can't tell him, or her. I don't like keeping things from them, but maybe this time …" They all nodded vigorously and assured him that this knowledge would not pass from their circle, to anyone. George took a whisky at that point, not his usual drink. The others opened some bubbly. Bill punched his arm, Alicia went to pat him on the shoulder and Moira even gave him a kiss on the cheek.

24
THE RIVER AND THE STREAMS

It was at this point, with the party conferences past, that the prime minister completed his plans for all the pre-election posturing and policy-announcing, and tried to get a grip on the less important business on his desk. Eventually, the continuing media enthusiasm forced him to turn to the minor irritation on the edge of the Cotswolds. He met with an adviser or several, consulted some of his batteries of lawyers, went for a walk with the dogs back home in the constituency, and decided not to play along.

Word came out from Downing Street that planning international rugby competitions was rather pointless when this whole thing would be snuffed out shortly. The parish council was ordered to call an extraordinary meeting, to be attended by one of the attorney general's top civil servants, who would explain in words of a single syllable the limits of a parish council's powers. There was no question of permitting any token independence. Meanwhile, behind the scenes, representations were made in regard to the Privy Council case, and those involved were nudged very strongly to get a move on and whip the wretched Prenderby into line.

News filtered back to Mutley Shepwell and gloom descended upon the village, even though it was bathed in unseasonable sunshine. The lowest point was reached when a cavalcade of dark official-looking cars rolled up to the village hall and the deputy attorney general herself descended, accompanied by a veritable pack of government lawyers. As they entered the now half-repaired Bonifer Room, the council sat in gloomy silence.

A week ago, they'd been totting up the royalties on Mutley Shepwell merchandise, and debating how best to sell off the new ".mutsh" domain on the Internet, now the hangman was arranging the noose, and their brief burst of freedom looked like being choked off. Alicia spent twenty minutes reminding the others that she had known all along this would happen, provoking a rare explosion of wrath from Alexander. Moira resorted to endlessly rearranging the tea things, while George retreated into himself so far that he even had to be poked to go out to the front door and greet their guests.

The deputy attorney general was Lady Jennifer Broadwell, an elegantly thin individual in sharply tailored suit, icily calm under her silvered-dark hair. Her thin, not to say gaunt, face was perfectly made up, her accessories as expensive as her suit. She looked around her very slowly, eyed the proffered mug of tea with ill-disguised scorn and made a brief speech about the irregularity of recent events. She ended by noting the parish council's request to be included in the Cotswold National Park, with access to the relevant generous grants, and commented that it was rather a late stage for such a request to be considered. Had the government wished so to consider it, furthermore, a problem had been discovered.

At this point, she handed over to the most junior of her team. He, Richard Brixham, was even thinner than she was, but there the similarity ended. Untidy blond hair, rather less well-cut suit, nervous jerks and twists and stammers, looking every inch a bundle of nerves as his boss's eyes bored into him. He began at a rush, confused himself, and had to begin again.

He then explained that he had found no support for the document said to have come from King John. It might be genuine but the burden of proof remained with those who wished to prove it so, and the government had no obligation to do the research for them. The room became funereal. He raced on. While that manuscript might not be genuine, he had discovered another that was quite definitely genuine.

This related to the second matter the parish council

had put forward, the claim to be a part of the Cotswolds. Not just a dubious manuscript, this one, an actual act of parliament from 1685, put through quickly when John Churchill was stamping out the remnants of the Duke of Monmouth's rebellion in the West Country. It gave wide powers to the judiciary to deal with any rebels who might be declaring their independence from parliament, or from the anointed king, and, he concluded triumphantly:

"The area covered went all the way from Devon to the Cotswolds – some of the rebels had retreated that way, apparently. It didn't include the rest of Oxfordshire, though. The pre-prescribed punishment for the ringleaders of rebellion was to be hung, drawn and quartered. After the fuss was over, they never got round to repealing the act. It's like getting hung for piracy on the high seas or arson in a naval dockyard. S-so, you see, if you're in the Cotswolds, as the leaders of a rebellion, you're liable to being hung, drawn and quartered, but if you're not in the Cotswolds, just in Oxfordshire, then the act doesn't apply."

He looked at his boss in humble triumph. She looked round the room in rather less humble triumph. "I'm sure His Majesty would consider commuting the hanging, drawing and quartering to life imprisonment." She smiled, showing off her perfect teeth. "Perhaps you might like to consider your response? Mr Brixham and his team will be ready to make time in their diaries any day next week for a meeting in London to sign the necessary papers to return matters to normal." With this, she swished out of the room at speed, her team scrambling to follow, leaving tea, councillors, Cotswold Cream biscuits, checked tablecloths, half-painted walls, confusion and despondency in her wake.

"Don't fancy bein' hanged," said Des. "A bit of floggin', maybe, in a good cause. But don't fancy bein' hanged."

There was a silence. "Mightn't be so bad, the hanging,

if they did it quick," muttered George, "It's the drawing and quartering first that bothers me." Mary Tranctard glared at him, with a look that could have refrozen a baked Alaska. Alicia, to his surprise, stepped to his side, defensively, only to be glared at in her turn by Richard. Even Alexander looked rather upset.

"They don't do it quick, that's the point," snarled Alicia. "Anyway, they couldn't do it these days. It's just the imprisonment."

"Will you all shut up? No one's going to jail," said Moira. "There's something we need to sort out quick. The Russian wanted a meeting but won't say why. We need to find out what that's about. Meanwhile, we need to see if Prenderby thinks this law really does apply, and if there's a way round it. Perhaps the European courts could oblige, or even Vatican law, after all we've left the UK to attach ourselves to Rome."

As they all gathered up their papers, phones, laptops, umbrellas, and other gear, George found Moira at his arm. "You didn't mean it, did you, George?"

"About them hanging us? 'Course not, no one's going to do that sort of thing in this day and age. Just a joke, trying to lighten the atmosphere, sorry, got it wrong."

"Don't be silly, we all knew it was a joke, just not one of your best. I was talking about not minding being hung. You didn't mean you wouldn't mind, did you?"

He smiled wearily, "'Course not. I'd rather die at home like anyone else."

Moira winced. "Not even, that, George, some of us would still mind even that, rather a lot." He looked a little surprised and she touched his arm in apology, and took her leave. The parish council returned for extra emergency meeting after extra emergency meeting, but could see no way forward, even with the Russian's help.

While the parish council was conferring with itself, Number Ten's publicity machine had gone into action, and news of the hanging, drawing and quartering being promised was soon in the news, local, national, international. Carefully placed leaks got the story into the papers exactly ten hours before Giles Prenderby's attempt to gain Mutley Shepwell observer status at the UN.

Unmitigated mirth broke out across all parties at Westminster, and in the London media, matched by impotent fury across several of the regional parties and their web and print outlets. In a few days this had overtaken all the stories the Russian's PR people had been assiduously planting. For a moment, even his consultants seemed baffled. The government was pushing their story hard, and winding up to saying that this was the end of the story, we'd all had the joke, and it was time to go back to business as usual. For a few days, this line took hold and seemed to be working powerfully.

There was consternation in Mutley Shepwell, amusement far beyond: Bill Stone more doleful than even his admirers had thought him able to be; Des Martin raging and offering to build a trench round the entire village, himself personally; Lady Venetia, like an English Cassandra, berating all the village for trusting the Russian, not listening to her, and making themselves a laughingstock to the nation. Gloom deepened into depression all round the village; even Moira Brenchley could not believe that they had sleepwalked into this.

The Tranctards would probably have been the most dismayed of all, had they been in the village, or even the country. Because of the awkwardness about keeping them in the dark over the dubious nature of the casket and the charter Mr Pronotkov had produced, the rest of the Guy Fawkes Club had carefully arranged for Mary to be made the foreign secretary of their little republic, so that she was almost always away at present, taking Richard with her.

A surprising number of people looked at his hulking figure and assumed he must be some sort of ageing bodyguard, rather past his sell-by date. One actually thought he was her butler, which amused her enormously. On the rare occasions they were at home, they were tied up with church business, which kept them neatly away from investigating any dealings with the Russian.

As the gloom deepened, Moira, George and Johnny received an invitation from the Russian to Shepwell Hall. They were greeted by English afternoon tea, taken to a rare level of perfection. Mr Pronotkov was as well-groomed as ever. His eyes regarded his visitors with that deep thoughtfulness and understanding they had come to know and rather like. Moira had once observed to George that if anyone they knew could have a promising second career as a hypnotist, it was their host.

Mr Pronotkov seemed uncharacteristically embarrassed. He hummed and he hawed, he twirled his teacup gently round through 360 degrees, three times in a row. He began uncertainly.

"My friends, if, that is to say, if I may call you my friends." They nodded politely (what else could they do?). "My friends, I have heard that you have reached a certain predicament with this most interesting project of yours. Your prime minister has come down against you, has he not? A difficult moment. The path ahead seems blocked. And yet it may not be. May I converse about this with you in the strictest confidence? I have invited you because I believe you to be as entirely confidential as I am myself."

"This is a matter of such delicacy that I would need your word that you would not share it even with your closest friends. One or two of your closest colleagues I have not invited today as I do not wish to put them in a difficult position. There is no reason for anyone to find what I wish to say difficult, and yet they may have such fine feelings, such delicate sensibilities, that it is hard for them to face some of the realities of this complex world. I do not hold that against them, I admire them for it, and yet it is better for all if we do not involve them, is it not?"

They stared at him, and he assured them that he meant nothing in the slightest bit immoral. He put it to them that it was a matter of public image, of politicians showing their understanding of the frustrations of ordinary people, of the political class addressing the alienation felt by Middle England. His voice was so reassuring, his seemed eyes so deep and understanding, that they almost believed his every word. They certainly wanted to believe him. One by one, they promised him to say nothing. Mr Pronotkov sat back and seemed to relax a little.

"Not wishing to see such a bold initiative reach such a sudden end, I have taken – how do you say? – the liberty, is it? Yes? Taken the liberty, then, of having begun some delicate negotiations with some of the representatives of your political parties, both government and opposition, to point out to them that there might be advantages to all sides in a temporary independence for our beloved village. The prime minister may have taken a certain position, yet politicians are often persuadable. It may be possible to negotiate, very discreetly."

"Contacts, you say in English," he mused, bestowing his deep, dark eyes on each of them in turn. "Contacts are what are needed in such situations. As it happens, I have some such contacts in your political world. The Woodvilles, they have very good such contacts. I have been in discussions with the Woodvilles."

"They've never cared about our village," blurted out Moira, "Wouldn't even help with our village hall appeals. Said we were the wrong side of the river."

"Ah, your little river, so small and yet so large in the minds of the English, with your boundaries and gates. 'Good fences make good neighbours,' is that not one of your poets? Yet they are on this side of the river now."

"Their precious research centre," said Moira, comprehension slowly dawning.

"Yes, indeed, their research centre. It certainly changes this situation for them. They have high hopes for it, for what they are developing there, but it is very expensive, all this artificial reality, all those robots. A, shall we say, more favourable tax situation would certainly make things so much easier for them. They appreciate this, they are working with me, and with their contacts, and mine, to find ways we can move forward together with your government. One of them is married to a cousin of the prime minister, I believe. The other went to school with your British foreign minister, and university with the leader of the opposition."

"They are delicately taking, how you say it? Soundings, they are taking soundings. It is all most delicate. The leaders of the parties do not wish to know of these things. They are better off kept in the dark. We must deal with treasurers, who must be very confidential, even from their bosses. It is all most delicate, yet they are hopeful. We can all be hopeful. It will require only the very smallest assistance from your three selves, on very minor matters, very minor indeed. Rest more easily, my friends, all these things can be managed."

Then, having assured them that he would keep them updated about the progress of these sensitive and highly confidential negotiations, he took them back to the village and asked about the current situation. They had to admit that it was highly confused. Selling things off the back of being independent was the simple bit; trying to work out the legal and tax implications was another story entirely.

Mr Pronotkov was keen to help. His people, he explained, would give these matters the closest consideration in their discussions with the politicians. It would surely be best for all parties to have the legalities of this unusual situation made clear. Bit by bit, he took them on a journey through some of the legal possibilities of a temporary independence.

It was a question of the right arrangements being made, so that any companies headquartered in Mutley Shepwell could be confident that they would attain tax haven status while still patriotically located in the heart of Britain. Johnny Berensford started tapping his teacup with the spoon at this point, without even noticing he was doing it. Moira was able to wrest the teaspoon from him, quietly, without even breaking his rapt concentration on their host. This tax freedom might be only temporary, but with certain careful manoeuvres on behalf of the accountants, several years' profits might be included in the taxless window. Johnny was practically on all fours by this point, tongue hanging out.

The Russian modestly mentioned that, in the strictest confidence, he wished to share with them that he had been in discussions regarding selling quite large parts of some of his Russian and Central Asian operations and reinvesting the profits in English companies. He portrayed it as a way of supporting this country he had come to love and, on that afternoon at least, they half believed him. To make this reinvestment financially viable, he needed a tax window such as the temporary independence of Mutley Shepwell might provide. All the political parties were keen to boost their coffers, and their public image, ahead of the coming election. He felt confident that an accommodation could be found that would satisfy all parties.

"All of them?" asked Moira. "Is that not a little over-ambitious? Will they not object to your support for their opponents?"

"In Russia, yes. In your country, on the contrary, we must, how do you say it? Butter the toast on both sides? That way, whichever side ends upwards, you have a friend in power; and, of course, both are equally buttered, that is what guarantees their happiness. It's a better arrangement for everybody."

His visitors walked back down to the village in something of a daze. Moira tried asking Johnny what "Both are equally buttered" meant. She got only a dark look in reply.

George was frozen in silence. Johnny tried to cheer him up: "It's not us doing this. Nothing to do with us. It's the Russian, none of our business. You heard him, we only give the tiniest bit of help, nothing major, nothing worth worrying about."

Moira softened as she looked at George. "We've crossed the Rubicon, already, haven't we? We didn't know where this was going to go, George, we couldn't have known."

George looked as if his thoughts were a long way away. He was looking south to the far hills. He murmured something inaudible in reply.

Moira went on, "Look how excited the whole village is. We've never had anything like this in our entire lives. What the Russian gets up to with the politicians, that's not our business, that's not our story. We can't stop now, George."

George looked at her with a face that seemed suddenly stretched gaunt, as if in pain. "The village, yes, the village," was all he said.

"You promised to keep this confidential," said Johnny. "You'll keep that promise, won't you?"

George slowly nodded. "We promised," he said. "You have to keep a promise. I need to go." He looked sadly at Moira as he walked away.

She was almost in tears as she turned to Johnny Berensford, but he was also far away. All he said was: "Pronotkov and the Woodvilles? Between them, they've got more money than God makes." Then he dashed off down the shortcut to his house, muttering to himself in a maze of accountancy speculation.

At this point, the story took a twist that the powers in Westminster had not foreseen. The media coverage shifted, at first subtly, then more decisively. Journalists who'd been enjoying a scornful laugh at the whole episode suddenly found that their hearts of stone had melted and they were full of compassion for these plucky little provincials. Politicians who'd been utterly dismissive started to U-turn, and discover the charming Englishness of the whole episode. At first, just a few of them, then a growing number. As momentum mounted, celebrity endorsements started to come in, for this brave little village and its rebellion. It started to get mentions on *Celebrity Big Aunty* and *I was almost famous once, get me out of here.*

As the winds changed in central London, the reaction in most of the rest of the country, after an initial hearty laugh, was rather in favour of Mutley Shepwell. "Plucky little rebels," "The Little Village with a Big Heart," "Standing up for the Forgotten Englishman," "The Village that Lives what the rest of us Dream" – these were just a few of the headlines. Most of the messaging, twittering, networking and blogging world took a similar line. So, increasingly, did the local press, all round the country. Campaigns were started for the village on MyBook and Twoogle.

A number of the new regional parties, the parties that had come out of UKIP, took this little village to their hearts. One or two even heralded it as an emblem of freedoms that once were and might be again, for the local and the little. Western Alliance MPs and MEPs had a group trip to the village to declare their support, with photos taken on the village green by the new flagpole. Not to be outdone, the Northern League sent messages of support, the various rival factions of the Eastern Union bussed in supporters to cheer and wave, even Midlands First sent declarations of solidarity. The verdict in many a local newsroom, and many a pub, was that independent villages were the future and to get clobbered by the government like this, well, it all seemed very unfair.

The old working men's club, which was almost derelict, was used for hospitality for international well-wishers, with the result that its walls were soon papered with posters in Basque, Catalan, Igbo, Canadian French, Kurdish, and Kashmiri. Rather overwhelmed by all of this, Moira, Alexander, Alicia and Des were interviewed most sympathetically by independent bloggers and journalists. They rather disappointed their interrogators by pointing out that all most of them really wanted was to be part of the national park, and it was just a shame that they'd been forced into extreme measures in the first place.

One grumpy old law professor up in Durham started digging up the charters of medieval boroughs and listing their freedoms and responsibilities on social media, as the start of a campaign to get ancient liberties reinstated. Social networks thrummed with sympathy for the poor little villagers. MPs started getting irate letters from constituents. The prime minister's own electoral agent asked him if he didn't think it was a bit harsh, and couldn't they be nicer to these poor but popular people.

In the village, the mood was lightening by the day as more and more people started to sense that their new opportunities were not about to be snatched away from them. At first, it was rather complicated to work out how to move on. Various people complained that they were a little lost with the legal and financial considerations.

Moira was the one most bothered by this: she had already been battling with a great number of applications from companies hoping to set up a temporary office in Mutley Shepwell to benefit from the village's new fame, there seemed to be endless ways of making money in this short window. She mused about just how many companies they could squeeze in, and how best to use the proceeds.

The empty half of the industrial estate was filling up fast with nameplates. Not much else, but a lot of nameplates. A few builders were making desultory attempts to clean it up and smarten it up. The money kept rolling in, so fast it was hard to keep up with the accompanying paperwork, and she was always totally scrupulous about paperwork.

Not only that, the long term future of that end of the industrial estate was almost sorted: Stephanos's cut of "Meet the Future," plus all sorts of donations from eccentric groups around the world, looked like bringing him in enough funds to complete his purchase and set up his religious commune, once the current bonanza was over. What the coachtrippers enjoying their rural history experience next door would make of it was hard to say.

Most of the village was in the dark as to why the media winds had shifted. Three of the members of The Guy Fawkes Club knew a reason, but did not speak of it. The other members of their little club, on the other hand, thought they knew the reason and were raising their glasses to the Russian. Alexander even invented a new cocktail he called the Gin Siberién.

The creation of a new country, even if still in progress, meant new elections, as the parish council decided its new name and became, officially, The Council of the Loyal Republic of Mutley Shepwell. Moira was easily re-elected chairman, of course, no one was more trusted in the village. The other votes threw up a few surprises, however. George was still there, with Alicia and Alexander and Bill. Mary, however, had come from nowhere to take a seat. Even more surprisingly, Stephanos, although only a recent immigrant, had run a nifty little campaign and got in on promises to share the wealth of the new republic with the people, as fast as it came in.

His ambitions now extended beyond commerce. He vowed to put a bonfire under petty rules and regulations, starting with Health and Safety. This went down very well in *The Old Bells* and *The Red Ship* both, because the current government had put through more Health and Safety legislation than any of its predecessors, and insisted that local councils confirm and conform in every way.

Hence, the parish council, in the last couple of years before its elevation to its new eminence, had been obliged to put through no fewer than 28 different Health and Safety policies. It would have been 29 had that last policy not run into furious debate over the precise height of the artificial elevations allowed to those engaging in the dangerous art of flower arranging. Stephanos had found fertile ground with his proposal to scrap the lot and start again, "with just one rule, Common Sense!"

He had a lot of freedom to stir things in the village because Moira was incredibly busy negotiating with the old country, the name the village had given to England. Some preferred to call it the near abroad, as opposed to the overseas abroad, with which Mary Tranctard dealt, as foreign minister.

Dealing with the near abroad was Moira's responsibility. Things were busy there, and the hotline from Westminster to the manor kept humming away. After their August of discovery, September of sunshine, and October of hope and fear, November was a time of stubborn negotiations, behind the scenes. George became almost a permanent resident at the manor, and was ushered into little backrooms unknown to those outside the inner circle.

In public, there was a very sudden restoration of respect and good humour. The spokesman at Number Ten suddenly went into reverse, and began talking about not using sledgehammers to crack nuts and the need to observe constitutional proprieties, observing that having one technically independent village in Middle England was not exactly causing grave problems to the country as a whole. The foreign secretary weighed in, saying that this was a government that could take a joke, and he didn't mind paying a state visit to Mutley Shepwell if the prime minister wanted one.

The prime minister himself kept silent: he wasn't going to give Giles Prenderby the satisfaction of a public climbdown, so he let his ministers make a joke of the whole thing. He assured journalists that the government had better things to worry about, although Mutley Shepwell would have to be dealt with, gently, in due course. The members of the coalition were sure they weren't in a terrible hurry to stop these village folk having their fun.

The Russian's PR gentlemen and ladies made sure the media were right behind this change of tack. *The News of The Times* even resurrected a famous headline, "Do you break a butterfly on a wheel?" (once used about a famous rock band), to support a gentler approach to these fine and independent-minded English folk. The rest of the press, online and off, queued up in support of this approach, with plenty of cheering for the eccentric villagers defying an age of conformity, and good old English stubbornness in the face of the bureaucracy of the state.

Meanwhile, the media moved its attention to the final chapters of the long-running saga of the coronation. The new king's desire to recast the entire coronation service, and much of the paraphernalia of kingship as well, in the image of a new, multi-faith nation, with so many different groups given a role in the actual coronation – this had long kept the Privy Council tied up in knots, and also required inordinate amounts of discussion in the Church of England's General Synod and Parliament's Ecclesiastical Committee, not to mention the House of Lords, in one of its last big debates.

Even to these deliberations, however, there comes an end, and that end was at last in sight, with the final items of new legislation within sight of the finishing post. It had been the race of the tortoise, rather than the hare, and certainly the most delayed coronation in history, but Britain was finally going to enjoy the celebration in the spring.

With the spotlight off Mutley Shepwell, it should have been easy enough to conclude arrangements for a spot of titular independence. The detail of the negotiations, however, was proving tricky. On the surface, all things were done in the most above board manner. Behind the scenes, however, and in the strictest secrecy, certain of the parties' representatives were happy to accept Mr Pronotkov's very reasonable acknowledgement that elections require funding, all of which must arrive in the most impeccably legal and correct manner. To provide the kind of funding they required in return for keeping Mutley Shepwell independent, and free of British tax, until after the election, exceedingly complicated arrangements were required.

The money could not be seen to be coming from any

source even slightly tainted, indeed any of the politicians involved would have thrown up their hands in horror and dashed their hats to the ground at the very thought (if only they wore hats). In fact, so delicate was this matter that only a very small circle knew of their existence.

The leaders of the parties were kept in the dark. Their treasurers kept the secret close, reassuring themselves with the thought that none of the political protagonists would wish to be anywhere near the negotiations, or to be informed of the detail of the negotiations, or to be informed at all, as far as any traceable paper trail or computer record went. These were negotiations without secretaries, without minutes, without records in any form at all. As far as Her Majesty's government and opposition were concerned, these discussions did not exist.

To find ways of channelling money to the relevant parties without its origin being discernable by any of those who monitor these things was proving incredibly complex. As Nikolai Marisovitch himself put it, in a rare poetic moment, the river must be split into a thousand streams, and all of them divorced from their source. Having said this, he seemed curiously disturbed by his own analogy.

Such weaving and unweaving of financial streams, it all took time, too much time. The Russian funder of all this English independence was getting annoyed with his lawyers. Not that Mr Pronotkov ever displayed what most human beings would call signs of annoyance. Only Nikolai could tell his boss was fed up. Much of the time, Mr Pronotkov stayed in close touch with the negotiations.

When business dictated his absence, negotiations dragged: the complexities were considerable but the teams employed to navigate these difficulties had to be kept very small, because of the extreme confidentiality involved, and frequent reference back to their principals was required. The Woodvilles seemed reluctant to deal with anyone but Mr Pronotkov, preferably in person, and certainly not via any medium of communication that could possibly be traced or recorded, and so communications were trickier when his attention was elsewhere, although Nikolai did his best to be go-between.

Moira, Johnny Berensford and Alicia were back and forth quite a bit to the manor in these weeks, trying to find out where things had got to, and where George had gone. George was immersed in negotiations. He was rarely free until the evenings, when he emerged from hidden basements, blinking owlishly and saying very little, except that many things were best not to know.

The only one of them who was able to provide George with any useful help was Johnny B. He turned out to have a keen interest in manoeuvring money discreetly, in tax-friendly ways. As a result, he became George's unofficial adviser, although even he was not party to the details being discussed. He assisted in other ways: he was rather good at coming up with tickets to major football matches for Nikolai's sports-mad sons, not to mention the latest kits and other merchandising. They even got to a point where Nikolai actually accepted an invitation to visit the brewery and sample the sinless stouts and ales produced there.

25
THE HEART HAS ITS VEGETABLES

George's dedication to the village was second only to Moira's, but even he had other commitments. He could rarely leave the manor during the working day, but sometimes those other commitments took him away from the pre-prandial socialising of the early evening. One Wednesday, for example, George had to miss the world's finest canapés for more important business.

He was looking after his grand-daughters Alice and Emma, and their golden retriever, Buttons. Their mother, Elizabeth, had promised to tweak Molly's programming for him. He was keen to stop his robot addressing him as "Sir." He preferred to hear "Good morning, George." Alicia had reprogrammed her machine to call her "Ma'am," but George hadn't dared to tinker with Molly since the time he tried to adjust her housekeeping algorithms and she started putting clean dishes into the dishwasher and dirty ones into the cupboards, while emptying his waste-paper bins into the sink. In the old days, he had never been able to programme his video recorder. Perhaps adjusting a robot was too much to ask.

Unfortunately, as so often before, Elizabeth was called away on business. This left her daughters free to play with Molly. They discovered that if they stole George's hat, Molly would chase them round the house to get it back. As even Emma could run just a little faster than Molly could roll, especially up stairs, this made a wonderful game for them. Finally, taking pity on his robot, George managed to get them away on an exciting expedition to the recreation ground, rain notwithstanding.

Then, when Elizabeth returned, George had to pop out to deliver a few newsletters for the parish council, a chore

Alice loved to help with. Even Mrs Mudgery came to the door to receive her newsletter when Alice was delivering it. On his return George found a daughter at the end of her tether, completely frazzled and threatening dire retributions on her younger child.

"I do love her, Dad, but continents have formed in less time than it takes Emma to eat her vegetables."

Unfortunately, Emma chose that moment to change from glacier mode to rioters of the French Revolution mode, and tipped up both her bowl and her drink, while complaining loudly at not getting fish fingers and potato curls.

Her mother, at that moment, was torn between supervising supper, changing younger daughter while putting the clothes said daughter had just got filthy through George's washing machine, answering a couple of her more urgent texts, fielding a phone call from her boss, and jotting down To Do lists and shopping list items on her phone. Frazzled, she shoved a new top over Emma's head and managed a curt "Naughty step, now if not sooner!!" and a vigorously jabbing finger in the direction of the step of that name, for emphasis.

Emma might have got away with a peaceful sojourn on the aforementioned step, had not her elder sister Alice, seeing their mother detained, felt it her duty to step into their mother's role. When it came to her younger sister's shortcomings, Alice sometimes seemed to feel that she was the last hope of civilization.

When she looked at her younger sister she knew herself to be the one sage of truth and righteousness who lived at 17A Cherryplum Lane, and so the full responsibility of correcting the erring young fell on her. For the entire period of Emma's sojourn on the naughty step, Alice lectured her with a list of her errors, wrongdoings and shortcomings.

George, having cleared up the mess, finally spotted the instruction session and told the instructor to go and do a puzzle instead. He turned back to his overrun daughter.

"At least Alice was good. Why don't I supervise the rest of Emma's glacial excavation process, darling? You go and get yourself ready and have a lovely time with Sally and Miranda."

Elizabeth smiled her relief and was gone. George was soon in the midst of the excitement of finishing vegetables, embarking on puzzles, and watching several shows on small children's television which left him completely confused. He wondered, not for the first time, if correct English had been banned from television these days.

The girls started playing up, and he was starting to lose track when his helper for the last part of the children's evening arrived. He had a kind of rota going with Alicia and Moira, whenever he found himself looking after Alice and Emma: both professed themselves very keen to help; neither had grandchildren of their own.

Moira may have seen generations of youngsters growing up under her care, as a revered head teacher, but she said she could always find time to help with one more. For Alicia, the lack of children had been a three-stage sadness.

First, when she was with Alex, they seemed too young and busy with their careers to worry about having babies, then they split up. Afterwards, with Patrick her partner, the subject was often on her mind, but he was the master of procrastination, in the matter of children and marriage most of all, and it never happened with him either. Finally, when Frank turned up, he was willing enough but complication after complication ensued, worst of all the trauma and sadness of miscarriages, perhaps that was what drove them apart in the end, perhaps the lure of someone younger, for whom having babies might be less problematical. Whatever the cause, children had never happened for her. She had become very attached to little Alice and Emma, and was ever ready to drop everything and help George out with his grandparental duties.

George would happily have shared his time with his grand-daughters with both of them together, but somehow things never seemed to work out that way, so he'd learned to alternate. When Moira came to help, things tended to get very organized. She'd even managed to free him from his last cleaning lady, of whom he'd lived in fear. George was used to being terrorised by cleaning ladies, old, young, short, tall, he'd been intimidated by them all.

He could never muster up the front to fire anyone, but the moment Moira came in the door his latest tyrant almost shrank visibly, and before he knew it, she had gone, and been replaced but someone much more amenable, personally vetted by Moira. Moira was similarly authoritative with the children, and all things ran like clockwork when she was there.

With Alicia, things were more creative, also more relaxed. Unlike Moira, she didn't have every aspect of Alice and Emma's time with her planned out in advance, yet they seemed to enjoy her company, if anything, even more. She also was firmer than George, with children or adults. She liked to remind him of a recent occasion when she'd been helping him with Morsel and the children, only for Mary Tranctard to pop by to inspect the young. Out of politeness, he offered Mary a cup of the tea Alicia had made for him, which he'd been drinking dutifully for twenty minutes.

Mary made a face. "You gave him that milk?" Alicia nodded. Mary wagged a corrective finger: "It's not exactly in its heyday, is it?" Alicia just laughed, knowing that George, unlike Moira or Mary or Richard, would never have said a word.

After Elizabeth had returned to collect her girls, George walked Alicia back, as he always did, carrying her bag. She mentioned that she'd be away over Christmas, staying with a niece and an old friend who now lived in Australia, and seeing a bit of the world en route.

"I'll be sorry to be missing all the excitement here.

When I planned this trip I had no idea what would be going on. I'll have to stay glued to my messages. Can you keep me posted on the major developments?"

"Of course, of course, glad to oblige. I'm not very good at all this modern messaging, but if you don't mind old-fashioned videocalls, I'm sure I could manage that. We'll miss you here. It won't be the same without you."

"Nice of you to say it. You'll have so much going on, though, you won't miss me at all," she said, a trifle wistfully.

"No, no, really, it won't be the same without you," and as he said it, he realised it was true, true now in a way it wouldn't have been six months before. The revelation shocked him so much that she left him open-mouthed and silent at her front gate, wondering why he had clammed up all of a sudden, and pondering once more the strangeness of men.

George wandered back in something of a trance, even going straight past Mrs Mudgery without greeting her, for the first time ever, which left that august lady quite amazed, and sent her speculating wildly. George had thought that he had left feelings like this far behind, buried in a dark oak coffin with Tabitha.

He'd appreciated Moira and Alicia's friendship, but not till now, when she was about to miss sharing the greatest moment in their village's history with him, had he had any idea how much he might wish to have Alicia by his side. He was sure she would always be far too grand to reciprocate, and yet hope refused to be quite crushed. His heart had been empty for so long, it felt strange to have it feeling nourished, suddenly full of emotions he had never thought to feel again. As he ate the vegetables his grand-daughters had left behind, his life seemed warmer and more substantial, somehow.

When he got back home, he just had to talk it through with Morsel. As was his habit when something really important came up, he felt the need to talk it out, and Morsel was the only possible recipient of his tumbling feelings. Unfortunately, she was in no shape to receive those thoughts, as he had recently got into the bad habit of giving her a little extra something when he came back after an evening out, and she was going into paroxysms of joyful anticipation.

She always got very excited at meal times, dancing around him till the food was delivered, and the thought of a bedtime snack sent her into overdrive. She danced about so much she fell over herself, looked very surprised, then jumped up with undiminished energy and pirouetted the rest of the way to her food bowl.

Once the necessary feeding had been accomplished, he addressed Morsel on the pressing matter. Morsel had a very pleasing way of cocking her head when he spoke to her, as if she really were listening very intently. The other thing he liked about talking to her was that he never had to worry about what he was saying or how he was saying it.

He did worry about his accent. His voice was a slightly odd mixture of very correct received pronunciation with a touch of a Wiltshire burr underneath, which emerged more strongly at certain times. His native burr came through on some sounds, while others were clipped to the precise dimensions of what used to be called BBC English, before the BBC discovered vocal diversity.

Back in the days when he'd worked for a posh London accountancy firm, before he went from poacher to gamekeeper and became a tax man, one of his less kind colleagues had commented that it was as if George had paid for elocution lessons and not got full value. George might not have had actual lessons but, as an insecure young man, he'd felt a need to posh up his accent, first to fit in with the City world he found himself in, and then with all his wife's friends and relatives.

She had grown up in West Hampstead, part of a set much richer and more cosmopolitan than he'd ever known. Had they not ended up working for the same firm, their paths would never have crossed. Her world was very different from his, much more cosmopolitan, and full of attitudes and values he was never quite at home with. Fortunately for him, it was a world she was keen to escape, and so they got jobs in Oxford instead, and eventually edged themselves back to Mutley Shepwell, most of the way back to his Wiltshire roots, and in both their views a better place to bring up children than where they met.

It seemed a long time ago now, as he reminded Morsel. Much in the habit of talking to the dog though he was, he'd never gone on for this long before, and her little dachshund head kept lolling off to sleep, only to loyally wake a few minutes later. By the time he'd finished their conversation, it was halfway to morning and he had been sitting in the same position for hours. In the dim light of the one desk lamp he'd left on, in the stillness of his memories, he looked as if he'd been there since before the house, and it had been built around him.

26
THE REPUBLIC OF CHRISTMAS

As November came to its damp and miserable end, two sets of negotiations, one public, one secret, started to converge on a track that might even lead to a conclusion. For nearly a fortnight, Moira and Johnny kept being summoned up to the manor for progress reports and consultations. When not there they were frantically busy preparing the ground down in the village for an announcement. As far as their friends and relatives were concerned, they almost disappeared from view. Then, two weeks before Christmas, they reappeared and summoned a meeting of the enlarged council of the republic – the assembly formerly known as the parish council.

"We have a deal," announced Moira. "We get to be a republic till a little before the election. The prime minister gets a press conference with all of us in Westminster now, and another during the election campaign, here, with all of us promising to smile and be good little countryfolk, acknowledging that he has treated our tiny village with lordly respect and seigneurial compassion, for the cameras anyway."

"Businesses headquartered here can apply for special treatment during that period, in view of our unusual circumstances, and their applications will be examined on a case by case basis by a special team from the top end of the Inland Revenue, reporting directly to the Chancellor, no less. Most important, we get to be in the National Park, confirmed next Friday, when the final boundaries are announced. That means that the NAP's draft planning permission for the fields on the west side of the village is automatically revoked, and any future planning applications go to the National Park, which knows how to say No, and not to the Nappy band, which only knows how to say Yes."

"Once the election's over we get a special visit from the foreign secretary to sign the treaty ending our independence, with full pomp and ceremony and all of us cheering, to give the new government a feelgood item in the news. If we can sign off on all of that tonight, we can break out the champers and all go down the pub to celebrate."

It wasn't quite that simple, of course. George and a few others rather objected to being bounced into things. The pub landlord was furious to find that the official name of their little statelet was down on the documents simply as Mutley Shepwell. He wanted the Republic of Mutley Shepwell: "I've been waiting all my life to live in a republic, even if I only get to live in one for five months."

This didn't go down too well with the more royalist members present, and started a massive argument, which ended only when weariness slowed almost everyone down. The landlord's proposal was agreed on a majority vote in the end, if only because he and Johnny Berensford were the only people left with enough energy left to argue. The other thing that swung it was the promise that they'd soon be back in a monarchy. This calmed the dissenters, who were persuaded that the marketing prospects were better for a republic.

George and The Old Tank wanted it down as The Loyal Republic: "We're not becoming a republic because we're disloyal to England. We're doing it because they're disloyal to England. They only care about London when they're at home, and their global Britain when they're abroad. They don't care about England. They don't care about people like us." Alicia sniffed her disapproval, to make it clear that she certainly wasn't 'people like us,' but most just nodded it through. It was the end of a long evening.

The Old Tank looked rather surprised to have got that one signed off. His success emboldened him to put in a half-hearted attempt to add a religious section to the treaty, outlining the republic's ecclesiastical independence. Bob Corns, funnily enough, was the only voice in support, on the grounds that the more ridiculous you made it, the more people saw through religion. Then Mary asked her husband if, while he was at it, he'd like to have heralds with trumpets announce his passage from the front door to his bicycle. At this point he gave up, to general relief. Everyone wanted to wind up the meeting by then.

There was just one postscript. Bob Corns put in a noble bid to make the republic a duty-free zone for all alcoholic products, and cigars. It was ruled very definitely out of court. That evening, he invited Giles Prenderby, the village's eminent legal adviser, to a very fine supper, washed down with his pub's finest beverages, all on the house, naturally.

The upshot of their discussions was that Prenderby invited the two lowly flunkeys who'd been given the job of tidying up the last bits of preparation for the signing to stay at *The Old Bells* the night before. These two unsuspecting innocents soon found themselves discovering just how good Beef Wellington can be. Before they'd got to that stage, they had already discovered a quality of champagne quite new to them. As for the wines that followed, they couldn't pronounce their names, and had no idea where on the map they came from, but they knew that they liked them. Actually, by the end of the evening, they couldn't pronounce many names. That didn't stop them toasting the Duke of Wellington for his beef, or from trying to learn a marching song his soldiers used to sing about their Iron Duke, with Bob leading the chorus.

At the very end of the meal, where they'd expect to be paying the bill, the landlord announced that it was all on the house, and Prenderby, as they were about to roll upstairs to bed, turned up with a couple of documents he'd been working on. He said these last couple of pages had been missed out in the earlier checking, asked them to sign here, and said he'd go through it with them first thing in the morning.

The next day, over a very fine breakfast, they found they'd signed an amendment creating the Mutley Shepwell Duty-Free Zone for Alchohol and Cigars. Their initial response was indignation. Prenderby, who was rather enjoying his breakfast, pointed out that if they wished to challenge the document now, they'd have to explain to their superiors how they'd come to sign it. At that point, they swiftly saw that discretion was very much the better part of public service, consoling themselves with the thought that the amendment genuinely did serve equity and natural justice.

The documents were couriered off to Whitehall and processed through by the powers that be with remarkable speed, mainly so that the prime minister could have a cheery good news announcement to finish off with before he went home for Christmas. The new republic's rulers were escorted to Westminster in a rather grand set of limousines, and duly smiled for the cameras and shook hands with a number of eminences they'd only seen before on the news.

The politicians enjoyed making jokes about the new republic and carefully steered the conversation away from the Russian and his residence in it. They preferred a narrative along the lines of "Jolly, eccentric English village meets good-humoured sympathy from understanding, popular government, and All Are Happy." Also, they liked to portray it as: "No need to vote for regional parties to get sympathetic treatment from the powers that be." "Westminster shows a human face" was one spin doctor's line. Another coined the phrase "The Republic of Christmas," to emphasise the seasonal bonhomie.

Johnny Berensford wasn't there, and nor were Mike and Jane Singer. They had been detained by a clause in the small print, in one of the documents that wasn't made public, the one about the special tax concessions. These applied only to a certain list of businesses whose owners could prove they lived in the parish, and had done since before its claim to independence. The owner of the manor was at the top of a short and select list. Since no one was being told about this, and they were all sworn to secrecy, they couldn't tell anyone else, but they were surely keen to get their own businesses registered, and Mike and Jane made sure that they got the republic's official souvenir company registered too.

The only person they mentioned it to was Becky, whose latest holiday job was assisting with their paperwork. The only person she told was Jimmy, in the hope that sharing something like that might make her seem a Woman of Mystery and Secret Knowledge. Jimmy had to tell Jem, of course, being as how they were best mates. Jem didn't mean to tell his dad, but it slipped out somehow while they were fixing his bicycle, and his dad happened to be an old bridge partner of Lady TCB. They happened to be playing bridge that evening and her ladyship's stiff upper lip curled somewhat disdainfully at the news, before another thought struck her, and she called for a break so she could make a hurried phone call.

Two days later, the result of her phone call arrived in the midst of a tipping down winter soaking, cursing loudly and wishing he was back in the South of France. "Good to see such loyalty to your ancestral home," his mother remarked.

"I've emigrated, and there was a reason for that."

"I know, dear, and where you should be we have a Russian billionaire, plutocratic brothers, and a village without guidance, which is having all sorts of silly fun with pretending to be its own little kingdom."

"Republic, Ma, isn't it? And they do seem to have done us something of a favour. Good thing I kept one of the companies headquartered here, with you in charge of it. I'm about to make you the majority owner too, no need to look so glum."

"Ah, those loving words, when you see your mother

again for the first time in a year, it's good to know what heartwarming thing comes first to your mind."

"You should come down to Montmere more often, the place is named after you, after all. Anyway, aren't you desperate to be a European now?"

"Very drole, Jamie dear. Now, you're sopping wet, why don't you get into some dry clothes while I get us something to keep body and soul together?'"

And so, even though she had once declared herself no part of the new republic, even Lady TCB became a temporary tax exile, while staying at home, thanks to the curious financial provisions of the treaty that created the loyal republic.

Her son may have wished only to connect with his computer and phone, but in his heart of hearts he must have known that he'd never be allowed to get away with it. Sure enough, only three days later, his mother had arranged a tea party at which to show him off to a few, select old friends.

After he had entered and had been introduced, Richard Tranctard had been foolish enough to opine that women's conversation tended to revolve too much round home, family and a few other topics. Mary replied, "Of course, men are never boring. When they're young, they talk about sex and sport; when they're middle-aged, they talk about money and sport; when they're old, they moan about their health, and sport. All that variety, who could be bored?"

Lady TCB asked her son if he'd like to comment. His rejoinder was that her conversation tended to revolve rather a lot around Russia, Russians, and their generally objectionable nature. She returned that she'd have been happy to leave them alone if they'd left her alone, but if they insisted on coming over uninvited, then they must expect resistance from someone.

Her son disloyally replied, "No need to be snobby about Russian immigrants, mother. We're all immigrants if you go back far enough."

"James, your ancestors came over with the Conqueror, we are hardly immigrants."

"Precisely, Ma, not just immigrants but uninvited, unwanted, and entirely illegal. The Conqueror was, and all his cronies. Trampled over the natives with his rugger boots on. 1066 and all that: nothing invited about it: illegal immigrants, our noble ancestors."

She gave him her minor key warning stare, which was about six levels below the highest danger rating; he knew every level very well, and knew exactly where he was on the maternal anger scale. This was the playful mock charge, a long way from real battle.

Down the hill, the Woodvilles' research centre was feeling rather full of the joys this Christmas season. The whole operation was benefiting greatly from its brief sojourn in a tax haven, and all this publicity had been a wonderful bonus. The various prototype devices were marching ahead, and the artificial reality was looking more real by the month.

The facility kept expanding, with new buildings rising up one by one, and unnumbered builders fitting them out. Lorries kept bringing in endless equipment and office furniture. Some unknown music lover decided to use the public address system to play carols in the afternoons of the last working days before Christmas. Humans and robots together were regaled with "Hark! The herald angels" and "O little town of Bethlehem," soaring above the usual soundtracks of the working day.

So busy was it that Bill Stone, as Buildings & Facilities Manager, was practically living there now. In fact, the company had given him use of one of the little flats that had been built for visiting scientists, so that he could be there at all hours (and escape from his brother). His job kept expanding, everything from receiving deliveries and supervising workmen to finishing off jobs at all sorts of odd hours. In addition, assisting the Security Manager was one of his duties, and when she was off site he was needed to manage that aspect of the operation. Whereas the buildings and facilities were still staffed by plenty of living, breathing men and women, security was almost entirely computerized. He hardly had any staff to manage, it was a case of supervising machines rather than men and women.

As he opened the gates for delivery lorries in the small hours, he felt like a cross between one of the lodge keepers of old and one of the robots he supervised. As part of their testing they had the robots doing an increasing amount of the work around the facility. He and the other staff were effectively acting as coaches to machines learning how to operate effectively under human supervision. Alexander Livingston and a few others were there at all hours too, both to act as voice models for the robots, and also to give them extra training.

Alexander said he felt like a lion tamer at the zoo, sometimes. Bill pointed out that these were rather tame lions, and Alexander had to agree that perhaps it was more like training elephants and performing seals, not that anybody trained animals in captivity any more – just as the real, living show animals were banned, the first artificial ones were being created to take their places. All more humane and hygienic, and the research centre was certainly playing its part, although its plastic pets were a long way behind the more mundane robots in the development process. All these technological wheels kept turning, day by day, opposite the church, beside the River Amble, which had watched many futures take shape along its banks down the years.

Up in the village, it was a unique Christmas. Mike and Jane's firm had found a way to turn the national flag into bunting, which draped the village hall and the pubs. The republic's coat of arms appeared in many a front garden, all lit up beside the usual plastic Santas and reindeer collections. The carol services were fuller than ever, the carol singers louder and more joyful, the pubs celebrated like never before, and charity collectors of all sorts prowled the streets. The church of Charles, King and Martyr, set up two very popular evenings featuring carols, mince pies and mulled wine, outdoors, in front of the church. Not to be outdone, St Martin's constructed a Christmas float, towed by a tractor, with not just a singing Santa but an entire choir dressed up as reindeer and elves, singing carols for all they were worth.

The council used its new found wealth to heat a marquee on the village green so the school's Christmas play could be enjoyed by the whole village. It had been written by one of the teachers and featured a retelling of the George and the Dragon story, in which the maiden about to be eaten by the dragon was replaced by an entire village about to be eaten, before Good King John – as he now certainly was known in Mutley Shepwell – arose from the grave and sent his faithful knight St Peter to liberate them from a whole array of dragons, all rather small and cute, as befitted a primary school play. All this dragon fighting then suddenly morphed into a kind of nativity at the end, with Mutley Shepwell rather than Bethlehem as the village chosen for the saviour's birth.

The gloomsters said all this was getting a bit carried away, and if they heard the Old Tank's sermon at the St Martin's, their opinions were revived. Richard Tranctard, when not trying to raise money for his hospice project, was now trying to use their new-found fame to rally support for persecuted and minority churches around the world, from the Middle East to North Korea. Some of the more responsible in the congregation wondered if they should find someone to restrain him, but most were sympathetic.

Mary told him to spend less time on international correspondence and more on the actual parish. She also enjoyed reminding him that charity begins at home and he had someone at home who could do with some actual help getting ready for Christmas. He still found time to deck St Martin's with the banners of persecuted churches from around the world. Mary was about to protest a little more, then paused for thought, and found herself so impressed that she even took time out from chiding him to help him, and George and Alicia and Des and Peggy, as they rushed to put the banners up in time for Christmas. To cap everything off, the skies bestowed a real, proper snowfall right on cue, as the light faded on Christmas Eve.

27
THE GOVERNMENT
OF THE REPUBLIC

In the New Year, the wide world was preoccupied with the latest scandal around ex-President Ronald Tramp. His plans for his latest venture caused a certain mirth. He was proposing to build a full-size replica of the White House in New York City, to be called the Tramp House. The replica presidential rooms would be a museum, the other parts of the interior would be replaced by seven-star hotel rooms, all gold and glitter, to which he proposed to welcome the jet-set.

Having tried to requisition part of Central Park for it, he ended up building on the Jersey shore. Meanwhile, his plans for his own retirement house were also making waves. He was building a mansion on Long Island. For security reasons, he had decided he needed a wall around it, and felt the neighbours should pay for the wall. They objected somewhat. He backpedalled, the proposed wall got smaller and smaller, he ended up trying to persuade the neighbours to pay for a white picket fence.

Across the street from the house, a plot of land had been bought by the comedians of America. After spending the years of Tramp's presidency biting the hand that fed them, they had belatedly acknowledged that he was their greatest modern benefactor. He may not have been God's gift to politics, but he truly was God's gift to political comedy. After he left office, they began collecting donations for a statue of the man who had done so much for them.

Back in Mutley Shepwell, the weather deteriorated, and some remarkably stormy nights shook the village, making the oaks and pines along the ridge groan and sway as unusually fierce winds came up from the west. Hats and umbrellas found life increasingly hazardous on windy evenings, and increasing numbers of small branches were torn down by the wind, and larger branches too.

The winter storms without were matched by a storm within, within the Village Hall, in fact. It was now, all of a sudden, thanks to the republican marketing drive, a beautifully redecorated, rather remarkably smart village hall, and so well fixed up that the worst winter storm could see it had no chance to batter its way through the immaculate new roof, and was left with no option but to pack up its clouds and go home. Inside, however, the storms kept rising higher, discord threatened to dislodge the rafters, from the bottom up.

As everyone returned to work in the new year, one thing that had been keeping the council of the republic very busy rapidly ceased, while two unexpected issues came to vex the village's peace. The thing that suddenly stopped was the attraction of the republic as a business location. Most of the companies which thought they could make money from the republic's fame were installed in the business park already, and with only a few months of independence to go, few new ones were arriving.

Other businesses that had been hovering in the hope that Mutley Shepwell would become Britain's only onshore tax haven were now slinking away, because the tax authorities were loudly insisting that no such thing would be allowed and the village was not about to be a mini-Monaco or an onshore Bermuda. The Inland Revenue had been very clear in the small print of the agreement that created the Loyal Republic of Mutley Shepwell that only businesses headquartered in the parish before negotiations with Her Majesty's government began would possibly be considered for favourable tax treatment.

What was not made clear, even to the lawyers who drafted the agreement, was why the exemption for those businesses had been made; the secret negotiations behind the tax arrangements were known only to a very small circle, who were all sworn to secrecy.

The business issue calmed rapidly and two more rose up in its place. The first was immigration. No one had quite foreseen that the loyal republic would find itself attracting asylum seekers, still less that some of them would be seeking asylum from London, Birmingham, Wolverhampton, and numerous points further north and east.

After the business relocation applications were cleared up, an ever-growing queue of personal applications appeared. Moira closed down the republic's International Commerce department, which consisted of a phone number and a dedicated laptop, kept in the store room of the village hall. The laptop in the store room became the Immigration & Asylum department instead. It stayed stationed at the same desk, next to the same phone, but Moira put a different sticker next to it so that anyone who happened to wander into the store room would know what the laptop was there for, and be requested kindly not to walk off with it.

The council of the republic had not expected anyone to apply for asylum in a country that was only going to last till May. Yet applications poured in and for a moment, pound signs glistened, as they thought of selling citizenship to just a few of the more well-heeled applicants. The Home Office lost little time in pricking their bubble, and making it very clear that no one from beyond the UK was remotely going to be allowed to claim asylum, or immigrate for any reason.

Nevertheless, there were a surprising number of people who seemed to fancy joining the republic, even for a few months. It was difficult for the Home Office to object, since their maps all showed Mutley Shepwell as part of the UK anyway, and they had just signed an agreement giving the parish council the right to decide who the true residents of the republic were (within agreed limits), and create for them purely honorary Mutley Shepwell passports.

It may have been the passports that were half the attraction. Mike and Jane had worked with some designer friends to make them really most attractive, with the Republic's coat of arms on front, Lord Bonifer's on the back, and all the paper and binding of superb quality, rather better than any boring old normal passport.

Some enterprising villagers had already put theirs on eBay as collectibles (having checked that they could get a replacement if they registered the first one as lost). The prices these unusual collector's items were reaching were so remarkable that the Council had quickly to make a rule that no one was allowed more than one replacement; if they wanted to sell both, they couldn't get any more.

So the parish council had to decide on how much internal immigration from within the UK to permit. This led to impassioned debates. The first rule they could all agree on was "No Londoners." The consensus was: "They've got their own country, and they can look after themselves." The second rule was "No Scots – they want to go, they can't come crying back," as Alicia put it, even though some of the applicants insisted they'd never wanted to leave the UK in the first place.

There was more division about other regions, until the volumes of applications got to the point where they were wondering about people from Birmingham swamping the village, let alone Manchester, Liverpool and Leeds. So large cities were ruled out. By that time, they were getting asylum seekers from Cheltenham and Winchester, alleging council persecution, and possibly wishing to escape council and other bills. They decided that no one not from a village could possibly qualify. That raised the question: how to define a village? The debates were so fierce and the prices they were now charging for passports so high (in order to keep the profits within the village; they weren't planning on letting the resellers make all the money), that only a few grants of citizenship had yet been made.

The one exception to the 'Villages Only' rule was a

gentleman from Walsall once known as Fred Smith, whose name, identity and indeed life had been radically changed by technology. He started with a second identity on Mybook, then Twoogle picked that up and renamed his account with them. This he enjoyed but then his other online accounts started to follow their big brothers' example and changed his account name too. At this point he applied for a credit card and the machine told him to reapply in the name they had from Mybook and Twoogle and the rest, so he did.

Then his bank and others started telling him to change his name to match his credit details. Before he knew it the police were convinced his passport was in a false name and he must have changed it. He found himself the object of an anti-terror investigation, and ended up stuck in limbo, not able to change his name or replace his passport. He turned up at the village hall one day, with only his story, an apple, and a suitcase, calling himself a refugee, and regaled the council one by one with the tale of his woes, till in the end they gave him citizenship in his original name.

Worse than these immigration issues were the planning problems the government's lawyers carelessly bequeathed to the council of the republic. One clause that had been included into the public section of the agreement between the republic and the United Kingdom with, perhaps, less thought than there might have been, was to give the council of the republic exclusive jurisdiction over planning issues until the general election, and that any decisions made by said council would stand thereafter.

This meant that everyone in the village who'd ever wished for an extension, a loft conversion, to sell off part of the garden for another house, to have a swimming pool, a tennis court, a stable, any form of building at all, suddenly felt great urgency to get their application approved before independence ended. The council was snowed under. It took a great deal of their time. One application in particular caused more trouble than all the rest put together.

Stephanos Stone and his assembled communards had put in their application to transform the western end of the old industrial estate into a kind of religious fairyland, with buildings in every style and colour, including no fewer than five pagodas and four other towers and spires. These nine lofty constructions were already beginning to sprout from the park's location, at the bottom end of Mutley. The commune's leaders didn't believe in waiting on the planners where the spirit led. Tucked away though the estate was, these nine high points would be visible for miles. Initially the council was disposed to say a firm "No."

At that point, Stephanos and his communards began a campaign of persuasion. Each meeting of the council of the republic was picketed by circles of chanting monks and gurus. Around them priests and others of the spiritually enlightened sang the songs of their religions, waved incense about, waylaid passers-by and handed out literature.

It got to a point where it was hard for anyone to get in or out of the village hall. The council would have reported Stephanos and his crew to the police for aggressive use of incense, if their republic had any police. They promised themselves that once part of the United Kingdom again, they would get a sound control order to cut the chanting down to tolerable limits.

Stephanos then upped his game, threatening to bring the spiritual planning campaign to that sacred event, the village fete itself, and embroil the whole thing in incense-driven protest. Fearing a riot, and begged by half the village for peace and quiet, the council gave in, on condition that all chanting, religious procession, singing of the songs of many religions, and other noisy manifestations of spiritual enlightenment should henceforth be kept within the bounds of the commune. To this Stephanos and his communards eventually agreed.

The immigration and planning issues led to heated discussion. A rather gentler and more sensitive discussion concerned the village fete. The fete was always the centrepiece of the Mutley Shepwell year. It had been held in the field just above the church for donkeys' years, at the end of August, come rain or shine, until now.

For this unique year, the Russian had offered to host the fete at the manor on the Saturday of their re-entry into the United Kingdom, just before the general election, on the last day that Mutley Shepwell was still an independent country. Certain traditionalists felt that the fete should stay as it had ever been; most felt that this was an opportunity not to be missed. The bright lights of fame are alluring, especially when they are about to be dimmed forever.

Just to complicate matters, the Mutley Shepwell Horticultural, Horological, Meteorological & Botanical Society was proposing to host its very first village show on that very same day, on the Village Green, and had arranged for it to be televised. In an attempt to pull things together, the Business Secretary of the Council of the Republic, that is to say, Jane Singer, proposed merging the two events and rechristening the whole thing as The Mutley Shepwell International Trade Fair, Fete, Show and Festival. All agreed this was something of a mouthful, however much it might bring in the punters from afar. It was agreed to shorten the name to The Loyal Republic's Fete & Show.

All were heading amicably towards an agreement for a shared event when *Goodbye!* Magazine offered an eyewatering sum for the exclusive rights to film and report on it. This offer came with major strings attached. No other photography would be allowed, mobile phones would be handed in at the entrance, the entire event would be choreographed by the magazine, so that it could be livestreamed across the web, as well as laid out perfectly in their magazine. Nobody liked this but the money offered was so substantial that half the organizing committee felt they should agree. It was, they argued, the village's last chance to cash in.

Supporters felt it was the best way to milk their last gasp of fame, and get some value for the village from the assembled dignitaries and others who would be signing Mutley Shepwell back into the United Kingdom. Some of the opponents felt that the day of their re-entry was really a day of shame, and should not be celebrated, rather mourned over by grieving villagers in the peace and quiet of their own homes. Still others felt that the sacred traditions of the village were being sacrificed on the Altar of Mammon. Neutrals were tugged this way and that by the interested parties.

Finally the council of the republic had decreed an open meeting, at which all villagers could speak, and then all could vote. The speeches became impassioned, the rhetoric flew higher and higher, at times it might have been the first French Republic, not that of Mutley Shepwell, although fortunately without the threat of the guillotine for the losers. The vote came and it was goodbye to *Goodbye!* magazine. Those who lost the vote sadly listed all the things the village could have done with the money; the winners said the village had done well enough and was in a good position to cock a snook at the hounds of celebrity culture.

Commerce did not rule the Village Hall all the time. Alongside it Moira, Alicia, Alexander, George and the Tranctards were trying to foster various projects, using the village's celebrity now to build connections for the future.

Moira's favourite project was UniLocal Radio. It was actually not delivered over radio waves, but over the internet, and it was a network of local stations all broadcasting from the same universal site, MyPlace: if you kept your device tuned in to the one site, the content changed as you moved from village to village, giving local news, views, weather, music and opinion, relocating its content automatically as it tracked your movements. If you preferred, you could select local news from anywhere in the world, but it would only ever play local music, local news, local views. The aim was to create a seamless network around the world, and Moira had put Mutley Shepwell into the forefront of that campaign.

Another venture, this one plugged more by Jimmy and Jem and Mary, was the Universal Holiday Exchange. This one was a non-profit listing place for anyone who wanted to rent their home or room, or sell their possessions. It was linking up smaller sites around the world to fight the big corporations, and Mutley Shepwell's few months of fame were being used to give the linkages a push.

The same with the new Infinite Arts Exchange, for artists and writers around the world to connect up. The effort and money going into plugging these projects caused great debate. Some felt the harvest of fame should be reaped only for the village's benefit, but a majority on the council of the republic insisted that they should use their good fortune for villages everywhere, especially in England.

The one place unmoved by the village's debates was the Woodvilles' research centre, where the construction of the future continued at an ever-increasing pace. What with all the delays, the robot training teams kept drafting in extra help, and Bill Stone, although meant to be supervising the facilities, found himself with more non-human trainees than he knew what to do with, while Alexander Livingston and the other voice models and interaction instructors were being pressured to work longer and longer hours with a greater and greater variety of robots.

The one thing that never varied in Bill Stone's day was his lunchbreak. He was enough his own boss to arrange his commitments so that he knocked off at one and went back to work at two, on the dot. He was enough of an old-style union man at heart to treasure this one last bit of work to rule. He left his office at one o'clock precisely, marched over to his little flat, just round the corner, ate his lunch and put his feet up for a twenty-minute siesta.

This last might never have been known had his immediate neighbour, on the other side of the partition wall separating one flat from another, not been laid up with flu for a week. On her return to work she commented to her assembled workmates, on the astonishing volume of his snores and their even more astonishing precision, starting as his head hit the pillow at one thirty-five, and ending on the dot of five to two, without the intervention of an alarm clock.

She marvelled at it, and some of her colleagues marvelled too. It may have been one of those colleagues whose hand slipped in the door of Bill Stone's flat at one thirty-six the next day, found his keys on the side table by the door, and took them back to his office, for seventeen minutes, returning them at one fifty-three precisely, just as the final snores reached their crescendo.

28
THE FIRE OF THE LAMB

"I've been reading the Book of Revelation," said Jem.

"Steady on, mate," said Jimmy, "They'll be coming round to lock you up short-ish. It's a nutter's book, y'know. It's this job, innit? Getting a bit much for you."

Jem did indeed look tired. After their unfortunate experiences at the manor, and the rather more fortunate cheque that resulted, he'd been liberated from holiday jobs. Liberated from a lot of things, in fact. They'd both negotiated a year out of their master's courses at university so they could make the most of the new republic's opportunities.

At first they tried to be travel guides for their own village. "After all, Mutley Shepwell's a foreign country for most people," reasoned Jimmy. Foreign or not, very few people seemed to feel the need for two student guides to show them the backstreets of their village. Since the village hit the headlines, there had rapidly developed plenty of online maps, gazettes, commentaries, photo-journals and other forms of assistance for the traveller.

Their first venture into business having come to naught, they were then fortunate enough to get nudged into the new tax haven status of the republic, just in time. Jem's mum was an accountant, and set up their first company for them, "Mutley Shepwell International Travel." Mike and Jane Singer and a couple of others showed them how to attract traffic, and they became the hosts to a number of travel ventures, which people liked to book tax free on a website hosted in Mutley Shepwell. Their business careers suddenly looked a lot more promising.

His and Jimmy's new online travel hub had now reached a point where they could use a bit of help, and it had become the holiday job for Ben and Becky, when they were back from university. To their own, and everybody else's, great surprise, they seemed to have a thriving little business going, at least until the election and the village's re-accession to the United Kingdom. Meanwhile, they could help Jimmy's Aunty Moira with her more altruistic ideas.

What was more, now they had some help they could indulge themselves a bit. Their first and foremost concern, of course, was to make the regular trips to Anfield they had always dreamed of. They were spending a weekend or two in Liverpool a month now, enjoying themselves no end and even starting to make friends up there.

Other than that, Jimmy's main occupation was to trek up to London to try to see Petra, who may have been regretting her decision to give him her number, judging by the number of excuses she found to cancel on him, or at least restrict their time together to a coffee somewhere smart, followed by a swift exit. Becky found it particularly rough that she was usually holding the fort back home for Jimmy during these trips. Each time he returned home with his tail between his legs, however, her demeanour became that mite more cheerful.

Jem's plan was to indulge his passion for history. Since he was keen and couldn't say no, he'd got enrolled by the local history society to do the legwork for a book they were going to produce on St Martin's and the old parish of Mutley. One of the spin-offs from being a republic was that Mutley's ancient gothic parish church, having been gently ignored for eight hundred years, could suddenly attract some funding.

The Historical Society had been wanting to do a project on it for years but could never get the money to do the thing properly. Now, all sorts of trusts had come through with grants, and so had the Russian and the Woodvilles. Johnny Berensford had come through as well, with a good wedge of funds, and arranged to pay Bill Stone to manage the building of a proper entrance to the Bonifer monument in his spare time, such as that was.

Now that this had become famous, it was going to be permanently open, in theory. The trouble was that the council of the republic and the church's own parochial church council were still arguing as to what would be the least offensive shape to have sticking up in the middle of a churchyard. It needed to be something of a monument itself, this extension to the original monument, and all sorts of people kept coming up with ideas for it, from glass pyramids to canvas pavilions to even a larger reflection of the original, containing an entrance hall and a mini-exhibition.

Bill Stone had arranged for a start, and got as far as some foundations, but he was far too busy to make progress. George, the Old Tank and numerous others were getting increasingly frustrated because he was taking ages to do not very much. Because he already had a full-time job as the buildings and facilities manager at the Reality Exchange, he couldn't give the role much time.

They wondered why Johnny had given him the job. The Woodvilles kept piling more and more work on him, and when he did get across the road he just kept tinkering about, saying he was changing their rickety corrugated iron surround into a more salubrious temporary structure, to protect the tomb until the various heritage bodies could be persuaded to agree on a permanent building.

Meanwhile, there was enough money to commission a very glossy book and website, with professional photographers brought in to illustrate it, and even to turn the back of the church into a little gallery-cum-meeting room, which could be done with rather less argument than the Bonifer monument aroused.

In the midst of this, the local historians were having the time of their lives, sending off articles to learned papers and far-off magazines, having their writing hosted by well-known web journals, and generally basking in this unexpected interest from across the world. They had found all sorts of different angles to explore in the history of their new republic and their funding allowed them to employ Jem to help.

This meant that the senior members of the Historical Society could stay at home doing their research in comfort on their computers, while saving up the bits you still had to get on your bike and go somewhere for until Jem was free. Jem was amazingly willing to be sent off yet again to the County Record Office, or the Bodleian Library, or some other repository of ancient facts with a bearing on their church and parish. He loved these jobs, kept being talked into doing more, while his long-suffering parents babysat Ben and Becky back at the company he was meant to be running.

As a new sideline, he had taken to poking round the church himself in spare moments, which was a new experience for him. He'd started getting very into Norman arches and early Gothic styles, to Jimmy's bemusement. He tried to take Becky with him on some of these trips, although her energies were more devoted to trying to get Jimmy to take her along on some of his, and then waiting, sad-faced, by the clock in the office, for his return. Perhaps it was the amount of time that Becky spent in the office waiting for Jimmy that had made Jem so keen to get out of it. All that said, it's a long way from church architecture to the Book of Revelation, and the mention of the latter made Jimmy very worried for him.

Jem remained unruffled by his friend's concern. "It's the crypt, Jimmy. Have you ever been down there?"

"Only go into the church at Christmas, what would I be going down the crypt for?"

"You know those beasts carved on the walls in the Bonifer tomb?"

"No. Mate, I'm tryin' to make a point here. I don't spend my life nosin' round in the dark. I got places to go, people to see. I got a life, in fact. You should get one too. You're getting old just a bit young. Come down Faringdon

243

with us tonight and let's have a few drinks." Jimmy's own historical interests had faded somewhat as other horizons expanded.

"No, I want to go and check that lamb. It's been bugging me."

"Bugged by a lamb? You're losin' it, mate." With that, Jimmy was off.

Jem sighed and went back to his laptop. Even with the screen extender set to highest res it was hard to read some of the scans from the older records. "I thought handwriting was meant to be better in those days," he mumbled to himself at last, and gave up on it and went back down to the church, to look at the Bonifer monument one more time.

There were indeed the dragon and the beasts still engraved on the wall: one had the sea washing round its feet, the correct complement of ten horns, seven heads (one wounded), ten crowns, some largely eroded, but all still just about visible. On the other side of the dragon was the second beast, feet firmly set on the earth, a well-known number in Latin numerals on its chest: DCLXVI. Jem knew 666 when he saw it. The beast looked like a giant lamb, but with two horns and the same markings coming out of its mouth as the dragon had, the same wavy lines.

After quite a lot of researching, that is to say, looking at poor quality photographs on the internet, Jem was pretty sure those signified flames coming out, although it was hard to be quite sure. He fingered one of the old Bibles from the church: "And I beheld another beast coming up out of the earth; and he had two horns like a lamb, and he spake as a dragon."

The strange thing was the other carvings. He would just have to go back to the crypt of St Martin's one more time to check something. He got on his bike and set off down the hill. That part of the ride was always a breeze, with the view opening out when you came out of the woods at the southern edge of the village. The sight of the river and the fields and St Martin's and the old stone bridge never failed to lift his spirits; the sight of the reality exchange looming through the trees of Traitor's Wood never failed to sink them again.

He leant his bike against the north wall and got out the key to the side door of the church. He always loved that key, so ornate, so scrolled, so large and so old for such a small door. The Old Tank had made quite a fuss about entrusting him with the spare, they only had two for that door, and it wasn't a key that was easy to replace. Every time he turned it in the lock he could hear a low grinding noise, as if the innards of the lock were grumbling at being brought out of retirement once again. They deserved a rest. The old key for the main door had been replaced with a modern one decades ago, but this last relic of a medieval locksmith still did its work after seven centuries.

He turned on the lights in the north aisle and then went down the little flight of worn stone steps into the crypt. It wasn't used for much, mainly because it flooded most winters, sometimes quite deep. They couldn't really store anything in it, and it smelt musty and faintly rotten, as if there were a family of dead rats decomposing discreetly in a distant corner, so nobody especially liked to go down there. It was a pity, thought Jem, because the pillars that held the crypt up were themselves rather wonderful, with Romanesque arches between them.

Then, in the centre of the crypt, unusually, rather than at the East End, beneath the altar of the church above, was the remains of a second altar. Legend had it that Sir Thomas de Thurslay himself had it built, so that prayers could be said there for the soul of King John, and his own. That all ended at the Reformation, and the altar had been left to moulder, all alone in the centre of that dark space.

Behind it were a strange collection of engravings on the walls, either side of an empty space where a grand carved crucifix had once stood. Shame it wasn't there any more. The records said it had been quite splendid once. In front of the altar, well in front, near the door, were two pillars, made of a lighter stone. On the left hand pillar were the arms of King John, on the right those of Sir Thomas. Each coat of arms was surrounded by images, mostly a pattern of alternating angels and knights on horseback, but with one other animal each: for the king, a dragon, for his chancellor, a lamb.

What was perplexing Jem was something that he thought he might have seen a little while before. It kept bugging him. A photographer had been taking photos for the new book about the church and everything was so filthy down here that she had insisted on a general clean before she'd take the photos. As the most enthusiastic, and the least good at saying no, Jem got the job.

When he got to the lamb, he was almost sure that his fingers could trace the same wavy lines coming from its mouth, hidden beneath an ancient layer of moss and grime. He didn't want to scrub the stone too vigorously, because it was getting crumbly in places, so he left some of the dirt, which made the hint of those lines indistinct. He still thought they were there, although the photographer hadn't been convinced. There was one other thing he thought he'd found, though: the angel next to the lamb's mouth seemed to have something in its right hand, it might have been a dagger but he thought not. It nagged at him and he finally resolved to take a chance on pulling off some of the looser chips of stone and giving that angel a final scrub.

When he finished he looked for a long time at the angel's right hand. He was almost sure he knew what it held, but not quite. Lost in thought, he made his way out into the Spring evening, not noticing that there were fresh tyre marks in the mud in front of the churchyard gate. Jem knew he needed some more software to work this all out, and fortunately the travel business and Mr Pronotkov's cheque had left him with plenty of readies to buy the programs he would need, and a more powerful computer to run them on. As he went back to his scooter, he was deep in his plans, and noticed nothing nearer than the thirteenth century.

Two quiet, watchful grey eyes watched him leave, from the shelter of the wood across the road. Traitor's Wood was full of brambles and hawthorn bushes on this side, they added to the screening of the buildings, so the Woodvilles had left them in place. Both inside the chain-link fence and outside it, brambles still ruled, with the ancient oaks and birch and ash above them, and willows along the riverside. After Jem had scooted back, the owner of those eyes slipped across the road to sniff around a little.

The rest of the village remained blissfully ignorant of all this. For them, the thing that dominated the later part of the winter was the endless rain. Mutley Shepwell had never seen anything like it. One cloudy day followed another and every second or third brought another wave of rain, not just British drizzle but proper, driving, soaking rain.

The paths through the woods beneath the village became quagmires, the ridge above the village was a wet and windswept and unwelcoming place to walk your dog, or yourself. The Amble itself began to rise. At first, amid the encroaching gloom, Des retained his usual cheerfulness. "The Amble never floods that much, not here, not in Mutley Shepwell," he assured all and sundry, in the pub, the village shop, in the street. But as the weeks went by and the rain kept falling and the Amble kept rising, inch by inch, up its banks, even Des began to wonder.

When February came, there was rumour of worse. Weather forecasters started to get excited, knowing that they were about to get their fifteen minutes of fame. Some even bought new suits. They started to talk about storms building over the Atlantic. Those first storms ended up going north or south, to Scotland or down to the Bay of Biscay. There was a brief lull then.

This came as a great relief to the council of the republic, because they had big plans for a special spring event in

March. It was almost the last chance to showcase their little republic before the media locked down into general election mode, and sideshows such as Mutley Shepwell began to be ignored once more.

29
THE RAIN AND THE PARADE

Jem finally got his software and his new computer, and he kept mapping out the various strange carvings in the crypt. It was all preying on his mind. One evening, he turned up in Faringdon, at *The Fool & Chain*, and poured out his thoughts to Jimmy over a beer or three. Jimmy was more interested in the closing chapters of the football season, and in the end Jem sank back into his beer and looked very thoughtful for the rest of the evening.

The following week he and Jimmy got dragged in to the preparations for the great media day. The one person Jimmy could never say no to was his Aunty Moira, and Jem could never say no to anyone, so they got lumbered. This meant he had no chance to investigate further, but Jem did put some ideas to Moira, who'd added to all her other hats by becoming the acting head of the historical society and the official village minister for heritage & culture.

The council of the republic were having a ticklish time. All the political parties wanted to send representatives to a pre-election photo shoot in Mutley Shepwell, with greater and lesser dignitaries present ("the greater spotted windbag or the lesser spotted weathervane," was Bob Corns's verdict). Jem asked what Moira and Mary had decided.

"All or none," said Moira, firmly.

Somehow, more than anyone in the village, she had managed to edge her way to the centre of the limelight and become the voice for Mutley Shepwell's story, the one who could explain how an obscure village could become, albeit temporarily, its own country. She seemed to be enjoying it, judging by the new wardrobe, in rather brighter colours than the old, the even more careful coiffing of the dark locks, the videoblog, and the consultancy roles she'd snapped up for several historical and local government organizations. But then, she had always been good at running things.

Moira was truly the plenipotentiary of the village firmament. By her decree, everyone agreed that, when it came to politics, Mutley Shepwell should be hospitable to all parties and partisan for none. Jem, Jimmy and all her other dogsbodies wearily accepted the various jobs that needed doing so that the politicians they wanted to keep on the right side of might be photographed with England's own independent village. This gave all those politicians a chance to demonstrate their sense of genial humour and appreciation for eccentricity, just in time for the election.

A whole day of glad-handing and photographic smiles was arranged, at locations including the church, the two pubs and the village green. It all became highly pressured because of the weather. After their winter of rain, they'd had a brief lull, but one last almighty storm had been building in the Atlantic. It was due to hit Wales and Cornwall with almost hurricane strength, then head across the country, still ferocious.

Torrential rain was forecast, with walls of cloud following up to dump more and more on. It was predicted to be one of the biggest storms England had seen in years, with near-record rainfall, and it was due to hit on the very evening of their big day. It was too late to change all the plans, and anyway there were no alternative dates possible before the general election. So everyone was in a tearing hurry, extremely keen to get the day's photography done before the storm arrived.

Almost everyone on the council of the republic got roped in, and they grabbed everyone else they knew to help. Jem was assigned duties at St Martin's, then escorting people up the hill to their next event. He additionally volunteered for a final role clearing away and locking up after everyone had gone.

Politicians came and went, suited in different shades of grey, with more brightly clad retinues, like partridges surrounded by peacocks. Jem twitched nervously in the background, then guided each group in turn up to their next stop and negotiated a lift back each time. Jimmy went through every shade of boredom. At last the final smiles had been plastered on to the final faces, then surgically removed once their owners were safely back in their cars.

Jimmy departed with the last car, and Jem was left alone, as the first clouds rolled in and gusts of wind began to make the treetops sway and the leaves start to jerk and tug at their moorings on the branches of the more exposed trees. It was the beginning of the forecast deluge, just the first outliers of the storm. The rain wasn't too much yet, but it soon would be.

The Tranctards had sensibly gone to stay with some old friends in Faringdon, with the water already lapping close to the front step of their vicarage, even before the storm. So Jem was left alone. He could feel the force of the wind building, as he walked round the church to look at the Amble. It ambled no more: in normal times a sleepy stream sitting deep within its banks, with rushes almost meeting in its middle at points, it had swollen and swollen.

Its pace had changed from its usual lazy dawdle to a brisk march, then continued speeding up till it was almost racing along. The churchyard had been a mudbath for weeks, and in the last few days the puddles had been starting to join up and form little shallow ponds, while the river had been transformed. As it swelled it edged its way up its banks, day on day, to unheard of heights. Just yesterday, it had been starting to lap at the top of its bank, and even beginning, rather rudely, to invite itself beyond. After a lifetime of courteous reticence, it had become an altogether more aggressive river.

Jem was fascinated. He could see the beginnings of the flood starting to reach forward and join up with the nearest pools and puddles, although it was increasingly hard to see very far as the rain got heavier, and the wind really started to whip in from the west. He watched in amazement for a minute or two, thinking of their quiet stream, hardly a river at all in its normal life, being transformed at last into a torrent. Jem shook himself, remembering what he had come for, pulled the hood of his kagoul more tightly round his face, and started back around the church to the side door by the crypt, to which he still had his favourite key. He let himself in by that little door, always a hard push to open it, even more so with so much moisture in the air.

Jem first went to a temperature and humidity-controlled box, brought to the church this day for their distinguished visitors to look at, and awaiting its return to the museum where it usually now resided. From it, very carefully, for he knew the necessity for extreme delicacy, he removed the curiously-shaped key they had found in the Bonifer tomb. Then he made his way down to the crypt, turned on the lights, and stared at the fire emerging from the mouth of the lamb.

What Jem had noticed about it was that it was directed to a point, like the fire coming from the lamb's mouth in the tomb itself. The other strange thing he had found was that amid the plethora of curious engravings at the back of the crypt, there was yet a third lamb, also with fire emerging from its mouth, to a point, and an angel beside it bearing a sword.

He perched himself on the step in front of the altar and fired up his computer. The altar had running round it a kind of tree of life design, with the stone carved to signify that ancient image. Age and damp had damaged the carving a little, yet it was still very fine.

Jem's new holoscreen buzzed softly into life. It had on it the kind of mathematical modelling software he'd been waiting for, to create a replica of this space he'd so carefully measured, with all its angles and distances. Once he'd checked that the new software had all the correct data in all the right places, he switched it into 3-D mode. In front of him, in green, a model of the crypt, the church and the Bonifer monument. He highlighted each of the three lambs, linked them in a triangle, and asked the software to pinpoint the centre of the triangle. He had a little trouble communicating with it to start with, but he made his point in the end. The computer thought for a moment, and then a cross appeared above the altar. How very appropriate, Jem felt.

When Jem went to that point, however, he saw nothing. The top of the altar was made of two stone slabs. The sides of the altar were made of four stone blocks, which had been decorated once with a mark like a hand with a hole in it, the hole being where the stones met, or didn't quite meet. At the top of the altar, however, the slabs still met snugly and there was no gap. Jem's latest acquisition was one of the new deep-level scanners that could even penetrate a few feet of stone. He got it out of his rucksack and starting calibrating it.

Meanwhile, up at Jem's parents' house, as the rain began to really hit the roof tiles hard, they were snuggled up on the sofa watching pictures of even harder rain falling on other people's roofs. They were fascinated as they saw the storm in the west slowly moving towards them. They certainly weren't expecting a knock on the door. It was Bill Stone, grey eyes even greyer through the rain.

"Sorry to bother you. Just needed to check something with Jem. Was trying to catch him before the storm."

Jem's mum was rather surprised by this, but she knew her son was deeply involved with all those in the History Society these days, and had been in discussions with Bill about the Bonifer monument. "He's at the Singers', I think, with Jimmy and the twins."

"Thanks," said Bill.

Five minutes later, he was knocking on the Singers' front door. Becky answered. "Sorry to bother you, looking for Jem."

"He's not here," she said, rather puzzled.

"Know where he is? I was hoping to catch him before the storm gets here."

"Wait a minute." She went back to where they were all glued to their holoscreens. Everyone was watching endless variations on howling wind and rain, except Jimmy, who was enjoying one of his favourite comedy shows. He waved at the screen and explained to Becky: "All this storm, you need a hearty laugh. And look at them: everyone else on TV is all about looks and grooming, all surface and shine. Comics, now, they have to have talent, so they can't pick them for looks. Only time you get a proper lineup of ugly mugs on TV."

Jimmy liked comedy, and comics. She had to poke him severely to get him to actually listen to her question. Finally, he detached himself from the screen enough to answer: "Still down at the church, I think. Funny geezer sometimes, old Jem, y'know how mad he is about all his measuring and his funny old things. He'll be up later."

She went back to the door, reflecting that it had been rather rude to leave Bill soaking in the rain. As she opened the door to tell him, something made her pause. Perhaps it was that she knew how much Jem hated to be disturbed when he was deep in his historical research, perhaps it was something about the night approaching, and the forbidding look of their visitor in his hooded coat, either way, she just said, "He'll be in later."

"I'll be back," said Bill, "After the storm." As she shut the door, he was already back in his four by four, switching the all-weather sensors to max, and rather than go home, he cruised back to a little layby just down from Jem's parents' house, where he installed himself for the present.

Back at the Singers', Becky was worried. "It's getting really bad out there. He's only got his scooter, he wouldn't be safe. Think we should go get him?"

"Good idea," said Ben, "my car will drive. Good chance to try it out in this weather, see if it's all it's cracked

254

up to be."

"Leave it a minute, and I'll come with you," Jimmy's voice muttered from the sofa, "Just want to watch the end of this, it's great. Just a few more minutes …"

Back down in the crypt of St Martin's, Jem was unaware of the storm building. He was very focused on the altar, and increasingly frustrated that however he scanned it, he could find no opening or secret chamber within. So focused was he on his search that he didn't hear the door opening behind him, or the quiet steps approaching, pausing behind the pillar to the left of the altar, then stepping into the open.

"Good evening," said Alexander Livingston. His grey eyes seemed amused, for some reason.

Jem jumped, and turned round swiftly, caught by surprise and not best pleased. He flicked his screen off. "Wasn't expecting you down here. Just finishing off some measurements."

"Can I help? Just finished off at the Exchange, tucked my robots up in bed, then I saw your scooter, thought I'd see if I could help."

"Thanks, but no. Just putting things together and packing up now. Need to get back."

"Do let me take a look at that model. I've been working on King John and this church for a long time and I've never been able to put a model like that together."

In spite of himself, Jem was chuffed. He flicked the holoscreen back on and the model started to rotate slowly round, in all its green glory. "Thought I had something with those three lambs, they're centred on the altar, but I've scanned and scanned and there's nothing there."

"Can you zero in on the three lambs?" Jem did so. "The angle each flame is at, where it comes to a point, where are they all pointing to, can you work that out?"

That was more complicated, but Jem managed in the end. "The chapel, it's the chapel. Does that mean something, do you think?"

"Might do, there's something we need to check in the Bonifer monument first. Let's scoot over there quick while we still can, leave all your gear, we don't need to photograph anything, I just need to check something I think I saw. Come on!"

Jem followed him, wondering what it was that was taking them through the driving rain. It was fiercer than it had been when he went into the church, and the wind was stronger too. The puddles across the churchyard seemed to be joining into one wide sheet of water, and when they got to the monument, a steady flow was coming down the stone steps into the lower chamber. There was a barrier round the entry to the monument which limited the flow, but it was starting to leak quite significantly, and the trickles coming in through each little leak were combining into a significant flow of water.

"Just in time," said Alexander, "Another few hours and this place will be flooded, and it could take days or weeks to clear it all out. Now, look, just stand there, in front of the top step, and look very closely at the top of the wall in front of you."

Jem did so, torch in hand, peering at the circle of light his torch revealed on the wall, but could see nothing unusual. He was just turning to ask Alexander what it was he should be looking for when something very hard hit him on the back of the head and he crashed forward down the narrow steps, ending in a jumbled heap amid the rising water beneath.

When he woke up, for a moment he had no idea where he was. He could feel himself being manhandled but couldn't tell who was doing it. He wished he could move, wished his head would just clear for one moment. Bit by bit, the fog in his brain lifted a little. He knew this place. He knew this stone. He tried to say something but no words came out, just groans. Even if he'd been able to cry out, no one could have heard, down below ground, with the howling wind and the hammering rain above. A torch shone in his face and by its light he saw stone walls all round him, no, not walls, sides, the sides of a coffin.

"Sir Thomas," he croaked.

"That's right," said Alexander's voice. The man was just a shadow behind the light of the torch, but his voice was clear. "It's an honourable resting place. I didn't want to leave you on the floor, besides, it's just possible someone might have taken a look, if anyone misses you before the flood's complete. With the lid back, there's nothing to see."

"No ... I won't, won't ..." Jem was trying to talk back, until a gag was pushed into his mouth.

Alexander continued. "Won't tell? I'm sure you mean it, and I really am very sorry. I just needed that 3-D model of yours, and the key, and I need silence until I'm long gone. If there had been another way, I would much rather, but I couldn't do the modelling myself and I needed it to know precisely where to look. I'll have to destroy the computer now, I'm afraid. I don't want anyone else seeing it, and you won't be needing it."

His hands were round Jem's jaw, checking the gag was firmly in place and tying it precisely. "Seems rather appropriate, don't you think, to give this rather splendid coffin an occupant after all these years? Bit of a waste to have it always empty, especially when you've shown me where the real one is. You didn't know that he changed his emblem to a lamb at the end, after he repented, did you? No one knew that, it took me so long to find out."

"Didn't totally repent, though, did he? Old Sir Thomas didn't get the money to build the old bit of the manor honestly, did he now? Or the church here? Way beyond a mere knight. Although he was the knight in charge of King John's treasure the day it was lost in the Wash. People forget these things, Jem, and it takes a real historian to find them out again, after all the centuries have rolled over them and buried them. I found that out. I was going to share, but not when other people are trying to cut me out."

"That's happened too often. Sometimes a man has to act. Mustn't stay to chat, when you can't even reply. I need to get to the chapel, before my erstwhile partners realise that I might have discovered their plans to cheat me. Not this time, not this time. No. Once again, young man, my sincere apologies, you might have had a brilliant future. Don't worry, drowning's kind, they say." With those words, he heaved the lid of the coffin back into place, very neatly, so it looked as if it had never been moved.

This is illegal, Jem thought to himself, inconsequentially, you can't disturb a grave. He was alone in a little world of stone, alone in the dark. He could hear the water flowing down into the chamber. It sounded quite deep already. He thought he could hear Alexander leaving, but it was so hard to know what was real and what his throbbing brain was making up.

Cold, wet, bruised though he was, the hurt on the back of his head kept dragging him back down into sleep. He knew he ought to move, but his body didn't seem to want to know, and it was so dark, so totally dark. He tried to arch up to push against the lid of the coffin, but it was heavy and hard, very, very heavy. Stone. Stone's heavy, he thought to himself, before the dark and the fog in his head pushed down and snuffed out the little bit of him that was still trying to cling to the light.

30
OLD FRIENDS AND NEW ENEMIES

Becky and Ben had finally managed to drag Jimmy away from his show, thanks to a phone call from Jem's mum to see if he was with them. When she found out he wasn't back yet, she was all for sending out his dad, but Becky assured her that she and Ben and Jimmy could handle it. The news of the parental phone call finally roused Jimmy from his sloth and they all donned their stoutest water-proofs, at speed.

Soon they were urging Becky and Ben's little car down the hill. Faster, faster, Ben shouted at it; slower, slower, responded the controls, which his parents had set up with a forest of restrictions, designed to prevent him doing things like driving fast round sharp bends in torrential rain, or, as he saw it, having fun. Fume as he might, the autopi-lot was in control.

Finally, they got to the church. The rain made it hard to see more than a few feet ahead, they were being pum-melled relentlessly from above. They could see Jem's bright green scooter, though, parked by the gate.

"Look," said Ben, "Whole graveyard's under water."

"He was takin' photos or somethin'," volunteered Jimmy vaguely. The front doors were locked, but they found the little side one ajar, then managed to track down the light switches. They started calling for Jem, but no re-ply. Ben ran round the side chapels and up to the East End of the building, still nothing. Jimmy then remembered that Jem had said something about the crypt. Becky no-ticed that the key from the Bonifer monument was missing from its case.

They went down into the crypt and were mystified: Jem's rucksack was there, alright, and some of his kit, but no Jem, and his computer had been smashed, thoroughly taken apart. Jimmy looked at it, mystified. "Wha'appen?"

Ben was ahead of him. "Maybe we find what happened to the computer, we find Jem. Can you get in to his cloud account?"

"Got all his passwords. But all this stone, won't have uploaded."

"Got a data relay on it, see. And I know he put one on his scooter, that'll have sent it on."

Jimmy nodded ruefully. "Good thing he's gadget mad. I haven't got any of that. Let's go look on the car computer."

They used Ben's ePad, which went everywhere with him, day and night, to get to Jem's cloud account, via the car computer. The security codes Jimmy kept on his phone allowed them to access it – he and Jem had backed up each other's passwords for years.

With that, they were able to get back to the last projection from the computer, the three lambs highlighted and the triangle over the altar. There was something else about the lambs, and an angel, but the data was corrupted at that final point. Ben was looking bashfully proud that he'd managed to retrieve the data feed back that far. Jimmy looked confused.

"Why was he looking at the lambs?" Becky replied, frowning with concentration. "He's highlighted the ones in the crypt, and there's the one in the Bonifer monument."

"Okay, let's look there."

They braced themselves and went out into the rain again. The water was rising across the churchyard, and it was starting to get close to the tops of their boots. Their torches carved little pathways into the wall of rain, but not strongly enough to gouge more than a few feet of twilight out of the darkness. When they got to the barrier round the Bonifer monument, they found it sagging but still just holding. "Won't last," warned Jimmy.

"What if it goes?" Becky asked nervously.

"Whoosh!" Said Jimmy as he followed Ben over the barrier, and reached back, very gentlemanly, to give her a hand.

The upper chamber was empty. Ben shone a torch down the steps into the lower chamber. "Cor, look at that, water's up to the top of the tomb."

"Top of the coffin, more like," said Jimmy, "Good thing Sir Thomas's bones aren't in there, or he'd be stew. Come on, nothing here." He turned away.

"What's that," said Becky, pointing down. "Oh, nothing, I think."

Beside her, Jimmy made a startled cry and knelt down so he could shine his torch into the corner of the chamber, where something small and dark was trapped. "Jem's cap!"

"How do you know it's his?"

"Know anyone else round here wears Liverpool cap, 'cept me? What's it doing there?" The cap was there, but no sign of Jem. They shone their torches all round the monument, watching the top of the coffin disappear below the water. Baffled, they headed off to check the church again.

As they got to the side door, Jem's parents' car skidded into view, rounding the corner into the churchyard via the gatepost, with a screech.

They all huddled together just inside the side door of the church to try to think what must be done. Jem's parents were seriously worried by now and had called the police, only to be told that there was no chance of any police vehicle getting anywhere near Mutley Shepwell till the storm had blown itself out.

"We had to come," said Jem's mum. "Have you seen any sign?" They told her about the computer and the cap.

Just at that moment, there was a knock on the door. They looked at each other, and Bill Stone came in, looking grim. "Saw you heading down here, wondered if I could help?"

Jimmy and Becky wanted to know just what he was doing chasing round after Jem through a storm, anyway. Jem's dad was more diplomatic, and got a reply: "Been trying to find Alexander Livingston, actually. I found out that he'd been getting some specialist software for Jem, very niche stuff, it looked. He's good with all that, isn't he, your boy?"

They were all now thoroughly confused. Jimmy took them down into the crypt and showed them the smashed computer, which Bill examined with interest. They explained about the triangle centred on the altar, and he gave it a cursory inspection. "We need Jem." They didn't need telling.

"The cap, show us the cap," said his mother.

"It's just floating, there's nothing there," explained Jimmy.

"I want it, even if there's nothing there, I want it," she said with great emphasis, in a voice that brooked no denial. Gathering up the remains of the computer and his other bits and pieces into his rucksack, she led them out of the crypt. Ben and Jimmy shrugged at each other, Becky ran ahead to be with Jem's mum. They all hunched their shoulders and went out into the rain, their torches stabbing dim beams of light ahead of them into the darkness.

Back at the monument, Jimmy braced himself and volunteered to jump in and get the cap. "No need, lad, I've got better gear, and a better light," said Bill. He did indeed have state of the art wet weather gear, and a torch and a headlight, both twice as powerful as anything anyone else had. Becky wondered why he came out so well equipped, as he gingerly lowered himself into the water.

He reached for the cap but the mini-wave he created sent it bobbing ahead of him on the little air bubble it had trapped, into the far corner by the head of the tomb. He lunged after it, and cursed as he blundered into the coffin itself, now under water. He had to actually climb on top of the coffin to reach for the cap, now right in the far corner. As he did so, he paused, then put his head down below the water level, then up to breathe, then down below again. "Jimmy, get in here!" He shouted.

With a lot of wincing, Jimmy did so. "There's something hitting the inside of the lid, I can feel it. Get across here and help me lift it," commanded Bill.

With a level of water above it, the lid was hard to lift. After their second fruitless attempt, Bill realised there was more: "It's sealed itself, it fits so tight, it's like an airlock – we need a crowbar." Jimmy was sent aloft, and had to get back into the church itself, where the tools that had been used on the monument were stored in a back vestry. Crowbars arrived, Jimmy got back down and they pulled together. As the lid slid off the coffin, they saw Jem's face just as the water rushed in to submerge him.

31
THE GHOSTS OF TREASURES PAST

Everyone was shouting and screaming at once. Jem's dad, his mum, everyone but Ben jumped in at that point to drag him to the surface. In the confusion, they almost dropped him back down into the water. They could hardly get him up the steps for getting in each other's way. Ben was too busy videoing and live-streaming proceedings to actually help, until he was fiercely ordered to desist his filming and do something useful.

Jimmy and Bill supported Jem between them back to the church, where they lay him down out of the rain. He was pale as Sir Thomas's ghost, and drifting in and out of awareness. Bill and Jimmy were desperate to get him to speak, his parents were desperate to get him to rest.

In the absence of an ambulance, they were ransacking the church for old vestry curtains and other warm items to wrap him in for the journey back up the hill, and calling an old retired doctor they knew in the village to beg to bring Jem to her on the way back home.

While everyone else was phoning and ransacking, Bill took his chance, with Jimmy at his side. "Who did it, mate?" said Jimmy, but Bill Stone just asked "Where is he?"

Jem was moaning about kicking, kicking, kicking the lid till somebody came, but he opened his eyes when he heard Jimmy's voice. It was Bill's question he answered, though: "Chapel – went – chapel."

Bill was off out the door in a second, with Jimmy and Ben tailing after him, in spite of Becky's protests. She stayed to look after Jem, who looked up at her with all the gratitude that any nurse in the history of the world could ever have wished for.

Before crossing the road, Bill Stone went to the boot of

his car and got out a shotgun and a packet of shells. Seeing Ben's face, he said, "No one's asking you to come. Stay back and look after the boy. I've got business to do."

"We're coming," said Jimmy with more courage than he felt, "Jem's been my best mate since we were knee high, whoever did this, we'll get him."

The boys started off towards the path along the river, only for Bill to peel off at the side gate to the reality exchange. "If you're coming, come the quick way," he muttered back at them, then started striding through the complex of oddly shaped buildings scattered between the remaining trees.

Scots pine and ash and oak and birch, every last tree suffered beneath that storm, with the security lights casting lurid shadows through them onto the steel and glass structures between. As they entered the complex, the first lightning struck. Ben ducked, as it seemed to be almost hitting the wood.

Bill was following a footpath till suddenly he turned, raised his gun, and moved off cautiously to the right. He was now heading for a massive, hangar-sized structure made of burnished steel and dark glass. It was shaped like a circus big top, except that there were square extensions at each end, and above them the steel rose into gothic arches stabbing the sky. Whereas all the other buildings had been dark, bar their security lights, the Big Top (as it was called) was full of light, and various humming noises escaped from it into the night. What's more, one of the big hangar doors on the river side was half open.

Ben and Jimmy followed, wondering what this building contained. Bill ignored the open hangar doors, went right, and disappeared inside a side door at the east end. They, very cautiously, followed on behind. As they entered, they were faced by a row of green cylinders with multiple arms and all sorts of gadgets on each arm. Beyond them were serried ranks of computers, from huge chest-sized servers to little flat tablets, rectangles of metal sitting on desks waiting for their screens to be fired up to come to life. Between the desks were all manner of small robots in every stage of completion, from things that looked like oversized hoovers to others that looked like mini-cars, humanoid designs, or pseudo-animal shapes.

It was a vast laboratory, scattered with every kind of electronic paraphernalia, littered across desks where its users had left it when they'd all been sent home that afternoon ahead of the approaching storm. In the distance beyond, the centre of that vast building was a much more open space, full of larger machines of all sorts of wonderful shapes and kinds, construction robots, security machines, transport and maintenance androids, and the rest.

Ahead of them, Bill Stone had his shotgun raised to his shoulder, pointing at someone's shadow across the building. "Step out with your hands up, or I fire." The lights went off and the Big Top was suddenly darker than the storm outside. Bill cursed and fired off a shot. No reply. He waited for his night vision to come in, then started stalking slowly forwards, turning his torch on for brief seconds to reveal his way, then turning it off again so he could disappear into the dark.

Jimmy and Ben followed him, they thought it was safer to keep close. They didn't dare to use their torches, just relied on the light from his. They sneaked forward, crouching low and trying for silence. At the edge of the laboratory area, creeping round all the desks and paraphernalia, they saw ahead of them the big, open space. Massive machines were scattered through it at intervals, looming up through the darkness ahead of them like ancient monsters frozen in the gloom.

"Keep down," whispered Bill, "He's somewhere behind the central control desk over there, and he may be armed too, for all I know." As he spoke he got up and started out into the darkness. They looked at each other, shrugged, and followed him. When they were ten feet out, arc lights came on above them, pinning them in a pitiless glare, brighter than daylight, destroying their night vision so they could see nothing beyond the ring of light surrounding them.

All three froze momentarily, and Alexander's voice, magnified by a sound system, rang out: "Behind you!" They turned almost involuntarily, and as they did so huge pincers reached out from the darkness and pinned them. Ben almost got away, but turned back to try to help Jimmy, and another set of telescopic arms reached across to block his escape. Bill got off one more shot before a huge metal hand reached down from above and broke his gun in half.

Alexander's voice again: "Did you find Jem?" He could see the answer in their faces. "Good. I never wanted to hurt him, believe me." They didn't. "Since my hopes of a leisurely getaway are now gone, I'll just ask my metal friends to put you in the cooler for the night." His tone changed to the voice he used for commands: "Take them to the printing room."

The three huge robots holding them, massive security prototypes, turned on their wheels and rolled off across the space to a large cuboid structure at the far end. Bill kept shouting commands at them, but they didn't react. Reaching up, they deposited them through a square gap in the roof of the cube, and they dropped ten feet to the floor.

Bill was cursing Alexander in every way he knew how. When the other two eventually got him to calm down, he explained: "Until two months ago, I had higher security clearance than him. Then Alexander got them to upgrade him so he could work on the next stage of development for the security and construction prototypes. That's what he said it was for. It means they obey him when the project managers aren't around."

"Maybe that's why he saw his chance tonight. The facility was evacuated as a precaution, including the guards, just for one night. The remaining security's electronic and cyber, except for me. He'd been getting very close to the head of security lately, he was only meant to be helping her tune in the security to the different robots' voice controls, but he seems to have taken his chance to learn the backdoors in the system. We were pretty lax, and now we've paid."

"Talking of backdoors," said Jimmy, "What about this?" Halfway up one wall there was some sort of maintenance hatch. It had all sorts of warnings on it, but the central section looked as if it could be unscrewed, given time. The people who made it probably hadn't been expecting any of their 3-D printing to try to escape. Unfortunately, the hatch had no fewer than sixteen screws at even intervals round the edge of it, and they didn't have a screwdriver.

They started using their keys and the coins in their pockets to undo the screws one by one, but it was hard work. As they began they could hear the noise of some particularly massive machines moving off, then the lights went out again, and they worked in the dark. The minutes ticked away. There were signs of tomorrow's world all around them yet time seemed to be slowing as it hovered around their little prison, the future in no hurry to become the past.

With three to share the load, they gradually worked their way through. Jimmy whooped as the last screw released. Bill shut him up swiftly. As they crawled out of the cube, they looked up apprehensively at the hulking machines that had imprisoned them, but without a voice to command, the machines stood at rest.

They crept out through the open hangar door, hunched into the wind and the rain and the darkness. The trees gave some shelter, as they slipped through them down to the river, where a side gate opened onto the path to the chapel. Bill knew the way very well, and crept from tree to tree without hesitation. Unable to see where they were going, the others followed him.

They had to use their torches now, just to see a few steps ahead. Once they got out onto the path and turned west along the river, they were walking into the teeth of the storm. Rain drove into their faces, blinding them, and they were practically crawling along. The wind whistled through Traitor's Wood, the trees howling like angry ghosts, spitting rage at those who disturbed their night.

Through the darkness, they could see a glow ahead, where the river bent to the north, and they knew it was coming from the little clearing where the ruins of Sir Thomas's chapel lay scattered. Beautiful it must have been once, but from early times it had had a bad reputation in the village. The legend of Sir Peter's betrayal had not been covered over by Sir Thomas's repentance.

The original almsmen whom that knight had paid to pray for his soul had not been succeeded by others, their cottages had been reclaimed by Traitor's Wood, and the chapel itself had been left to decay. No one wished to worship there. It was a ruin before the Reformation came to England. A ruin it remained, and a very picturesque one, but only parts of the walls remained now, with willows growing through them, and ivy twining round the remnants of stone.

As they turned the corner to the wood, they saw the chapel was lit by the lights built in to the construction robots themselves, focused on a spot at the west end of where the church had been. It had once been a cross-shaped Romanesque structure in Cotswold stone, unusually square, almost the shape of a Greek Cross, with no tower but perfect symmetry.

Instead of a tower it had been built with a small spire of solid stone, said to indicate an ancient pagan burial site beneath. The spire had long since fallen. Now what remained of the walls was being tumbled down by two huge robots. Around the tumbled stone, entire willow trees had been torn away. Truly, the Woodvilles' prototypes were excelling themselves this evening.

Alexander Livingston was sitting in the driver's chair, on the shoulders of the bigger of the two giant construction machines, shouting commands into the howling gale. He must have seen their torches, for he barked a command. Out of the darkness they saw shapes moving, like giant ghosts coming out of the storm to get them.

Ben dived behind a tree, Jimmy stood irresolute behind Bill Stone. Then another bolt of lightning flashed down to the south and by its light they saw two more security-style robots, edging forward to block their passage. These were long-legged, with red radar eyes and four long arms apiece, each arm with different implements attached. In the lightning-punctuated dark, they looked like futuristic reconstructions of ancient, monstrous mailed knights, protecting the chapel's secrets.

"Go wide," snarled Bill, "They can't move in the woods, their tracks aren't that good. And their sensors will be pushing it in this weather. Go round them." He led the way, but at this point Traitor's Wood was overrun with brambles and nettles, so progress was terribly slow. When they got to the edge of the clearing, they saw, in the bright lights focused down by the big construction robots, a huge hole.

It had been dug near the west end of the church, just outside what would have been the entrance. Sir Thomas had not even allowed himself burial in his own chapel. From that hole, the smaller machine was lifting up an ancient yellow skull, and other bones, before Alexander gave it the command and it turfed them out onto what remained of the chapel's stone floor. Then it reached back into the hole, and its scoop came up with Alexander standing in it, cradling some sort of metal casket. He stepped over the bones of the man he had studied for so long as he moved to collect a black rucksack, then turned to the river.

Bill bellowed his rage and set off across the grass, but before he could get there one of the security robots, whirring up behind him, fired off some sort of net and he found himself rolling on the ground, entwined, halfway between the edge of the wood and the ruin of the church. Alexander seemed to be laughing, and he ordered his two massive machines to the water's edge as Jimmy and Ben raced to release their colleague.

The net was weighted and had wrapped itself into tangles. They yanked and twisted and cursed to get it loose. Finally, Bill free, the three of them managed a kind of shambling run through the rain. There they saw a sight that would have been impossible before the storm. Normally, the Amble was such a tiny and shallow and docile stream, it would have been very hard to sail the smallest dinghy down her, but swollen by the storm she had turned into a raging river, for one night.

At the edge of that river, Alexander had an inflatable with a powerful motor, tugging at its moorings, eager to go. The machines' lights were focused on it, giving him something to work by. He laughed as he released the last rope, cradling a metal casket that seemed to gleam in the harsh light, and raised a hand in farewell as they shambled towards him.

Bill Stone made a dive for a trailing rope, reached for it, his right hand close – but too late. He grabbed a rock and threw it after the boat, just a hopeless gesture. Alexander didn't even look back as he sped away down the foaming river. As he rounded the bend, lightning struck the river beyond him, turning its surface silver for a moment. In that blast of light the casket he held suddenly gleamed and they saw him silhouetted, standing tall, looking to the future he was racing towards, without even one last dismissive glance at his past.

The three of them stood there in the rain, wetter than they would ever have thought it possible to be, then turned to begin the slow walk back.

32
WHAT LIES BENEATH

Up the hill, no one knew what was unfolding by the river. For those whose roofs didn't leak and whose internet stayed working, it was a cosily exciting night, and so was the day to follow. The rain continued to hammer down, the wind very slowly lessened, till by the next evening it was just a stiff breeze driving merely heavy rain into the faces of the braver souls of the village, who were just starting to venture out in numbers.

Before that, along with almost the whole of the rest of the country, they had all stayed in and watched the pictures of the worst storm in decades. "Not like 1987, though," as Des reminded people, until the broadcasters announced that it was worse, and he went into a corner and sulked over his beer.

A night and then a day of stormy winds, branches down, trees even, the south of the country was paralysed from Cornwall to Sussex. With such a downpour landing on top of waterways already threatening to flood, rivers burst their banks across the Southwest. In Mutley Shepwell, few saw the extent of the damage at first because almost everyone stayed in.

Their south-facing hillside was exposed to gales from the southwest, and their village took a hammering. Lady Venetia's Union Jack was blown from its flagpole and sent high off to the east. No one ever knew where it landed, except that it was somewhere beyond the bounds of the republic. Roofs lost tiles, sheds lost roofs, and trees came down all over the place. Alicia spent most of the night in her little barn with her beloved sheep; George didn't venture farther than the village shop, except to look in on Mrs Mudgery and her neighbour Norah, who was ninety years old and housebound, to check that they were alright.

On the Friday, it was still a storm, though mostly diminishing, but word started to get around about the events down at the church and the research centre. Police cars were seen in the village – a rare event. As the physical gale wound down, the gale of gossip wound up. The village was discovering that it had slept through the most exciting night in decades.

The last of the storm finally blew out on Saturday morning. That second night had begun with the rain still heavy, the wind still driving hard. Early next morning, very early, for he woke up extremely early these days, George woke to the sound of quiet. He couldn't hear the rain any more, nor any wind.

He looked out of his bedroom window and his bedraggled garden was witnessing the first peeps of sunshine it had seen in days. The storm was well and truly blown out, the last clouds were being ushered off to the east by a lighter breeze, and a very welcome blue was taking over the sky.

As a church warden, George Sneed often woke up worried. After the last two nights, he had good reason: what damage had that storm done? He should go down to St Martin's to take a look. They might have got the money in to fix the roof, but they hadn't been able to arrange the right kind of builders yet, for a medieval roof is not a job that can be given to any old cowboys. They'd had to leave it patched up, and the patches were vulnerable. George had reason to worry.

He had other practical concerns too. Even before the storm, the Amble had been lapping over its banks and into the south side of the churchyard, and it might be up to the church by now. Fortunately, the entrances into the church were all raised a couple of steps. This was difficult for wheelchairs but those medieval builders knew their business and their river. The water had never yet made it into the church itself. The churchyard had become swampy a few times, although never worse than that. But after a deluge like this one?

He needed to go and see. It was a gloomy day, low clouds over the ridge, drizzle gently dropping with a dull, depressing patter. After Morsel's usual routine of pirouetting to her breakfast bowl, and a rather more sedate repast for himself, it was still grey half-light as he stepped out of the house. No one was about. He got his old Renault moving, wondering if it really did grumble more than it used to when he started it up, and if he should get one of these new-fangled self-driving things.

He took it down the hill, taking the bends between the copses very cautiously. Some pines and birch had come down further up the hill, and one oak, he noticed, across a field to the west, together with a lot of branches. He had to steer carefully around a couple of large ones that had fallen partly into the road, but nothing actually blocked it. He crawled cautiously down the hill, through Beggar's Copse and then between Tansey Wood and The Ride, with its avenues of oaks mostly still standing tall, less one that leaned against its neighbours at a drunken angle, and another that was completely down.

He came round the last corner at the bottom end of Tansey Wood and looked down across a couple of bedraggled fields to St Martin's and its churchyard. Except that today, instead of a churchyard, he saw a grey lake, with the tops of the larger tombstones gloomily protruding above the surface. The Amble had risen with a speed he would not have believed, and the whole of the churchyard was a sheet of grey water, and the fields either side of it too.

The top of the arch of the old stone bridge broke the surface of the waters, but the road approaching it on both sides was well and truly a highway for fishes. And in the middle of that lake, St Martin's seemed almost to float on the water, St Martin's-in-the-lake, not St Martin's-in-the-meadow. In fact, just for a moment, as he looked through his fogged up windows, through the early morning mist and the half-light, he could have sworn that the church seemed to be floating away, down the river, leaving its moorings after a thousand years.

George got out of the car, wiped his glasses clear and looked again. In that grey-half-light, with the drizzle blurring his spectacles, this time the flow of the Amble made it look almost as if St Martin's was gently but stubbornly nosing its way westwards, against the stream. George just stood and stared, with shock being succeeded by sadness for the good ship St Martin's, buffeted once again as it tried to forge its own way forward; and finally a certain pride, with the reflection that their church had withstood much from the hand of nature and the hand of man down the years, and it would see out this flood as well.

George's problems were large, but straightforward enough. For the police, on the other hand, the complications were just beginning. It was certainly the oddest kind of attempted murder they'd ever heard of. With all the other pressing matters demanding their attention, fallen trees blocking roads, houses rendered unsafe, verges, roads and even railway lines washed away or ruined, it was hard to spare resources for an investigation when the victim was recovering quite nicely and no one had any idea what had actually been stolen.

The Woodvilles were kicking up a terrible fuss about all the damage to their research centre, but it was their own management who had employed Alexander Livingston as a consultant, then upgraded his role and security clearance to the point where he could take over their empty facility in the window of opportunity presented by the storm. It was hard to see whom else they could blame, although that didn't stop them pushing very hard for compensation.

Then there was the curious role of Bill Stone. At first he insisted he'd just had a feeling Alexander was up to something and had been trying to track Jem down purely with a wish to help. That story seemed unlikely from the start. Once the police got to searching Alexander's house, they discovered that he had recently been in partnership with Johnny Berensford.

It turned out that the two of them had together paid for several very detailed searches, with the latest in ground-penetrating scanners, on that very area in the Wash where King John's royal treasure had disappeared, all those years ago. In fact, Alexander's share of the bills remained unpaid, as the bailiffs explained when they arrived to disturb the police. Quite a lot of other bills also turned out to be unpaid. It seemed that Alexander had been splashing out rather lavishly in the expectation of his hoped for future television riches, without waiting to see the ink dry on the contract first.

It turned out that the person Johnny Berensford and Alexander Livingston found to help them in this matter was none other than Bill Stone. When he was quizzed about this, his answer was "So what? We looked where it should have been, eight hundred years ago, we found nothing. So what? Eight hundred years is a long time, mud moves, the tides don't stop. So what?"

Bill admitted that Johnny and Alexander must have joined The Guy Fawkes Club in the hope of finding clues to King John's treasure, but he still insisted that he himself had been an innocent partner, until the police tracked down a record of how much he'd owed Johnny Berensford since his last business went bankrupt. Bill Stone crumpled then. They saw tears falling, and things began to tumble out.

It took a lot of patient questioning. Gradually they heard his story: he said he'd had no choice, his debts meant Johnny could have taken his farmhouse and the last bits of land he had left from the farm his family had farmed for so long. He swore he would never have hurt anyone, that was just Alexander. Johnny had thought Alexander might double cross them and try to run off with King John's loot, so he'd ordered Bill to keep an eye on him. Bill didn't trust either of them. He insisted he was different, and keen to help the police with their enquiries

The officers of the law found that Alexander's researches into Sir Thomas de Thurslay had gone to the extent of finding out that Sir Thomas had hired wagons from a Lincolnshire monastery in precisely the month that the king's treasure was lost. It had taken Alexander years to trace the monastery's broken rolls of accounts through the stately homes and museums and Cambridge colleges to which they'd been dispersed in the 1500s, when the monastery was dissolved. Finally he'd tracked down that one vital item, on the back of a reused piece of vellum, half rubbed away to make way for later accounts. Bill said he knew nothing of that.

Johnny Berensford was also in denial. In his case it was rather angrier. He was insulted, he said, that anyone might think he'd had anything to do with something so shady. He was an honest brewer, and his lawyers would have something to say to anyone who suggested otherwise. Treasure hunting was not a crime. He was still loudly proclaiming his innocence when the police received a cache of files from an anonymous donor, who signed him or herself off as "A defender of mankind."

Most of the files were audiofiles of meetings between Johnny Berensford, Bill Stone and Alexander Livingston, so it wasn't hard to guess who'd sent them, even before someone noticed that the name Alexander means "Defender of man." The meetings had gone into great detail about their pursuit of King John's lost treasure, much more than Bill had admitted to. They'd paid for a survey of the spot where it vanished, using the most cutting edge equipment to probe further down into the silt of the Wash than anyone had ever done before, under the pretext of looking for archaeological remains.

All Alexander's many years of research had added up. He had tracked down the receipt for the wagons Sir Thomas had hired. Most importantly, he had used all the latest LIDAR and RADR data to reconstruct a plausible route the guards and wagons could have taken that fated day in October 1216. It seemed to have taken him years, working his way back through centuries of maps to try to understand where the salt creeks and the marshes and the rivers would most likely have been in those days. Without the radar and scanner data it would have been impossible, and even with it he'd needed endless study to work out the maps of the past from the data of the twenty-first century.

After all of this painstaking research, it was almost understandable that Alexander had felt his years of work deserved to land him some serious treasure. Instead, he had escaped with just one casket. Bill and Johnny had ended up stealing nothing, whatever they may have intended.

Whatever was in that casket, it could not have been more than a fraction of what King John lost in the Wash. The audio files mentioned copies of letters Alexander had found in France, in which Sir Thomas de Thurslay promised his children that if they returned they would be "provided for" on a princely scale. Those letters never said how, and the "defender of mankind" made no mention of what was in the casket.

Everyone was puzzled, except for Richard Tranctard. He laughed, and pointed out that the two tombs next to the church referenced only a fraction of the story of the Book of Revelation. "He needed to look for the rest of the story," said The Old Tank, with a certain satisfaction. "I told him he ought to study the Book of Revelation but he never did."

The police were not entirely convinced by this line of reasoning. They did, however, start to cheer up now that they had at least a couple of suspects under their gaze. They got a lot more cheerful when they started investigating Johnny Berensford's tax affairs. After a short investigation of those, they sent a car to bring Johnny in.

33
SMALL EARTHQUAKE
IN MIDDLE ENGLAND

Jem's first words when he woke up after his near-death experience were to ask for the Liverpool scores. It was the business end of the season, after all, and there were some very important games happening.

"We love you too," said his mum. "It's all okay, the police are dealing with it, we just want you to rest, darling."

He stared at her, and his next thought was for Becky. When reassured about her, he got round to asking, "What happened to Alexander Livingston?"

His dad patted him on the shoulder. "Good to see you haven't lost your curiosity then. He's gone, got clear away, with the help of some of the robots at that miserable research centre." Jem did get curious, then, and wanted the full story of the rest of that momentous night. His father started in on it, but his mother insisted on rest.

His dad obediently abbreviated the story, ending: "Of course, Alexander might have addled your brains a bit with that bash to the head, but they were pretty addled anyway, weren't they?" His wife swiped him playfully, and kissed her son. Jem felt a pressing need to think, so he shut his eyes to keep his parents out, and then the morphine and the sleep came up to drag him down again.

Over the weeks that followed, his family were glued to his bedside, and plenty of friends came to visit, most often Jimmy and Becky. With Jimmy, of course, the conversation was mostly about Liverpool. Usually they argued about the team, the manager, the results, the referees, and the unfairness of the footballing gods.

At this moment, however, Jem was obsessed with a strange idea. He wanted to persuade their club to build a unique memorial by populating its newly finished stadium with 96 metal statues of fans, statues like those at Crosby beach: fans forever walking in; fans always watching from the steel rafters above the seats; fans seated atop the players' tunnel, with a foot hanging down that the home team could touch for luck as they came out; fans looking down above the players' entrance, so the players would have to pass beneath their feet; fans walking up a long steel staircase into the sky from the highest point of the stadium.

Jem's view was, "It's class, see, it's class. Wouldn't get that at United, or City, or Otherton."

Jimmy thought this mad vision was probably due to the blow to the head, but he felt it his duty to argue with Jem about it, because he felt the best way he could support Jem was by arguing with him. That was how their friendship worked.

To help the argument go better, Jimmy suggested putting the statues of four angels on top of the stands, Liverpool angels, with a fifth, even larger, to welcome away fans with a drawn sword, in front of the gates. To his horror, Jem actually liked this suggestion, and didn't even argue about it. Jimmy shrugged and said to himself, "Jem likes his little dreams. Jem needs his little dreams."

When not talking about their shared faith in Liverpool, Jimmy was full of business ideas: "Mate, it's perfect. Soon as you're better, we'll start the Mutley Shepwell Murder Trail. You can show 'em round. We'll call you Dead and Alive, the buried guide. How often do you get shown round a murder scene by the victim? D'you think they'd let the punters have a turn each in old Sir Thomas's tomb for an extra fiver? Or could we put a skeleton in it, as part of the show?"

Jem thought probably not. Becky thought Jimmy's bedside manner needed a bit of work. They both thought that "Murder Trail" was a bit exaggerated in the absence of a successful murder, but Jimmy told them, "That's marketing for you. Sell, sell, sell."

Everyone else was enjoying the last days of the republic. The great storm over, Spring had finally sprung, and the gentle sunshine, the new growth everywhere, the daffodils and crocuses and wild flowers, all helped Mutley Shepwell to look its best at that point in the year. A minority were interested in the election, but for many that was just the prelude to the completely unique, once only, ever, Loyal Republic's Fete & Show, as it had finally been named. The planning was intense and controversial. Different attractions vied for centre stage. They had to plan in the great signing ceremony signalling the end of the republic as well.

Mike and Jane got roped in to all sorts of things, mainly because they couldn't say no. George was still buried in the depths of the manor most days, finishing off tax arrangements no one else really understood. He had to continue to leave Morsel with Alicia quite a bit, even though the Sailor situation was getting very difficult. When he came back to find Morsel hiding under the sofa, with Sailor glowering down, he felt things had gone too far. The previous evening Moira, with a side glance at Alicia, had politely informed him that, with all her work for the fete and show, she regretted that she wouldn't have time to look after Morsel any more.

George was wondering what could be done for the little lady, who required the gentlest of care. Fortunately, Alicia was ready with an answer: "Mary was here earlier, and saw how these two are. She offered to have Morsel to stay down there when you're away. Their cat, Hadrian, is a lot more polite with dogs."

Which was how George came to be trundling back and forth across the churchyard quite often that Spring, across a sea of mud to start with, which gradually turned into a sea of wildflowers. Somehow the inundation had given new fertility to the ground. It also made a wonderful excuse for the churchyard mowing crew to give it a break till this wonderful display of floral colour had run its course.

The mowing crew had previously called themselves The Mutley Rollers, in honour of the ride-on lawnmower that was their pride and joy. In the village's days of fame they had promoted themselves to being The Knights of the Lawnmower, and were now changing their name again, either to The Mutley Rollers AKA, or After the Flood. There must have been a couple of frustrated gents in there who'd really wanted to be in a band.

The Vicarage had seen a strange transformation since Mary moved in. When the Old Tank lived there alone, it had hosted a strange conglomeration of his parents' and grandparents' furniture, alongside assorted mementoes and curios of a life lived in many places, together with carpets, curtains and walls in varying states of genteel decay.

When she agreed to marry him she teasingly suggested it would be best to throw out the lot and to redecorate the whole house. She had the money to do it, after all. They debated decoration and furniture room by room, with good humour but much determination. She got her way with the living room, in patterns that he called 'floral' and she called 'practically abstract.' He got to keep the dining room as it was, old uncomfortable mahogany chairs, oak cabinets, completely redundant panelling on the walls, and all.

Initially he refused to change his gloomy bedroom, so she threatened to move into the main guest room next door and told him he could visit her room, but she wouldn't be visiting his. He gave way and kept his old bedroom as his dressing room and den. The front hall ended in a compromise with her decoration and his furniture, the kitchen was her domain, the spare bedrooms his, the paintings a bizarre mix of his and hers, intermingled with the photographs of two separate lifetimes, juxtaposed with artistic care. All in all, it could leave visitors feeling slightly shell-shocked, but George had got used to it.

Richard Tranctard answered the door, but there was no sign of Mary, with whom George had made the arrangement. The Old Tank grinned, "Can't talk to her now, she and two of her oldest friends are sharing stories. – When will they be finished? About next Tuesday, if past form is any guide."

George agreed to leave Morsel in his care instead, and deposited her in the kitchen. She looked doleful but not as frightened as when left with Sailor. She looked up at Hadrian and wagged her tail politely at him. He responded with a magnanimous wave of the paw. This was a feline who exuded an air of immensely self-satisfied benevolence. He might patronise a dog, but he'd never lift a claw against one. Mary used to sum up Hadrian's philosophy of life as "If Jesus was on earth today, I'd be his cat."

Mary Tranctard was pretty heavily involved in the fete and show herself. Soon after her marriage, she'd joined the Horticultural Society and soon became so enthusiastic that her husband felt the need to warn her, "You're going native." Spurred into action by that remark, she immediately offered to fill the Horticultural Society's vacancy for secretary, a position they'd been trying in vain to fill for months. Soon afterwards, for the first time, she overheard herself being referred as "a villager" for the first time. She never looked back.

She was more often at Moira's side than her husband's now. Not that she and Richard weren't getting on, when they were together, there were even moments when they were almost complimentary. She still had plenty of her husband's follies to regale her friends with, but some days she even verged on the positive. For his part, he grinned more than he used to, and exuded an air of quiet content, while still doing his best to get a rise from his wife. Sometimes, she still rose like a well-trained trout, but not so often as she used to, and her formerly acerbic commentaries on life were becoming noticeably more mellow.

Moira herself was a blur of movement. She viewed the combined fete and village show as the grand finale of their days as an independent country, and she was determined to make it the perfect ending. She was also working hard to extend the reach of UniLocal Radio, working with Jimmy and others on the Universal Holiday Exchange, with the Tranctards and the Singers on the Infinite Arts Exchange. In the midst of such grand ambitions, Jem and his little injury, and the strange events in Traitor's Wood, had all flowed rather fast into the backwaters of people's memories, while the main streams of village life raced past with great enthusiasm.

The police came to question Jem but found he didn't have much to tell, and was pretty uncommunicative. When Becky came to question him, on the other hand, he revived remarkably, and found all sorts of things to say. When he ran out of facts, he embarked on speculations, when he ran out of speculations he asked about every aspect of her current activities.

She and Ben had emerged as the leading lights of his and Jimmy's business; with Jem out of action and Jimmy off in London half the time enjoying his sudden celebrity – Petra had decided she didn't mind being seen with him if the press were there – Becky and Ben had suddenly, to everyone's surprise, been promoted to management.

They'd persuaded their parents to let them defer the rest of their last year at university, so they could actually manage a business between them for a while, which Mike and Jane had to admit was good experience, even though it meant their parents worrying greatly and being told off by their twins for hovering over them whenever decisions had to be made. Not that Mike and Jane had that much time left, because they'd got roped into the committee organizing the Fete & Show. It's not often you get the Foreign Secretary coming to open your village fete and the Deputy Leader of the Opposition closing it, not to mention the Lord Lieutenant of the county and a minor royal, representing the King, giving out the prizes. The rest of the country might have been mad about the election, but the village was gripped by fete and show fever.

Moira was in her element, organizing away. The biggest challenge came when she asked Mick if the metal bashers could make a stage – they were going for a medieval theme, with the best in show being crowned, a children's parade of princesses and knights, and a hog, sheep and cow roast, on giant spits.

She told him all these plans with the enormous enthusiasm that had propelled the school forward all those years. He looked at her, put down his hacksaw, took off his goggles, and said, "No. Customers. Busy." Then he walked off into his inner sanctum, the store room at the back of the shop. Not only was he a man of few words, he hated arguments and retreated to his den whenever faced with the possibility of one.

Moira turned to Sally, but she was highly resistant, protective of her man, full of lists of customers waiting and deadlines approaching. The whole medieval theme for the fete was in jeopardy: Mick's team were the only people who could deliver it. Moira had to turn to her last resort: she invited Sally round for afternoon tea.

Four days later, Sally found herself cornered in Moira's summer house behind a table beautifully laid, with Alicia's famous Bakewell tarts, Mary Tranctard's grandmother's own recipe Ginger sponge, Jane Singer's Christmas special apricot flapjack, and Moira's own handmade shortbread, with all their owners pressing these creations on her enthusiastically. Not only that, Lady Venetia arrived with Cook's famous Victoria Sponge, adorned with strawberries from her own garden. Family pride prompted her to feel that if the manor was to be the host of this great occasion, the thing should be done with all fit splendour.

Her arrival was the last nail in the coffin of Sally's resistance. Surrounded by such pressing charm and urgent appeal, she crumbled, and found herself saying the fatal words, "I'll see what I can do. I can usually get round him somehow."

Her hostesses sipped their tea with a new satisfaction,

and got on to the details of planning this great medieval event, and how all that metalwork would be put to good use. The one thing Moira and her inner cabinet were silent on was the grand finale. It was a village tradition that the grand finale of each fete should be a surprise. Each year the participants were sworn to secrecy, and this year the only thing the committee would say was that it would be bigger and better than ever.

Two of that fete committee were rather preoccupied with a matter of their own that both of them thought a great deal about, but neither knew how to talk about. George and Alicia found ever more excuses to see each other, yet when they did the conversation kept circling round the same old topics. They met on republic and fete business, but their time alone seemed far too limited.

Alicia decided that to help them have the time for more extended conversations, she needed to be able to have Morsel to stay again, but Sailor's feline terrorism was a stumbling block. Morsel had been traumatised by him and by the great storm, to the point where George felt it necessary to investigate dog therapy techniques. Morsel wasn't objecting, as dog treats were involved. The Tranctards, however, had no time for such coddling of pets, and, benign cat though Hadrian was, his feline benevolence reached only to extending a paw from on high in benediction. George began to worry about Morsel spending so much time at such an unsympathetic vicarage.

Alicia was also sure Morsel needed more tender care, and sure that she could provide it, but felt duty-bound to be loyal to Sailor. The answer came when she heard Bill Stone lamenting that Stephanos was having a problem with mice and rats in the new religious commune he was trying to set up at the west end of the industrial estate. Some of the buildings were in such a decayed state that rodents were a major problem. Sailor was known as the best mouser in the village. Alicia pricked up her ears and offered Sailor on loan.

She didn't expect it to last, as cats don't usually like a change of territory. Sailor, however, was soon tucking in to the feast with such gusto that he didn't seem to pine for his old home at all. Alicia was less upset than she thought she would be; Sailor had been her ex-partner's cat first of all, and had been dumped on her along with a raft of bad memories. Besides, in his absence, she was free to make her house Morsel's second home, with George busy so much of the time at the manor.

George enthusiastically accepted Alicia's offer of additional dog-sitting help, which came with a great deal of conversation attached, and a number of offers to stay for lunch or supper, all gratefully received. He felt he should ask if he could take Alicia, and Morsel, out to lunch at *The Dumbrell's Dimbrell*, as a way of saying thank you. He didn't know how much Alicia would dress up for a simple lunch, but was duly impressed when she did, so impressed that she found herself waiting in the car as he popped back home to fetch a tie.

By the time coffee arrived, his hand was hovering just above the salt cellar, wondering if it dared to stretch past the pepperpot, and meet hers. Then Morsel made a grab for a sausage the little boy at the next table had dropped, and the moment was gone. There were plenty of other moments, yet, amid all these opportunities, George's tongue remained tied, and Alicia was too traditional to step up and speak first. However much time they shared, the words they heard in their hearts would not be spoken aloud.

Elsewhere in what remained of Great Britain, the general election was brewing up nicely. The new parties for the regions were looking to make their best showing yet in terms of the popular vote, while still in danger of getting about two seats between them in the House of Commons because of the cruelties of first past the post.

The Northern League and the Western Alliance were the most confident, but even they were worried, while the other members of the Alliance of the Regions were positively despondent. With the vote so split there was a real danger of the established parties taking over their accustomed seats in the commons, and business remaining as usual at Westminster, even though vast swathes of the country were voting for alternative parties. All sorts of ideas for new kinds of relationships with Europe floated in the debate, new sorts of links between regions that could bypass London entirely.

The Tories were looking positively smug. On the government side, the prime minister was trying to make up for the loss of Scottish support by laying the groundwork for a coalition, meaning that he had to be terribly nice to all the rest of the parties, making it an exceedingly dull election, except for the bashing of Tories and the Tories battering back. The new parties were trying hard to liven things up, but their local roars were reduced to squeaks in the media coverage.

Back in the village, people were finally beginning to talk about the old country's election. What had once been a two-way fight had now become at least four-way, and in some areas five or six parties were in with a realistic chance. "All adds to the fun, eh?" said the landlord, one evening at *The Old Bells*. He was running a kind of sweepstake on how many seats the different parties would get. After all, the loyal republic would be rejoining the old country shortly.

Meanwhile, in a small cell in London, Johnny Berensford was singing a new tune. The thought of being put into such accommodation on a permanent basis, far from his own alcoholic creations, had had a magical effect on him. His cell was clean and neat, but it was small, and the food far inferior to what he was used to, not to mention the company. The rooms he was questioned in were positively unfriendly.

He missed his farmhouse, he missed his beer, he missed his partner, he missed Chatsworth the cat, most of all. He even missed his friends in the village more than he thought he would.

As he sat under those harsh lights, his stock phrase, "Look, I'm just a brewer," rang more and more hollow, and the patient faces and voices taking turns to sit across from him kept coming and coming with more and more questions, till, one day, something broke, and Johnny started talking to his lawyer about a deal. In return for a reduced sentence for his tax and other offences, he might be prepared to spill the beans on an altogether greater crime.

Once Johnny Berensford started to negotiate, his custodians became more lenient about visits. They were amused to discover that the visitor he wanted most was his cat. Chatsworth was not amused to be summoned from her home, but was given no choice. Johnny's partner arrived at the prison carrying the love of his life, snarling in her basket.

The guards searched Johnny's partner and the cat's basket but gave only a perfunctory inspection to the flowery elaborate collar Chatsworth was wearing. They might have given it more attention had they known that Johnny would never have allowed such a flamboyant excrescence anywhere near Chatsworth's neck when they were at home, though he didn't seem to mind it here. Had they reflected on just how small computer chips are these days, they might have looked a good deal closer.

34
THE FATES AND THE FETE

It was the day of the Loyal Republic's Fete and Show. The manor's fine lawns were lined with more stalls than had ever been seen in the village. All sorts of outside companies had been willing to pay handsomely to be present. Village organizations, of course, paid but a peppercorn rent for their stalls.

The St John's Ambulance occupied one corner, the Scouts and Guides sold burgers and confectionery in another. St Martin's ran a Pimms, strawberries and ice cream café. The church of Charles, King and Martyr offered mindfulness coaching and health food at its stall. The Brownies sold brownies, the Cubs ran the bouncy castle, with a little grown up help. Overton Kingsby's finest DJ was playing easy listening tunes in the background. The smells from the various spit roasts were starting to permeate the air, except in the rose garden where the various gardening stall-holders were selling all sorts of plants.

Jimmy was going round with Becky. Petra had decided that his days of fame were done, and ditched him for an aspiring rock singer called Byron Dashforth-Shelley, whose band, Nirvana's Gadflies, had flirted with the edges of the charts several times lately, and whose live shows had an enthusiastic following of fashionistas. His father was an earl, which may have helped. At least, inviting her to the family stately home didn't seem to have damaged his chances with her, although it may have worsened the chances of his father taking him to their friends' shoots that winter.

"Asked her out yet?" said Jem. "She won't have me, might as well have you." He said it with bitterness, but under control.

"Nope."

"Going to?"

"Never do that to you, mate. I'm just helping her keep away from anyone else till she wakes up to yer shining virtues. Now clear off and take yer personal raincloud with you."

Jem tried to say thank you, but in the end just punched Jimmy on the arm, and said: "Make sure you give up on Petra before you collect your pension." Then he went off to the Historical Society stall. He relieved Des Martin, who ambled off to the Scout tent for a drink.

Jem finished his stint on duty in time for the grand finale that had been so much whispered about. Speculation had been rife for weeks. The committee had proved entirely leak-proof, unusually so. Jem's curiosity had got the better of his misery and he was prepared to return to the company of his fellow human beings, cruel though that could be, in order to see the show. First, however, he had to sit through the remainder of the prize giving. It wasn't often, or indeed ever, that they'd had royalty giving out the prizes, rather minor royalty though it was.

"How many cousins do they have?" sniffed Elsie to Mrs Mudgery behind him. Fortunately Mrs Mudgery's loyalty to the royal family overcame her disdain for their hangers-on, and she remained, for once, silent.

Everyone was waiting for the big moment, everyone except the manor's owner himself, who had been due back from central Asia that morning, but had found himself unavoidably detained at the last minute. The only other absentee was George Sneed, who had unaccountably failed to turn up, with the flimsiest of excuses, and was missing the village's great celebration.

The prizegiving featured rewards for all ages and stages. The newest and most curious prize was the Bishop Johnson Recycling Prize for Children. It was a gold-plated mobile phone on a plinth, donated by Mary Tranctard in memory of her father. The Old Tank could have claimed to have donated it too, since it was his old phone, which he'd put through the wash.

Mary had taken it off him with glee, pointing out compassionately that anyone still walking around without a waterproof phone in this day and age deserved to have that happen to them. She'd then had the prize made and enjoyed seeing the Lord Lieutenant present it to Unicorn class from the Village Primary School, for making an entire replica classroom out of cardboard boxes and fast food packaging. It had been optimistically intended as a prototype classroom for production in hotter, drier climes. Unfortunately the winter rain had reduced it to sludge before UNICEF could visit, so its potential for the hotter parts of the world remained unexplored.

At last the final prize was being bestowed, the Headmaster Fisher Prize for the Best Trained and Disciplined Garden in the Village. Moira herself had been wont to win this on a regular basis until the committee introduced a rule that no one could win any prize more than five times in total, forcing the gardening elite to vary their events and branch out into flowers and vegetables new. Bottoms shuffled on plastic seats as the assembled audience anticipated the final unveiling of the biggest and best-ever grand finale. Moira stepped up to the microphone, flanked by the Foreign Secretary and the Deputy Leader of the Opposition.

As she did so, there was a series of loud bangs on the other side of the manor house, hidden from their view. Everyone turned to look. Two helicopters appeared above the house. Men in black started to abseil down, onto the roof and onto the lawn this side of the big house.

"Best fete ever!" shouted Ben.

"What a grand finale!" shouted Jimmy back.

"Where did they get helicopters from?" asked Bob Corns.

"Better not have blown all our money on their little exhibition," declared Mrs Mudgery.

More bangs were heard from beyond the house, closer now, and louder, very loud. The helicopter engines and the bangs, together, rose to a deafening crescendo. This began to seem like an unscripted part of the show. Faces looked at each other as a terrible doubt dawned.

Then one of the Borises appeared at an upper window, holding what looked like a gun. He pointed it, there was yet more noise, two of the men in black went limp, others raised metal objects of their own, also looking suspiciously like weapons. The Boris at the window jerked convulsively and fell forward, bouncing off the wall of the house onto the flowerbed. The people nearest the house suddenly felt a pressing need to move back. Shouts, squeals and screams filled the air, almost drowning out the gunfire as another Boris reeled back from another window.

Most of the crowd were scattering, ducking behind shelter, or heading for the exits. While the lesser spotted villagers beat a retreat, however, a few hardy souls were enjoying the spectacle. The landlord still held his pint, leaning on the bar of the drinks stall, Des at his side. The Old Tank also refused to be separated from his beer and his plate of pie and chips, for all Mary's attempts to get him to be sensible. She asked, in exasperation, how he'd ever managed not to die young. Ben and Jimmy were edging round the podium to get a better view.

Half the men in black had hit the ground now, and were running very fast into the house, firing as they went. Others swung in through the big, leaded windows, with a mighty smash.

All around them was screaming and confusion. The dignitaries on the podium had been unceremoniously thrown down by their own bodyguards, half the throng were trying to run away, others hiding behind any shelter, however flimsy. At this very moment, the parade arrived: six knights on white horses, wearing Lord Bonifer's coat of arms on their shields, leading a wagon carrying a scale model of the village towards the podium where it was meant to be received by Sally Smith, dressed up as Britannia, as a symbolic representation of the return of the village to the United Kingdom.

Instead, the horses reared or bolted, the wagon was overturned, Britannia was nearly shot by the Foreign Secretary's bodyguard as she hove into view brandishing a trident. There were a last few seconds of screaming and confusion. Then a black-clad officer announced over a loudspeaker that the manor was secure and the danger over. He even apologised on behalf of His Majesty's Government for the confusion.

"No manners, some people," said Mrs Mudgery to Elsie, angrily. She'd helped to clean that house in days gone by, so she took it personally when she saw it being messed up.

Others were wondering about the house's owner. "He's not goin' to like that, worra mess," observed Des sagely.

"I don't think he'll have a lot of choice," replied the landlord. "Maybe he won't be coming back, after all."

George's daughter Elizabeth had grabbed her children to her and ducked behind the podium, but her daughters were more phlegmatic, and peered through round the corner to get a view. "Dat man is bwokened," said Alice to her Mummy, pointing to one of the soldiers who fell.

"A little bit brokened, darling," replied her mother, "Just a little bit."

As everybody gathered themselves together, some headed straight home. Others remained in sight of the manor's doors, all of which were now guarded by the men in black. There was a great deal of discussion of this unprecedented end to the fete. As the analysis went on, a third helicopter hove into view and descended very noisily onto the lawn.

From it stepped several senior-looking army officers in smart uniforms and someone who looked very familiar. It was George Sneed, himself, in person, walking into the manor alongside some soldiers carrying what looked like explosives. The village commentators moved into over-drive when they saw that.

Mick was alarmed to find that the Foreign Secretary's bodyguard actually had shot his wife, in her role as Britannia, but the shield and the breastplate between them slowed and deflected the bullet, and it just grazed her ribs. She was hospitalised and shocked, but soon recovered. After he had recovered from his own shock, her husband was so proud of his own metalwork that he hung up that shield and breastplate ever after in the sales room next to the workshop, and delighted in showing them to prospective customers as evidence of the quality of workmanship Mick's Metal Bashers produced.

The explosions in the village, however, were as nothing to the cascade of uproar that rippled out across the country as the media discovered what the men in black had found. It turned out that George Sneed's long, anguished night of doubt had resulted in him deciding to keep some of his old friends in the revenue secretly apprised of the dealings with the Russian. They in turn had informed contacts in the security services, and waited their moment. All the vital documents and computer files were kept in a single strongroom, deep down beneath the basement of the manor.

The security services had been waiting for Mr Pronotkov's return from business abroad. They wanted to capture both him and the evidence when they swooped, and have the whole business completed before the village's great day out. Instead Mr Pronotkov unexpectedly decided not to return, and George discovered that the crucial evidence was about to be spirited away by Nikolai Marisovitch. Perhaps Mr Pronotkov had discerned that he was being investigated. George sent out an emergency call: they needed the men in black immediately if the evidence was not to be destroyed.

Hence the rather unusual timing of the raid, which indeed found a treasure trove of records of Mr Pronotkov's careful dispersal of his riches into the rivers and the streams of political funding. What it did not find was evidence incriminating the Woodvilles. They had kept all of that at their own place, and somehow stalled the raid descending on their own manor until all vital evidence was gone. The Woodvilles had got clear away but Mr Pronotkov's part of the story was there to be read.

At this point the even-handedness of Mr Pronotkov's blessing of the main parties became their curse. In the days remaining before the election, the police were able to unfold enough of the scheme to pour mud over key financial sections of the major parties, and the lightning speed of modern media took the story round the world, just in time for the election. The major parties might protest, legitimately, that hardly anyone had known of these goings on, but they were holed below the waterline nonetheless. Those in charge of their finances had to resign in the last days before the election, while the evidence was displayed in front of the cameras.

The party leaders might protest their innocence and, in the end, be exonerated, but the mud stuck to their rosettes too, by association. They were part of the same organizations so, even if personally innocent, part of a system that was guilty. It may be that only a handful of people in either party had known of the scheme, nevertheless their leaders were held responsible in the court of public opinion. The media had a field day reporting all this, which turned the election, for them, from exceptionally dull into enormously fun.

The winners were the regional parties, who had not been important enough to receive the Russian's largesse. Instead of looking at winning just a seat or two, the new parties found themselves riding the biggest wave they'd ever seen. Their opponents' numbers collapsed in front of them. Even if most who left the old parties were not interested in the new, the shocked and the stay-at-home made all the difference to the voting on the big day.

The Friday after election day Britain woke up to the most mixed, muddled, multi-faceted representation in Parliament it had ever had. After all those years mocking curious continentals for their coalitions and the time it took to manufacture them, Britain's rulers found themselves with a coalition jigsaw of unparalleled complexity. There were multiple different outcomes possible, everyone needed to negotiate with everyone else. Leaders of regional parties who'd thought they would be lucky to gain a single seat suddenly found themselves kingmakers. The landscape had been transformed.

Back in Mutley Shepwell, Bob Corns raised a glass to his fellow members of The Guy Fawkes Club. "Who'd have known what we'd have started?" he mused. "We may have used a different kind of gunpowder, but we sure put a bomb under parliament."

Only one Mutley Shepwellian was not pleased. The news of the raid on the manor was music to many, but poison in Johnny Berensford's ears. The secrets he had been prepared to spill had been revealed already, in far greater detail than he could ever have supplied. His bargaining card was gone. He became at most a supporting witness.

A few days after the election, Johnny was offered a deal by the police, but it wasn't the deal he wanted. He stalled for time. He haggled for more visits from his cat, with it always wearing that flamboyant floral collar. The prison officers were getting more and more relaxed with Chatsworth, and with him. He kept negotiating and the wheels seemed slowly to be turning. Until the day the wheels suddenly stopped turning, when Johnny Berensford vanished.

35
REGRETS AND NEGOTIATIONS

"We've done our part," said Moira. "Isn't that right, George?"

George still hadn't got over the shock of finding that Alexander Livingston had been ready to kill. Come to that, treasure clues in the crypt had been a bit of a surprise too, even if the treasure itself remained elusive. Whatever had been taken away in that small casket, it could only have been a fraction of what King John lost.

Richard Tranctard had smiled when he heard about the little casket and reminded them all that the four horsemen were only the beginning of the biblical apocalypse. He pointed out that the full story included seven seals, seven trumpets, seven angels, seven golden bowls, and asked them why Alexander would ever have thought that the four horsemen could be anything other than the start of the story. A fraction of the story, a fraction of the treasure, was his view..

"Cheer up, George," said Bob Corns. "We need you and Mary on good form to keep her cousin Prenderby on our side if we ever get our hands on that gold. We'll need a free lawyer. The Crown seem to think it's theirs, if found, but it's got to be ours, right?"

"Might as well be in the Wash if we don't get it," said Richard Tranctard, rather uncharitably for a clergyman. "Mary, what about that cousin of yours, have you persuaded him to waive his fees?"

"Giles Prenderby? You'd have more luck asking a crocodile to lend you its teeth."

"A true lawyer, then. We may be needing you, George."

"Don't put all that on 'im," protested Des, "It was you who had the big coronation protest, isn't exactly going to leave Buck House in a good mood with us, is it?"

Richard Tranctard waved a dismissive hand. "You think they'd hand over King John's treasure, if we ever find it, whatever I might have said? You have another think coming, my friend. Anyway, I simply pointed out what piffle the new coronation service is. Someone had to say it, and we weren't part of our new king's dominions at the time, so I could."

"Not any more," said his wife. "Now, when outraged archdeacons come after you, don't look to me for help. Your own silly fault."

"I don't know, dear," Richard replied. "I was thinking of forming a Church of England resistance movement. We could throw flour towards the powers that be when they get too politically correct, while making sure to miss. Wouldn't want to actually get them messy, poor things. I thought you'd be a rather good terrorist-in-chief."

"Only at home, my sweet, you're the only person who deserves terrorizing round here." She said it with surprising softness, knowing how shocked he had been to discover the web of the Russian's deception that had lain beneath their loyal republic. He had been driven to unusual cynicism ever since. She took him aside: "Come along, my old dinosaur, let's take you home."

"Still want to go home with a mug who doesn't even know when his own conspiracy turns properly criminal?" Richard Tranctard may have preached forgiveness in his church, but he found it hard to forgive himself for starting a plot that had ended up with the Russian subverting British democracy.

The Old Tank might have wished the major parties to fall, but not like this, and not with his own hand helping corruption infiltrate his country's democracy, however unwitting that help. Mr Pronotkov's schemes may have been foiled, thanks to George, the Russian himself might be unwelcome on British soil ever again, yet Richard still could not believe what he had started, and the Woodvilles had got away scot free.

Mary softened as she looked at him. She knew him well enough to spot the emotional cracks in his granite exterior. "You may be a dinosaur, but you're my dinosaur. Your faults are God's and mine to forgive. You tell everyone else about God's forgiveness but you can't forgive yourself. How does that add up? Besides, somehow, with all of that, you're still registering top marks for customer satisfaction, did you know?" His craggy face softened and they walked home arm in arm.

Later, Peggy was walking home down the High Street when Jem came past her, walking down it, rather fast. Unusually, he didn't pause to say hello, but kept going, head down. She wondered what was wrong with him.

He couldn't have told her, or anyone. He wished he'd been back in hospital with Becky chatting away to him and listening as he told her his hopes and plans. Buoyed up by her sympathy, he'd gone up to her parents' house with a bunch of the best roses he could find in Faringdon. They'd wilted slightly by the time he managed to pluck up his courage, but he thought they still seemed fine enough.

When she opened the door to him, he thrust them at her, and started into a speech about maybe becoming more than friends, only his speech stumbled to a halt when he saw the look on her face. She only got as far as, "Sorry, Jem. I'm just really touched, but I've just never – it's good to be friends …"

The last words landed on the back of his head as he turned back down the path, faster than he had come. He didn't see the pain on her face at the hurt she had caused, nor hear her mother's words about girls with no judgement who let their heads be turned by funny jokes and nice looks, and had no idea about solid worth.

Instead of going home he turned onto the path along the ridge, stepping off it to avoid any contact when anyone else happened along. Then he snuck home when he knew his parents would be out and helped himself to their drinks cupboard, vanishing up to his room afterwards so that all they heard on their return was rather louder snoring than usual.

36
DAYS OF TEA AND ROSES

A couple of weeks later, there was a rather more relaxed afternoon, the school's summer fundraising bazaar. Alicia was on duty at the Women's Institute cake stall, relaxing after the first rush of customers had denuded the tables in front of her. Caroline Masterson, who had been helping with her, had stepped over to help the Evergreens with their ice creams, which were melting a little too fast in the heat. George ambled across from the Scouts' tent, with two glasses of Pimms in hand.

"Refreshments for the workers," he said.

Alicia thanked him. "How kind. Good day for the school?"

"Seems so, so far. Ah, how are the WI getting along?"

"We're almost out of Victoria sponges. The chocolate cakes and brownies are selling steadily, but the fruit cakes aren't doing so well, and as for the flapjack …."

"I've always been partial to a bit of flapjack. Let me take a little off your hands, and maybe a fruit cake while I'm at it. Lovely hot day, isn't it?"

"Lovely."

"Does terrible things to the garden, though. My hostas were struggling already, and the penstamens are in trouble too, now." George looked downcast.

Alicia was most sympathetic. "Oh dear, I am sorry. Could I help? I've always been lucky with hostas."

"I'm sure luck has nothing to do with it. It would be very kind of you if you wouldn't mind coming over. Ah, could I offer you a bite of lunch?"

She graciously accepted. Lunch on Tuesday having been arranged, they discovered that they had been walking as they were talking, and found themselves veering away from the cheerful crowd. They decided to carry on walking. With the government in temporary charge of the manor its gardens had been left open for village visitors. They decided to make a tour and they somehow found their feet taking them down through the rose garden, still rather short on roses this early in the year, and on through the next yew hedge to one of the finest of the woodland walks.

One walk led to another, and in between walks, gardening concerns remained prominent in their conversation. George and Alicia had to spend a great deal of time getting the planting right in his garden. It had been neglected for far too long, and the weaker plants, in particular, needed a great deal of attention.

It wasn't the penstamens' fault. They were soon mended, but the hostas proved a harder struggle, with even George reduced to cursing the health of the local slugs, under his breath of course. It took several visits to set them straight. By the time they were as they should be, George and Alicia had become worried by the state of the roses, particularly the Rambling Rector and the Ena Harkness. This proved a more prolonged project.

It was in the midst of this struggle that Alicia happened to mention that if one wishes to see roses at their best, there is nowhere like Mottisfont Abbey. It is the National Rose Centre for Old Roses, after all. George wondered, in reply, if she might like to accompany him there, and she graciously consented so to do.

As they slowly inspected their way round the walled garden, George stopped to lean against a pergola for a moment. "A cup of tea, perhaps?"

"Lovely. Is it over there?"

"This way, I think. It is very nice to be looking round this place with you."

"Lovely to be visiting with you, George."

"I am, ah, enjoying spending a little more time with you. The roses look better when you're beside them."

"How kind, George."

"I was actually wondering how you would feel about spending a little more time together?"

"We are spending quite a bit of time together these days, George. How much time, exactly, had you in mind?"

"Ah, I hadn't quite got that far as yet, but, definitely, a bit more."

"A bit more?"

"Quite a bit more?"

"Quite a bit more would be lovely, George."

They found themselves withdrawing from the main currents of village life, for the moment. Others remained rather more concerned with the rest of the nation and national events. *The Old Bells*, for instance, was about to be renamed *The Old Republic*, and was now decorated with the shields, breastplates, trident and other metalwork Mick Smith had made. The conversation in it remained much the same, however; a pub by any other name smells as sweet, and sounds the same.

"Country looks like a patchwork quilt," said the landlord. It seemed that every pundit had their own ideas for the best coalition to be stitched together from the regional parties and the remains of the old ones.

"We've turned into Belgium," said one disgruntled Tory as he faced all sorts of demands for regional government.

"Bring back the Scots," said another.

"Get rid of the Welsh," said a third.

Mutley Shepwell got a lot of namechecks on the national news, as the harbinger of a new spirit of local independence. Media interviewers who wanted a quote from the little village at the heart of the big storm tended to go to Moira, and she was spending more and more time up in London.

She came back one day and announced she was stepping down as head of the parish council and moving to the Midlands to be a special adviser to one of the heads of the new parties, who were still locked in coalition talks. She laughed as she told them: "Six months of leading our little independent council, and I'm a world expert on the new politics. They talk about the triumph of localism and wheel me in to tell them about it. It's all the village, though, it was never me, it was us."

"Why leave the village? Why now? You've done so much," asked Mary. Moira looked away, across the room, at George, and said nothing. Mary looked back, with sympathy in her eyes, and nodded slowly.

Moira looked thoughtfully at Mary and said, "There is one thing. Could you look out for Alicia for me? And for her sheep?"

Mary looked baffled. "Sheep? What is it with those animals? Why does she care so much about them?"

Moira lowered her voice to a whisper: "She told me once, why the sheep."

Mary looked back, question marks written all over her face.

Moira looked troubled: "Might be good if I told you, as I won't be here for her any more. If I did, you couldn't tell anyone, not Richard, not anyone."

Mary nodded, "Of course."

Moira went on: "A long time back, in her London days, there was a partner who meant more to her. They were engaged, she said, trying for children. She had three miscarriages, three late miscarriages, one after the other. Then he left her. He wanted children. She says she doesn't blame him." Mary touched her arm and thanked her, and promised she would look out for Alicia.

Then Richard turned up and started trying to enlist Moira's support for his latest idea to raise the funds for the hospice he dreamed of. His latest plan was to ask the government to stump up the funds as an advance on the village's share of King John's treasure, assuming that said treasure would actually be found before too long. His wife stared at him, with more warmth in her eyes than her words might suggest: "No more crazy schemes, you old fossil. The rest of the dinosaurs are dead, and you will be too if you don't stop hatching mad eggs."

He quietened down, for about three and a half minutes but couldn't help telling them that he'd found a potential site for the hospice in the hamlet of Hanging Bishops. He'd asked his bishop to sponsor the project and that patient worthy had agreed. He wanted to build it as a place of beauty, on a grand scale, surrounded by gardens, soothing to mind, heart and soul, but was finding the funding hard: not many of the moneyed had the appetite for such enterprises.

Stephanos, on the other hand, was finding funders everywhere from the USA to Tamekstan for his rising commune of world religions on the old industrial estate. It looked as if monks in a rainbow of coloured robes were going to become a curiously regular site at the back end of the village, where, before the failed experiment of the industrial estate, pigs had once been penned and the Cabbage Improvement Corporation had begun its quest for the perfect cabbage.

The enthusiasm levels varied from one part of the commune to another. When it was rumoured that one of their groups had expertise in the use of hallucinogenic drugs in seeking the divine, fervent seekers appeared from as far away as Bristol and Birmingham. It was all now legal, after all. At the other end of the estate, in a run down former garage, the smallest of the communes was occupied by a South Indian cult that espoused lentils and celibacy as the path to purity and perfection. No one was arguing with them; no one was joining them either.

Just when Moira was preparing her farewell party, Bill Stone came back to the village, very uncertainly, late one evening. The police had decided to believe him in the end, and his help with their investigations had left him with only a suspended sentence. The research centre, funnily enough, didn't want him back, but he got to keep what was left of his farm. For a few days he hovered uncertainly around the edges of the village, passing old neighbours in awkward silence. Then the Tranctards went to see Jem and his parents, and the five of them turned up at Bill's door with a box of his favourite chocolates. Jem presented it:

"You got me out of that tomb, Bill. We know Johnny made you do the rest."

Then they took Bill down to *The Old Republic*. The pub went silent. Richard Tranctard stepped up to the bar:

"A drink for my old friend?"

Bob Corns stared at him for a long moment, then nodded. "Alright." He didn't just pour it he took it round the bar and delivered it himself, with a pat on the shoulder: "On the house, Bill."

After that, bit by bit, Bill Stone became a part of village life again. He was quieter than he had been, and went very shy when he felt tension in the air, but given the right cues he would unfold slowly into his old self again. He really started looking a lot more cheerful when he heard Stephanos would soon be leaving him for the new commune of all religions. Bill was very happy to wish Stephanos and his fellow communards well, and leave them to it, and have his home back to himself again.

In the midst of all this, wedding invitations began to appear. Half the village was invited, it seemed, to the marriage of George Sneed and Alicia Cornwell, at St Martin's, at the end of September. George had got as far as holding Alicia's hand on that trip to Mottisfont Abbey to see the roses, a visit to Hidcote Manor Gardens had ended in a kiss, and he finally plucked up the courage to propose while standing next to the moat at Sissinghurst, after a trip to the White Garden.

On their return, Morsel had greeted Alicia with almost as much excitement as she reserved for him, and even rolled over for Alicia to tickle her tummy, which George took as almost an official blessing. His daughter and granddaughters seemed very pleased too, which was almost as important.

The last blooms of summer had done their stuff, and George and Alicia were ready to face autumn and winter together. The reception was to be a modest one, at *The Old Republic*, with speeches by both of them, and a final exit by hot air balloon from the pub garden.

"George, who'd have thought it?" said Peggy to Des. Rumour had it that *Goodbye!* magazine had even put in a bid to photograph the first wedding in the village since it lost its independence, but George had said an unusually firm no, so *Goodbye!* had gone back to its staple diet of sports stars on the decline, minor celebrities on the way out, and media personalities going through lean times.

As the invitations arrived, Jem was back down in the crypt at St Martin's, still measuring and cataloguing the strange carvings. He didn't hear the door opening behind him and stayed hunched over till the sense of someone's presence made him swing round and lift his head. Becky was standing there with two glasses and a bottle. He went red enough to match the wine.

"Been missing you," she said. He looked down. She went on, rather breathlessly. "My mum says I'm mad not to give you a chance. I keep thinking about you, wondering how you are. I think she might be right. I might be mad. If I was sane enough to give you a chance, would you be mad enough to give me a chance?"

He didn't look up. For a long heartbeat he stayed exactly still, as if not breathing, then he nodded and looked up. "Yup." His voice was choked and his head went down again. She poured the wine and very hesitantly came and sat beside him before the altar and held out a glass for him. He took it, looked at it, raised it, "To us?"

"To us. Give it a try, eh? Just a try."

"Let's see where we go, let's hope it's good."

They leaned back and drank their wine. The village started to get used to seeing them together, while their parents held their breath and their friends speculated wildly. Things were awkward between Jimmy and Jem, but Jimmy was off travelling half the time, which eased things.

Jimmy was busy anyway, with the Universal Holiday Exchange, with Aunty Moira managing him from long distance. Moira had got Jem involved with the team developing a local history aspect to UniLocal Radio, so he was busy too. They weren't sure they'd ever get back to university.

George and Alicia's wedding caught the general imagination, with much astonishment at this unlikely match, and indeed at George's unlikely turn as financial spy and whistleblower. Apart from anything else, it took everyone's minds off the general indignation about the failure to catch Johnny Berensford and Alexander Livingston.

In the case of Johnny Berensford, he had turned up in France. The French government, had stated, with regret, that the particular tax offences with which he had been charged were not part of the EU's extradition treaty with UK - and they were not minded to take a generous interpretation of that treaty, unless the UK should be minded to take a less generous interpretation of certain other tax matters, annoying to the EU. So Johnny remained very happily at large. He was trying to introduce his brewing techniques to the French at Avignon, which seemed to him an appropriate location for the pope of beer, having been a residence for popes in the past.

Alexander, on the other hand, had found his way to Russia, whose authorities explained that, had the young man in question actually been killed, there would be no question at all that Professor Livingston would be extradited. They had heard, however, that the young man had not only made a full recovery but actually become something of a celebrity as a result of his adventure, so they found it hard to see what real harm had been done.

According to the strict letter of the law, of course, he should be extradited, but by the time he was located he had become engaged and then married to a Russian woman, an old friend from his younger days, and that changed matters. In vain did the former council of the republic point out that when Johnny and Alexander's crimes were committed, the Loyal Republic had been fully European, and, according to British law, part of the EU. The EU, of course, had never accepted this change of status, and its authorities were unyielding, as were Russia's.

Fortunately, people had the wedding to take their minds off this injustice. All round Mutley Shepwell the excitement mounted. When the day of the wedding came, half the village was out in its finery. Alicia looked radiant, her usual reserve cast aside for once, while George exuded shyness.

She had gone for a rather elegant 1920s-style wedding dress in ivory silk and he was in morning suit, feeling strange to be standing before the altar in it again after all these years, strange but good. It seemed a bit late in the day for any giving away, so they entered from each side of the church and met before the altar. The Old Tank was at his most sonorous and resonant, the choir at its very best, the congregation ready to cheer if given half a chance.

At the back, Peggy was sobbing happily next to Des, with Mary Tranctard suppressing the odd tear on the other side of her. Mary mused, "I always used to cry at weddings, until it came to my own first one. After that I found it amazingly easy to be dry-eyed. Once I found out the dreadful truth, the tears just stopped. Since marrying Richard, I seem to be leaving the dry lands again. Funny how fond of them we get, isn't it?" And she no longer directed her gaze at Peggy, but up to her husband at the front. Des just shrugged and went back to happy memories of yesterday's fishing.

Across the aisle, Bob Corns was wondering how he'd ended up in a church again, looking across to the door of the crypt, and wondering if he should help Jimmy out with that new Mutley Shepwell Murder Trail the boy was trying to launch. Not that there had actually been a murder, but, as Jimmy pointed out, near enough was good enough if it meant calling the thing a murder trail rather than a "knock on the head and make a good recovery" trail. He was so lost in all these musings that he found himself the only person not cheering as George was told he could kiss the bride. He made up for his lateness with an extra loud war whoop, then fell back into reverie for the rest of the service.

As George and Sarah came out onto the steps through the west door, the golden afternoon sun caught their faces and made them shine. Bill Stone, in full chauffeur's uniform, was waiting in one of Mary's vintage Bentleys to take them up the hill to start their life together. They had decided to live at Alicia's. It would have been hard for her to move in with his memories and his ghosts. With Sailor gone to terrorize the rodent population of the industrial estate, the last obstacle had been removed. Morsel had been sent ahead to settle in and adjusted so well that Alicia had already been promoted to her Number Three friend, after George and her food bowl.

Before entering in to domestic bliss, however, there was the little matter of the honeymoon. They were going to Italy and, to cheer up The Old Tank, George had agreed to leave a flag of the republic somewhere in the Vatican City, where it might linger in remembrance of past independence and future dreams.

First, the reception, the photos, the speeches. They agreed with each other that they'd feel calmer when their speeches were over, although Alicia found that something about George's presence was having a soothing effect already, and he certainly felt more at peace to have her there. In the late afternoon sunshine, for those waving them off outside the church, his grey hair seemed to light up silver and almost match her silver-blonde. They were so focused on each other they forgot to turn and wave as the car turned right past Traitor's Wood.

When they left the reception, they found that instead of

the usual ritual of sabotaging the car, their friends had found four huge flags of the republic and draped one on each side of a hot air balloon's basket, so, as it rose into the air, the flag of the Loyal Republic flew above the village, higher than it ever had. George and Alicia looked down on their village, with the setting sun reddening the sky to the west, and the crescent moon silver, high up in the sky to the east. They watched the rooftops recede and the Amble flow past St Martin's, quiet once more as the bridge watched it pass.

ABOUT THE AUTHOR

David Pickering lives in Oxfordshire, England, where he and his wife and son provide staff services to two cats and a golden retriever. When his services are not required by the pets, he works for three village churches.